METROPOLITAN

Walter Jon Williams is the author of many successful science fiction novels, including *Hardwired*, *Days of Atonement*, *Facets* and *Aristoi*. He lives in New Mexico.

D1514003

Voyager

WALTER JON WILLIAMS

Metropolitan

HarperCollins*Publishers*

Voyager
An Imprint of HarperCollins*Publishers*
77–85 Fulham Palace Road,
Hammersmith, London W6 8JB

A Paperback Original 1995
1 3 5 7 9 8 6 4 2

A catalogue record for this book
is available from the British Library

ISBN 0 00 648023 3

Set in Meridien by
Rowland Phototypesetting Limited
Bury St Edmunds, Suffolk

Printed in Great Britain by
HarperCollinsManufacturing Glasgow

1

A burning woman stalks along the streets. Ten stories tall, naked body a whirling holocaust of fire. Terrified people on Bursary Street crumple into carbon at her passing, leaving behind only black char curled into fetal shapes. The heat she radiates is so powerful that structures burst into flame as she passes. A storm of paper, sucked out of buildings by uncontrolled drafts, spiral toward her and are consumed. Uncontrolled rivers of flame pour from her fingertips. Windows blast inward at her keening, at the eerie, nerve-scraping wail that pours from her insubstantial, fiery throat.

In a city that girdles the world, all-devouring fire is the worst thing imaginable.

Aiah hears the sound first, a scream that raises the fine hairs on the back of her neck. She gazes in shock out of the office lounge and sees the woman turn the corner onto the Avenue of the Exchange; and for a moment she sees the woman tripled, multiplied by the mirror glass of the Bursary Building and the Old Intendancy, and for a horrified moment gazes into three burning faces, three hollow sets of flaming eyes, three expressions of agonized torment in which she can read the woman's last remnant of blasted humanity begging for help, for an end to pain . . .

Aiah turns to run and the window blows inward with a breath of wind that sears Aiah's neck and flings her to the floor, and at the same moment she hears the first shriek from Tella's baby and the foolish, urgent ring of the phone—

The burning woman's scream rises to Aiah's throat.

GRADE A PLASM LEAK IN FINANCIAL DISTRICT.
143 DEAD. 2000 INJURED.
PLASM AUTHORITY INVESTIGATION ANNOUNCED.
DETAILS ON THE WIRE.

As the escalator lifts Aiah from the blue passageways of the pneuma station the liquid-silver words track across the sky, telling her things she regrets she already knows. Between the worn metal treads of the escalator steps lie drifts of ash, a percentage of which may be human. On the surface, a cold wind blows black cinders between the sluicegates of buildings.

IS YOUR FAMILY SAFE? DO YOU CARRY ENOUGH INSURANCE? More words, addressed in this instance to a more local audience, crawl in mirrored image up the gold glass wall of the Bursary Building. Insurance underwriters hawk their wares from hastily assembled booths on the sidewalk.

'You safe, lady?' one asks. 'You probably got a bunch of kids, right?'

Right. Barkazil women are supposed to spend their lives pregnant. Aiah hunches deeper into her jacket and walks over to the new lottery seller at a new, improvised kiosk.

Both the old lottery seller and his kiosk had been turned to charcoal. Aiah had bought a ticket from him every working day for the last three years and never known his name.

A police motorcycle glides by with an efficient turbine whine. Glass crunches underfoot as Aiah walks across Exchange to the Plasm Authority Building with its jagged crown of bronze horns and its gaping windows. There are white paint circles on the pavement, each with a bit of soot in the center that marks a casualty, a human being turned into a carbonized husk. The pigeons have already scattered droppings on them.

2

She knows what waits in her office. Tella's crying baby, the smell of dirty diapers, stale coffee in the stale-smelling lounge with its broken window now covered by plastic. The inevitable message cylinder on her desk, because three months ago, trying to score a few points with higher authority, she'd volunteered for Emergency Response.

And then, after the message is answered, long hours in shivering cold, far underground, searching for plasm that will never be hers.

More words track across the sky. *Snap! The World Drink*, followed by the green-and-white Snap logo. The resources necessary to track all that across the sky during shift change are staggering, more than she'll make in her life.

A silent aerocar crosses the sky between Aiah and the logo, rising from the roof of the Exchange. It inverts so the driver can view the city below, enjoying a view Aiah knows she'll never see.

In a city that girdles the world, what is the worst thing imaginable?

Not having anyplace to go.

THREE MORE INDICTED IN TRACKLINE SCANDAL
INTENDANT PROMISES CLEANUP

The Plasm Authority Building is broad and high and powerful, built for the creation, storage and transmission of plasm. It stands in careful relationship to the other buildings of the financial/government district, relationships in which weight, design and core construction are carefully balanced. The carbon-steel supports form an intricate generation web insulated from the exterior by white granite. Its thorny crown of transmission horns reaches into the sky like grasping fingers. The outside bronze collection web, with its roots deep in bedrock, curls over the granite in shining arabesques, brutally functional ornamentation meant to attract, gather, and disperse any plasm threatening to endanger the building itself – break any attack into fragments, deprive it of will, then store it for use by the Authority's own heresiarchs.

If the burning woman had touched the building with her tendrils of flame, she would have cried and trembled and vanished, her energies sucked into the building's structure before being dispersed through the city grid.

But she hadn't touched the building, had in whatever was left of her reasoning mind known that the bronze traceries meant danger. Instead the Jurisdiction had to divert its resources to her destruction, had snuffed her by brute force, a burst of power transmitted from the bronze transmission horns.

The building is less impressive when seen close up. Fifty other anonymous employees enter with Aiah beneath the bronze-sheathed, grime-encrusted archway mosaic that shows the Goddess of Transmission Dispensing Her Glory to the People. With twenty of the new arrivals – she doesn't know one of them – she experiences the peculiarly liquid motion of one of the building's hydraulic elevators.

On the tenth floor the first thing Aiah hears is the wailing of Tella's baby. The halls are covered by brown ribbed plastic runways intended to protect crumbling floor tiles. The doors are of battered metal painted dull green. The furniture is battered metal painted dull gray. The walls are green with a gray stripe. The ceiling is tin and its holes reveal wiring. There are no windows.

Welcome to the civil service, she thinks. Welcome to a secure future.

'Hi,' Tella says. She's changing Jayme's diapers on the top of her desk.

Aiah wants to shout down to the insurance hawker: *See? Jaspeeris do too have kids!*

Baby stool glints greenly in the fluorescents. 'Big meeting at ten,' Tella says.

4

'I expected.'

'How's your neck?'

Aiah touches her scorched nape beneath pinned-up hair. 'All right.'

'At least you didn't get any glass cuts. Calla from Tabulation was looking right at her window when it blew in. She almost lost an eye.'

'Which one's Calla?'

'Auburn hair. Married to Emtes from Billing.'

Aiah doesn't know him either. She looks down at her desk, the computer with its glowing yellow dials, the scalar, the logbook.

Gil's picture in its gleaming wetsilver frame.

The baby gives another shriek. Tella smiles, half-apologetic. 'Healthy lungs, huh?'

Tella hadn't wanted to leave her kid in the Authority's creche all day, looked after by disinterested functionaries and subjected to every epidemic sweeping Jaspeer. She'd asked Aiah if she minded her keeping Jayme in the office, and Aiah had said it was all right.

She'd said it reluctantly. She had been raised in a big family, not only siblings but cousins and nephew and nieces all jammed together in tiny government apartments in a Barkazil neighborhood – it would suit her perfectly well if she was never around small children again.

No less than three message cylinders sit in her wire basket. Aiah opens them, finds they're all about the meeting, all from different supervisors.

Evidently there is chaos at the top.

Her computer's yellow dials glow at her.

She peels lace back from her wrist and pens a reply on each message, puts each back in its cylinder, and looks on her plastic-covered list to double-check each supervisor's pneumatic address. She dials each address on the little gears on the end of each cylinder, then feeds them, one by one, into the pneumatic message system. Each is tugged from her fingers by the hissing suction of the tube, and she pictures them bulleting through darkness, destination as fixed as that of passengers on the trackline shuttle.

In a city as big as the world, what is the worst thing?

To be twenty-five years old, and to know exactly how one will spend the rest of one's life.

EARTHQUAKE IN PANTAD.
40,000 BELIEVED DEAD!
DETAILS ON THE WIRE!

Aiah has learned to ignore the pain the heavy black ceramic headset inflicts on her ears. At least the headset blots out the volume that comes from Jayme's healthy lungs.

'09:34 hours, Horn Twelve reorientation to degrees 122.5. Ne?' The tabulator on the other end of the line has anything but healthy lungs. There are gasps between each word, and a dry cough punctuates each phrase. Occasionally Aiah can hear him suck on a cigaret.

'Da,' Aiah repeats. '09:34, Horn Twelve reorientation to degrees 122.5 confirmed.' 09:34 is about six minutes from now. She jots in her log as she speaks, then dials the numbers into her computer. Inside the metal matte-black console there are clicks and whirrs.

122.5 degrees. That would be Mage Towers.

'09:35, Horn Twelve transmit at 1800 mm. tfn. Ne?'

'Da. 09:35, Horn Twelve transmit at 1800 mm. Till further notice. Confirmed.'

1800 megamehrs. That was a lot of demand even for Mage Towers. Who wants so much? she wonders.

She wonders if it's Constantine.

Aiah writes the numbers into her log, and notes that column six of her transmission scalar is free. She dials column six into her computer, then slides the algorithmic scale on the scalar until it points to 1800. She pulls an insulated cable from her cable bank and plugs it through the scale into the socket behind, pinning the scalar in place and completing an electronic circuit.

There are no more calls for power until 09:34. Aiah fidgets with her lace and feels the back of her neck burn. To avoid thinking about the burning woman she looks at the picture of Gil in its frame.

09:33. Computer gears whirr. A little mechanical flag at the top of column six clicks over from white to white-and-red. Atop the building, the huge bronze transmission horn shifts slightly to 122.5 degrees.

A minute passes. The flag clicks over to all red and the electric circuit on the scalar goes live, triggering another, far bigger plasm circuit within the webbed steel skeleton of the building. Power pours from the transgression horn. Mage Towers begins reception of the colossal charge of plasm.

Tfn. Till further notice. Enough plasm to fly Mage Towers halfway to the Shield.

Aiah reaches out her hand, touches the face of the scalar, hoping to get a taste of power, light a glowing candle in her backbrain, charge her nerves with a taste of reality . . . and of course nothing happens, nothing, because the plasm isn't hers, because she lives in a building filled with the stuff and she can't have any of it.

She wonders if it's Constantine on the other end of the circuit.

Probably not. Probably this is another sizzling salute to consumerism, a thundering display for a soft drink or a new brand of shoe.

What's the worst thing in a city that covers the world?

To live forever with the object of desire, and not to possess it.

2

All leaves are cancelled: everyone's going to be working shifts-and-a-half. Mengene has the meeting only vaguely under control: panic's infected everyone from the Intendant down and there's a lot of shouting. Aiah, far too junior to shout, sits across the shining glass conference table from Niden, the only other brown Barkazil face in the room. She was hoping for comfort but it turns out he has a streaming cold, and she winces every time he coughs or sneezes, mentally willing the viruses to the nasal membranes of upper management.

Visible through the wall behind Mengene, a floating billboard drifts past. *Why so tense?* it asks.

Sometimes advertisers have a sense of humor.

'Oeneme thinks it has to do with the new construction of Old Parade,' Mengene says. He touches his little blond mustache. 'The Unity Hospital is being demolished, there's an office building going up one and a half radii away, and there's an excavation for a new trackline station right in the middle of the street. The configuration is a little irregular—'

'Irregular? There's a map, isn't there?' Denselle booms. He's a fat man who loves his own voice. Fat blooms of lace spill from his jacket cuffs.

'Not yet.'

'Why the hell not?'

Mengene sighs. 'Because Oeneme's office didn't send one.'

'Couldn't you get one yourself?'

Mengene ignores him and begins giving out assignments, work team numbers. Aiah begins to realize that her own name hasn't been mentioned. She holds up a hand, is ignored, finally raises her voice. '*Mr Mengene!*'

There is a moment of silence.

'I haven't been given a job,' Aiah says.

Mengene looks at her. 'I know,' he says.

'Then why am I here?'

Mengene is annoyed. 'I was getting to you. You've got a special assignment.'

Her heart leaps, but she sees daggers in others' eyes. What right has *she* to a special assignment?

Mengene can see the daggers as well as anyone else. 'It's Rohder's idea,' he says, and the others instantly lose interest. Aiah's hope fades. Rohder is a cobwebbed relic of the old Research Division, far gone in abstruse speculation and philosophy, but with too much seniority to fire.

The others receive their briefings. The boardroom chairs are big, heavily padded, with fan-shaped backs adorned with a huge gold chrysanthemum. They make it far too easy to feel drowsy. Aiah closes her eyes, finds herself thinking of Gil, of his short-fingered, powerful hands, the way they touch her.

Mengene finishes. Aiah waits for the others to file out and for Mengene to light another cigaret. Mengene sits, blows smoke, gestures for her to join him at the head of the table. She gets out of her chair, walks up the room. Sees her reflection in the wall's gold-plated crysanthemums, automatically pats her hair.

'It was Rohder who snuffed the flamer,' Mengene says. 'He was inside Transmission Control when it happened, saw the thing coming on an exterior monitor and dropped his butt in the hot seat. He'll get commended, but handling that much plasm at his age put him in the hospital.' He

9

shakes a cigaret partway out of his pack, offers it to her. 'Smoke?'

'No thanks.' She sits down next to him. Behind him a peregrine dives past, squab in its sights. If she'd blinked she would have missed it.

'Rohder called me an hour ago from the hospital. He says that when he dropped the shoe on our flamer, he got an impression of her sourceline. He says he got a fairly clear impression the transmission was coming from the east.'

'Old Parade is not east,' Aiah says.

'The sourceline dropped below the horizon somewhere this side of Grand City. He says he *saw* it.'

'From inside Transmission Control?'

Mengene looks uncomfortable. 'That's what he says.'

'On an exterior monitor?'

Mengene gazes fixedly at the tip of his cigaret. 'In his mind's eye.'

Futility wails in Aiah's nerves. She's going to spend days underground searching for an old man's hallucination.

'Rohder's good, you know,' Mengene says. 'He's solid, a real wizard. I worked with him, back when he set up Research. Bailed out before the whole department crashed. But the crash wasn't Rohder's fault – too much interference from above. You can't come up with a new field-tested theory of plasm use in a few months.'

'If this is so solid,' Aiah says, 'why are you sending only me on it?'

'Because I don't work for Rohder, I work for Oeneme, and Oeneme thinks the problem's on Old Parade.' Mengene drives his cigaret like a nail into the titanium ashtray. It spins lazily from the momentum. Aiah wonders if Mengene's just set up Oeneme to take a fall, perhaps on behalf of the Intendant. And whose fault will it be if Mengene's little plot doesn't work?

The scheming Barkazil, of course. Everyone knows

they're always looking for advantage, scheming, setting up a chonah or two. Aiah knows the situation well enough to know that she has no allies.

'The credit will be entirely yours,' Mengene says.

Escaping the credit is clearly something she needs to think about.

Mengene swabs away cigaret ash with his lace cuff. 'I've drawn you a two-man support team,' Mengene says. 'They'll be available right after midbreak. I know you're inexperienced with source-finding, but they might be able to guide you through—'

'I'll want an overflight with transparencies, densities, and patterns.'

'Of course. I'll call down to Records for you.'

'Our maps aren't always current if they're not our district. I'll want a map from— what's the substation between here and Grand City? Rocketman?'

Mengene looks surprised. 'I think so. I'll call Rocketman, if that's what you want.'

Sometimes, she's learned, Jaspeeris are amazed when something intelligent comes from her lips. She's learned to cope with the phenomenon.

Still, she can't ask any questions she truly needs the answers to.

Special assignment. What joy.

> *Speech is human, silence is divine*
> – a thought-message from His Perfection,
> the Prophet of Ajas

A few hours later, wearing an official yellow jumpsuit and hardhat, Aiah climbs out of a trackline car at Rocketman Station. She's followed everywhere by her two assistants: Lastene, a young kid with pimples, and Grandshuk, a grizzled man so short and squat and powerfully built that she suspects some ancestor may have had his genes twisted.

Rocketman Station, the station run by the Trackline Authority, has the same name as Rocketman Substation, the Authority plasm station. No clue as to why either is called 'Rocketman' – most of the names for these neighborhoods are so old they've lost all meaning.

The trackline station is ancient and deep below the surface. An old mosaic on the platform, once-bright colors grimy and chipped, shows how the aboveground must have looked at one time, bright whitestone buildings shining under the gray Shield, some with odd ball-topped antennae broadcasting plasm in the form of shining gold zigzag rays.

No rockets in the mosaic, though.

The tunnel to the substation isn't properly walled, just screened off with steel mesh. Aiah's boots boom on temporary flooring that was probably installed decades ago. She ascends past layers of human strata, all visible through steel mesh: old brickwork, scrolled iron stanchions, water pipes, brown stone, concrete, sewer pipe glistening with condensation, gray bricks, red stone, white stone.

Everything a generator of plasm, of geomantic power.

Mass creates its own energies – for that matter *is* energy, albeit in another form. The disordered pile that is the world-city, the structures of iron and brick and rock and concrete, generates its own intrinsic power. The power accumulates slowly within the structures themselves, fills them like rising water entering every crevice, and lies latent unless tapped. Geomantic relationships have been shown to matter more than mass itself – the design of a building, or the relationship of buildings to one another can multiply power generation, concentrate or direct it to one place or another. The metal structures of buildings, reaching down into bedrock and up toward the Shield, gather and concentrate that power, make it available for use and broadcast.

And the power – plasm – resonates within the human mind. It is susceptible to control by the odd little particules of human will, and once controlled, can do almost anything

– on the small, microcosmic end, plasm can cure illness, alter genes, halt or reverse aging, create precious metals from base matter and radioisotopes from precious metals. On the macrocosmic end plasm can create life, any kind of life a person can think of, can invade a target mind, destroy a person's will and make him a puppet for the manipulator, can burn out nerves or turn living bones to carbon ash, turn hatred to love or love to hate, can wreak death in any number of obscene forms, can fling missiles or bombs or people anywhere in the world, all in a snap of the fingers. Can blow buildings down in a tornado wind, carry sky-scrapers through the air for a thousand miles and set them down feather-light at the point of destination, create earth-quakes to shiver a hundred structures to the ground, can grant earthly power beyond the wildest dreams, can do anything except punch a hole through the Shield that the Ascended Ones set between the world and whatever exists outside of it.

But you have to get the stuff first. And it's collected, distributed, metered, taxed. There's never enough. Govern-ments require colossal amounts of plasm as a foundation for their own power. Complexes like Mage Towers or Grand City charge their tenants horrific sums, all because their buildings are constructed so as to concentrate and transmit plasm efficiently, and the tenants – geomancers of astounding wealth and power – live there because they can afford it. Because they can afford to call for power tfn, to let the meters run.

Never enough. But buildings are always going up, or tearing down, or going higher, or remodeling, and the con-figurations are always changing, mass achieving new bal-ances with mass, producing new potentials. That's why plasm divers burrow through the foundations of the world, through abandoned cellars and long-forgotten utility mains and rubble-filled inspection tunnels, all in hope of finding a source that's off the circuit, that hasn't been metered yet, a source of plasm that can be tapped or sold or used to fulfill the diver's uttermost dreams.

And if it goes wrong, Aiah thinks, if the diver takes on more power than she's trained to handle, maybe you have hundred-foot-tall flaming women wailing down the street, burning off a hundred years' chance accumulation of plasm in one horrifying, burning instant.

At Rocketman Plasm Station it takes a while to establish Aiah's credentials, since Mengene never made the promised call. The archives are kept in a room below street level, and are reached through the wide Battery Room where the station's power is contained in huge plasm accumulators and capacitors, three times human-height, gleaming copper and brass layers with shining black ceramic. Controlling them is a black metal wall filled with switches, dials, and levers that monitor and control the vast power stored here, that cause it to flow and surge at the drop of a contact. In the corner, near the control bank, is an icon to Tangid, the two-faced Lord of Power.

The two controllers sit in comfortable chairs in front of the control board and spend their days reading magazines. Their job is almost entirely automated, but the union insists they have to stay here in case of an emergency, and their contract even gets them hazard pay, just in case terrorists burst in the door waving machine-guns and demanding a dose of power.

Aiah is escorted to the archives. Lastene and Grandshuk follow like obedient hounds. She's back in the Battery Room a few minutes later, she and her team carrying bundles of maps, transparencies, and updates, all wrapped in official orange Authority strapping. She sits at a table near the controllers and drags them open.

The overflight maps are chromographs taken by aircraft, jigsawed carefully together, and carefully scaled to give an idea of relationships. Transparent celluloid overlays are supposed to show what's underneath. Some of the cels are

14

so old that they've yellowed or deteriorated. Anything that can alter plasm generation is supposed to be in the overlays or the updates. It's all pleasant fiction.

It's easier to let entrepreneurs do the work — that and greed. The Authority knows that the total of plasm stolen is enormous, impossible to keep up with. But if a plasm diver finds anything new, sooner or later someone will turn him in for the reward and the Authority will find the source and wire it into the circuit.

Aiah spends an hour looking at the maps. The area between the Exchange District and Grand City is vast, hundreds of square radii. She sets her dividers against the map scale and marches out the relationships between the various structures, then puts down the transparencies one by one and tries to add in their effects. The maps swim before her eyes.

It occurs to her that her job is impossible. Mengene, she decides, is up to something. Maybe he *wants* her to fail.

Aiah decides she wants to think about that for a while.

She looks up at her crew, who are reading the controllers' magazines. 'You can leave if you like. I'm going home.'

Grandshuk looks at his partner, then back at Aiah. 'We were sort of hoping to draw some overtime.'

'I'm on salary,' Aiah says, 'I don't get overtime. But you can take yours in the bar across the street if you want. I'll meet you here right at the beginning of work shift tomorrow.'

Grandshuk looks at his partner again, then nods. 'If that's okay with you, then.'

'Yeah, sure. Have fun.'

She looks down at the maps again, the yellowed transparencies that mark utility mains, old tubeways, the foundations of buildings long since demolished by wrecking ball or by earthquake. If she dove anywhere, *anywhere*, she'd probably find some plasm. Make an announcement back at the office, hey, problem solved. Get her pat on the

15

back, go back to her yellow-eyed computer and scalar and the wails of Tella's baby.

No, she decides. That's the sort of thing her brother Stonn might do. He'd even think it was smart, at least until another Grade A screamer started blowing out windows on Exchange.

There has to be a way around it, she thinks. A cunning way. A Barkazil way.

She's one of the Cunning People, she thinks. It's time to get those cunning genes into action.

3 DRUG DEALERS TO HANG
2100, VIDEO SEVEN
LIVE FROM HAGGUL PENITENTIARY
Let Justice Be Served!

Her cousin Landro works in a hardware store in Old Shorings, the neighborhood where Aiah spent her girlhood. That's an hour-and-a-half commute from Rocketman, and in the wrong direction from where she lives at Loeno Towers. Aiah tracklines out carrying a heavy satchel full of maps, wearing her jumpsuit and hardhat – she is feeling unlovely and unloved by the time she drags her feet up the broken escalator to the entrance tunnel, but as soon as her feet touch the sidewalk she feels her heart begin to lift.

A vocal group sings somewhere, the sound floating out of an upper window. Aiah finds herself smiling. A cold wind pours down the narrow corridor between buildings of soiled red brick, all so old they lean over the street like old women leaning on their sticks.

The street is narrow and closed to vehicle traffic. The buildings have shops on the lower floor, apartments above. Most buildings have metal scaffolding extending their fronts out over the sidewalk and into the street. Officially speaking, the scaffolding is supposed to support the old brick walls, but the scaffolds are all inhabited, divided up

16

into cubicles where people sell clothes or gadgets or toys, lucky charms or advice or vegetables raised in roof gardens. Sometimes poor people live there, with plastic sheeting for roofs and walls. It's all illegal, and the scaffolding and its contents will turn into missiles in the next earthquake, but nobody in this part of the Scope of Jaspeer has cared about building codes for a very long time.

Aiah did much of her growing up here, in public housing a few blocks away. Cooking smells hang heavy in the air, familiar Barkazil spices. Hawkers smile and offer home-made musical instruments, pigeon pies, incense, scarves, lucky charms, handbags, and watches with phony labels. No end of music, music everywhere, booming from ampli-fiers turned out the windows, slippery Barkazil rhythms competing with the boom of plastic sheeting in the wind. Children play football in the street. Old men drink beer on front stoops. Young men stand on street corners to protect the neighborhood from whatever they think is threatening it, presumably other young men.

At a scaffold shop she buys a meal of hot noodles with chilies and onions and a bit of meat for seasoning. She has to put down a five-clink deposit for the cheap ceramic cup with a chip on its rim. It's the sort of meal her grandmother was always warning her against: the meat is supposed to be chicken grown in a vat or on someone's roof, but it might well be sewer rat.

Aiah doesn't care — it tastes wonderful.

A flying billboard hawking cigarets soars overhead with a siren wail. It's illegal for plasm displays to make that much noise, but in certain neighborhoods the noise statutes never seem to be enforced.

Landro sees the yellow jumpsuit first, and he looks at Aiah a little warily until he recognizes her. At once he gives her an expansive hug, answers question about his girlfriend and various children, hers, his, theirs together.

'I thought you worked in an office now,' he says.

'I'm underground for a few weeks.'

'Have you seen your mama?'

Annoyance dances along Aiah's nerves on little insect feet. 'No,' she says. 'I just got here, and . . .' Deep sigh. 'Actually, I'm working.'

Wariness enters his eyes. 'What do you mean?'

'I was hoping you could give me some answers. About diving.'

Landro gives a look over his shoulder at the store manager frowning from behind a screen at the back of the store. 'Why don't I show you some samples?' he says, and takes her over to the paint section.

Upper management, Aiah thinks, is everywhere.

'I'm not looking to get anyone in trouble,' he says, and hands her a card with paint samples.

For several years Landro was a plasm diver, feeding his discoveries into local circuits through meters he'd carefully sabotaged, supplying local adepts with the amounts of plasm necessary to keep their predictions reasonably on the mark, their love spells boiling, their curses suitably calamitous. Till the Authority creepers caught him and sent him to Chonmas for a six-month stretch.

'I don't want to arrest anybody,' Aiah assures, 'I just want to find somebody's source. I need to know what to look for in a meter that's been cracked.'

'There must be a dozen ways.'

'Just the most common. Probably small-time stuff. Little meters, apartments, and small offices.'

Landro licks his lips and tells her what she wants. He used little magnets to retard the dials on the continuous-flow meters, and the gear-driven ones were gimmicked with special gears of slightly different sizes than the ones called for in the specifications. Aiah nags him until he tells her just where the magnets were placed, just which gears were swopped.

'Thank you,' she says, and kisses his cheek.

'See your mama,' he says.

'I'm working now,' glad for the excuse, 'but I'll see you all on Senko's Day.'

He looks after her doubtfully as she hoists her map case off the floor and heads out. She'd like to stay in the neighborhood a little longer, but chances are she'd run into another relative, and then her mother would hear about it.

Besides, considering that it's shift change, it's at least a two-hour ride to her new neighborhood.

Aiah is thankful for the noodles by the time she gets home. She can't afford to eat out in her neighborhood, and she really can't afford to buy groceries there, either; she usually buys food one stop up the pneuma line and walks home from there.

But she doesn't take the pneuma this time, because it doesn't connect to Old Shorings. Instead, she has to use the trackline and transfer, Circle Line to Red Line to New Central Line – and every single car on Aiah's journey is overdue for service on its suspension and tires. It's a tooth-rattling ride, and by the end Aiah's kidneys ache and her bladder is full. She has to walk a block and a half from the trackline station to her apartment at Loeno Towers. Hydrogen-powered cars hiss by on soft polymer wheels. Black clouds cruise under the Shield like hunter-killer craft, threatening a rain strike at any moment. It's dark enough so that some of the stormlights go on.

Loeno is a new apartment complex built on the rubble

of a decayed residential district, sixteen tall black glass monoliths, housing maybe ten thousand people in all. The place is expensive and Aiah and Gil could barely afford to buy it.

Now, it turns out, they can't afford to sell.

Well-dressed neighbors look at her with well-contained surprise as she walks to the elevators – assuming they notice her at all in the course of the day, something she doubts; they're used to seeing her in her gray suits, heels, and white lace.

The elevator carries her briskly to the thirtieth floor; from there it's a hundred quick steps to her apartment door.

Aiah steps inside and feels her boots sink into carpet. The first thing she notices is that the yellow message bulb on her communications array isn't lit. The apartment is one largish room, with a counter between the living area and kitchen and a small shower and toilet. There's a small room for a pocket garden, with grow lights and a tub of loam for vegetable cultivation. Through the black glass wall is a spectacular view, mostly of other black glass windows. It's the largest area Aiah has ever had entirely to herself.

She throws the map case onto the bed she hasn't bothered to convert back to its sofa configuration in weeks, sits down on the disordered sheets and unclips her boots. She rubs her feet, locates a few places that will blister if she isn't careful.

Tomorrow she'll wear a more appropriate style of sock.

There's something in a jumpsuit pocket that feels uncomfortable, and she unsnaps it to find the chipped ceramic cup that held her noodles. She forgot to redeem it for her five clinks. She puts it on the bedside table.

Aiah takes a shower and wraps herself in a velour bathrobe. One of the tunes sung by the vocal group in Old Shorings plays itself faintly in her head. She looks at the message machine again, just to make sure Gil hadn't called when she was in the shower.

No luck.

An aerial advertisement shines through the black glass window, tracks its yellow light across the room. *Vote No on Item Fourteen*, letters snaking between the Loeno Towers. She's never heard of Item Fourteen before.

She sits on the bed, looks first at the life-size portrait of Gil on one wall, then the icon of Karlo on the other. The two poles of her personal universe. From the armrest control she turns on the video and lets the oval screen babble at her. It's some kind of silly action chromo with Aldemar blowing up half a metropolis. She wishes Gil would call. She'd call him, but she never knows when he's going to be near a phone.

There had been a time, she remembers, when she'd really wanted to be alone. Wanted to be away from her huge, anarchic family, from their oppressive high spirits and noisy poverty and hopeless irresponsibility. In a place just like this, high and remote and sealed from the world by black glass.

She and Gil had been together for a year when they'd bought the apartment on Loeno Towers, pooling their savings and still having to borrow half the down payment from his parents. They were both successful for a while, working hard, saving, allowing themselves one shift out every week, a few carefree hours when talk of finances was carefully banned.

And then Gil got his transfer, a lateral movement across department lines that led to a job two thousand radii from the Scope of Jaspeer, far out in Gerad territory. The job was supposed to be temporary, lasting no more than two months, but now it had gone eight months with no real end in sight. Gil had been home only three times. His travel bonus wasn't enough to cover his expenses: things were expensive in Gerad and his income was garnished twice to pay two different sets of taxes – a bookkeeping problem that was supposed to have been solved by now, but somehow wasn't.

Gil had been sending what he could, but Aiah couldn't make up the difference on her own. Payments were falling behind, each by another day or two. Late payment penalties were piling up.

She considered acquiring a roommate, but Gil was against it. It would be, he explained, like admitting defeat. He still expected his new job to end any week now, and he didn't want to have to evict someone who'd just settled in. Roommates were against the Loeno protocols in any case, and she'd have to smuggle the person in.

Not but that she couldn't. She was one of the Cunning People, after all.

And she couldn't sell the place either. Loeno Towers had been built in expectation of a rise in demand for upper-middle-class housing and the demand hadn't come. A third of the apartments were still vacant, and the rest were going for bargain prices. If she sold, she'd have to sell at well below what they'd paid.

Gil wouldn't consider selling in any case. He'd say it admitted defeat.

Defeat was a stranger to Gil's mindset, but not to Aiah's: her whole culture, the entire nation of Cunning People, had all outsmarted themselves spectacularly three generations ago, and after that self-destruction no amount of cunning could piece together the wreckage. Even the Metropolis of Barkazi was gone, the once-sovereign commonwealth now carved into districts governed by former neighbors. Defeat and fragmentation was in the air Aiah breathed as a child. When she'd won her scholarship to the Rathene School, and then to the university, every single relative told her nothing good would come of it. *They're teaching you to betray your people*, her mother insisted.

Well, maybe they were. She had been awed by the Jaspeeris, by the utter simplicity of their optimism. Infected by their certainty, she'd signed up for geomancy classes, even though her scholarship didn't cover the plasm fees required.

The two years of theory went well, but after theory came practice, and she'd run into a stone wall: she simply couldn't afford her own discipline. So she shifted to administration and after graduation applied to the Plasm Authority. At least the civil service hired Barkazils, and in the back of her mind she'd thought that in working for the Authority she'd at least be learning something about plasm.

When she'd met Gil, she found him the most certain man she'd ever met; for a while Aiah thought Gil and his people had somehow found the magic her own ancestors had inexplicably missed. He was pale-skinned and Jaspeeri and practiced optimism as if it were a religion.

'All Barkazil heroes are losers,' he pointed out once, after she told him a few stories from her people's tradition. 'Have you noticed that?'

No, not till he mentioned it. Then she thought of Karlo, the greatest Barkazil hero, who had been offered the Ascendancy and refused it, and who had been walled off by the Shield along with everyone else; and of Chonah, who tricked her brilliant way through life until she lost everything and threw herself off a building, and in so doing got herself promoted to immortal in charge of hustlers; and of the Metropolitan Trocco, who got involved with Thymmah the prostitute and . . .

Well. The point was made.

Gil has no loser heroes. His role models all Ascended, or became Metropolitan of some district or other, or at the very least scored a winning goal in the last seconds of the big game. He read books on how to succeed by concentrating on the proper successful thoughts, and gave her solemn instruction in how it was all supposed to work.

'The human mind generates its own plasm,' he said. 'You just have to get it working for you.' It's not what they taught her in her geomancy classes at the university, but she figured she didn't have anything to lose by believing.

Successful thoughts. She'd thought nothing but successful thoughts for months, and the bills still arrive on the commo almost daily.

For a moment she considers asking her father for help. She's only met him three times in her life – he'd left the family when she was two. A couple years ago, just after Aiah had started at the Authority, he'd called her, a voice on the phone she didn't even remember, and asked if perhaps they might have dinner.

She didn't remember the face, either: he was a middle-aged stranger, plump and fairly well-off, the half-owner of a machine shop. After leaving Aiah's mother he'd remarried and had another family; Aiah has a pair of half-brothers she's never met. They managed to spend a pleasant hour together in the restaurant, and have met for dinner twice since and spoken every so often on the phone.

No, she decides, she won't ask her father for help.

After all these years, she doesn't want to feel she owes him anything.

A yellow flash lights up the room. Aiah assumes it's another advertisement until, a few seconds later, thunder rattles her black glass wall.

On the video news, Mengene is leading a jumpsuit-clad team into some utility mains on Old Parade. Oeneme appears and makes reassuring sounds at the camera. Aiah can't figure out why he looks different until she realizes that, for the video, he's laced himself into a corset.

Aiah's eyes slide from the oval screen to the little door set into the wall by the apartment entrance. The door set into the dark grained polymer paneling, the door with its little silver lock that only Authority keys will open.

Loeno Towers is set up to deliver plasm to each room,

not huge amounts like Grand City, but enough to get a lot of things done. That was part of the fantasy once: when they got ahead financially, Aiah could resume her geomancy studies.

Aiah thinks about what her cunning cousin told her about meters.

She rises from the bed and drifts across the room. One lightning flash after another lights her way. As a member of the Emergency Response teams she has a passkey, just in case she has to cut off someone's power. She opens the door, looks at the meter for a while. The Authority's yellow-and-red seals look back at her.

Her mouth is very dry.

She could open the meter with the same key, observe the silent gears that haven't moved since she'd bought the apartment. A couple substitutes placed just so, the gear ratio reversed, and her fortune is made. Aiah can bleed the plasm off into batteries, then sell it.

But of course she'd get caught. Sooner or later someone would notice that the seals were broken on the gearbox. Sooner or later one of her clients, perhaps even a relative, would turn her in for the reward.

And that would bring what remained of the dream to an end. The Authority would never employ anyone convicted of stealing plasm. The civil service would close, and she couldn't imagine anyone else hiring her either. Then it would be back to her old neighborhood, to be surrounded by her family, a new child every year or so, the check from the government every two weeks . . .

Her loser heritage fulfilled.

Maybe it was inevitable. At least then, one way or another, it would be over.

She closes the little door, goes back to bed, and tries to summon cunning thoughts.

None appear.

* * *

There's a deep subsonic rumble as the pneuma's hidden machinery inhales, a sound like the breath of a god, and then something kicks Aiah in the spine and the car is fired along its tube like a message cylinder through the Authority's mail system.

Aiah rubs sleep from her eyes. She's up early in hopes another look through her maps and transparencies might provide an answer.

She started with the earliest of the transparencies, one that showed a perfect rectangle of new apartment and office buildings going up four hundred years ago. And then it occurred to her to wonder what was on the site before. What was it that could have occupied that perfect six-block rectangle between 1189th and 1193rd Streets?

An old factory? A government building? Industrial park? Whatever it was, there had to be remnants, old foundations, utility connections, piers, rebar . . . a lot of mass for which there was no longer any real record.

Then she checked her largest-scale map with her dividers, marching them across the jigsawed chromograph sections, and found that the site was exactly 144 radii from Bursary Street, where the flaming woman first appeared.

One hundred and forty-four, twelve squared. One of the Great Squares. A flamer's sourceline, its umbilical cord to its energy source, might have fallen into that ratio naturally. A Grand Square like 81 would have been better, a square of a square, but she couldn't hope for everything.

The discovery set a little signal humming through her nerves. Now she'd check the archives and see if she could find out what had been on that site before the housing went up.

Her ears pop as the pneuma dives under an obstruction, a deep structure or subterranean river. On the front of the car is a video screen, a wide bright oval intended to keep the passengers tranquilized. It's covered with a slab of bulletproof glass and fixed to the car with heavy stainless steel bolts just in case anyone has a notion to remove it.

The car's speakers are wretched and buzz insistently. Aiah can't hear any of the dialogue, but it doesn't matter. She knows the story by heart.

There's the winsome blond apprentice with her white even teeth and innocent heart. There's the old master with snowy eyebrows like pigeon's wings, his manner gruff but his heart of purest hammered gold. The master answers the apprentice's every naive question, imparts vaguely optimistic philosophy, explains the ways of geomancy, and offers brusque advice on the winning of the hero, who as the son of the Metropolitan is about a thousand social strata higher than the heroine but who, luckily for the apprentice, is in deep trouble.

At the story's climax the apprentice climbs into the hot seat in some Transmission Control office, takes a copper transference grip in each hand, and screams, 'No *time to explain! Give me full power* now!' And the next thing you know the villain is thwarted, the Metropolitan's ass is saved once again, and the apprentice and the hero are wrapped in a clinch in his rooftop arboretum. Fade to black. The end.

Aiah's seen the film a hundred times, and during her adolescence probably read a thousand books with a similar plot. And all she can think when she sees one now is, *If only it were that easy.*

If only there were really these kindly old masters to explain everything, to predict the future unerringly, and guide you through life with a few homespun maxims. If only you didn't have to pay impossible sums for all the plasm consumed during training. If only the heart's advice were infallible.

But the system is rigged, and now, with the voices of her Barkazil ancestors chorusing *I told you so* in her head, she can't understand how she ever figured it wasn't. Those who have access, whether to money or plasm, keep it to themselves, and so far as she can tell that's true everywhere. Maybe the Ascended Ones are different, but they're outside the Shield. The only way she'll ever finish her training will be to risk prison by stealing the raw material. The only way she'll ever find a teacher will be to pay him wads of cash she doesn't have, or megamehrs of plasma she'd have to steal, or – maybe if she's lucky – she'll only have to trade him her body. And the only way she'll ever meet the son of a Metropolitan will be if he runs over her in his flashy Bolt 79D automobile.

Maybe she can find the flaming woman's source. Maybe it'll get her noticed if she actually does her job well.

It's not something anyone seems really to expect of her.

There's a blast of air as the pneuma car brakes, then a belly-queasing wrench as it drops out of the system to the designated platform. Humming electromagnets cut velocity further. Bright station lights pour through the windows, gleam from the Pneuma Authority's blue-tiled walls.

Time to go to work.

It's a four-block walk from the pneuma station to the trackline leading to Rocketman, then another kidney-punching ride to Rocketman Station on a car riding on its metal rims. After a forty-five minute search through the archives, she finds an old piece of paper, one that comes apart along its creases as she unfolds it. It describes an old plastics plant at a site called Terminal, one sold for scrap so that a 'mixed neighborhood' could be built on the site.

Triumph hums in her nerves.

She may be onto something here.

*   *   *

Two trackline stops east from Rocketman is Terminal, a station that isn't, actually, the line's terminal. Another one of those names come adrift from its original meaning.

From street level, Terminal is just like her old neighborhood, the leaning old brick buildings, scaffolding, the throb of music and cry of children and smells of cooking.

But the food is spiced differently, the music bounces to a different beat, and the faces are pale and Jaspeeri and suspicious. There are Jaspeeri Nation stickers in some of the shop windows. A warning trickles up her spine as the import of all this begins to penetrate her consciousness.

She concludes that her official yellow jumpsuit will protect her. But still she's glad for the company of Lastene and Grandshuk as she begins her search over the old factory foundations.

Success, right away. She checks three buildings in a row and finds gimmicked meters in every single one. A plasm diver has been operating here.

There's some contraband coming up from below, clear enough. Maybe not the source for the burning woman, but *something*.

The third building she tries is an old office structure converted to residence. The building superintendent, a broad-beamed man in green gabardine pants, agrees to let her into the basement – not that he's got a lot of choice – and one level below the street she's surprised to find an old blue-tiled stairway leading down. Blue, the color of the Pneuma Authority, not the yellow of the Trackline Authority. An iron-barred door bars the entrance, closed with chain and a fist-sized padlock. A battered tin sign says TERMINAL, with a fistmark pointing down.

'What's that?' Aiah asks. She feels so close the plasm might as well be pulsing through her veins.

The superintendent plucks at his suspenders. 'Entrance to an old pneuma station.'

Her mind swims as she tries to remember whether or not this was on any of her old overlays. 'When did they close it off?'

A shrug. 'Long before I ever got here.'

'Do you have the key?'

The superintendent only laughs.

'Do you have any bolt cutters?'

'No.'

'Shouldn't be hard to find bolt cutters in *this* neighborhood,' Lastene says, and the superintendent scowls.

Grandshuk just walks up to the padlock and gives it a yank. The chain rattles, and the padlock falls open. Lastene barks a surprised laugh.

Grandshuk unwraps the chain and pushes the barred door open. He looks at the superintendent.

'Somebody's been down here,' he says.

The superintendent looks innocent. 'Nobody I know. Maybe one of the tenants. Or their kids.'

Aiah switches on her headlamp and torch. 'Let's go,' she says.

Heavy boots echo on the stair as the party descends. Memories rise in Aiah: the Plasm Authority has an apprenticeship program designed to acquaint budding executives with their jurisdiction from ground level on up. After college she spent two years underground, doing the sort of jobs that Lastene and Grandshuk do every day. She'd hated it at the time, but it taught her more about the way plasm is distributed than anything she'd ever learned at the university.

There are footprints on the soiled tile steps, most of them tiny; children have been down here, and a few adults. On the second landing there's an old bedroll, empty food tins, used fuel cells for a chemical stove, and an untidy pile of plastic liquor bottles. Grandshuk kicks at the bedroll and

Aiah's leaping light catches a mouse as it scurries away.

'Years old,' he says. There are baby mice, Aiah sees, living in the bedroll. Her nerves wail as Grandshuk methodically crushes them all beneath his boot.

At the next landing water erosion has caused the tile wall to collapse. Aiah and Grandshuk peer into the little cavern revealed, see chunks of old concrete, brick, a leaking water main. No real plasm source.

Any footprints are now washed away by a water cascade that pours merrily down the stairs. Aiah walks carefully on the slippery tiles, keeps one gloved hand on the corroded rail. Something swims away as they approach a lake at the bottom of the stairs. The water level goes over Aiah's ankles. It's cold and she begins to shiver as damp soaks through her socks.

A level corridor sloshes along for about half a pitch, then divides. UPPER PLATFORM, one sign says. The sign for the other is missing. The water all pours off that way, so its level has to be lower. Aiah looks at Grandshuk. His face is yellow in the light of her lamp.

'Procedure says we don't split up,' she says.

'That's crap,' Grandshuk says. 'We know people have been down here. Nothing's going to cave in.'

Aiah hesitates.

'I can't feel my feet any more,' Lastene says. 'Let's do whatever's quickest.'

Aiah shines her light down the river. It's the most danger-ous way: if they're to split, two people should take that route, and one the other.

She's the leader, she thinks, the downward path should be hers.

On the other hand, she'd really like to wring out her socks.

'You two go down that way,' she says. 'If it's more than a hundred paces, come back and wait for me here. I'll check the upper platform by myself.'

They don't seem to resent her giving herself the driest job. Grandshuk and Lastene begin wading down the corridor. Aiah watches them descend, silhouetted against their own lights, then takes the other corridor.

Within ten paces she's on the old platform. Her bootfalls echo in the dark. Wet squelches beneath her soles.

It's a pneuma, all right, the oval tunnel makes that clear enough, and there are runners instead of tracks at the bottom of the pit.

The ceiling is supported by a row of iron stanchions, fluted, each with clawed feet bolted to the concrete platform through a frayed old pad of asbestos insulation. Light supports hang from the ceiling, the light fixtures themselves long since scavenged away. Chunks of wall are missing where fixtures have been torn out.

Aiah wets a finger, holds it up. No obvious air currents: the pneuma line is probably sealed off farther down the track. She slowly walks the length of the platform, examining everything carefully in the light of her torch.

She stops, redirects the light. Her heart lurches.

There's a streak of reddish dust floating down the length of one of the station's support stanchions. She looks closer, sees that powdery rusted iron seems to have migrated to the surface of the stanchion, pooled around the clawed feet, overrunning the asbestos pad and pointing straight across the platform.

Electrolytic deposition. Sometimes this happens if there's an electric current in an atmosphere heavy with electrolytes, but that water spilling down the stair was fresh, not salt. Hairs rise on the back of Aiah's neck.

Connections. What is that stanchion trying to connect itself to?

She flicks the light from the stanchion across the platform, sees a doorway. The door has long been removed, and there's a little gnomon in the doorframe where a lock was once placed. Her heart is in her throat. She walks to the doorway, flashes her light in.

It was a public toilet. The fixtures and even the pipe have been removed, leaving gaping holes in the walls and floor. There's been a cave-in – an old L-shaped iron brace has fallen through the roof, probably in an earthquake, and now lies cantwise along the length of the room.

Aiah approaches hesitantly, pans her light along the room.

Empty eye-sockets stare back at her. Aiah's throat clamps shut in terror and suddenly she can't breathe. Something – pulse probably – crashes in her ears. The room swims in front of her. She leans against the doorway for support.

The burning woman. She remembers the terror-filled face, humanity consumed in flames. The plasm exploded through the woman's mind, and though it soon had a mind of its own it retained the diver's pattern.

She takes a long series of deep breaths and steps forward, tottering on her heavy boots. She tries to focus her mind on theory, on a scientific theory of what's happened here.

Earthquake drops brace, disrupting the plasm well. The quake probably caused enough damage to the mains and meters above so that a small amount of missing plasm wasn't detected.

The plasm had been building for years, most likely, till one lone plasm diver found it and triggered a blowhole that exploded through her body and brain and ran amuck in the world outside.

As she approaches the beam Aiah tries to keep her eyes away from the corpse, from what the plasm has done to it. There's probably a small amount of plasm collected here since the catastrophe, most likely a detectable amount. She unhooks the portable meter from her belt, connects an alligator clip to the brace, focuses her helmet light on the dial, and watches wide-eyed as the needle almost leaps off the logarhythmic scale.

For a moment she's aware of nothing but the pounding of her own pulse. The plasm well is brimming over and immeasurably powerful, fully capable of burning every nerve in her body if she's careless.

It's not a one-time thing. She's found a glory hole, a lost well worth millions. That old plastics factory, all the iron and steel in its foundation, and who knows what *that*'s connected to besides the pneuma station.

With trembling hands she pulls the alligator clip off the brace, then gropes her way back to the door, trying to keep her eyes off the body. Once outside on the platform, she leans her back against one of the torn walls and tries to collect her breath, her thoughts.

The burning woman stalks through her mind. Her shrieks echo in Aiah's ears.

Some time later she hears the clump of boots, sees lights dancing in the entrance tunnel. She begins walking toward her team. A torch dazzles her, and she raises a hand to block the light.

'Anything?' Grandshuk's voice booms loud in the empty space.

Aiah takes a deep breath.

'Nothing,' she says. 'I found nothing.'

3

The lower platform, Grandshuk says, is the final station of the old eastward-bound pneuma line, hence the name Terminal. The leaking water pours across the platform into the pits where the old passenger elevators once were – apparently the old drain system works perfectly well, because the lake isn't very deep.

Grandshuk wants to go down the tunnels, lots of old metal and brick down there, but Aiah wants to get her team off the platform as soon as possible.

There are big empty spaces behind the station, where complicated machinery, salvaged long ago, once turned the pneuma cars around and shot them to the upper platform. And there have to be air shafts that fed the compressors, and other stairways to bring the passengers down.

'If the diver found a source, she'd need to get it to the surface,' Aiah says. 'If we can find a connection in one of those shafts, we can track it back to the source, ne?'

She takes the other stairways up, finds they've been cut off by new construction. The air shafts are huge, empty, drafty things, brick planted with old iron rungs leading to the surface. The rungs are wet with leakage or condensation and covered with rough flakes of rust. Aiah insists on textbook safety procedures, the team members clipping and unclipping safety lines as they clamber up and down. Drizzle mists down on her hardhat as she climbs. Her thighs ache with the effort.

All the deliberate work takes time, and Aiah can use time to map the place thoroughly in her mind, to work out all the possible access routes to the station. She doesn't want to keep walking down that waterfall again and again.

In the darkness, it's very easy to close her eyes and see the burning woman pulsing on the insides of her lids.

The shift passes, then a few hours of the next shift. Finally the team drags itself back up the waterfall to the basement of the apartment building. The superintendent has long since vanished.

'I want to get in a couple hours' research first thing tomorrow on how far those tunnels extend,' Aiah says. 'We don't want to walk for ten radii tomorrow.'

'We clock on at o8.oo,' Grandshuk says.

'Fine. Clock on by all means. But you don't have to meet me here till 10:oo.'

A flash of paranoia makes her look at Grandshuk carefully, just to see if there's a look of suspicion in his eyes, but all she can see is weariness.

Outside there's a solid wall of black cloud under the Shield. Chill rain pours down in solid sheets. The streets are full to the gutters and black, with the emergency lighting on. But it's no more wet under the street scaffolding than it was in Terminal Station, so Aiah stays fairly comfortable on a walk to the nearest hardware store. She gets a strange look from the man who sells her a big padlock, then notices the Jaspeeri Nation sticker only on her way out.

She returns to the Terminal Station entrance and puts the bright new padlock on the chain, then puts the key in her pocket.

A glory hole, Aiah thinks. A river of power, vast and strong and limitless. And she's the only one who knows about it.

She doesn't know what she's going to do with it yet, but she's thinking hard. She's one of the Cunning People, after all.

* * *

Aiah leans against the wall of the Loeno elevator. Streaks of dirt run down her face and jumpsuit. Neighbors frown at her politely: she's leaving dirty smudges on the elevator mirror glass. When the door opens she wearily shoulders her tote bag and marches out.

It's well past the start of third shift. She figures she'll get about five hours' sleep.

After she left Terminal she went back to Rocketman to do the research she'd promised to do the next day. She finds documentation that relates to the transparencies that should have been in the map file, but which disappeared or decayed or got misfiled. The old pneuma had been constructed for the purpose of bringing workers to the plastics factory from their company housing forty radii away. When the factory closed the whole pneuma had been decommissioned, its equipment salvaged but the tunnels left in place. New construction probably cut the tubes somewhere, but Aiah doesn't bother to research the location; she figures that tomorrow she'll lead Grandshuk and Lastene as far downtube as the next station, then switch to the other tunnel and return. A futile mission, but at least it has the virtue of keeping her team busy and away from the transphysical power well humming away on the upper platform.

Her feet ache at the thought of the long walk.

As she enters the apartment she sees the yellow bulb glowing on her communications array. Aiah drops the tote bag with a thud and walks to where the array is inset into the wall. She has a hard time focusing her eyes on the dial, which shows three messages. She presses a button and hears a whine as the etching belt begins to roll and then a grinding noise as the play head moves to the first position. She's got to lubricate that play head soon.

One message is from Tella, informing her that there's another meeting at end of work shift tomorrow. The second is from her mother and complains that Aiah was in Old Shorings and hasn't paid a visit. The message, which promises to be fairly long, as usual cuts off in mid-word, either because her mother's wall unit is faulty or because she forgot to keep her thumb on the transmit key.

The third is from Gil. When she hears his voice Aiah closes her eyes and leans her head against the grain of the polymer paneling and lets her breath slip past her lips, just lets the weariness and sorrow flow.

He's sorry she's not home, he says. He'd like to hear her voice. He misses her. The acquisition is looking more complicated every day but he's working double shifts and he hopes to be back soon. He had this unexpected expense – to do with his apartment lease, something called 'bed money' – and the company should reimburse him eventually; but this month's cashgram is going to be a little short.

He wishes she were home. He loves her. Maybe she can call him early tomorrow, an hour or so before first shift. Maybe in a month or so he can get some time off and come home for a few days. Goodbye.

Aiah opens her eyes, lets the room come back into fragile focus. A plasm ball with the logo for Gulman Shoes rotates past her window. She looks down at her feet, sees her bulky tote bag, and she remembers what she's carrying in it.

She picks up the tote, carries it to the kitchen table, opens it. Its main contents are three plasm batteries, layers of copper and brass and ceramic coated in white insulating plastic. Heavy things, miniaturized versions of the giant capacitors in the basement of Rocketman Substation.

Aiah plans to bleed off plasma from the glory hole, sell it somewhere – she doesn't quite know where just yet, but Old Shorings is never far from her thoughts. Then, after she's raised a little money, she'll have to think of something else, because she can't keep shuttling batteries around forever.

She adds to the tote a blanket, a file, some light machine oil, some cleaning rags – then, after some thought, one of her old college textbooks on plasm use. She takes a shower, thinks about drying her hair, decides not to. Shieldlight is breaking through the rainclouds overhead, so she unfolds the brushed aluminum crank from the wall, cranks the window polarizer a few times, darkens the room. She falls into bed and reaches for her alarm clock so she can set it a little early and call Gil, and then her hand freezes in mid-air.

What, she wonders, will she tell him? That she's found a plasm source worth millions, that she's going to tap it slowly and bleed it off, that with luck she can make a fortune but she'll most likely end up in prison? She can also tell him the damn plasm source is so powerful it may just blow on its own, cause another catastrophe for which she'll be responsible.

She can't even imagine his reaction. Whatever it would be, she knows, it would be utterly reasonable. He would break the situation down, make a list of logical steps. Is it too late to turn back? he'd wonder. Probably he'd want her to find a lawyer, follow his advice. Or maybe just find a psychiatrist, who knew?

Aiah picks up the alarm clock, sets the wake-up time fifteen minutes early.

She'll tell him she's working on proper visualization of her successful thoughts.

Aiah dreams of the burning woman, of her terrifying progress down Bursary Street, her passage leaving a river of fire. She hears the screams of the woman's victims, cries echoed by the woman's own wailing cry. And then the burning woman turns onto the Avenue of the Exchange, and Aiah relives the moment when she sees her standing there, flame pouring from her fingertips, the central figure mirrored and re-mirrored by the glass walls on either side of her, three views of the burning face, the hollow eyes, the lips parted in a scream that never ends . . .

The face is Aiah's own.

The woman's scream rises from Aiah's throat as she wakes.

The room is silent around her. The building, its vast webbed structure built for the generation and containment of plasm, broods silently, gathering power.

The three batteries sit waiting on the table, awaiting their fate.

The connection to Gerad is bad, full of other voices, half-heard conversations that act as a chorus to Aiah's words. But her heart aches even at a distorted version of Gil's voice, a voice fogged with sleep and weariness, and Aiah doesn't dare look up at the kitchen table with its tote and plasm batteries, reminders of what she's planning.

'I'm sorry I missed you,' Aiah says. 'I was working.' She tells him about the plasm blow out, the fact she's working shifts-and-a-half underground.

'Did you catch the part of my message about the apartment lease? The bed money thing?'

'Yes.'

'I can't send you as much this month. I hope that's all right.'

She can feel the anger entering her voice and can't quite hide it. 'It's fine with me, Gil. But the people we owe money to might think otherwise.'

'Who do we owe money to?'

She can't believe he has to ask. She gives him the short list, then hears a brief silence broken only by a stray voice, one from another conversation, saying *What in the prophet's name?*

'There's got to be something wrong,' Gil says finally.

'Yes. We could barely afford this place before you left. Now we can't afford it at all.'

Gil's tone was patient. 'We worked out a budget.'

The heavy plastic-and-metal headset is hammering her

skull, pounding places already chafed by her hardhat. 'Yes, we did,' Aiah says. 'Based on you sending me a certain amount every month, which you have not done.'

'You're saying it's *my* fault now? How is it my fault that I've had all these expenses?'

Aiah has to take a breath or two. 'I'm not laying blame,' she said. 'I'm just telling you how things are.'

'Things are expensive in Gerad,' Gil says. 'You should see the place I'm living in – it's pathetic, maybe three mattresses wide, but Havell got it for me and I'm stuck with it. And I'm obliged to take all these other people out, buy them drinks, and the prices are rigged in the places catering to executives, because they're all owned by the Operation, so . . .'

'You have to take people out?'

'That's how business is done here. It's all done over meals and at clubs. And the company only reimburses part of it, and . . .'

'I think you need to stop doing that kind of business, Gil.'

'The quicker I get it all done, the quicker I get home.'

'We're going bankrupt,' Aiah says.

There's another silence. *Banshug wouldn't do that!* says a voice on the phone.

'I'll try to come home,' he says. 'Soon. There's got to be a way to work something out.'

For the first time Aiah looks up at the plasm batteries waiting in her tote bag.

'Soon,' she says. 'I need you soon.'

I need you to save me from this, she thinks.

Aiah locks the pneuma station grill behind her, then walks down the old stair to where the water spill begins. She holds to the rusted iron guardrail as she carefully treads down the little series of waterfalls. She realizes her steps are slower than they really have to be.

She comes to the bottom of the stair and her shifting helmet light catches a glimpse of writhing liquid silver – a flash of belly scales, of needle teeth – of something moving in the shallow lake, and her heart gives a terrified leap.

The serpentine thing writhes away at the touch of her light. Aiah waits, one insulated glove clamped on the rail, torchlight beams stabbing at the water while her pulse drums in her skull.

Whatever the thing was, it's gone. A kind of resonance effect generated by untapped plasm sometimes gives birth to creatures unhealthy, unnatural; or maybe someone actually built the thing, and then set it free or allowed it to escape.

She hesitates for a long time before she dares to put a foot in the water. Whatever the creature was, it doesn't reappear.

The platform seems larger than the day before, the shadows darker, angles stranger. Aiah's thundering heart sounds louder in her ears than the sound of her echoing boots. She remembers the dead woman's hollow eye-sockets, remembers she's been dead for three days now and this isn't going to be pleasant at all. Aiah hesitates outside the door to the old toilet, sweeping her hand torch over the platform, trying to make sure nothing's there.

She's just delaying things, she knows. Either she's doing this or she isn't. She takes a breath, turns, enters the room.

The dead woman lies on a mound of broken concrete next to the canted brace. Aiah sees a dark spill of auburn hair, heavy boots, one hand dangling, the other still fiercely clamped on the brace. The mouth is open, a perfect oval of an endless scream. Her hollow eyes grow larger as Aiah moves closer. Aiah's steps slow, then halt. She doesn't want to get any closer.

Aiah's nostrils twitch obsessively, but she detects no odor of decay. The woman seems curiously shrunken inside her olive-green overalls.

Aiah's heart thunders in her chest. She takes a step closer, then another. The woman's skin seems stiff, parchment-like, the lips shrunken, long teeth visible in shrunken gums. There are no eyes in the hollow sockets, nothing there at all.

Aiah kneels by the body, reaches out a hand that freezes in mid-air. Air spills from Aiah's lungs in a soft hiss.

The woman is mummified, she realizes. Moisture drawn out, nerves burned away, soft organs like the eyes just *gone*. All consumed by the Bursary Street holocaust as surely as the lives of its other victims.

Aiah's already wearing insulated gloves. Carefully she reaches for the woman's arm, takes it gently, pulls the clawed hand away from the hot brace. There's no resistance, no rigor; the arm seems to weigh nothing at all. Aiah opens her hand and lets the arm fall.

Sister, she apologizes, *I'm sorry*.

She takes the blanket out of her tote, lays it next to the plasm diver, and then rolls the body onto it. She picks the body up – it weighs no more than a heap of dry rags – then moves it around the fallen brace to the back of the room, where it won't be seen in the first flash of someone's torch.

The auburn hair is disordered. Aiah tries to arrange it about the hollow-eyed face, happy she's wearing gloves when a fingertip scrapes across a withered cheek. Then she covers the body with the blanket.

Aiah stands, open-mouthed stare still in her mind, and feels the weight of the surface world about her, all the foundations and beams and brick and concrete, all of it inadvertently generating power, the plasm waiting in its well like water, poised in this old iron brace like a drop at the end of a faucet . . .

She has things to do, and time is passing.

Feeling a prickly psychic pressure from the corpse right behind her, Aiah moves her tote behind the brace and takes

43

out the battery leads, then attaches the alligator clips to the fallen brace. She's not about to touch the brace itself if she can help it. She watches in fine surprise as the batteries fill almost instantly, as the little indicator on top, reacting to the plasm field, goes from red to purple to blue, and then begins to give off an ominous, unearthly cerulean glow, one just like the pile of a high-pressure fission reactor, and potentially just about as dangerous.

She leaves the batteries in place, takes the tote, ducks under the brace, and leaves the room. She approaches the fluted iron pillar on the platform, carefully examines the electrolytic footprint, the rusty indication of iron trying to find its way to a powerful nearby circuit.

Aiah gets out oil and rags and her file and tries to scour the footprint away. Her arms and back still ache from yesterday. Her feet hurt. She finds herself panting for breath, sweat dripping from her nose, and she's barely started.

She thinks of plasm waiting in its batteries.

Aiah returns hesitantly to the plasm source as her mind works through the idea. She hasn't handled live plasm in four or five years, not since the one lab course at college she'd convinced herself she could afford and had to drop in mid-term.

She snaps off one of the alligator clips from a battery, takes the battery to the platform. She opens her old college textbook to one of the plasm-control diagrams she used then, the Trigram. She kneels on the platform and feels her heavy boots pressing up against her buttocks. She puts the open book in front of her and props her hand torch up so that it shines on the pages. Then she strips off one of her insulated gloves and holds the battery lead with one hand, keeping her fingers carefully on the insulated wire and not daring to touch the bare metal of the alligator clip.

Suddenly this seems the most ridiculous thing in the world. Stolen plasm, a battery, a college textbook she hasn't looked at in years – the potential for harm is absurd.

Still. The battery shouldn't have *that* much power.

She looks down at the Trigram, tries to fix it in her mind, fix the pattern of it, the balance of energies. *Human will*, dry lecture-voice echoing in her mind, *is the modulator of plasm*. Time to get her will moving, to visualize some successful thoughts.

She can't remember any of the chants she learned in training.

I am the power. The power is mine. Idiotic, but it's all she can think of. And the point is focus anyway, not what's actually said.

The power is a part of me. The power responds to my will.

She closes her eyes and the Trigram glows on the inside of her lids. Carefully she inches her fingers up the battery lead, touches bare metal, and . . .

It's like a peregrine falcon diving off a building ledge for the first time, a moment of shock, then surprise at finding herself in her natural element, the wind rustling through pinions, smoothing the feathers at the base of the neck, the airy medium itself responsive to her will, to the merest inflexion of a wing.

. . . it's *effortless*. It's *easy*. . .

The Trigram burns in her mind like fire, the same blue radiant color as the battery indicator. She can taste power on her tongue.

The weariness is banished from my body. My body is whole and well and powerful. The energy pulse is so powerful that the words seem redundant, but she guides the Trigram on a mental journey through her body, urging the weariness away, banishing fatigue toxins, flushing tissues with energy.

Aiah opens her eyes, sees through the burning pattern of the Trigram the fluted iron pillar with its telltale upwelling of rust. She stands, one hand still clamped on the metal

45

clip, and she tries to remember the atomic composition of iron oxide — is it Fe_2O_3 or Fe_3O_2? It doesn't matter, she decides, she should use the atomic number, but now suddenly she can't remember it. Six? Eight? She seems to remember eight.

She reaches to the pillar, feels the cool red dust under her fingers, then projects her power through her fingertips, another ridiculous chant running through her head, O^8 *out!* O^8 *out!* O^8 *out!*, and maybe the plasm knows more about atomic composition than she does, because to her amazed delight she sees the fluted rust shrink, turn dark, become iron — poor iron, spongy and brittle, but iron none the less.

She moves her hand up the pillar, plasm flowing through her body into the rust, transmitting it . . . and then the power fades, and she gives a little cry of disappointment as she feels the last of the battery's contents drain away.

Aiah stands on the platform, mouth half-open in amazement. Power still tingles in her nerves. Her heat throbs like a turbine. She raises a hand, touches her breast, feels an aroused nipple. Her vagina is heavy with arousal. An astonished laugh escapes her throat.

The little hints of power she was permitted in school were nothing compared to the touch of this miraculous reality.

She almost dances back to the glory hole, fills the battery, returns to the platform. Brings the Trigram to her mind, connects again to the circuit, projects her power to the iron pillar. Aiah burnishes the rust away, then stands for a moment, reluctant to let the circuit drop. She puts the alligator clip carefully down on the concrete platform, then stands for a while, enjoying the power that hums through her veins.

Aiah peels back the jumpsuit's elastic wrist, checks her watch. She doesn't have much time left.

She glances up and down the platform again. The gaping

lavatory door mars the stripped concrete wall. What if Lastene or Grandshuk decided to take a look inside? Hell – what if one of them just wanted a private place to piss and wanders in?

She fills the battery again and tries to focus the power on the doorway, on creating an illusion of an unbroken concrete wall. Her first attempt is translucent and wavery, but after she charges the battery another time she succeeds in producing a satisfactory wall, complete with the little lines of plaster that remained when the original tile was stripped away by the reclaimers. She has to put an arm through it to make absolutely certain that she didn't produce an actual concrete wall.

She leaves the battery just inside the door, its copper contact touching the illusion, feeding it.

How long will it last? She has no idea, though it probably won't stay there for long. Just an hour or two is all she needs.

It's only then that Aiah realizes she forgot to use the Trigram as a focus. She was so dizzy with success that she forgot proper procedure.

Better not do that again, she admonishes herself. It could be dangerous.

It's time to leave but she really doesn't want to go – the whole experience has been far too glorious, too satisfying. The last thing she wants to do is play troglodyte in some damp dungeon.

She makes certain all her gear is hidden behind her illusory wall and heads for the surface. Plasm still energizes her body, she feels she could run a hundred radii without stopping to catch her breath.

When Aiah comes to the shallow little river between the platform and the stairwell she doesn't hesitate. Any scaly monsters, she figures, had better watch out.

Grandshuk and Lastene are waiting for her outside the barred door. Lastene looks surprised as she mounts the stair. She looks down at herself, sees the wet boots, the fresh mud scars on her jumpsuit. She turns the key in the padlock, opens the door.

'I got uneasy about that cave-in and leak,' she said. 'I went down to take a look at it, see if there was something we missed.'

'That violates procedure,' Lastene says. He seems suspicious, though probably only that Aiah might have cheated him out of some overtime.

'Anything there?' Grandshuk asks. He hasn't bothered to shave today. He has to turn his broad, powerful body sideways to get through the door.

'Nothing,' Aiah says, repeating her most successful thought. She keeps wanting to laugh. 'Nothing at all.'

Aiah wonders if the plasm she gives herself is like a dose of push or amphetamine, if the buoyancy she feels will wear off and leave her exhausted and hung-over. But it doesn't. She burns the energy off over the course of the day, but by the time she returns to the Authority Building for the meeting she feels much fresher than she would have coming down off any drug.

She's done everything possible to make the day uneventful. The illusion she'd built held up through the brief time it took to lead Grandshuk and Lastene down the upper platform, and the rest of the first half of the shift was spent in the tunnels. After the midshift break they finished exploring the old air shafts, then came up to the surface to start checking meters all over again.

She opens her locker in the Response Team assembly room and gazes in faint surprise at the gray suit, lace, and heels she'd worn three days ago, before she'd changed into the yellow jumpsuit. It seems the costume of a stranger.

Aiah goes to the changing room and puts on her suit and tries to comb her ratted hair. The sight of herself in the mirror makes her wish she'd carried a little of the plasm with her so that she'd make herself look beautiful, or at any rate presentable.

She needn't have worried. Mengene and the others, after the better part of three days underground, barely have the energy to greet Aiah as she walks into the room. She seats herself far away from Niden's cold and waits for the meeting to start.

Mengene's opening address is rambling and circular, but Aiah soon realizes the point of it is to decide whether or not the Authority ought to declare victory and go on to other business. A few small plasm leaks have been discovered on Old Parade, leaks that could conceivably have built up, over time, into a big enough charge to produce the Bursary Street display.

'Any indication that any of these sources were tapped?' Aiah asks. 'Any sign of plasm divers?'

The others give her weary looks. They've all been under Old Parade and they already know the answers. 'No,' Mengene says. 'But that doesn't necessarily mean these sources couldn't have caused the conflagration. Sometimes a large enough charge of plasm will react to the massed consciousness of the population at large, there doesn't necessarily have to be any one person to direct it.'

That's official policy, Aiah knows, but she doesn't know if she quite believes it. She suspects that any events attributed to collected consciousness are in fact the result of a single consciousness who left no traces.

The discussion proceeds listlessly. Nobody really wants to bring up the possibility that if the Authority announces it's found the source and dealt with it, and then another flamer runs mad on Bursary Street, any number of careers could get torched right along with the financial district.

Eventually there's a compromise. An announcement will be made – 'in order to calm public fears,' as Mengene puts it, not to mention taking political pressure off the Authority – but the search for plasm sources will continue at a

49

reduced scale. No more extra shifts, and people can spend alternate days at their desks. Mengene turns to Aiah.

'Have you found anything?'

'I found a promising source, one off the charts,' she says, 'but there wasn't anything in it.'

'Right. You can join us on Old Parade, then.'

Aiah tries to control her leaping exultation. No more worrying about Grandshuk or Lastene stumbling across the glory hole by accident.

There's a source of unlimited power, and only Aiah knows where it is.

One of the Cunning People should be able to take it from there.

She walks down Bursary Street, flame shooting from her fingertips. People scream and wither and die. Buildings explode outward at a wave of her arm. Glass shatters at her scream. Power roils in her bones like a lake of fire.

Her own screams wake her. Heart thundering, Aiah sits bolt upright in her bed, imprisoned in her silent tower of glass.

4

The trackline car jolts and drives another blow up through Aiah's legs and straight into her kidneys. Standing in the crowded end-of-shift car, she's exhausted from working on New Parade for eight hours, but there's still a bubble of energy in her spine, a phantom of yesterday's plasm that keeps her on her feet.

She's heading out to Terminal again, to pick up her batteries. Two days from now is Senko's Day and, unless Emergency Response insists she work underground on the holiday, she hopes to spend the day with her family and maybe sell some plasm.

The trackline car jolts again and the lights flicker, then go out. The man standing behind Aiah passes the back of his hand over her thighs and buttocks. It's normally the sort of thing she'd ignore – he's not going to feel much through her waterproof jumpsuit anyway – but the spark of plasm dwelling in her makes her consider action, maybe a little upward jab of her elbow . . .

The lights come on again but not fully, a strange yellow half-light that reveals nothing but sallow long-nosed Jaspeeri faces, and Aiah's suddenly aware of the fact she's the only brown-skinned Barkazil on the train, that she's heading into Jaspeeri Nation territory without the formidable presence of Grandshuk backing her, and that maybe getting groped in the underground is going to be the least of her worries. Maybe, she thinks, she ought to acquire some protection. One of her relations could get her a firearm.

At the next stop, when the crowd eases a bit, Aiah moves to another place. From here she can see the platform with its spread of advertising: the new Lynxoid Brothers chromoplay, the new Aldemar thriller, an ad for cigarets, others for beer, for Gulman shoes ('Meet for the Street'), and a new chromo called *Lords of the New City*. She's heard some of the buzz about this last item, because it's directed by Sandvak and is supposed to be based on the life of Constantine. The lead is played not by an actor but by the opera singer Kherzaki, who's supposed to give the role a unique quality of grandeur.

Constantine was always in the news when she was younger. *Lords of the New City* isn't the first chromo made about him and the wars in Cheloki, just the first to garner such prestige. His name and image and cause had hypnotized half the world. When she was in school she had a picture of Constantine up above her desk, and she'd read his books *Power and the New City* and *Government and Liberty*.

One of her cousins, Chavan, had even been inspired to go off and fight for Constantine – though he ended up getting arrested for petty theft in Margathan and never got as far across the world as Cheloki.

Horn Twelve transmit 1800 mm. tfn.

She can't imagine what Constantine is doing in Mage Towers. Jaspeer seems far too tame for him.

Maybe everyone gets old, she thinks. Maybe he's just sitting up there using his talents to create aerial displays for Snap! or Aeroflash cars.

The trackline car lurches away from the station. Terminal is two stops up the track. It's time for Aiah to start maneuvering through the packed commuters toward the doors.

Jaspeeri Nation territory. She'll try to be careful.

Whatever 'careful' means in this situation.

As Aiah comes up she finds the building superintendent drinking on the stoop with some of his cronies, big men with beer bellies and callused hands. The superintendent looks at her sourly.

'Still got business in my basement, lady?'

'Yes.' She begins to shoulder her way through the group of men. Powerful shoulders and pendulous guts loom at her like sagging buildings. She tries not to flinch at the powerful smell of beer.

'You find anything down there?' the super asks. Aiah stops, looks at him.

'Why? You lose something?'

A couple of the men snicker into their beer. The superintendent scowls.

'I'm just looking after my building,' he said. 'I don't like having people wandering around.'

Aiah shoulders past him, steps into the building foyer, turns to face the superintendent. She knows she doesn't dare let him gain the upper hand, that she needs to put him in his place now. 'You never stopped anyone wandering around before,' Aiah said. 'There were people *living* down there.'

The man shrugs. His friends watch in silence, their amusement gone, their eyes shifting from Aiah to the superintendent and back, charting the little shifts in power.

'You weren't controlling access,' Aiah says, 'and you've got gimmicked meters in your building. Maybe you know where there's a plasm source down below. Do you?'

The superintendent looked into the street. 'Those meters could've been cracked years ago, before I ever got this job. There hasn't been an inspection in all the years I've been here.'

Aiah's heart is racing. Maybe she should quit now, before she provokes him into doing something she won't like, like calling her superiors to complain. But something – instinct, maybe, or the euphoria of plasm – urges her to press on.

53

'The building owners are going to get fined no matter when the meters were fixed,' she says. 'They won't be happy with you. And if you want me out of your basement, you can tell me where the extra plasm was coming from.'

The superintendent stares fixedly at the street. 'Don't know nothing.'

Aiah shrugs. 'I get paid no matter what,' she says, and heads down to the pneuma.

Now, she wonders, was that *careful*?

Not particularly, but it was necessary.

Down below, beneath the iron and brick and concrete, Aiah can hear the plasm calling, a blaze of fire in the cold wet darkness.

A charge of plasm carries Aiah, rung by rusted rung, up the old air shaft. Subterranean rain pours off the corrugated channels of her hardhat. She's decided to use an exit that won't compel her to carry charged plasm batteries past a collection of resentful drunks.

Aiah flexes her legs and raises a heavy iron grate she'd had Grandshuk loosen two days before. She unclips her safety line and emerges into the weak yellow light of a utility tunnel, a concrete-walled oval, below street level, lined with color-coded electricity, steam and communications pipes. A row of low-intensity bulbs, each glowing dimly in its metal cage, illuminates her crouching walk as she moves in what she calculates is the direction of the trackline station.

She hears street noises above, finds steps molded into the curved concrete wall. She plants the toes of her boots into the concave steps and hoists herself up, then cautiously nudges the manhole cover over her head. She doesn't want to drop a truck on herself, but she can't hear any traffic noises or vibration, and she suspects the street is for pedestrians only.

Aiah pushes up with both hands, carefully shoves the

manhole cover out of its inset steel socket. Peering out of the oval crack, she sees furry socks on feet jammed into old carpet slippers. She pushes the cover a little more, sees an elderly male face peering down at her through thick bifocal lenses.

'You like some help, lady?'

'Thank you, yes.'

He's a retiree earning a little money by renting a piece of concrete in front of a crumbling, scaffold-draped brownstone. His wares are displayed on an old gray metal door propped up on concrete blocks – a sad collection, timeworn kitchen utensils, battered children's toys, a few yellowed books held together by tape.

Plasm seems to flush Aiah's muscles as she drops the manhole back into its socket. 'You're pretty strong,' the old man says, and sits in his folding chair. 'Wanna buy something?' he says hopefully.

Aiah scans the rubbish on the old steel door, sees a few cheap metal lucky charms on metal necklaces. One is in the shape of the Trigram, a useful tool transformed into worthless popular magic. 'I'll take that,' she says. The old man takes her money and she puts the charm around her neck, tucking it into the high collar of the jumpsuit. The symbol of power sits cool on her breastbone.

Aiah asks direction to the trackline station. 'Just around the corner,' the old man says, and Aiah thanks the man again and heads for the station. Along the way she scents cooking smells and stops at another scaffold-stall. There's a pink-cheeked maternal woman behind the counter who smiles at her and looks apologetic.

'Oh, sorry,' she says. 'We sold out of the stew, and the new batch isn't ready yet, and the pigeon's been on the fire too long and has gone all dry – I'd hate to sell it to you.'

'No problem. Thanks anyway.'

Aiah sees another stall across the street and buys a bowl of soup with pasta and vegetables fresh from someone's roof garden. It has too much comino, like most Jaspeeri food, but otherwise its warmth and its taste is gratifying to someone who's just hoisted herself up from the underground with three heavy plasm batteries in her sack.

As Aiah stands by the stall and eats her soup she sees the pink-cheeked woman sell stew and skewered pigeon to three different passers-by.

Aiah feels her cheeks burn.

She isn't used to being shafted by people who smile so helpfully.

She returns the empty soup bowl to the vendor and stalks toward the trackline station. A group of young Jaspeeri men stand on a streetcorner and watch her in sullen silence. Jaspeeri Nation territory, she thinks. Barkazils not served.

At least, Aiah figures, now she knows the neighborhood, and her place in it.

5

Two days later it's Senko's Day. Aiah has the day off, since Mengene's moved the plasm search to a lower priority. Aiah dresses in blacklight colors, fluorescent red and green and gold, and carefully arranges her hair in the ideal long ringlets that are too much of a bother the rest of the time. She wears the bracelet with the little etched ivory disk that Gil gave her, and the metal lucky charm under her blouse. Then she hoists her tote on her shoulder and heads for the trackline station. If she can mix her holiday with business, so much the better.

Aiah drags her heavy tote up from the underground and discovers the streets already full. The weather is fine, with only a few light clouds beneath the Shield. Women in bright, flowing gowns pose artfully on balconies. Bellowing men in tufted headgear, bare chests striped with paint, swagger down the street carrying containers of beer and wine. Apartment dwellers have turned their sound systems onto windows and balconies, and the amped sound ricochets along brick and concrete, rattles windows, jumps inside the skins of the revelers. Bass rhythms rock the pavement beneath Aiah's feet. Aiah finds a grin breaking out on her face, and her steps are lighter despite the tote's strap digging into her shoulder.

The street is closed to traffic and already strewn with litter. Aiah bobs a zigzag course through people dancing on the pavement, then past a group of stiltwalkers, all dressed as fabulous animals with horns and sweeping tails made of soft plastic foam.

A series of booms overhead, accompanied by dazzling

flashes, heralds an advertisement for *Lord of the New City*. Kherzaki's huge, determined face scowls down out the sky.

Aiah's cousin Elda has an apartment overlooking the parade route, one where the inevitable scaffolding has been turned into regular balconies with scalloped wrought-iron rails – a nice place, because her husband Nikov was a member of the Operation who got assassinated, and the Operation has an excellent insurance plan that's been taking care of Elda and her kids ever since.

Aiah and many of the family wrote off Elda when she married. After what had happened to Henley, Aiah couldn't believe Elda could marry someone like Nikov. But now that Nikov's ashes are safe in their little cement cubicle far underground, certain elements of the past can be buried with him. If Henley could forgive, Aiah supposed that she could as well.

Aiah can hear the high pitch of conversation and the throb of music as soon as she steps off the elevator. She enters through Elda's open door and is swept up in a whirl-wind of embraces. Small children clasp her knees. She greets them all and manages to drop the heavy tote behind the sofa where it won't attract attention.

And then she encounters Gurrah, her mother, the only person who greets her with a frown. 'You didn't come see me the other day,' Gurrah says in her thick-tongued Barkazil accent; and then she makes a show of reluctantly embracing her daughter.

'Mother,' Aiah says, 'I was *working*. I wasn't up here for a social call.'

Gurrah sniffs. 'Landro told me what you were working at. Looking for ways to put your people in prison.'

'I was looking for ways to keep someone from blowing up Bursary Street again.'

'Were you there when it happened?' asks her sister Henley, and Aiah gratefully turns to her. Henley is as tall as Aiah, a year older, and carries herself with an uncommon grace of movement that Aiah has always envied.

Henley is pregnant again, Aiah knows. At least, she thinks, Henley's husband is a reliable sort.

'Yes,' Aiah says, 'the flamer blew out the window of the room I was in.'

Henley gasps, puts a hand to her throat. The hand is swollen and deformed with arthritis.

The keen edge of a useless anger touches Aiah's throat at the sight. 'I had my hair pinned up,' she says, 'and it burned the back of my neck. Got a few glass cuts, too.'

She lifts her hair to demonstrate. Suddenly Gurrah is a model of concern.

'You didn't tell me,' she complains, and insists on Aiah bending over so that the neck can be examined. The last thing Aiah sees, before she bends over, is the amusement in Henley's eyes.

Aiah can't remember ever taking Gurrah seriously. Aiah is the fifth of seven children, and followed the older sibs in treating her lightly. Gurrah is an expert on dramatics, alternately devastated or exalted according to circumstance; but none of the drama ever seems to be about anything in particular, though it revolves round the necessity of Gurrah being the center of attention at all times.

Gurrah's fingers pinch vertebrae. 'You need to eat more,' she says. 'You're all bones.'

'I eat plenty.' Aiah straightens and tosses back her hair.

'Aiah!' It's one of her cousins, age six or so, waving from the scaffolding overlooking the street. 'Come see! It's the Lynxoid Brothers!'

Aiah gratefully steps out onto the scaffolding and watches the orange-skinned Lynxoids dance along the street below, passing out packets of candy to the children. Plasm displays sweep the sky overhead, hyping liquor, tobacco, entertainment. A leaf drops onto her cousin's hair, and Aiah brushes it off. The roof of this building is covered with mulberry trees because the landlord raises silkworms.

The first parade goes by, the Warriors, ranks of marchers in paint and sequins and nodding foam plastic plumes, some in marching bands, others carrying toy weapons made from the iron that, in the Barkazil tradition, Karlo gave to Senko in order to defeat the Lord of the Trees.

Aiah leans on the metal rail and scans her relatives discreetly as they watch the Warriors below. Some of them would know of a place to sell her plasm – the question is who, and how discreetly? She likes Elda – now that she's a widow, anyway – but any contacts she'd have would be in the Operation, and that's unacceptable. Aside from family history, if they found out about her source, they'd own her.

Landro? He had the contacts once, but so far as she knows he's been on the safe side of the law since his term in Chonmas. Any of his knowledge might be years out of date.

Her brother Stonn? He's been in and out of jail all his life and might know people, but he's a minor criminal at best and she has no regard for his intelligence or discretion.

The Warriors Parade passes and the people below surge into the street. The family drifts off the balcony in search of refreshments. Aiah takes a glass of beer, drifts and chats and watches the others carefully.

Aiah's grandmother enters, with Aiah's cousins Esmon and Spano and a woman Aiah doesn't know. Esmon looks fabulous, with billowy, immaculate lace and a coat glittering with green and gold sequins. His buttons are expensive, polished ivory.

'You should be in the Warriors Parade,' Aiah says as she kisses his cheek.

'After the new year I'm joining the Griffins,' he says. He introduces Aiah to the stranger, a small, sturdy woman in a red turban decorated with gemstones in expensive settings. Aiah recognizes the Trigram, the Mirror Twins, and other geomantic foci. She's Esmon's girlfriend, and her name is Khorsa.

It's pretty clear, Aiah figures, who's dressing Esmon these days.

She clasps Khorsa's many-ringed hand and gazes down into lively, interested eyes rimmed dramatically with kohl. The eyes narrow a bit at Aiah's touch.

'*You've* been somewhere interesting, ne?' she says.

Aiah prefers not to pursue this. She moves toward her grandmother and gives the old lady a hug.

'Would you like a seat out on the scaffold, Nana?' she asks. 'I'll get you one.'

'I'd rather have a glass of wine.'

Aiah gets her grandmother Galaiah a large tumbler of red and a folding chair overlooking the street. The old woman takes a drink of wine and gazes fiercely out over the revelers. A couple of great-grandchildren venture onto her lap and snatch at her cheap holiday beads. As she dangles the beads in front of them, Galaiah looks at Aiah and cocks an eyebrow.

'You have that *passu* of yours with you?'

'He's still in Gerad.'

Galaiah sniffs. 'At least he works.'

Aiah's hand strays to the ivory disk on her bracelet. 'He works hard, Nana.'

Galaiah shakes her head. 'Pushing paper isn't work.'

Nor is going out and getting drunk with Geradi executives, Aiah thinks, though the job seemed to require that as much as anything else.

'Esmon seems to be doing well,' Aiah says.

'It's his woman,' dismissively. 'She's a witch and makes good money.'

'Does she work for the Operation?' A lot of witches do.

'She's on her own. Works with her sister, some kind of priestess.' Galaiah takes another drink and deftly prevents a descendant from toppling off her lap. 'If she was working for the Operation, she wouldn't be able to support Esmon like that, eh?'

'I suppose not.'

Galaiah grins with coffee-stained false teeth. 'Esmon better not step out on her, I'll tell you that. Witches have ways, ne?'

Aiah hesitates, casts a glance inward. 'Is she reliable?'

Galaiah gives Aiah a sharp look, one the children on her lap promptly imitate. 'Why? You need a love conjuring to bring your longnose home?'

'Nothing like that. But everyone needs—' Aiah hesitates again. 'Needs *something* from time to time. And I'd rather get it from someone who isn't a *pascol*.' Which is a Barkazil term for a confidence player or someone who makes her living by her wits. The word is usually meant to be admiring, and is etymologically related to *passu*, the person from whom the *pascol* gains her living.

Galaiah looks at Aiah as if she were a simpleton. 'Khorsa's a witch. She runs a place called the Wisdom Fortune Temple, takes money from unhappy and desperate people and promises them miracles. How much more *pascol* can you get?'

Aiah nods. During the course of Aiah's girlhood her mother must have belonged to half a dozen tabernacles, all of them more or less the same. Somewhere along the way Aiah figured out why Gurrah was here, Gurrah and most of the others. They were people who were failures or bewildered or maybe just unhappy, and they didn't understand life all that well, or reality; and they needed to feel magical, special somehow, because if they weren't magical they weren't *anything*. And being Barkazil made it worse, because Karlo's children were *supposed* to be magical, supposed to be better than everyone else. The Cunning People. And if you were supposed to be cunning and weren't, and brilliant and weren't, and magical and weren't, where did you go?

62

The Wisdom Fortune Temple. Or something just like it.

Aiah looks down at the street. *How much more* pascol *can you get?* Galaiah is, as usual, to the point.

Galaiah is a survivor. When the old Metropolitan Fasta died and Barkazi went smash, Galaiah brought her children out of the wreckage and to Jaspeer while her husband was fighting street by street as a member of the Holy League of Karlo. While her husband spent six years in a Fastani prison, Galaiah brought up her children alone, in a strange metropolis. And when Aiah's grandfather had finally been released on the collapse of the Fastani and the occupation of Barkazi by the Regional Federation, she nursed him painstakingly back to health, only to have him drop dead of influenza a few years later.

Elda, indoors, sets down a tray of pastry, and Galaiah's grandchildren begin to squirm. Galaiah lets them down and they dash for the sweets. Galaiah takes a long drink of wine and looks up at Aiah.

'You in some kind of trouble?' she asks.

Aiah blinks. 'No,' she lies.

'Those longnoses treating you all right at the Authority?'

'As well as can be expected.'

'You're not pregnant, are you?'

Aiah is surprised. 'No,' she says. 'I haven't even . . . it's been months, Nana.'

'Good. Plenty of time for babies later, when you've got a man from your own people.'

Aiah smiles. 'Yes,' she says, 'of course.' Somehow even Galaiah's bigotry seems so much more acceptable than that of other people, possibly because she never pretends to be anything other than bigoted.

There's a crash of drums from down the street, the amplified cry of the Barkazi fiddle. Children begin to shriek.

The Transvestites Parade is next, men wearing giant false

63

breasts and enormously wide flounced skirts, women with absurdly padded shoulders and yard-long phalloi. The scaffold balcony sways with the weight of the onlookers' good spirits. Alcohol swirls in Aiah's head. Maybe she should have eaten something before drinking.

After the Transvestites come the Tree Spirits with their elaborate green hairstyles and giant satirical balloons, portraying all human endeavor as absurd, pointless or crazy. The balloons sway past, vast and round, just tantalizingly out of reach of the little children. Aiah finds herself looking at Khorsa, at the jeweled charms on her turban. The tiny woman has worked her way to the front of the balcony, and has propped one of Elda's children on her hip so he can see better. Her eyes glitter with delight as the balloons parade by.

Well, at least she's good-humored, not like the slit-eyed, mask-faced members of the Operation, all merciless calculation, or the outrageously dramatic witches who offer to remove curses and intervene with the ancestors' spirits for a few hundred dalders, and all without plasm.

After the parade passes Aiah approaches Esmon, but he's surrounded by admiring relatives and in no position to talk privately, and she sees Khorsa drifting toward a freezer chest of beer. Aiah approaches, takes another beer for herself. Khorsa fills her glass and smiles at her.

'Esmon seems happy,' Aiah offers.

'I hope so.'

'You're a – what is it? – a priestess?'

'My sister's a priestess. I'm a geomaterga. I do magic, she talks to the gods.'

'Do you go to school for that?'

Khorsa puts her hand on Aiah's arm and smiles.

'No. It sort of runs in the family. My mother founded our teaching, and my sister and I have inherited it.'

'Does the Operation bother you much?'

It's as if a mask drops into place – Khorsa's smile is still

64

there, but the amusement behind it is gone, and the eyes are like a wall of glass.

'Why do you ask?'

Warning sirens sound in Aiah's mind. 'I don't know,' she says. 'Just making conversation.'

She will *not*, she thinks, sell plasm to this woman. Maybe Khorsa isn't the Operation, but there's some other angle that Aiah doesn't know about and doesn't want to get messed up in.

Khorsa looks at her keenly, frowns, shakes her head. 'We've kept them out,' she says. 'Once you buy their unmetered plasm, they're into you forever.' She sips beer, looks serious. 'A lot of our clients come from among their victims. They always want us to soften the street captains' hearts. But,' shaking her head, 'of course the Operation has no heart.'

'No,' Aiah says, thinking of Henley. 'It doesn't.'

Khorsa gives her a shrewd look. 'Why are you asking? You're not interested in religious teaching, are you?'

Aiah shakes her head, smiles. 'Perhaps not today.'

A drum rattles outside. There's a subdued cheer.

'Strange,' Khorsa says. 'All this celebration and joy, and what we're celebrating is really the greatest tragedy in human history.'

'Yes?'

Khorsa lifts her head, a bit defiantly. 'Well, Senko failed, didn't he? He beat the Lord of the Trees and the Prince of Oceans, but when he challenged the Ascended Ones they destroyed him, and they put the Shield over our heads to keep humanity from ever challenging them again, so . . .' She waves her arms. 'Why do we celebrate? Why aren't we all weeping?'

Aiah looks at her. 'Because we get the day off?'

Khorsa laughs. 'Maybe so.'

'Perhaps I should contribute to party supplies. Excuse me.'

The little elevator passes the landing four times, each time jammed too full for Aiah to get on board, so Aiah walks down the twelve flights to the ground floor and steps out. There's a liquor and cigaret store on the far corner, and Aiah crosses the street to reach it. The sky overhead sizzles with plasm displays. A stiltwalker strides past roaring and pounding his chest, his foam-plastic tail floating out behind him. A group of twisted people dance on the corner to music booming down from the scaffold above — they're short and gray, with hairless, glabrous skins. A cold finger slides up Aiah's spine at the sight. She hasn't seen this variety of genetically tampered before.

Aiah buys a case of beer at a marked-up holiday price, and a large plastic bag of salty krill wafers. While she stands in the long cashier line behind some local groover girls, she hears the booms and thumps of the Assassins Parade marching this way.

She follows the groovers out of the store. Police are clearing the street, so Aiah crosses at the corner and glances up to see old Charduq the Hermit up on his fluted pillar at the old Barkazi Savings Institute. A warm memory rises in Aiah at the sight. She'd assumed Charduq had died years ago. She waves at him and calls out.

'Hi, Charduq! Remember me?'

The old man's eyes twinkle from deep within wrinkled sockets. He's bald except for a long beard that reaches to his lap. His naked skin is deep brown from constant exposure to Shieldlight, and he lives entirely off what people drop into the plastic bucket he lowers on a rope for offerings. He's been sitting on one of the Savings Institute's ornamental pillars for as long as Aiah can remember.

'Hai-ee, Miss Aiah!' the old man calls. 'You haven't visited your old friend for years! Where have you been keeping yourself?'

'I graduated and got a job with the Plasm Authority,' Aiah calls up.

'You live with a longnose lover, I hear. Is he rich?'

Aiah smiles. Everyone in the neighborhood passes the time of day with Charduq, and he learns everything sooner or later. The hermit is supposed to be contemplating the All, but instead he's become the most perfect gossip in the world.

'No,' Aiah says, 'he's not rich.'

'Then what good is he?' Charduq pats the pillar next to him. 'Come up here, dearie, take off your clothes and live with me. I've been preserving my potency for years – I can make you happier than any *passu* Jaspeeri!'

The hermit giggles and makes the penis-and-vulva sign with his fingers. Aiah bursts into laughter. She takes a beer and puts it in the old man's offering bucket.

'You've been up on that pillar too long,' she says. 'You want a girl, you'd better cut that beard and get a nice job.'

'You'd be surprised how many girls want to stroke my beard,' Charduq winks. He hauls in the rope and the bucket zooms upward. He's got another bucket for waste which he lowers twice a day; whoever's the junior clerk at the Savings Institute gets to empty it for him to keep it from stinking up the sidewalk.

Aiah waves goodbye and heads through the crowd. The Assassins are marching past, shadowed by fat, satisfied-looking balloons – all prominent celebrities or political figures – and all stuck with balloon daggers, arrows' or hatchets. Tuphar, Aiah recognizes, Gullimath the football-player, Gargelius Enchuk, and Constantine, who looks surprised at the number of daggers buried in his back . . .

Constantine, she thinks, stopping dead in mid-stride, and then, *of course*.

She dances through the dense crowd, then, after the elevator fails to turn up, and up the stairs to Elda's flat. By the end of the trip she's dripping sweat and her lungs are pumping like a bellows. She takes one of the cold beers and holds it against her forehead and tries to absorb the welcome chill. Then she drinks it down.

She steps out onto the scaffold balcony and finds herself standing behind her mother. The Assassins Parade is about half over. One of the balloons is sagging, losing hydrogen; it looks as if its phony dagger has actually punctured it.

Gurrah turns, looks at Aiah over her shoulder. 'You sell that plasm to the witch lady?' she asks.

Aiah feels herself flush as other relatives turn to gaze at her. 'You looked in my bag?' she says.

Gurrah's voice is loud in justification. 'I thought there might be food in there. I didn't want it to spoil.'

'Yeah,' Aiah says. 'I always put my food behind the couch.'

'You sold the goods to Khorsa, ne?'

'No. I'm not selling anything.'

'Where'd you get it? You take it from work?'

Aiah tries to glare. 'No,' she says. 'I didn't.'

'I hope you know what you're doing, working a chonah like that. You get caught, bad things happen when you steal from the *passu* government.' Her mother's voice is rising, carrying to everyone on the balcony. Aiah lowers her voice almost to a whisper and hopes her mother will follow her example.

'It's not a chonah. I'm just doing someone a favor. Don't make a fuss.'

Gurrah's voice rises above the sound of the parade. 'I shouldn't make a fuss?' she demands. 'My daughter finds out how to gimmick meters and starts selling plasm and I shouldn't wonder about it? I—'

'*Thank* you,' Aiah rages, 'for making everyone here think I'm a thief!'

She turns, stalks away, drops onto the empty sofa. Her pulse throbs in her head like a runaway engine. Out of the corner of her eye she sees Gurrah draw herself up and look mortally offended, and then Aiah sees a trace of doubt enter her expression. Maybe it hadn't occurred to her that her daughter *wasn't* a thief. She begins to look anxious, perhaps wondering if she's missed something.

Too late, Aiah thinks. Too damn late.

Among the relatives Aiah can see little knowing glances being exchanged. She hates being the subject of scrutiny, or pity, or speculation – whatever it is. She bolts up from the sofa, goes to the cooler, takes another beer.

Maybe it's time to go.

She takes her tote and wanders out into the hall, finds the elevator miraculously standing empty, and takes it to the ground floor. The last of the Assassins have just marched past and the crowd is pouring out into the street, and Aiah goes with them. She buys a sandwich from a vendor, bread filled with vat shrimp spiced to perfection and hot from the fryer; and by the time she's finished eating, the Dolphins Parade is starting, led by the huge red fiberglass float of King Crab waving his pincers over the crowd. People dressed as fish and crustaceans prance past. Some minor video actor is the Lord of the Dolphins this year, one Aiah knows is supposed to be famous; he stands on his float and tosses presents to the crowd, cheap plastic puzzles, whistles, crackers, toy drums.

Aiah finishes her beer and drifts with the crowd. A stilt-walker offers her a drink from his wine flask. The Griffins and the Jaspeeris march past – the last are a burlesque, Barkazils mocking Jaspeeri over-seriousness and manners. The briefcase beaters leave her in stitches, people in suits with great gouts of lace pouring out of the sequined collars and sleeves, who chase each other and whack each other with briefcases. Overhead, the sky sizzles with patriotic displays and bright advertisements.

She wanders into a bar, eats some bread chips and lets people buy her drinks. Video screens show extravagant parades from all over the world. A procession marches past outside while she's in the bar enjoying herself. She feels more relaxed than she's been in years – hell, she's probably going to prison, she might as well have a good time while she still can.

Aiah pushes out of the bar onto sidewalks ankle-deep in rubbish. Her shoes stick to the concrete as she walks. Music rackets out of a basement club, and the line is fairly short; Aiah joins it. There's a special on some fashionably new cocktail, two for one, so she orders a pair of them and, while she's waiting, cruises the dance floor.

The band is solid in its grove, glorious, the musicians sweating harder than the concrete wall of the old cellar-turned-club. Aiah returns to her table after two dances and finds her drinks waiting for her. She sips one, gets an invitation to dance, says yes.

There are a lot of men in the club. The one who interests her is Fredho – he's utterly skilled on the dance floor, and when they spin to the music he makes her feel like a much better dancer than she is. If he can't find a partner he dances by himself, spectacular spins and high kicks, hand-stands and splits. He wears an expensive white raw silk jacket over his bare chest, and the jacket's got to be a gift because he doesn't give a damn what happens to it; it's smeared with dirt from the floor and the satin lining is coming to pieces as he thrashes around inside it. His skin is the fine brown color of burnt sugar, and his chest is smooth – lucky, because Aiah doesn't want to be reminded of Gil's hairy chest, not when she's thinking what she's thinking. And Fredho is nice – arrogant enough, but not demanding. At one point, ending a slow dance, he asks if she'll take him home. She leans back in his arms, looks at him through slitted eyes, tries to make up her mind. 'Maybe later,' she says, and leans forward to lick a trail of sweat off his chest – something she's been thinking about for several minutes now.

He shrugs, lets her go back to her table, dances alone for a while. Aiah wonders why he wants to go to her place, if he's got a woman waiting at his own, and then she decides it doesn't matter. Anyone living with someone like Fredho knows well enough what to expect.

Later comes soon enough. She and Fredho take the trackline to the Loeno, and in the seat they're all over each other, kissing, nibbling, teasing. The other passengers don't know where to look.

Aiah takes Fredho up into her black-walled tower and fucks him three times. Next day, after the alarm jolts her from sleep, she finds that Fredho has gone. Gone along with him is all her money, the plasm batteries, and the ivory bracelet that Gil gave her.

Head pounding, she looks at the picture of Gil on the wall and promises him that, real soon now, she's going to get smarter about all this.

6

Aiah has a breakfast of coffee and vitamin pills and drags into work twenty minutes late, but so does half the staff and no one offers a comment. While she spends her pre-break at her battered metal desk, insulated from Jayme's shrieks by her headphones and her hangover, she considers her situation.

After lunch she has to go out onto Old Parade with Grandshuk and Lastene. She spends an exhausting post-break dragging herself through muck-filled tunnels and scrapes a shin on a broken pipe.

After work she buys new plasm batteries and heads for Terminal.

Plasm pours through Aiah's body, filling every cavity like warm rising water. The Trigram glows in her mind, a deep luminescent blue, power pulsing through its design. Existence leaps into focus as her clarity sharpens, as her senses quicken – it's as if she's just plugged into the well that waters the world. Perceptions extend through the darkness, and Aiah is suddenly hyperaware of the texture of the scarred concrete walls, the invisible supporting web of metal behind the walls that stand out like bones on an x-ray, the rapid heartbeat of some animal, a rat probably, that sleeps curled under the crumbling platform.

She hadn't noticed this effect before. Too overwhelmed by the whole experience, probably.

Aiah directs the plasm through her body, burning off fatigue toxins, pouring energy into herself. She's practiced at this by now, and by the end of the procedure she feels like a bottomless well of potential, of power. Her senses seem to extend to the Shield and back.

Her plasm battery is fading, so she takes another of the three she's just charged. She tries some elementary visual effects, bright streaks of color that splash themselves along the length of the platform, will o' wisps that shine softly from corners, bright light glowing from the old, empty, gutted sockets that pockmark the ceiling.

She tries to create a picture of Constantine, imprint it on the wall opposite, but the result is so ridiculous, worse than a child's scrawl, that she wipes it.

She exhausts the second battery and goes to the third. Decides to try something new, to attempt to reach out westward to the Metropolis of Gerad. She calls into her mind first the Trigram, then an image of Gil, invokes his kind blue eyes, his gentle, thick-fingered hands, the feel of his fine freckled skin against hers, the touch of his furry chest against her cheek . . . and at that particular memory a chill sad finger touches her heart, a sensory image of Fredho, the taste of his sweat and skin, but the fire in her nerves and mind is too pure, too powerful, to permit sadness for long; and instead she tries to send her spirit westward, a message to Gil wherever she may find him.

And for a moment she touches him, a fleeting connection to his psyche, so immediate and surprising that it startles her and makes her lose the contact almost immediately. She knows that he's in a bar, or club, surrounded by other men; she knows he's moderately drunk – she can taste watery beer on her tongue, feel it swim in her head. She knows that he's bored.

That boredom, she decides, wins him a lot of points.

Carefully she probes again, more gently this time, invoking him, calling up his image. Gradually he comes into focus. He's startled, she realizes, by the moment of contact. She calls up her thoughts: longing, sorrow, desire. She tries to wrap Gil in her tendresse as if it were a warm fuzzy towel. And, slowly, she finds him relaxing into reverie, into a yearning that answers hers.

The moment fades. Aiah realizes that tears are falling from her eyes. She blinks them away and looks at the battery and sees that it's drained. Apparently long-distance communication takes a lot of power.

Contact's affect slowly recedes from her mind. Aiah takes the batteries into the old toilet in order to recharge them. She connects the alligator clips, sees the charge indicators go through their swift rainbow shifts to blue.

She spends another half hour working with the plasm, accustoming herself to its charge, always with the batteries as a buffer.

She's decided that she needs to do something about the open door. If she puts up an illusory wall with plasm from the batteries, it will eventually fade. She has to connect the illusion to a live circuit.

Aiah takes a deep breath, puts on an insulated glove, and takes a plasm pen out of her jumpsuit. Carefully, with her insulated hand, she clears rubble from the area where the brace fell. Then she uncaps the pen, draws a line – carefully shaped, crosshatched just so, to guide the power properly – down the last few feet of the beam, then out across the concrete floor.

The plasm pen is cheap alchemy: it contains a metal-based ink that allows plasm to travel along the length of the ink-streak, but only in controlled amounts depending on the metal content of the ink and the width of the drawn line. The pens are available in varied sizes and densities to permit different amounts of plasm to move along their lengths.

Aiah crabs sideways along the concrete, drawing her line. She reaches the threshold, draws a line along it, then steps out onto the platform and looks at the result.

Allow a moment to dry. That's what it says in the instructions.

She allows that moment, then another. Aiah starts to take off her glove, then hesitates. Her throbbing heart seems to fill her chest.

Aiah pulls off the glove, lets it fall to the platform. She takes her little metal Trigram out of her collar, holds it in her hand, stares at it, tries to hold it in her mind. She kneels by the doorway, reaches out a hand, hesitates, reaches out again.

She touches the line, and the Trigram screams and reaches out to seize her.

Her senses roar with the potential on the other end of the line, the yawning well of elemental power separated from her by only a thin line of metallic ink – and she could overcome that, she knows, just spend the energy to create a transmission line of plasm in the air, just as she does every day at work, beam a ray of plasm from the brace to her own mind, just as she radiates the stuff from the Plasm Authority's transmission horns to receivers throughout the city.

The empty-eyed face of the plasm diver flashes into her mind.

Aiah jumps back, breaks the contact. Sensation pounds in her head. Sparks flash across her retinas. She takes a deep breath, tries to calm herself.

She just wasn't expecting it, she decides. This time it'll be easier.

She crouches by the line again, looks at the little metal Trigram in her palm. It isn't hard to keep the figure in her mind, not when it's been branded into her visual centers by a roaring blaze of elemental energy. She touches the ink line with her finger.

The Trigram flows with color, deep silver-blue. The plasm roars at her from across the narrow gap of torn cement. Carefully Aiah walls it off in her mind, tries to concentrate only on the small trickle of plasm coming along the ink trail. Then, just as she's done before, she creates an illusory wall over the toilet doorway, an insubstantial barrier of wracked and pitted concrete.

Aiah takes her finger off the ink line, steps back, holds her breath. The illusion holds. She watches it for a few minutes and makes certain it doesn't move or distort, doesn't fade. And, more importantly, doesn't become a raging blowtorch of plasm that threatens to consume the district.

The power is still a pleasant buzz in her nerves. Aiah gathers her gear and carries it up to street level, climbing through the manhole cover she'd used before.

She drops the manhole cover back into place and stands blinking in bright Shieldlight. The old man and his rickety table of junk are long gone. Only a few people are on the streets. Aiah looks at her watch and discovers that she's spent most of the second shift underground. It'll be third shift in another few minutes.

A few high clouds drift overhead. All fatigue is burned away. Her feet seem light on the pavement even in their heavy boots, and she feels as if she could run for miles. She wonders if she'll be able to sleep. She wonders if she'll even need to.

No wonder, she thinks, the people with access to plasm are so long-lived.

She turns down the tunnel leading to the Terminal trackline station, and her nerves give a little warning cry as she sees dark figures silhouetted against the yellow tiled walls. Three men, dressed in canvas pants and baggy loose shirts and heavy boots. They're sharing a ten-pack of beer and smoking cigarets.

Aiah's plasm-driven feet have bounded partway down the tunnel before her mind's foreboding catches up with them, and by then it's too late. She keeps walking and tries to force a civil smile. The three men look up at her, unshaven faces cold in the light of the overhead fluorescents.

'What are you doing out here, man?' one of them demands, a burly man with a beer gut peeping out from beneath his short-tailed shirt.

'Working,' she says. The man seems surprised to hear a woman's voice.

'Got a job, huh?' A skinny kid with tattooed arms and pomade in his hair. 'More'n we've got.'

'Maybe you've got *my* job,' the first man offers.

'Nation!' the third man says. He's sitting on the concrete floor and leaning against the crumbling yellow wall tile, bare arms resting on bent knees. His eyes are closed as he half-sings, '*Nation, nation, migrants from our nation!*'

Jaspeeri Nation, she thinks, oh lovely.

'I'm leaving,' Aiah says. Adrenaline wars with plasm in her veins as she passes the fat man. She's taller than he is but still he seems to loom over her. Her stomach turns at the power of the beer on his breath.

'Out of our *nation*, bitch,' the fat man says. He takes a step toward her as she begins to walk away from him.

Aiah's grown up in a neighborhood like this and knows the worst thing she can do is run. She plants her unwilling feet and stares into the fat man's eyes. Tries to radiate the power of plasm at him. And then tries to speak around the pounding heart that seems to have lodged in her throat.

'I work for the state, okay?' she says. 'Don't fuck with the government, because then the government will find endless ways of fucking with you. And if the government doesn't the union will. Understand?'

The fat man hesitates, just looks at her and tries to think. Then he scratches his unshaven face and takes a step back.

'*Nation!*' screams the sitting man, and then he leaps up and throws a beer bottle that smashes into the yellow wall tile a few feet from Aiah. Foam spatters the side of Aiah's face and she bolts.

Bolts cursing herself as she runs, because even after the bottle smashed she could still have walked away and probably managed it without pursuit. Now that she's panicked they're chasing, excited as a pack of dogs that have tasted blood. Heavy boots pound after hers. Her only hope now is to get to the ticket taker and hope she'll be let into the booth . . .

She swings around the turn at the bottom of the tunnel and crashes into a barred metal gate that's been drawn across the tunnel in front of the ticket booth – the station has been closed on the off-shifts due to lack of traffic. Stunned by the impact, Aiah bounces off the gate, then tries to rip open the zipper on her tote because she knows at this point her only hope is the plasm waiting in the batteries.

The skinny kid runs up before she can drag the zipper open. Aiah swings her tote and smashes him in the chest with its weight. He gives a yell and falls. And then the fat man is on her and smashes her full in the face with a fist the size of a ham. Starshells burst inside Aiah's skull and she goes backwards, cracking the back of her head against the barred gate. Her hard hat clatters on the concrete. Aiah falls in a sprawl of arms and legs and hugs the tote to her chest, trying to protect herself as boots and fists begin to fall. Pain explodes her nerves as a metal toe-cap connects with a kidney. Aiah finds the zipper with her hand and tugs, pushes her hand inside the tote. Someone's hand gropes her crotch. The fat man aims a boot at her face and misses, sitting down suddenly as he overbalances with the force of his kick. A beer bottle clatters on the floor. Aiah feels a plastic safety cap under her fingers and pulls it off the battery terminal. Touches her thumb to the battery.

The skinny kid screams as a ball of plasm melts his face. His hair pomade explodes into fire. The fat man is halfway to his feet before Aiah gestures at him with her free hand, a gesture like a fist, and the fat man flies backward as if hit in the chest by a wrecking ball. Aiah can hear the crack of his head as it hits the far wall.

The third man, the bottle thrower, stares in horror at

the burning boy, and then clumsily, drunkenly, turns to run. Aiah points at him and gives him a push between the shoulder blades, a shove that flings him skidding face-first onto the concrete.

Aiah staggers upright, half-blinded by tears and pain, and finds her hat. The skinny kid is clutching at his liquified eyeballs and staggering down the corridor, shoulder thudding against the wall. For some reason the hair pomade is burning bright blue. Clumsy with pain and the weight of her tote, Aiah runs past him, past the other man lying on his face, and out of the tunnel into bright Shieldlight.

The old brick buildings reel around her. She takes a deep breath of free air and staggers down the street, looking wildly for a cab. Screams keep echoing out of the tunnel. Aiah pulls her hat down over her face.

Aiah finds a cab on the next block and asks to be taken to Mudki, a financial and business district fairly close by. One side of her face is swollen and she turns it away from the driver. The Transit Authority's Mudki Station is a complex of different intersectioning tracklines and pneuma stations and will be open at all hours; the tangle is complex enough for her to disappear in there, take the Red Line to the New Central Line and home.

Covering her trail. At least her mind seems to be working along fairly rational lines. Unless the authorities deploy a plasm hound, she should get away free.

Until she returns to Terminal, of course. There will be people looking for her, maybe some very serious people.

By the time she arrives at Mudki she's trembling so hard that she spills her change on the floor of the cab. She bends down, picks it up, pushes it across the wide shelf behind the driver's seat. As she walks beneath Mudki's fortress tower office blocks, she slips a hand into her tote to give herself a dose of plasm, tries to burn away her jolt of adrenaline, the liquid fear pouring like acid through her veins.

The plasm helps to clarify her mind. As the Red Line car jolts away, Aiah coldly plots her next moves. Evasive methods of getting back to the old Terminal Station, procedures for avoiding anyone who could identify her.

It can be done. And with luck it only needs to be done once.

The sensation of clinical detachment lasts until she gets home, until she sees the gleaming yellow light of her communications array.

She presses the play button, hears the etching belt begin to roll, the grind of the communications head that she's forgotten to lubricate, and then there's Gil's voice. There's a lot of noise in the background, clattering and loud music. Gil sounds bewildered and lost.

'I'm calling from a club, and I don't know why because it's costing a fortune ... but I miss you so much that I can't stand it, and I just wanted to tell you that ...'

Now, in the silence of her black glass tower, Aiah feels free to go to pieces.

7

Next day Aiah can barely move. One side of her face is so swollen that the ballooning flesh seems a part of someone else. Only the pain reminds her that this disfigurement is hers. Deep purple bruises bloom over her body. Her ribs feel as if they're displaced an inch to the left. When she tries to walk a bolt of pain shoots up her leg; she takes off her sock and finds someone has stomped on her right foot: two toes are swollen and black, and the nails broken. She doesn't even remember it happening. She doesn't think the toes are broken, but she can't be sure.

Aiah limps toward the bathroom mirror. She can't even look at herself: she's like a member of the twisted, one of the grotesque ones. And, she remembers, she's supposed to spend the prebreak leading her team through tunnels under Old Parade.

Aiah hobbles to the plasm batteries, returns to the mirror, hesitates. She's apprehensive about tampering with herself this way, of making actual physical alterations.

How did the twisted get twisted? Just this way, some of them.

But still, healing is the most common plasm art. How much talent does it take?

Aiah puts a hand on the battery, feels her heart lift with the onrush of the goods. She raises her metal charm to her swollen cheek, touches it lightly to the sensitive skin. Tries to will the pattern into herself, compel the tissue to heal, edema to flush from the torn tissues. The mummified face of the plasm diver floats into her mind, and she resolutely banishes it. *Slowly*, she thinks, *gradually*.

The battery empties partway through the procedure. Aiah looks at herself, sees the swelling noticeably reduced, the purple bruise lightened. She seems to be on the right track.

Aiah reaches for another battery.

A few minutes later the two-tone chime of her array interrupts her. She decides to ignore the call, but when she hears the first grind of the communications head she realizes it might be Gil, and she leaves the battery and limps to the array. She picks up the headset and holds an earpiece to one ear, and hears her mother's voice. '*Here's what I thought*,' Gurrah says, and Aiah doesn't need to hear any more. She returns the headset to its hook and goes back to the bathroom.

The communications head grinds on as Aiah continues her attempts at healing – apparently Gurrah's remembered to keep the message key depressed this time. Aiah's cheek warms as plasm flows through it. She straightens, takes her hand off the battery, brushes the skin with her fingertips.

Acceptable, she thinks. There's an abrasion she can't seem to heal entirely, and a little bruising around the eye, but she can cover these with cosmetics. The grotesque swelling has faded entirely.

And now the rest. She treats her foot, her bruises. Skill grows with practice. As a conclusion she pours energy into her body, banishing the after-effects of pain and fatigue.

Better. The battery indicator glows purple, so there's still a half-charge in it. Aiah puts on her jumpsuit and hardhat and leaves for work, arriving late to find Lastene and Grandshuk waiting. She leads them off on the day's assigned search. Far underground she finds an isolated, uncharted pipe with a small plasm potential, and she notes it on her charts and marks it with a red tag.

Making the city a little richer.

After lunch bought from a streetcorner vendor Aiah returns to the Avenue of the Exchange. From a hardware store she buys a pair of alligator clips, then after buying her usual one-dalder lottery ticket passes warily under the mosaic of the Goddess of Transmission. She wonders if anyone waits in her office. She changes in the Emergency Response Team locker room, puts on the suit and lace she'd worn the day before.

She doesn't even know how frightened she should be. She considers this fact and wonders if it is not pathetic.

No one waits in her office, not even Tella and her baby, though the room has a faint odor of uric acid. She sits down at the scarred metal desk and throws her computer's start switch, watches the yellow dials begin to glow. Promptly at 1300 she puts on her headset and tells the operator her station is open.

It isn't a very busy postbreak and she has a chance to make a few calls. Her authority as a member of Emergency Response goes unquestioned; she has some flimsies sent up in a pneumatic message cylinder with the account numbers of everyone at Mage Towers. Once she has Constantine's account number she calls another department and has another set of flimsies sent up with his records. These are sufficiently thick that they have to come up by messenger, not by tube.

When she isn't monitoring the computer or setting up transmissions, she spends her time studying the patterns of Constantine's plasm use.

He doesn't call for transmission very often, she finds; the normal plasm relays within Mage Towers are for the most part sufficient for his needs. But that's only because he lives in a place like Mage Towers, where huge plasm connections are available: his weekly bill for plasm is greater than Aiah's yearly salary, and he pays them on time.

He has money, and apparently lots of it. Considering that he'd left a shattered Cheloki behind when he finally withdrew, a deserted pile of rubble only now beginning a recovery, Constantine seems to have come out of the deal with his bank balance to the good.

So much the better, she thinks.

Plasm, in Constantine's system, is the foundation of a nation's wealth as well as the guarantee of the people's liberty. She wonders how much cold cash a glory hole like Terminal would be worth to him.

Her phone rings – the outside line, not one of the Authority tabulators – and she unplugs her headset from one socket and into the other.

'Da,' she says.

'Aiah?' Her grandmother's voice. 'You were never home when I called.'

Aiah's heart gives a leap. 'I'm working a lot of overtime,' she says. 'Looking for that leak.'

'Your mother is a fool,' Galaiah says, 'but that doesn't mean she's wrong, ne? Are you in some kind of trouble?'

Aiah tries to keep her voice level. 'No,' she says. 'No, I'm not.'

'You can talk to me, you know. I won't tell Gurrah. Or anyone else, if that's what you're concerned about.'

Aiah hesitates, wanting badly to be able to tell Galaiah of her discovery, her plans, her terrors.

Then the other line buzzes. 'Excuse me, Nana,' she says. 'There's another call. I'll be right back.'

She shifts her headphone jack to the internal line, hears a familiar cigaret-husky voice call breathlessly for a ten-minute plasm transmission at 044 degrees.

'Da,' she repeats. '1530, Horn Five transmit 044 degrees at 08 mm, transmission to cease 1540. Confirmed.'

She programs the transmission into her computer and scalar, then shifts the headphone jack back to the outside line.

'Nana?'

'I'm still here.'

Aiah takes a breath. One hand covers the flimsies on her

84

desk, as if hiding them from her grandmother's sight. 'I'm not in any trouble,' she says, 'and my only real problem is that Gil has been gone too long.'

There is a little silence on the other end, and then, 'If you're certain.'

'If I ever need help,' Aiah says, 'you'll be the one I call.'

Best keep family out of it, she thinks. That way, if it all goes wrong, she'll be the only one to pay the penalty.

Aiah works till her break, tells the tabulator she's off, and then makes her way down to the third sub-basement, where all the phone lines and switches stand in scarred gray metal cabinets. With her alligator clips she makes a few jumps and connects her office phone line to the outside through extension 4301. It's the office of Rohder, the man who snuffed the Bursary Street flamer and who is now in the Authority Hospital. Any calls she makes out of the building will be billed to Rohder's office.

Back when she was a kid, her family used to steal phone service this way.

She returns to her office, jacks her headphones into the outside line, and carefully presses bright steel keys one by one.

'Da?' The voice is male and disinterested. The answer is immediate, faster than Aiah anticipated, and it startles her. She takes a breath and tries to calm the sudden pounding of her pulse.

'I would like to speak to the Metropolitan Constantine, please,' she says.

And, as she speaks the words, she feels an invisible circuit being connected, some indefinable flow of potential being created between herself and Constantine . . . things falling into place, a little act of subcreation . . .

Not least among the things being created, she realizes, is a new Aiah.

8

Mage Towers rears above Aiah like a tribe of fabulous threatening giants: a double circle of high black-glass pinnacles, so many-sided they might as well be round, each studded along its height with horns and protrusions and scallops of metal intended either to gather plasm or to repel an assault. Dark storm clouds, heavy with rain, scud low in the sky, impaling themselves on the baroque, spiraled bronze transmission horns that thrust toward the Shield from the crown of each tower. The towers' twin circles are arrayed in careful geometries, each tower certain fractions of radii from each of the others, all with the intention of building and gathering plasm, and the entire complex built so as to take advantage of a confluence of relationships with other buildings, some of them many radii away.

'No, I need to speak to the Metropolitan Constantine personally . . .'

Glass doors, ornamented with gold scrollwork, part as Aiah approaches, and she enters a tunnel beneath Tower Seven. There is a soft, thick carpet under her new boots. An abstract mosaic floats gentle patterns down the slightly concave walls, swirling gold and black designs, suggestive of a descent into a sable and amber sea. At the end of the hall is a desk where a pleasant Jaspeeri woman, placid smile and expensive honey-colored soft wool jacket, checks Aiah's identification. 'Elevator bank four,' she says, and presses a discreet button that opens another set of gold-traced glass doors.

'My name is Aiah. I'm an executive with the Plasm

Control Authority. I need to speak to the Metropolitan Constantine concerning his plasm use . . .'

The tiles leading to the elevators are patterned with geomantic foci. The walls are mirrored, with black metallic streaks. The elevator doors are brass polished to a perfect, undistorted reflection. Aiah's knees buckle slightly as the elevator begins its swift ascent.

'Yes, I will speak to Special Assistant Sorya if you like, but I need to make an appointment to see the Metropolitan Constantine personally . . .'

The elevator sways slightly as it rises – neither the elevator shaft nor anything else in this building is perfectly straight. The architecture is warped slightly in order to draw power. It requires exacting, expensive engineering and is fraught with inconvenience, but the inconvenience probably doesn't matter overmuch to those who live on a diet of plasm.

'Yes, Madame Sorya, you may have a callback number. My office is in the Plasm Authority Building on the Avenue of the Exchange. My extension is 4301.'

Aiah's stomach lifts as the elevator brakes to a swift halt, and she shifts her feet to regain balance. The polished bronze doors slide open in silence. Two men stand in the anteroom outside – immaculate lace, dark, bulky suit jackets, polite and attentive expressions. There is a certain intensity about their eyes.

Aiah shows her ID card. 'Aiah,' she says, 'from Plasm Control.'

One of them shows her a metal detector wand. 'I hope you won't mind submitting to a search?'

Aiah realizes she's holding her breath and lets it out. She steps out of the elevator into the long anteroom. Her boot heels click on polished bronze-and-black tile. She offers her briefcase to one of the men, then stands back and extends her arms to either side.

'Not at all,' she says.

'Madame Sorya, I have been reviewing the Metropolitan Constantine's record of plasm use. I believe that with one of our use plans, I will be able to save him twenty to twenty-five percent off his plasm bill, but I will have to explain the use plan to him personally . . .'

The metal detector rings at Aiah's belt buckle, at buttons and zips, and at the cheap metal charm that, with a bit of embarrassment, she pulls from beneath the band of lace around her collar. The other guard waits with polite attention for this business to conclude, then glances in Aiah's briefcase and finds nothing but papers.

'Follow me, please?'

The anteroom is mirrored, with tables and chairs and fresh-cut flowers in crystal vases. Aiah glances at herself in the mirrors, adjusts her throat-lace, brushes ringlets into place. She wants to look a certain way – a successful woman, businesslike, in charge – and she wears a suit of gray tailored wool that is the single most expensive purchase Aiah has ever made, and which she's bought on credit. She's taken two days off from work, days devoted half to shopping, half to research. She's spent hours sitting in a booth at a local café, one with the black-and-red *Wire* sticker in the corner, plugging coins into the machine and calling for all available information on Constantine. She's printed out everything and stared at the plastic flimsies till her eyes ached. She was surprised to discover his age, that Constantine is over sixty when he doesn't look older than his thirties. That's what living around plasm does, Aiah thinks.

He hasn't been idle since losing the war in Cheloki. He's been an advisor to governments. Supposedly he's had a hand in a few wars and revolts here and there, though usually on the losing side.

Still trying, she hopes, to build the New City.

Aiah's heart throbs smoothly, driving adrenaline power to her limbs. She has to keep reminding herself to move slowly, deliberately, and not with the twitchy speed her adrenaline-charged body demands. Her throat is dry, her palms moist.

One of the guards pushes at a wide metal door that swings open on noiseless hinges. Everything, Aiah realizes, moves silently in this place. She steps through the doorway into a long drawing room. Its far wall is glass, with a view of rooftops that stretches to a cloud-shrouded horizon. Planted in front of the view is a curved steel brace, scalloped and ornamented but still unlovely and inconvenient, one of the compromises in polite living undertaken by those who live their lives in a power generator.

A green-eyed woman watches Aiah from a doorway. Her hair is streaked blonde, her chin is sharp, her stance artful, weight on the back leg, the front foot drawn up in a dancer's pose, toes pointed almost accusingly at Aiah as they rest on the rust-red carpet. Her apricot-colored gown leaves her arms and clavicles bare. The belt that rests low on her hips is composed of gold links, each link forged in the shape of a geomantic focus.

Aiah slows as if she's run into a wall. A flush prickles her skin. The woman's presence has an almost physical impact.

Aiah looks down at her wool suit, its fibers the precious product of sheep raised on rooftops or penned in alleys, fed vegetable matter grown in vats with resources that might otherwise have been used to support human beings . . . the garment Aiah had thought extravagant now seems ridiculous in contrast to this place, this person. The other woman's gown is probably worth twenty times the value of Aiah's suit.

'You've been around plasm, haven't you?' the woman says. She speaks with an indefinable accent. Her green eyes narrow. 'Emergency surgery, from the look of it.'

Aiah restrains herself from lifting a hand to her cheek. When she'd inspected herself in the mirror before breakfast she'd seen only minute signs of the beating, and then only because she knew where to look.

'I had an accident,' Aiah says.

The woman says nothing, continues her inspection. 'No live plasm now,' she says. 'Only residual. No lifeline. No foci, no time bombs, no traces of mental intrusion.'

'Who are you talking to?' Aiah asks.

The woman lifts her pointed chin. 'Someone you don't know.' She nods. 'Come with me, please.'

As she steps back Aiah sees a wire leading from her hand to the other room and realizes the woman was dipping the well, reading her with a plasm connection. Aiah should have recognized that sense of warmth, that prickling of the skin. Aiah's boots glide silently on the plush carpet as she follows the woman through the door into a spacious office room equipped with an elegant glass-and-alloy desk and a terminal and a silvery spiral stair. The green-eyed woman unjacks her wire from a plasm connection in the desk, then coils the wire around her fist as she mounts the stairway. Aiah follows and is halfway up the stair before she realizes that the central pillar is structural, that it's a plasm-generating inconvenience artfully disguised.

Upstairs is another empty office, though this glass desk has some loose flimsies on its gleaming surface. The woman knocks at a door, then enters without waiting for an answer. Aiah follows and is face to face with Constantine before she realizes it.

There's a strange little moment of adjustment in which Aiah has to reconfigure her mental image of the man; now she realizes that every chromograph she's seen, every flat-screen video image, has diminished the reality. Constantine is a powerful man, a head taller than Aiah, with great bull-like shoulders and a barrel chest that an opera baritone might well commit murder to possess. His hands and wrists were made to bend iron. His skin is blue-black. His face is a little fleshy, not unattractively, and his tight-coiled hair is oiled and braided and worn over the left shoulder, the braid tipped with ornamented silver. Aiah recognizes the symbol worn by a graduate of the School of Radritha.

Lord of the New City. Lord of Creation, looks like. She knows there are people who worship him, literally, as an avatar of Senko.

She is beginning to see their point.

Constantine wears loose black trousers stuffed into suede boots, a plain white shirt, a thigh-length leather vest worked with obscure symbols. Aiah recognizes some of them as geomantic foci, but the others are unknown.

No need for lace, Aiah thinks. The leather and suede alone must have cost—

'You want to save me money?' he says. The voice is deep and, for the moment, expressionless.

'Yes, sir.' Aiah tries to speak slowly, not permit the adrenaline that burns through her veins to blurt out the words.

'How unusual in a bureaucrat,' Constantine says.

He turns without a word and pads back into the room, drawing Aiah after. He has a delicate way of walking, poised and balanced, that makes her think of armored warriors who have to adjust to the inertia of their combat suits, as if he's somehow carrying more weight than is otherwise apparent . . .

It's a long room, big enough to contain any three Loeno Towers apartments the size of Aiah's. One whole wall of the room is transparent and looks out into a huge conservatory that must cover most of the tower roof: there are full-sized trees under arching glass, all heavy with fruit, and above them the curved, shadowy shapes of the tower's huge transmission horns. Colorful birds flap among the high branches. A battery of huge video sets, all dark, looms down from high wall mountings.

Constantine walks to the far end, steps behind a desk and sits in a big chair that seems all chrome rods and black tanned calfskin. There's the sigh of pneumatics, the creak of leather. Constantine puts his big hands on top of the desk.

'Tell me, then.'

She catches movement out of the slant of her eye and her heart gives a surprised leap. A huge spotted cat is walking through the ferns of the conservatory, padding purposefully toward the glass wall. Shieldlight gleams from jewels in its collar.

'It's Prowler,' the woman says. 'He's seen me. May he come in?'

'Yes.' Constantine's eyes haven't left Aiah. She drags her attention from the glass wall and tries mentally to reassemble the presentation she'd so carefully prepared, the plan she was going to offer him. She glances left and right, sees chairs.

'May I sit?'

'It's going to take that long?' Unsurprised. 'Very well.'

As she draws up a chair she hears a little hiss behind her, the sound of a sealed door opening. There is a waft of warm air, the scent of fruit and vegetation and decay. Aiah tries not to react to it, to the somber eyes of Constantine that haven't moved once from her face.

She opens her briefcase, pulls out the flimsies that detail Constantine's plasm use. Something patters on the glass ceiling of the arboretum: the promised rain.

'Your use patterns,' she says, 'demonstrate that much of your plasm use is second or third shift, so you're already getting much of it at off-peak rates.'

'I do not keep conventional hours,' Constantine says.

'I thought perhaps you were attempting to economize.'

Constantine's eyes shift briefly, somehow encompassing the long room, the huge conservatory, the expensive furniture, Mage Towers itself. *Do I need to economize?* he seems to ask.

The eyes return to Aiah's face. It is not an unfriendly stare, but there is no warmth in it either. Not even expectancy. Just a frowning challenge: *give me something useful, or go away.*

Aiah licks dry lips. 'I can enroll you in a plan that can get you a minimum of 1500 mm per hour at a cost fifty percent off the top rate – there's a lump sum payment of a million up front. Or you can go five million out front, in which case you can forget any hourly charges.'

Constantine doesn't change expression. Rain is a constant drumming overhead. 'That sounds attractive,' he says.

'I take it you're interested?' Aiah hears a cough behind her, a growl. That big cat. She tries to keep her mind on business.

'Who did you say you are exactly?' Constantine asks.

'I work for the Plasm Authority,' Aiah says. 'I'm a Grade Six. One of your people checked my ID, but perhaps you'd like to see it.' She reaches into her briefcase, takes her identification, holds it up. Constantine's eyes don't even flicker toward her picture, instead remain focused on the original.

The blonde woman ghosts up by Aiah's side. The big spotted cat is with her, butting her hip with its huge head while she scratches its ears. Its rasping purr sounds loud as a portable generator. Humid breath bathes Aiah's cheek, and she can scent raw dead flesh.

'I thought perhaps you were working for a private individual,' Constantine says. 'Someone with his own building or other plasm generator, who needs an installment of money so badly that he's willing to sell future plasm at below market rates.'

'It's something like that,' she says.

'What's the problem? A gambling debt? If it's to the Operation, then your principal can just sell them plasm.'

'And then never *stop* selling it to them,' Aiah says. 'That's how the Operation would work it. But no, nobody's in debt to the Operation.'

'Then why this great generosity?'

Aiah allows herself to smile. Her heart sounds in her ears louder than the purr of the great cat. 'I'm an admirer of the New City Movement,' she says.

Constantine makes a surprised sound deep in his throat, a growl that sounds as if it might come from the cat. The blonde woman gives a brief, trilling laugh.

'The New City Movement,' Constantine says, 'was dead when you were in diapers.'

'Not that long ago,' Aiah says. 'I remember you.'

'The movement was a stillbirth.' He shifts in his seat. 'None of us realized it, that was all.'

The big cat approaches, sniffs Aiah's hand. Aiah restrains the impulse to snatch it away. She glances at the green-eyed woman, then faces Constantine.

'May we speak privately?' she says. 'I was hoping for a private interview.'

Constantine absorbs this, leans forward, clasps his big hands on the desk as he gazes at Aiah. 'Madame Sorya has my confidence,' he says.

Sorya. The Special Assistant, Aiah remembers. She and Aiah had spoken on the phone, and it had taken Aiah a lot of effort to get past her.

Thunder speaks nearby and the building trembles. Aiah glances at Sorya again, sees the green eyes regarding her casually, without interest. She turns back to Constantine and takes a breath.

'The plasm is mine,' she says. 'I'm the person who needs the money, though it's not for anything so romantic as a gambling debt.'

Constantine says nothing, just continues his stare. Aiah resists the impulse to fidget, keeps her hands still, her shoulders square to her target. 'You may remember,' she says, 'the flaming plasm apparition that appeared on Bursary Street a few weeks ago. There were deaths.'

'That was you?' Constantine's voice shows no amusement, but Sorya trills another laugh. Aiah feels herself flush.

'No,' Aiah says. 'But since I'd volunteered for the Authority's Emergency Response team, I was sent out to look for the source.' She pauses, presses her hands firmly to her thighs, onto the rich gray wool. 'I found it,' she says.

'Congratulations,' Sorya says. Constantine says nothing, just continues his open stare.

Resentment skates along Aiah's nerves. Constantine isn't doing anything, isn't saying anything. He's making her do all the work.

Draw him out, she thinks. Make him respond to her.

'What would you do, Metropolitan,' she asks, 'if you found a renewable plasm source that powerful? A glory hole worth millions, that no one knows about?'

His response gives her nothing. 'What I would do is not the issue. But I suspect we are soon to find out what *you* did.'

The cat leans close and sniffs at Aiah's ear. Aiah's stomach turns at the moist touch of his breath, at the stench of a thousand dead animals. Aiah fights the sick feeling in her belly, the cry of despair and futility that rises in her heart.

Stick to the program, she thinks, and lightning illuminates the conservatory in pale corpse-light.

'Were I given such a thing,' Aiah says, 'I would know I couldn't use it myself. So I would offer it to someone . . .'

Sorya laughs again. 'For a million.'

Aiah clenches her teeth. 'For a sum considerably less than its value.' The cat's rumble is loud in her ear; maybe even the *cat* is laughing at her.

Constantine leans back in his chair. Leather creaks, pneumatics sigh. 'Ah. I knew – *we* knew –' with a nod at

Sorya, '– from your peculiar insistence over the phone, that you wanted to see me for some reason other than some little metering problem. At least it isn't some,' he lets weariness show in his eyes, 'feeble attempt at romance. You are not as tedious as that.'

'Thank you.' Aiah speaks as coldly as she can.

'You want to sell me power,' Constantine says. 'But what use would I have for it? I reside in the Scope of Jaspeer on sufferance. Your sad little republic is stable and old and possesses neither imagination nor conviction, and it considers me an adventurer. It is cautious; it spends a certain amount of effort monitoring my activities. I make this government uneasy, and it would as soon see the last of me.'

His tone is perfectly level, as opaque as his manner, and betrays neither interest nor passion. Maybe, Aiah thinks wildly, I am *boring* these people.

The cat, at least, is bored with her. It sits and begins to lick its paw.

'What better way,' Constantine continues, 'to dispose of its unease, than for this government, or one of its agencies operating on its own, to send a provocateur to my home to tempt me with some grand illegality?' He steeples his fingertips. 'How much easier it is to believe this story than to believe that some young woman has discovered a vast source of power, and wishes to sell it.'

'I have it,' Aiah says. 'I can show it.'

'This proves nothing.' He sits in his chair unmoving. 'If you are who I think you are, tell your government I am uninterested in these games. I have no ambitions, and no spare millions in any case. If you are who you say you are, I wish you success in finding a buyer. The Operation, I know, is always interested.'

Aiah's nails drive through wool into her thighs. Pain leaps through nerves, tautens her voice. 'I won't do that,' she grates. 'Never to them.'

Constantine's somber pupils grow wider. 'Why not?' he asks. 'The Operation is at least as respectable as I am. Probably more so.'

'They,' Aiah lets out a breath. 'They hurt my sister. I won't deal with them.'

Constantine just looks at her. Waiting, as always, for her to reveal herself.

'They control all the clubs here,' she says. 'And entertainment. And . . .' She waves her hands. 'You know that.'

He says nothing. Aiah hates him for making her tell this story, for bringing up the memories, the rage, and all of it for nothing, because he's not going to take the offer, he's just bored and looking for entertainment, and Aiah will provide it because she's too desperate to simply turn and leave.

'She — my sister Henley — she worked for them. Just as a waitress, in a club. She was expected to dress a bit provocatively, but she wasn't required to — there was nothing more than flirtation involved, and flirtation pays well — she was going through college, getting a degree in graphic arts. And when she'd saved enough, she tried to leave, and when she came to pick up her checktube . . .' Fingernails bite into thighs again. 'The manager had her hands broken. Not just her hands, but wrists and elbows. You don't do graphic arts with broken hands, do you? And then she got arthritis, and . . .' Aiah finds herself snarling, her voice shaking with anger. 'Henley wasn't under contract to him or anything, she didn't *owe* him anything, and she was just a *waitress*, the manager just did it because he *could*, because he was having a *bad day* and she made him angry. So . . .'

She shrugs. Hate lies bitter on her tongue, and she can't tell who she hates, herself for groveling this way or Constantine for making her do it. 'So I won't sell to the Operation. And I guess I won't sell to you.' She makes a gesture that encompasses the room, the conservatory, all of Mage Towers. 'You've retired, or taken up gardening. Maybe you only saw me because you were bored. The New City Movement is dead. Pardon me for still believing—'

He holds up a hand. Lightning etches his features. Thunder rocks the tower. 'You don't know what it is you're asking,' he says.

'Apparently not.' The sarcasm comes easy enough.

'This is not,' he says, 'a *little* business you wish to engage in. You do not deal with *little* people.' There's anger in his voice, and Aiah takes a mean satisfaction in having put it there. 'And *you*,' he says, 'you have put yourself in our hands. We could *take* this source of yours, and you could disappear.'

At the threat Aiah feels the hair on her arms prickle. 'You couldn't get to it without me,' she says. 'Nor could you use it.'

'Are you that certain?' Sharp teeth gleaming in his black face.

'I've taken precautions,' Aiah continues. 'Left documents in places where they'd be found.' True enough, in its way.

His lip curls. 'Where *I* couldn't find them?'

'Metropolitan,' Sorya says. There is a warning in her voice.

'Whatever *little* dreams you have, put them aside,' Constantine says. His eyes, alive now, burn into hers, though his body is still relaxed in his leather chair. 'Can you run with giants?' he demands. 'Or at any rate such giants as this sad and barricaded world can engender?'

Hatred still burns in Aiah's words. 'I haven't seen a giant yet,' she says.

'*Constantine*.' Sorya's alarm is clear.

Constantine rises from his chair, and Aiah involuntarily shrinks from him – she's forgotten how huge he is, how powerful, and she sees now that he's got a copper t-grip in his hand, and that there's a wire leading from it to some plasm source – Constantine is armed, and active, plasm-light glowing in his eyes, and with a fast, ferocious gesture he thrusts one massive hand toward Aiah.

And that is the last she knows, for quite some while.

When Aiah comes to herself she's standing on a wet street-corner busy with end-of-shift traffic. She looks up wildly, sees black glass reflecting receding storm clouds, the black pinnacles of Mage Towers cutting the horizon above a red-brick apartment building. They must be a full radius away. Someone runs into her from behind.

'Oh. Sorry.' She turns to see a businessman with a furled umbrella already hurrying away. Automobiles, silent except for the splash of tires in the wet gutters, glide past on efficient battery power.

600 DIE IN APARTMENT BLAZE. Words imprint themselves across the sky. DETAILS ON THE *WIRE*.

Beneath the burning plasm floats a figure: humanoid, with long wings, its body sheathed in bright metal. One of the twisted, an avian soaring in its element.

She looks up in awe. She's never seen an avian before.

She swallows the sudden lump in her throat. Perhaps it's an omen.

The avian flies out of sight. Aiah looks down at her palm and sees writing there. *Alveg Park, 1000, tomorrow. Hardhat.* The printed characters, written on flesh, are badly formed, but they're clearly her own.

She seems to have made an appointment with herself.

But how, she wonders, did she know to look at her palm just then? It was not a natural gesture under the circumstances.

Her eyes leap to the horizon again, the jagged teeth of Mage Towers. He's been in my *head*, she thinks.

You do not deal with little *people.* Constantine's words. Apparently not.

She looks around, sees a trackline station of the New Central Line that will take her home. She walks toward it, reaches into her pocket for her Transit Authority pass . . .

And to her astonishment, she lifts from her pocket a drawstring bag that clinks, full of money.

9

A cold wind shoulders its brusque way through Alveg Park, its breath moist with impending rain. The park sits atop District Hospital Seventeen, a cavernous medical complex roofed by a recreation center almost a full square radius in area. The surface beneath Aiah's heavy work boots is crumbling orange brick interlaced with exposed silvery bits of worn rebar. Trees sit in concrete tubs, bark scarred with pocket-knife carvings despite sharp-tipped circles of wrought-iron bars meant to protect each trunk. Some of the carvings are decades old. The shade provided by the trees is erratic, and a makeshift arrangement of faded canvas awnings, once brightly colored, is strung on steel poles above the old benches. No one sits on the benches today, not beneath the heavy canvas flogging louder than thunder in the hard wind.

Aiah doesn't have to go through the hospital to get to the park: there are big exterior elevators, graffiti-scarred steel cages, that lift the public to the park. Most of the park's inhabitants are pigeons, though there are also a lot of children at this hour of a Saturday, and there are a few adults in the ball courts, braving the weather, practicing or playing pick-up games.

Aiah can't picture Constantine in a place like this, though it otherwise seems like a reasonable place for a clandestine meet, without taller buildings nearby and with interrupted sight lines that would make observation difficult or obvious. Still, she feels conspicuous in her hardhat, boots and yellow jumpsuit. She doesn't know who's going to be meeting her. And, as the place is huge, she doesn't know where she's supposed to be met, so she wanders, chilled even in her jumpsuit, and feels lost. Fried-food smells from a vendor make her mouth water. She was too nervous to eat breakfast. She stops, buys a fish patty on a seed bun, and is pleased the vendor has Barkazil mustard. She adds the mustard, bites down . . .

'You are Miss Aiah?'

The speaker is one of the twisted, a huge slab of a man with a face like a piece of black armor, small eyes sunk deep beneath plates of bone. He has a Cheloki accent, which, Aiah now realizes, Constantine does not. The big man is taller even than Constantine and wears casual clothes, a giant blue windbreaker zipped up to the chin. If it's to make him inconspicuous it fails. Aiah tries to swallow her mouthful, finds it's too hot, nods instead.

'My name is Mr Martinus. I'm to transport you.'

Aiah manages to swallow her food. 'All right,' she says. 'This way.'

Walking after him is like following a moving wall. She has to make little skips to keep up with his long strides. He leads her through the park and past a section fenced off as an exercise yard for hospital patients, but which looks more like something in a prison complex, barren and old and grimy. As Aiah walks by, two young men in wheelchairs, bundled against the wind, grimly wheel themselves back and forth, a little circuit to nowhere.

Beyond is a rooftop landing field. A pair of small helicopters, emergency orange, wait with blades drooping, and a pair of aerocars stand on their pads. One of these is orange, with the hospital logo on its flank, and the other is a gleaming black, with an opaqued cockpit, and a serial number beginning with the three-letter code for a private vehicle. Martinus heads toward the last.

'Is that car yours?' Aiah asks. It's a Sky Dart, she recognizes, the classic TX3 from before the Dart company went downscale.

'I have the use of it,' Martinus says.

'Can you land it here? This is a *hospital*.'

'No one prevented me. It's a public pad, even if it's only the hospital that uses it.' He punches an access code on the aerocar's twelve-key pad and the cockpit rolls open. It's a four-seater, with twin controls. Martinus turns to Aiah and helps her into one of the front seats, then takes the other himself.

Aiah's never flown before, and nervousness stirs in her blood. She looks down at the sandwich in her hand and wonders what to do with it – her appetite is long gone. She puts it in her lap and fumbles with the crash webbing, and Martinus reaches over and fits the clasps with quick, efficient movements of his enormous hands. Aiah sees heavy slabs of callus over his knuckles and realizes he's spent a lot of time practicing to hit people – or maybe, she thinks, it wasn't all practice.

Fear crawls like a spider through her belly. Maybe she won't come back from this. But no, she thinks, if they wanted her dead they could have . . .

Martinus dons a headset and begins moving through a checklist written in wax crayon on slick, erasable plastic. A starter ratchets, coughing like some exotic animal, then turbines whine. Martinus peers out to watch the turbines gymbal, then checks control surfaces. He frowns diligently at the checklist as he jacks wires in and out of sockets to reconfigure the car's computer to its new destination. He gets a series of amber go-lights across the instrument panel, then reaches for the controls.

Suddenly the air is alive with plasm. Aiah can feel the hair on her arms stir. The turbines howl, and then the car is airborne, moving on a stream of plasm to its destination. Aiah's stomach is left behind; the smell of the cooking grease on her fish sandwich suddenly revolts her. The turbine noise fades. Aiah remembers to look out of the cockpit and sees the city far below, the long gray roofs going on forever, all the way to the horizon, their monotony occasionally broken by the skyscraper complexes, Mage Towers or Loeno or the area around Bursary Street, rising toward the aerocar like foreshortened claws. It's a bit frightening to see that far, to see a distant horizon unblocked by a frowning office building or the brick wall of an apartment.

And then she's descending, tall buildings reaching up toward her. Directly below is the flat concrete surface of a pad marked with a large target symbol, and Martinus uses the turbines to do some fine maneuvering, one eye fixed to the padded rim of a thing like a bombsight that lets him view the landing park below. The sharp wind buffets the car, making Martinus frown, but he lands with supreme gentleness, and then taxies the car to a parking area and shuts down the turbines.

His eyes scan the sky. 'No one following,' he says.

The landing pad is built atop a parking structure meant to service the office buildings that surround it. Aiah follows Martinus into an elevator that takes them below ground. She still carries her sandwich, she can't seem to find a place to get rid of it. They step out of the elevator and wait for a long moment, and then a large car pulls up, a stretched-out Elton painted a subdued gray. The car's design is purely functional, with no ornamentation at all, and that's more impressive than all the chrome in the world; it suggests luxury and ease and pampered living, economic security so all-encompassing it eliminates the need for display. The windows are opaque and marked with a fine crosshatching of bronze wire: armor against plasm attack. The Elton's turbine sings softly. Martinus opens a rear door and waits for Aiah to enter.

Sorya sits in back, her penetrating green eyes fixed on Aiah. Her blonde hair is tucked up under a knit cap, and she's wearing overalls over a gray sweater. The overalls are black and shiny and tailored, with silver buttons, and they're belted fashionably at Sorya's slim waist. Aiah wonders if there are boutiques for such things.

'Hello,' she says, and sits by the other woman. The door closes behind her with a firm metal thunk that makes Aiah think the car might be armored.

'Sorry to interrupt your meal,' Sorya says, and looks at the sandwich. Aiah feels her cheeks flush. The car has a trash container and Aiah drops the sandwich in it, drops the silvered metal lid.

'Any trouble?' Sorya asks.

'Should there have been?'

Martinus gets in next to the driver. There is a soft singing sound from the two big contra-rotating flywheels in the built-up area behind the front seat, and the car smoothly pulls away.

'Certain formalities,' Sorya says. 'Sorry.'

Aiah sits stiffly while Sorya searches her, pale competent hands probing her body for batteries, recorders, antennae. She manages to avoid twitching as Sorya clinically explores her crotch. Sorya finishes the job, then settles back in her seat.

'You'll have to give us directions to your glory hole,' Sorya says.

'Ah.' A chauffeured Authority worker, Aiah thinks, now *that's* inconspicuous. 'Let me think. Just head in the direction of Terminal.'

Saturday first shift, she thinks. Around midbreak. Lots of people on the streets. She wasn't going to be able to sneak Sorya through the old apartment building. They would have to use the tunnels, and she didn't dare use the nearest access, not with the possibility of being recognized by one of the men who'd attacked her.

'Will Constantine be joining us?' she asks.

Sorya looks at her. 'Constantine is far too fastidious to do his own dirty work, ne? I hope you're not disappointed.'

Aiah shakes her head. 'In fact, I'm relieved.'

Amusement twitches the corners of Sorya's mouth. 'Why?'

'Because if he were with us, there's no way I could hide him.'

Sorya's laugh trills out. 'Very good,' she said. 'You are perceptive.'

'It will be hard enough hiding *you*.'

Sorya's brows arch. 'How so?'

'You're beautiful, which means people will notice you no matter what. You're dressed better than anyone we'll meet today – certainly better than anyone I've ever seen go down a manhole. And Mr Martinus is not inconspicuous, either.'

Sorya judges this. 'Perhaps you have done this sort of thing before.'

'No. But I'm learning.' Aiah looks at her. 'And at least you didn't bring the panther.' Aiah looks out over Martinus's broad shoulder, sees a wide avenue moving smoothly past, office blocks half-deserted on a Saturday, pastel neon adverts scribed across empty black windows. 'Another thing,' she says. 'Do you have climbing gear? Safety lines, harnesses, carabiners?'

'Will we need them?'

'Only if we want to do this safely. I don't want to return you to Constantine in a damaged condition.'

Sorya seems amused. 'Tell us what we need, and we'll buy it on the way.'

Sorya carries a checktube charged with a significant amount of cash, because even when Aiah gets extravagant with her requests the gear is purchased quietly, without complaint, the checktube plugged into the cash register, little gears singing. The purchases set Aiah's mind running in fiscal channels.

'Don't think,' she says after she returns to the car, 'that you've purchased this source for the money I found in my pocket yesterday.'

In fact it had amounted to five thousand dalders, all in untraceable coin, enough to clear Aiah's debts and still have plenty left for the bank.

'Take it up with Constantine,' Sorya says.

'I'm taking it up with his representative,' Aiah says. 'You know my price. No amount of interfering with my head will change that.'

'*That*,' Sorya says, 'was not my idea.'

'It was dangerous. I could have suffered brain damage.'

'We stopped short of that,' Sorya says. 'But we needed to know if you are what you say you are.'

Aiah gives Sorya a skeletal little grin. 'And am I?'

'All we could tell,' smoothly, 'was that you *believe* what you told us. You could still be delusional, or you may have overestimated the strength of the power source.'

'Oh. Thank you.'

One pale brow arches. 'Miss Aiah. We don't *know* you.'

'Get on the Trans-City heading west.' To the driver. 'That'll be quickest.'

She directs the driver to Terminal, then begins making wider and wider circles around the area in hopes of finding a business district where there won't be quite so many people on the street. She doesn't, but she does succeed in locating a subterranean parking garage from which she's fairly certain she can gain access to utility tunnels. While the chauffeur leans on the fender of the car and smokes a quiet cigaret, Aiah uses her Authority passkey to unlock a scarred steel door and leads her party past the building's plasm meter and into the tunnels.

The streets are a regular grid here, fortunately, and with only small hesitation Aiah manages to find one of the pneuma's crumbling brick-lined air shafts. Underground rain drizzles on her hat as she waits at the bottom for the other two to work their way down the slick, rusting iron ladder. When they arrive at the base of the shaft, they seem thankful for Aiah's insistence on safety gear.

The platform waits in silence, Aiah's bootmarks the only sign of humanity. Martinus glides along the concrete, alert, silent as a cat despite his size. Sorya looks around expectantly, and Aiah smiles.

'Watch your step,' Aiah says, and walks through the wall.

It's some moments before Martinus follows, a suspicious hand bulky in one pocket, presumably folded around a weapon. He looks around the empty concrete room, gazes at the fallen brace, then steps back to the platform, the illusion closing behind him like a beaded curtain. Sorya is with him when he returns.

'Careful,' Aiah says. 'Don't step on the guideline.'

Sorya steps away from the line on the concrete, then turns to contemplate the plasm curtain. 'A nice piece of work,' she says. 'Yours?'

'Yes.'

'They're hard to keep stable.'

'I didn't have much trouble,' Aiah says, faint surprise tingling in her mind at the mention of the stability problem.

'It wasn't this one who made the screen?' Martinus has found the plasm diver. He pulls back the blanket and stares at the body with professional detachment.

'No,' Aiah says.

Martinus looks up at Aiah. 'Did you kill her?' he asks, and a chill rolls up Aiah's spine at his matter-of-fact tone.

'No,' she says, and wonders if she's said it too quickly. She lowers her voice, tries to speak slowly. 'She was the Bursary Street flamer. When I found her she was like that, with her hand on the brace.'

'Ah,' coldly. 'I suppose this kind of death can happen accidentally, but when I've seen it, it's always been quite deliberate.'

Sorya stands next to the brace and looks at it with cautious respect. She takes a portable meter from her pocket, attaches the alligator clip. Her eyes glitter as the glowing dial illuminates her face from below. Aiah sees a new regard enter Sorya's face as she reads the meter.

The blonde woman raises her other hand, bites the forefinger of one glove, pulls her hand out, then quickly puts the bare hand on the beam. Aiah's nerves give a cry, and she takes a half-step toward the other woman, an unvoiced protest on her lips.

Sorya turns to her and smiles. There's a cold light in her green eyes, something bright and inhuman drawn from the iron brace. She takes her hand off the metal.

'Very well, Miss Aiah,' she says. 'I think we can do business.'

The Elton takes Aiah all the way to Loeno Towers. Underground muck gets all over the seats, but Sorya doesn't seem to notice. Cleaning upholstery, Aiah figures, is pretty clearly for other people.

As the car pulls into Loeno's drive, Sorya turns to open a compartment in the shelf behind her seat. Her arm and shoulders strain as she brings out a heavy suede bag, then gives a tight smile and tosses it into Aiah's lap. Aiah can't prevent a convulsive jerk of her body, a protective curl, as the jingling weight crashes onto her thighs.

'Ten thousand,' Sorya says.

'I don't sell this cheap,' Aiah said.

'I didn't say you would,' Sorya says. 'It's an advance. But I don't mean to imply that Constantine has any spare millions lying around, either.'

'Tell me another joke,' Aiah says. She permits herself a contemptuous look at the money, at the Elton, at the chauffeur who has parked the car under the building's awning and has left the car to open Aiah's door.

'Oh, he's *worth* millions,' Sorya says. 'But ready money is another business.'

The door opens at the chauffeur's touch. There is a brief singing, a brief vibration, from the contra-rotating fly-wheels.

'Don't do anything foolish with it,' Sorya says.

'I don't do foolish things with money.'

'Don't buy a new car. Or new diamonds. Or ten thousand lottery tickets. Nothing that will call attention to you.'

Aiah smiles at her sweetly. 'Can I get new shoes?' she says.

Sorya returns the smile. 'Two pair, if you like.'

Aiah lets the smile flick off. 'Remember what I said.'

Sorya reaches into a pocket for a slim cigaret, poses for a moment with the white stick between her fingers. She's fond of striking poses, Aiah thinks.

'And I'd advise you,' says Sorya, 'in all friendship and sincerity, to remember what Constantine said, Miss Aiah. We are not *little* people.' She arches a brow, produces a platinum lighter glittering with diamonds, and with an effortless touch of her thumb turns on a delicate, golden flame.

'Money isn't a little thing,' Aiah says. 'Good day.'

The chauffeur closes the door solidly behind her. As she walks through the door she sees her fellow tenants looking at her, at the grimy Authority worker in her yellow jumpsuit and hardhat stepping out of a chauffeured Elton, and Aiah concludes her standing has risen a bit in the status-conscious world of Loeno Towers.

Sincerity and friendship. Of the things Aiah had sensed from Sorya, these were not among them.

As she walks through the building lobby Aiah can see, repeated over and over again in the mirrored walls, the long gray Elton pulling away. Her neighbors watch with interest. This, she thinks, is not a discreet conspiracy.

The sack of money tugs at her arm. Solid. Heavy. Real. All coins made of exotic alloys that could only be made with magework, so that they couldn't be counterfeited.

Not *little* people, Aiah thinks.

So maybe they believed they were giants.

Aiah plans to find out if giants are a match for one of the Cunning People.

10

Aiah watches as Constantine stands with his big hands curled around the jigsaw curves of the baroque iron terrace rail. He stares moodily at the city below while wind twitches at the collar of his black open-necked shirt. There is a coiled, restless energy in him that seems to inflate his presence, that dwarfs the terrace. His words are directed outwards, a rhetorical question addressed as much to the wind as to his guest.

'What is it, Miss Aiah, that you want?'

'Many things,' Aiah says. 'Money will do.'

His head turns slowly and he looks at her. Aiah tries not to let her breath catch in her throat: his look is so intense it seems to crawl up the map of her nerves. 'What can money do,' he says, 'that I cannot?'

'Are you offering me yourself?' The thought is so absurd Aiah has to smile. 'What would I do with you? You're a little large for my closets.'

'I am not offering myself, but what I am,' Constantine says, 'and that is not inconsiderable.'

It's Sunday, halfway through first shift. The previous day, after Sorya had made her report, Constantine had called Aiah, in person, to invite her to a late Sunday breakfast.

Sorya herself isn't present, and neither is her panther. Breakfast had been served by a silent Jaspeeri, a stranger. There had been a huge bowl of fruit, presumably grown in the conservatory or someplace like it, and Aiah had never seen or tasted anything as mouth-watering: fruit with skins bright as if they'd been polished, the flesh filled with juice, flavors alive and sparkling on the tongue ... the pathetic bruised stuff for which she pays fortunes in stores are nothing by comparison. She'd had to restrain herself from gorging.

'What can you offer me,' Aiah counters, 'that money cannot?'

'Wisdom, I hope,' Constantine says. There is cold self-mocking irony in his face. His eyes leave Aiah, shift out over the city below, and Aiah feels relieved, as if a searchlight had just passed over her.

'Any wisdom in particular, Metropolitan?' Aiah asks. 'And how much do you think it's worth?'

The wind flutters Aiah's lace. Constantine pushes his hands into the pockets of his charcoal-gray slacks. He gives another little grimace as his eyes rove over the city.

'Once I thought being right was enough,' he said, 'and then I learned I was incorrect, that mere rightness is not wisdom.' The hands in his pockets form fists, begin to gnaw the fabric. 'I learned wisdom in the worst possible way, watching everyone I loved die, everything I cared about be destroyed.' His voice is relentless, his gaze a pensive stare into the past. 'Watching it all happen slowly,' he continues, 'over a period of years, and knowing all the while it was my fault. What sort of wisdom do you think I gained?' His eyes flash to Aiah again, challenging.

'I can't say, Metropolitan.' She can't imagine herself with that kind of self-knowledge, the weight of that kind of responsibility dragging her down.

'What do you think I will do with this plasm of yours?' Constantine shifts his course, a probe in another direction.

This is *business*, she reminds herself.

'I don't know. It isn't my concern.'

'Not your concern. I could use these goods of yours to create another flaming woman on the Exchange. Destroy this smug little Jaspeer of yours.'

Aiah licks dry lips. 'I would suggest, Metropolitan, that such a project is beneath you.'

Laughter booms from deep within Constantine's barrel chest. Sly delight crosses his face, a suggestion that Aiah and he have just shared a wonderful jest. 'Well said, daughter!' he says. 'An encouraging sentiment!'

He pulls his chair out from beneath the breakfast table and mounts the chair by easily kicking one foot up over the chairback, then sitting down, a simple, dancelike movement that belies his true age. 'I could do it so much better now, you see,' he says. 'I thought if I could simply seize power in Cheloki, then my ideas alone would guarantee success, would deliver my corrupt, hapless metropolis to a new age. Would create progress, create an impetus toward change that it would be impossible to stop. But I'd been away from government too long. I'd forgotten how entrenched it all is, how many interests depend for their very existence on human inertia, how thousands of years of living in a shell —' he jerks his chin upwards toward the opalescent, enigmatic Shield, the eggshell skin of the world, the wall stretched across the whole of the sky, a barrier, but a barrier that gives light and life ' — how the shell has made us timid,' he continues, leaning closer as if including Aiah in a confidence, 'timid as all creatures who live in shells. And I've never realized how other governments would view mine with alarm, would feel terrified by anything that threatened their placidity, anything that demonstrated their smug satisfaction for what it was, delusion and hypocrisy,' the words roll on, hypnotic, intense, as if he were drunk on them, and by now Aiah is beginning to feel a little giddy herself, 'hypocrisy because they were happy to do business with my gangster family as long as we were looting our own people, our own economy, driving our best away or putting them in prisons, but as soon as I tried to liberate them, to transform the whole metropolis into an evolutionary instrument . . .' He hesitates, his ferocious intensity fading as he catches himself in mid-screed. He barks a laugh, makes a dismissive gesture with his hands.

'See what a fool I am?' he says. 'I can still get caught up in it, still believe.' He spreads his hands. 'That I matter. That any of this matters.'

Aiah props her hand in her chin, leans across the table toward him. 'What *will* you do with the plasm?' she asks.

He frowns. 'Some good, I hope. But *access*, that is the problem.'

'Metropolitan?'

'That disused terminal is hard to get to, by Sorya's account. And if I were to use it, I'd have to send work parties down there, build accumulators, string cable to carry the plasm to where I could use it, or work some way to broadcast it from a building.'

'There's an easier way to do it, Metropolitan.'

'Yes?'

'The Authority buys plasm at fixed rates, then resells it. What you do is create a dummy company, one that owns a building at a fictional address. You create a fictional history to go with that address. And then you get yourself a phony work order to install a meter, get another saying the job's been done, then sell the plasm from Terminal through that company. You take the money, then buy plasm for yourself here with it, and do it quite legally.' She smiles. 'If you have someone at the Authority to keep all the paperwork straight, you could go on that way for years.'

'I see.' Cold amusement glows in Constantine's eyes. 'But I lose something that way, don't I? I'd sell plasm to the Authority at a rate considerably below that which I'd pay to use it. What if I simply wanted to use the stuff at Terminal, not sell it?'

Aiah checks for a moment, rethinks. If Constantine actually wants to use the plasm at Terminal, it almost certainly has to be for purposes that would get his meters shut off here at Mage Towers. Something well over the border into illegality.

Interesting, she thinks.

'You don't have to go to the pneuma station to tap that potential well,' Aiah says. 'All you need to do is find another part of that old plastic plant – it's all strung together. Tap any one part, you tap the entire structure. You might be able to find some of the structure using standard utility tunnels, with a little digging, anyway. There are hundreds of old tunnels down there, many of them so old they're off the map.'

'Hm.' He frowns.

'But on the other hand,' Aiah says, 'the disused platform would make construction easier.'

'I foresee nothing but difficulty,' Constantine says. 'I'd need a control facility, a battery station, broadcast horns.' He shrugs. 'I may have to buy a building in the area, remodel it to the necessary specifications. And that means working through dummy companies, hiding the money, coming up with a plausible cover. A complicated business.'

Aiah leans back. This is a scope of effort she hadn't quite contemplated. 'You seem to have funds available, Metropolitan,' she says.

'I can spend only a certain amount,' Constantine says, 'before it becomes more cost-effective to buy my plasm from the Authority like any other mortal. If I must buy a building, you, Miss Aiah, would get less money.'

Aiah considers this. The sky above brightens with an advertisement for jewelry, the sky glittering with diamonds that reflect rainbows. The advertising over Mage Towers, she observes, has a somewhat greater cachet than that over Old Shorings.

'There's always the way I first suggested. Reselling through the dummy company. It's a sure profit-maker. That's how the Operation sanitize their plasm, when they can.'

'Profit.' Constantine is disdainful. 'Profit is not why I do what I do.'

'Either money matters, or it doesn't,' Aiah says. 'If it doesn't, why are you haggling?'

He looks at her stonily. *Got you*, she thinks.

'If it's a building you want,' Aiah says, 'perhaps you need only rent a warehouse.'

'Perhaps.' He leans back in his chair, moody again. 'You know this metropolis better than I. Perhaps you could make the arrangements.'

'Not I.' Aiah bares her teeth in a smile. 'I'm the wrong color for that neighborhood.'

Constantine laughs, puts his black hand on the table next to Aiah's brown one. 'If you're the wrong color,' he says, 'what am I?'

'Too intimidating to deal with, I imagine. But not me – I've already been attacked once.'

The laughter vanishes from Constantine's face as suddenly as if it had been wiped away. 'Who?' he says.

Aiah shrugs. 'Three men. Maybe they were Jaspeeri Nation, maybe just sympathizers. I—' She swallows, hard, against the fist that's suddenly closing about her throat. 'They beat me. I struck back – with plasm. Two are probably in the hospital. I don't know about the third.'

Constantine's hand stretches a few inches, takes her hand. 'I saw you had been injured,' he says. 'I thought perhaps this lover of yours . . .'

'No. He's a gentle man.'

His big hand closes around hers as if it were that of a child. His brows contract. 'You've risked much, daughter,' he says. 'This must mean this business is important to you.'

'It is.'

'Very little, these days, is of such importance to me,' he says. His look turns a little challenging. 'What does this matter so much to you?'

Aiah takes a breath. Constantine's hand is very warm.

'It's a contracting economy, and I'm a foreigner – treated as foreign, anyway, even though I was born here, and so were my parents. To most of the people here – certainly to those men who attacked me – I'm disposable. My own people were destroyed as a nation generations ago. Anything resembling normal family life was devastated by twenty years of civil war, and my people haven't recovered.'

There is a haunted look in Constantine's eyes. His fingers grip Aiah's. 'My own people,' he says, 'the Cheloki – have I done that to them?'

'I,' she hesitates and wonders why she feels an impulse to comfort him. 'I can't say. The Barkazils have unusual ideas about themselves that may make their situation unique.'

Constantine senses the weak comfort in Aiah's words. He drops her hand, stands, steps to the rail. He gazes out over the city, eyes moving restlessly; and his voice rumbles so low in his chest that Aiah strains to make out the words.

'There was so much more at stake than lives and misery,' he says. 'A metropolis misgoverned – how absurdly common is that? Why should it be important to me? Why should I lift a hand?' He turns to her. 'It was only a first step,' he says. 'I wasn't aiming at the mere salvaging of a metropolis, but of the entirety of our miserable world. Only,' he gives a mocking smile, 'I miscalculated that very first step. And so more misery was brought into the world, and war and conflagration, and so Cheloki died, smothered in its own rubble. And though my training is in detachment, in a body of doctrine that tells me to seek only knowledge, to know only my mind and the reality of plasm and not the world – *still*,' he grips the rail again, fingers sawing against iron, '*still* I care. I bleed for my people, and I want to find a place for them.'

He spins abruptly with the surprising swiftness she had

learned was a part of him, moves toward her with a purposeful intent that makes her inwardly quail as he suddenly looms over her, remorseless and gigantic as one of Mage Towers suddenly free of its foundations. She can scent his hair oil, sense his body heat.

'Will you help me do that?' he demands.

She puts a hand up, a pointless effort to shield herself from the power of his presence. 'I don't know what you're asking.'

'I want you to help me use this gift of yours. Not just ask for money and run away, but help me *use* the power. You said you admired the New City – help me bring it out of the ashes.'

She looks at the silver-tipped braid that hangs over Constantine's shoulder, the complicated device of the School of Radritha, a figure of a hovering bird surrounded by a complex, interwoven plasm focus. She looks at it, tries to focus her own thoughts.

'I don't know what you want,' she says.

He barks a sudden gusty laugh, then steps back. 'Nor do I,' he says. 'Not precisely. There have been . . . projects . . . suggested to me. I have said neither yes nor no.' He begins pacing again. 'I did not know whether I was truly interested. Or perhaps I am merely afraid.'

'I can't give you courage, Metropolitan,' Aiah says.

He seems amused by this. 'Indeed not. But you can give me the benefit of your advice.' He sits again, containing for the moment his powerful presence in a chair. 'I need to know how to make use of this discovery of yours. How best to find it, tap it, deliver it.'

Surprise stirs along Aiah's nerves. '*You* are the mage, Metropolitan,' she says. 'Not I.'

'My training is in the higher use of plasm, not in the practical arts,' he said. 'In the past I have had competent engineers to serve me, but now . . .' He shrugs. 'I will need help. You understand the local systems, the way Jaspeer is wired together below the ground, and none of my people do.'

'I'm an outsider myself,' Aiah reminds.

'That perspective will also be useful.' He leans toward her. 'I hope to learn from you,' he says, 'but I hope to teach as well. During our association, you will have access to the plasm at Terminal and, if you like, Sorya and I will teach you methods of using it.'

Aiah's mind staggers beneath the weight of this offer.

'Are you serious?' she asks, the best she can manage after long moments of silence.

'Of course,' simply. 'You obviously possess intelligence and talent – I will teach you what you can absorb, and without all the mystic drivel the great sages of the universities would think necessary.'

Aiah's thoughts swirl alarmingly. 'Money,' she says, returning to fundamentals. 'I still want money.'

There is a glow of amusement in Constantine's eyes. 'Money,' he says, 'very well. Let us talk then about money. Elbows on the table –' he plants his arms on either side of his plate, and with a smile shows her his empty hands, '– and nothing up my sleeve.'

It's the sort of thing a Barkazil learns from the cradle, the cut and thrust of fine-honed argument, the bluff, the hedge, the last-minute condition reluctantly recalled to mind. It's hard to say who's the *passu*, who's the *pascol*, since Constantine is good at this as well, enjoys the bargaining simply for its own sake, and has a hundred tricks of rhetoric to draw on. But in the end, since he's always had money available, Constantine doesn't really care about it, it doesn't have a reality for him, whereas Aiah cares deeply about the cash, and knows exactly what every half-clink is worth, and that makes a big difference.

Aiah finishes the bargaining with two hundred thousand dalders, more than she ever thought she'd get – the original demand of a million was pure outrageous bluff. Still, she has to remind herself that she doesn't have it yet. Raising that much cash discreetly, Constantine reminds her, is a time-consuming business; and he also wants to give her some advice about hiding the money, so that the tax police won't descend on them all.

'Tomorrow,' Constantine says, 'we will begin our lessons.'

He calls for his car to drive Aiah home. And, before they leave the terrace, Constantine smiles as he puts fruit in a basket, and wordlessly hands it to her before she leaves.

She hates to think he already knows her this well.

11

The Elton limousine is parked at the northwest corner of the Authority building, and Martinus's slablike figure stands by it. Aiah feels a prickle between her shoulder-blades as she steps toward the car and wonders if any of her co-workers are watching, but she finds herself straightening her shoulders and lifting her chin as she walks, swinging her briefcase at the end of her arm, and when Martinus opens the door for her she can almost hear Constantine's amused voice in her ear: *Let 'em look.*

If he doesn't care about subtlety, why the hell should she?

A basket of fruit, cheeses and a chilled bottle of wine wait in the back. Aiah smiles.

She could really get used to this.

Martinus climbs into the driver's seat, and the door closes with that too-solid chunk. 'Mr Martinus,' she asks, 'where are we going?'

'To the Metropolitan's apartment, miss,' he says.

The contra-rotating flywheels whirr, and the Elton makes a quiet, efficient acceleration. Aiah relaxes gratefully into the plush seat.

'Did you have a pleasant Sunday?' she asks.

In the rearview mirror Aiah can see Martinus's eyes regarding her from within armor-plated sockets. 'I didn't have the day off, I'm afraid.'

'Sorry,' she says. 'I hope it was pleasant anyway.'

Martinus's look seems to soften a degree. 'It was a more active day than most,' he concedes.

Indeed, she thinks, and files the datum away.

She notices alligator clips falling out of her jacket pocket, and tucks them back in. She'd taken them off the phone lines on quarterbreak.

The end-of-shift traffic is thick, and Aiah eats a bright pink plum, a handful of grapes, and drinks a half glass of wine – it's dry, so dry it's almost hard to believe the stuff is liquid. The wine is like the most fabulous air she's ever tasted, and the contrast brightens the taste of the fruit on her palate, makes the juices seem almost to sizzle on her tongue.

She could indeed get used to this.

She has another half glass and hopes it won't make her stupid.

Constantine has guests, waiting for the elevator in the mirrored anteroom, who leave as Aiah arrives. One is a hook-nosed man with tufts of gray hair sprouting over his ears, another a younger man in a quiet blue suit and modest lace, and a third some kind of bearded clergyman in a flat round cap of velvet and a gray cassock. He's wearing ecclesiastical jewelry with symbols and devices, though none that Aiah recognizes. He and his friends all have copper skin, dark eyes, wide cheekbones. The strangers smile at Aiah with polite disinterest as she leaves the elevator, then make room for Martinus as he looms in her wake.

She can't really picture the clergyman and Constantine having much to say to each other.

The door is open so she enters the parlor, walking past one of the bulky-suited guards she'd met on her first visit. The other guard is standing in a doorway in the parlor, a doorway Aiah hadn't particularly noticed before. He's looking away. 'They're gone,' he says, 'and the Aiah woman is here with Mr Martinus,' and then he turns toward her and looks a bit startled, he hadn't realized the door was open. 'Sorry, miss,' he says.

'Close the door,' Martinus says, a cold voice that grates

along Aiah's spine, and the guard vanishes, but not before Aiah suddenly understands why the anteroom is mirrored: it's two-way glass, so that Constantine's security can observe anyone leaving the elevator.

Another little datum, she thinks.

The guard leads her up the spiral stair to the long room fronting the arboretum. As she comes to the top of the stair Aiah can hear, through the open door, Constantine's deep voice alternating with Sorya's.

'I wouldn't trust those people for a second,' she says.

'I don't trust them at all,' Constantine answers.

Hearing the voices, the guard hesitates. Sorya's voice rises in pitch. *'Why are you negotiating with them, then?'*

Aiah walks past the vacillating guard and stands within the open door's frame, waits for them to notice her. Constantine is dressed in soft formal gray and white lace, Sorya in a broad-shouldered red silk jacket over form-fitting pants splashed with bright color. There's a buffet set up, fruit displayed in crystal bowls as if they were works of art, gleaming copper chafing dishes, abandoned glasses smudged with fingerprints. Aiah detects the stink of spent tobacco.

Sorya and Constantine circle each other as they speak.

'If this business were only a cocktail party,' Constantine says, 'I would have Martinus kick them out, and not gently. But it is *not* a cocktail party, and they can help us.'

'I've given you reliable people to work with, and you choose this rabble?'

Sorya catches sight of Aiah then, and lightning flashes in her green eyes. Aiah's hands tighten on the grip of her briefcase, but she holds Sorya's gaze.

'If you deal with them at all,' Sorya adds coldly, 'you're insane.'

And then she leaves, heels clicking on marble. Her bare arm brushes against Aiah's sleeve in the doorway, and then her step hesitates, and her voice comes low in Aiah's ear. 'Learning something, missy?' she says. 'I hope so.'

Aiah keeps her gaze fastened on Constantine. His face is somber, chin tucked in, but there's a glow of amusement in his eyes.

'Come in, daughter,' he says, then adds, 'your education is commencing, I believe.'

Aiah lets her breath out and realizes she's been holding it for some while. She steps into the room, glances at dirty dishes and napkins.

'My luncheon seems to have run overlong,' Constantine says. He takes off his jacket, throws it over a chair, rolls up his sleeves. 'Have some supper, if you like,' he says.

'I ate in the car.' Her glance drifts across the buffet, sees a centerpiece of extravagant flowers, and displayed before it a thin gunmetal box propped up to exhibit its contents, a necklace of gold and platinum, its central orb aglitter with diamonds. Constantine sees the direction of Aiah's gaze and lazily prowls to the buffet, picks the necklace up with one finger and holds it out.

'I gave this to Sorya just now,' he says, 'a Forlong piece, and then curiously enough we began to fight. I wonder why.'

'Your disagreement didn't seem to be about jewelry.'

'The words concerned one thing, the passions another.' He holds the necklace toward Aiah, dangling it at the end of a finger. 'It seems not to be to Sorya's taste. You may have it, if you wish.'

Aiah's mouth goes dry. A little voice wails in her head, a plaintive whine of greed that wails out numbers, dalder amounts in the tens of thousands, then multiplied because it was crafted by Forlong. She looks at the glittering nest of diamonds, looks at Constantine, sees a little cold smile on his lips, a dangerous light in his eyes, and wonders if this is some kind of test, if he means to discover her character, if there is a *correct choice* involved. Dare she refuse his gift? And dare she take it, knowing it's Sorya's?

But then, as she looks at him an understanding slowly enfolds her, and Aiah knows she can have it, that at this point Constantine truly does not care what happens to the thing, and for some unknown reason that knowledge chills her, a cold that floods her bones. She licks her lips.

'Metropolitan,' she says, 'I don't think I'd feel safe with it.'

He shrugs, looks for a trash receptacle, and throws the necklace in. There is a liquid sound as it strikes uneaten food. Aiah has to suppress a part of her that wants to run screaming to the trash and dig the necklace out.

'Sit here,' Constantine says, 'and we'll begin.'

'We're doing this here? Not at Terminal?'

'I don't feel like climbing about in a cave. The plasm from Terminal will pay for any losses I incur.'

Perhaps, Aiah thinks, she ought to have held out for more money. She puts her briefcase down and sits on the chromium-and-leather sofa, sinks deep into soft calfskin. Constantine takes a copper transfer grip from his desk, then sits next to Aiah and fixes the t-grip into a slot on the couch. Surprise tingles through Aiah as she realizes she's sitting on a live well.

And then she looks up at the battery of video displays hanging overhead and realizes she's in a kind of command center, that the video is for remote plasm manipulation. It had all been discreet enough, or strange enough, that she hadn't noticed what the room was really for.

She turns to Constantine, ready to begin, and realizes that all his height is in his legs. Seated, she is the taller of the two.

An irrelevant datum, but there it is.

Know your passu. A Barkazil proverb.

Constantine looks at her. 'Sorya tells me that, in the old pneuma station, you used a guideline when you created a plasm screen. To insulate yourself from the source?'

'Yes,' Aiah says. 'Or I used batteries. I didn't want to end up like the flamer.'

Constantine nods. 'That was wise of you. I'll act as your insulator, then. I'll use the t-grip, and feed you such plasm as you can control. Agreed?'

Aiah nods. 'Should I use my focus?' she asks.

'If you use one normally, yes.'

There are people who don't use one normally? she wonders. But she unbuttons her collar, pushes the lace aside, and fetches out the little metal charm. Constantine's expression doesn't change when he looks at the little trinket in her pale palm – no sign of condescension or pity – and Aiah's heart warms toward him.

'I should point out,' he says, 'that in exchange for this education and use of plasm, I will ask you to do me certain services. And these services will be illegal.'

'Why start worrying about it now?' The answer is ready in her thoughts, and it amuses him.

He takes her wrist in one powerful hand. His touch is clinical. Aiah isn't certain if she likes that or not.

'You're skinny,' he says.

'So my mother tells me.'

His fingers close about her pulse. The other hand takes the transfer grip, and suddenly Aiah senses the snarling presence of plasm, a vast electric beast suddenly glowing in Constantine's mild eyes, and hairs lift on the back of her neck.

'Do whatever it is you do to get yourself ready,' he says, 'and we will begin.'

Aiah feels as if her mind is lit from within. Wherever she turns her thoughts she seems to know things that weren't apparent before: connections are perceived, facts tumble into place, and knowledge presents itself, neatly displayed, as if on a silver salver.

Throughout the lesson she's aware of Constantine hovering in her mind, guiding her movements, making suggestions, feeding her power. He approves of her choices, *approves*, and a spirit of fierce liberty possesses her. It's as if she's never felt approval before – and perhaps, on consideration, she never has.

An idea forms, and she wordlessly suggests it to Constantine. Again comes the unaccustomed, glorious sensation of *approval*, of liberation – and without quite realizing how, she jumps away, through the glass rooftop of the arboretum, along the arcing transmission horns and up. Her mind free of her physical location, as she'd experienced only once before, tentatively, when she reached out to Gil in faraway Gerad.

There's a wild soaring sensation as she springs upward from the transmission horn into the sky, bounds free of solid matter. Jaspeer's regular road grid falls away beneath her, dropping far faster than it had in Martinus's aerocar. The visual details fade as she climbs, but the *awareness*, the *knowledge*, of what's below never seems to leave her mind: steel and stone, brick and concrete, the ponderous matter that encloses and shelters and sustains all the world's fragile life, that generates plasm and powers her ascent.

Scattered white cloud drops below, overlaid on the world like one of the Authority's transparencies, and joyously Aiah continues her ascent. She can see the world curve away on all sides, the implastic gray mass of the city that wraps the globe, that stretches to every horizon. And then she looks up, and her mind staggers . . .

She hadn't intended coming this close to the Shield. But there it is, seemingly just above her, at this distance not opalescent gray but burning featureless white, the source of light and heat for the world. Aiah senses its enmity, its roaring *power*, an energy not merely the opposite of plasm, but plasm's destroyer, the raging enemy of all things earthly, power that will, if she touches it, snuff her out in an instant — and in the face of its fury she falters, loses command of herself, and her spirits reel. The horizon tumbles sickeningly about her. She can't tell her direction of motion — is she falling or still rising? And if so might she come in contact with the Shield, and be obliterated?

Panic reaches for her throat with clawed fingers.

Ah. Constantine's presence speaks softly to her inner ear. *Stabilize so. Now down, and slowly.*

The spinning stops. She and Constantine are drifting downward, away from the Shield, safe as if he were holding her arm while descending a stair. In a corner of her awareness, she knows that, far below, her heart throbs furiously in her body, her breath rasps in her throat.

– It's requiring rather a lot of plasm to maintain our lifeline to my apartment, Constantine tells her. Aiah can sense the amusement in his voice.

– Next time, he continues, we'll have to do this from underground.

– We can go back if you like, Aiah sends. Reluctantly.

The bright clouds rise toward them.

– We may as well stay. To Aiah's relief. We can play up here, with no ill consequences to anything below.

Plasm adverts, brief flares of incandescence, flash below over the city.

– Plasm is of incalculable value, Constantine says, and do you observe how we use it? To reduce tumors and to advertise shoes, to wage war and to entertain children. For purposes either absurdly foolish or deeply profound, and virtually nothing in between, a characteristic plasm shares with everything else of great value.

– I see your point.

– One might say *this* exercise is foolish, these aeronautics on the end of a plasm tether. But I find it useful, if for no other reason than it instructs me concerning your nature: that is, given some small encouragement, the first thing you desire is to take flight.

Aiah wonders if, back in Mage Towers, the blood burns in her cheeks.

– And what better desire to keep in your heart? Constantine continues. There are too many people who fence their minds with walls of stone and concrete, but to your credit you are not of these.

– No, she sends, no walls for me, it seems I'm transparent.

Amusement chimes in her senses, then fades. Aiah intuits that he is regarding her closely.

– You seem calmer now, he says.

Aiah is aware again of his fingers riding her pulse, and wonders if the whole purpose of this discourse was to control her panic by keeping her thoughts busy.

– Perhaps we can commence some actual instruction now, Constantine sends.

– I'm sorry if I'm wasting time with all this.

– No time was wasted, he says firmly. We have learned much, and I no less than you.

Though now there is much else to do, Aiah's surprise at this judgment fades only slowly.

Black, empty faces of video monitors gaze down at her. Constantine has removed the t-grip and put it away, but Aiah still sits on the sofa, immersed in the lingering sensation of plasm.

Constantine moves back and forth along the buffet, putting food on a plate. He pours sparkling wine, holds it to the light for a moment, then slips. He turns to look at her.

'Well,' he says, 'I believe all you need from this point is experience. You have the talent.'

Aiah looks at the plasm focus in her hand, lifts her eyebrows, begins to speak, to say something like, 'Have I?', but an inner knowledge amounting to certainty keeps the modest commonplace from her tongue.

'How do you know?' she says instead, and puts the focus back around her neck.

'I gave you all the power you asked for,' he says, 'and you wasted none of it. When you took flight, you carried your anima intact, with a fully-formed mentality and a full sensorium.'

'I lost control,' Aiah says.

He frowns, shakes his head. 'Inexperience only. You weren't closer than a hundred radii from the Shield, but without any other point of reference you thought you were much nearer. And even when you panicked, your personality didn't fragment – your sensorium stayed intact, and your anima. Telepresence may well be your forte.' He smiles, poured another glass of wine, and offers it to Aiah. She takes it, looks at the amber fluid with its tiny streams of bubbles rising, each bursting free as it explodes on the surface.

Constantine drops next to her on the couch, chews meditatively on a sweet bread. 'Do you know how they'd teach you to fly in the schools?' he says. 'You'd be put through a long procedure to evoke a spirit body and then endow it with senses. You'd spend an hour or so giving it sight, and hearing, and taste and so on, and then you'd very carefully walk – *walk* – through the doors, and down stairs, and out into the street. It would cost you a fortune in plasm, but that's the way you'd learn to do it, step by tedious step, and perhaps after a year or so of walking about they'd let you imagine yourself in an aircraft and take a few hesitant swoops through the air . . . and they're cautious because most people are afraid of any real power, any real taste of liberty, and when they have it they just go to pieces. But *you*, my daughter,' he sips the wine and smiles, 'you knew what you wanted, and you did it, and all I did was feed you the power, and make a small

131

correction when you lost your concentration. You had no fear, no hesitation, and you were capable of imagining everything you needed – and these qualities are the true attributes of the mage, not the miserable university degree, written on plastic and hung on a wall, that demonstrates only your ability to overcome the limitations imposed by your instructors.'

Aiah drinks her wine. Bubbles explode like little worlds on her tongue, implying a universe of expanding possibility. Plasm does a dance of power in her brain.

'You must decide what manner of abilities you wish to cultivate,' Constantine goes on. 'Creation, illusion, chemistry, communication. You're courageous enough to be a combat mage, I think, but I wouldn't wish that on you. A combat mage survives perhaps twenty minutes of battle before obliteration.'

Aiah looks at him. 'Who would employ me? I have no credentials.'

A dismissive sound puffs from Constantine's lips. 'With my training? With my recommendation? And with your ability? You may write your own future, Miss Aiah. Burn it across the sky in letters a radius high, if you so desire.'

Aiah reclines against the soft black calfskin. The wine warms its way, an expanding radiance, through her veins. 'I can't picture it,' she says.

Constantine shrugs. 'It's as I said: only experience is lacking. Experience, as well, in knowing what you want, as opposed to that which you have had to accept.' He rises from the couch. 'I believe Sorya wants to speak with you before you leave. Take a plate of food with you – this may take a while.'

She rises, steps toward the buffet, sees her image twisted in the curved surface of the gleaming copper chafing dishes.

Constantine's voice turns meditative. 'Perhaps, if you are to work with Sorya, I should tell you something about her.'

Aiah reaches for a plate, hesitates. 'Yes?' And now recalls

the earlier scene that plasm had driven from her mind, the diamond necklace flung in the trash.

Constantine looks pensively at the arboretum, green reflections in his brown eyes. 'She comes from an oligarchic family of Carvel, belonging to the Torgenil faith. Do you know what that means?'

The Torgenil, Aiah knows, are a religion given to extravagant, colorful ceremonies. Though the main branch of the religion is thought respectable enough, some of its offshoots had unsavory reputations relating to necromancy, experiments in twisted genetics, human sacrifice. But she knows little of their beliefs and thinks it best to say, 'No, Metropolitan.'

'Briefly,' Constantine says, 'the Torgenil hold that we are damned and living in Hell. That we are exiled from paradise and hope of redemption, that we are so corrupt we can only contaminate the souls of the elect, and that the Ascended Ones therefore created the Shield to seal our tainted lower world from their own. The Torgenil ceremonies, with their color and ecstasies, are not rites of worship but celebrations of despair. And despair motivates as well the vicious rites of the cults associated with the Torgenil: if nothing matters, if no hope exists and we are damned no matter what our actions, then why not perform all, why not exercise power in its most depraved form?'

He sneers, gestures largely with the wineglass, then gusts a contemptuous laugh. 'Were I to know myself damned, I trust I could behave with greater pride than that.'

'Sorya is a part of this?' Aiah asks. A cold finger touches Aiah's spine as she remembers Sorya's cold eyes alight with plasm in the darkness of the old underground terminal. Suddenly the notion of Sorya participating in rites of blood sacrifice and plasm resurrection is not quite beyond belief.

'Sorya has left that faith, and all others, behind,' Constantine says. 'But not the attitudes instilled by that faith, and by the oligarchs of Carvel among whom she was raised.' He looks down at his wineglass. 'She knows power, and all ways of raising it and using it. She can make use of people – use them with consummate skill, such that they often do not realize they are being used – but, because her view of people is conditioned by despair, she does not think to look for the good in them. She can use a person, command him or dominate him or persuade him through hope of reward, but she cannot inspire him, doesn't look to raise him above himself.' He looks meditative, pauses for a long moment. 'It is curiously small of her,' he says finally.

Aiah looks at Constantine, her mind aswim with questions. He sees her look and smiles. 'Try the poached eggs with truffles,' he says, and lifts the lid of a chafing dish. 'I think you will find the sauce quite accomplished.'

'Thank you.' She takes a plate and puts food on it. She doesn't even recognize half the food items on display. She hesitates, puts the plate down. Plasm still buzzes distantly in her nerves. 'Metropolitan?' she says.

'Yes.'

'What about the plasm diver?'

'What about her?'

'What happened to her? Why was she . . . destroyed?'

His eyes turn inward. 'Who can say? Some inner flaw, perhaps, magnified by the plasm. Perhaps she was caught unawares. Or perhaps she *intended*, deliberately, to use the plasm for destruction, but her plans went awry. I've found that people who are destroyed by plasm are the ones who, perhaps all secretly, desire to destroy themselves. There is a perverse impulse in them that seeks out failure, that turns their own lives to poison.' He approaches Aiah, puts both hands on her shoulders, looks at her closely. 'Forget the diver. Her fate is not yours, I promise you that. I have seen enough to know you do not have that dark seed in you.'

He kisses her, lips warm against hers for a long moment, and then turns back to his desk. 'Sorya must be getting impatient,' he says over his shoulder. 'Don't forget your briefcase.'

Aiah, motionless for an instant, wonders what promise it is that she tastes on her lips.

She gathers her briefcase, plate and glass, and carrying them leaves the room and awkwardly descends the spiral staircase. She finds Sorya in the parlor, sunk in an armchair with her boot-heels resting on a low, heavy table of marble.

The spotted panther, Prowler, is stretched luxuriously across a sofa like a huge, dangerous kitten, asleep with its belly-fur displayed and its paws curled in the air.

Aiah wonders if she should tell Sorya her necklace is in the trash. She suspects it isn't the sort of news Sorya would welcome.

Still, perhaps it's better than to let Sorya think Aiah walked off with her jewelry.

Sorya lifts an eyebrow. 'Ah,' she says. 'Are we a mage now?'

Aiah decides not to mention the necklace. 'Not yet,' she says. She can taste Constantine on her lips.

Sorya draws in her legs, tucks them under the chair. 'While the Metropolitan deals with grand strategy,' she says, 'it would seem I am confined to matters of engineering. Perhaps you would favor me with your maps.'

Aiah draws up a chair and opens her briefcase. The table is made of 'broken' marble, patterns of cream and deep brown wrenched by subterranean forces into new, contorted shapes. Aiah covers the pattern with her maps of Terminal, her official transparencies and the old transparency she found at Rocketman Substation, then puts her food plate on the corner of the table. Sorya takes the yellowed celluloid in her hand, holds it up to the light. Then she places it on the map.

'It's difficult to tell estate agents what we want,' she says. 'An empty building, in such-and-such a neighborhood, with a deep cellar and neighbors who will not ask questions, nor mind a little reconstruction and digging . . .'

'I can pull the records on any sites you find promising,' Aiah says.

'Very good.'

The transparencies are, Aiah explains, incomplete and out of date. Sorya doesn't seem overly perturbed by this revelation. Aiah makes a note of certain addresses, eats bits of the food off her plate. Even cold the food is superb.

Sorya leans back. 'Good enough,' she says. 'That's a place to start. One thing left.' She reaches for a portfolio-sized case she's leaned against the sofa. Prowler stirs, ropy legs stretched to full length. Shieldlight glints off unsheathed claws. Sorya drops the portfolio on the table, then reaches to rub Prowler's soft belly. The cat's purr rumbles vastly.

Aiah opens the portfolio. 'Batteries, control systems, switching stations, supply cables,' Sorya says. 'I need to know how to disable them – not destroy them, just keep them out of action for some hours. Whatever damage is done must be quickly repairable.'

'Ah,' Aiah says.

Another interesting datum for the files.

The plasm systems have an unfamiliar name – Ring-Klee – and so far as Aiah knows aren't used in Jaspeer, a fact which occasions in her a certain relief. She flips through the large sheets looking for cutouts and finds them.

'Here,' she says. 'If the control board suffers certain kinds of damage, the operators' instructions are overridden and the accumulator contacts are mechanically returned to a neutral position. There's a lengthy procedure required to restart; it should take several hours, and that's only if there's qualified personnel available.'

Sorya's green eyes glitter with interest. 'Thank you,' she says. 'Can you give me a better idea what sorts of emergencies will provoke this response?'

'It would be easier if I had an operators' manual. Is there one?'

'I can obtain a copy.' Sorya seems not so much to stand as to uncoil, rising sylphlike from her seat. The cat stands as well, shaking its shaggy head. 'Thank you for your advice. I'll call Martinus to drive you home.'

The fruit and cheese still wait in the Elton, and a fresh bottle has replaced the one that was opened. Aiah contentedly fills her glass and savors the wine as it crosses her palate.

'Mr Martinus,' she says.

Martinus's eyes meet hers in the mirror. 'Yes?'

Aiah searches for words. 'The Metropolitan made a gesture earlier,' she says. 'A necklace belonging to Miss Sorya ended up in the trash under the buffet table. I think the necklace should probably be retrieved — you would know best to whom it belongs.'

Martinus's expression doesn't change. 'Yes, miss,' he says.

Aiah leans back against the plush headrest and closes her eyes.

She breathes in, and the air tastes like wine.

12

'Will this suffice, d'you think?'

Constantine stands on a stained concrete floor in the midst of an old factory built of red brick. Arched windows high above the floor let in a grayish light; a double row of round iron stanchions helps support a tented ceiling. There is a smell of must and urine, and a scattering of old mattresses and blankets in grimy corners; people have been living in here.

'Suffice? I suppose,' Aiah says, and watches pigeons flutter among the iron roofbeams.

It's second shift, and Constantine and Martinus brought Aiah here after work. In the last few days Aiah's had three lessons at Mage Towers, sitting on the soft leather sofa with Constantine's big hand lightly enclosing her wrist, each lesson followed by a detailed discussion with Sorya, complex analysis of sabotage, diagrams and plans and manuals, talk of intrusion and subversion and explosives, and these conversations, somehow, seem more unreal than any of the phantoms she's been conjuring.

Constantine hasn't kissed her again, hasn't touched her in any way other than to hold her wrist during the course of her lesson – and even then, in the midst of feeding her plasm and offering instruction, she's had the sense that his mind, his deeper attention, is elsewhere.

'We'll convert it to a warehouse,' Constantine says, 'and what will we warehouse? Plasm accumulators, I believe.'

His security, Martinus and two other men, walk in a widening circle about Constantine and the Elton. Their grating footsteps echo in the big room. Constantine walks to the north wall, turns, takes five paces toward the center of the room. 'Below me,' he said, 'should be the foundation of the old plastics factory. Can we reach it?'

Aiah frowns. 'Is there a basement?'

'Yes.'

The elevator is frozen in place, so Aiah takes the old concrete stair. She's come straight from work and isn't dressed for this, and she steps carefully in her heels. The low basement supports the factory floor on arches of crumbling brick. Rusting lathe equipment, old boxes, and olive-green metal cabinets stuffed with moldering records are piled under the low arches like carelessly flung toys, leaving only a few cobwebbed paths amid all the rubble. By the light of her flash, Aiah finds an electric switchboard with stained hemispherical brass buttons. She presses them and to her surprise lights come on, faint yellow bulbs in metal cages.

She moves to the north end of the basement and prowls amid the rubbish, looking for a route to the foundations. A fat long-tailed rat, displaying no sense of hurry, ambles across her path and disappears among the rubbish. Something plinks into a wide, shallow puddle of water. Aiah sees an old water pipe hanging loose in its brackets and runs her flashlight beam along it, and then feels a tingle creep along her nerves as she sees a faint trail of rust angling down the length of a brick pillar, not from the pipe but from the lighter metal of the bracket. Electrolysis, just as she'd seen on the pillar in the old pneuma, a trail of oxydized metal pointing like a finger to a hidden source of power.

Aiah steps closer, reaching out a hand, and then something uncoils from the pipe and hisses at her.

She jumps back, crashes into a pillar, almost falls. The thing is pale, glutinous, sluglike, and the length and thickness of her leg; its lips are red, like those of a woman in a fashion ad. Aiah scrambles away, heart hammering against her ribs.

By the time she returns to the factory floor her fear has turned to annoyance and anger. She swipes grime from her suit as she walks to where Constantine waits by the car.

'Yes,' she says, 'there's access, I think. But there's a monster down there that needs killing.'

Constantine lifts an eyebrow, then gestures to one of his guards.

Aiah points out the creature from a safe distance, then holds hands over her ears as the guard takes aim with his pistol and fires.

The factory gate opens and the Elton glides out. While one guard closes and locks the door behind them, Martinus and the other guard seem taut, alert, their eyes intent on the streets. Then the first guard jumps into the front passenger seat and the limousine pulls away.

Constantine, accustomed to these sorts of precautions, pays them no attention and instead reaches into the pocket of his soft leather jacket for a notepad. He and Aiah sit opposite each other in the back of the car, Constantine facing the rear.

'What are we going to need?' he asks.

Aiah swabs at her skirt with a handkerchief and contemplates cleaning bills before she recalls she can, these days, afford them. She wonders what the monster had been originally, before it began to resonate with the hidden plasm: a rat? Mouse? Slug? Or worse, human? There had been tramps living in there. Maybe a drunk or addict had found something else more addictive.

She feels a chill on her neck at the thought.

Aiah clears her throat, and with it her mind. 'Clean out all the rubbish, first of all,' she says. 'There may be access that we simply can't see. If not, break up the floor, then we'll get a better look. The track of the electrolysis points straight to our goal. But you'd better have your people work with insulated equipment.'

'There are other basements in the neighborhood,' Constantine says. 'There must be other bits of electrolysis happening, perhaps other monsters. All clues to what lies beneath. The sooner we tap that stuff and put it in batteries, the better.'

The Elton pauses at a corner, and suddenly alarm courses through Aiah's veins. She shrinks into her seat, turns away from the scene outside, hand raised to shade her face.

'What's wrong?' Constantine's response is instant.

'One of those men,' she says. 'He attacked me.'

Constantine leans forward to peer through the window. 'Which one?' he says. 'You don't have to hide – he can't see you through the smoked windows.'

A metallic taste of fear still coats Aiah's tongue. Reluctantly she turns to the window and sees again the skinny man, the bottle thrower, seated on a piece of scaffold pipe and talking with some friends. 'The thin one,' she says. 'Peaked cap, green pants.'

Constantine's eyes are intent on the target. He addresses one of the guards. 'Do you see him, Khoriak?'

'Yes, Metropolitan.'

'When we turn the corner, get out of the car and find out who he is.'

Khoriak is pale and blond and won't look too out of place here. He begins to take off his jacket.

A truck, stuck behind the Elton, begins to blip its horn. Constantine looks at Aiah, nods at the thin man and his companions. 'Have you seen his friends before?'

'No. The other attackers were hurt badly. Maybe they're still in the hospital.'

Constantine looks over his shoulder at the driver. 'Drive around the corner, Mr Martinus.'

'Yes, Metropolitan.'

Khoriak has taken off his jacket and lace, and opened

his collar. He puts his pistol and holster on the dash, then, as the car drives partway down the block and slows, he steps out, closing the door with that too-solid sound, armor dropping into place. Constantine leans back in his seat, eyes heavy-lidded, and gives Aiah a lazy smile.

'Forget the man,' he says, 'and his friends, too. The problem is over.'

Aiah looks at him, her heart still leaping. Over? she wonders. How?

'I'm sorry,' Constantine says, 'but there's no time for lessons today. I have . . .' he pauses to search for a word, 'a conference. But tomorrow, I will send Mr Martinus at the usual time.'

Tick tick tick . . . Tella's child clicks back and forth in his automated swing, each clack of the gears pacing off another torpid moment to the end of the shift.

'Tell me about him,' Tella says. It's a slow period, with few calls on Aiah's computer. There's something wrong with the air circulation again, and Aiah's windowless office is hot and close and smells strongly of the sleeping baby's diapers. Aiah spends her spare time reading, a text on plasm theory, while Tella works puzzles and talks with friends on the phone.

'Who?' Aiah asks absently, and her eyes turn to the picture of Gil in its wetsilver frame. She feels a pang in her heart – though not, perhaps, the usual pang.

'The man who picks you up after work. In the big car.' Tella smiles. 'Are you doing a little stepping out? I wouldn't blame you, the way Gil treats you.'

'Gil treats me perfectly well,' Aiah says automatically. 'It's not his fault he's away.'

'Who is he?' Tella's white smile is relentless. 'Gelen from Tasking says that he's a Barkazil.'

Who? Aiah wants to ask, not having heard of Gelen from Tasking till this minute. Not that it matters – Tella's network of friends in the Authority is complex beyond comprehension.

'He's not a Barkazil,' Aiah says, 'he's Cheloki.'

'Is he rich?' Tella asks. 'He must be, to drive an Elton. You're dressing better, I've noticed.'

Aiah fluffs an annoyed hand through her chin-lace. Two suits, she thinks, a pair of shoes, and now she's a kept woman.

She wonders what Tella would say if she'd come to work wearing the diamond necklace.

Tick tick tick. The swing marks off the seconds to Aiah's answer.

'The man Gelen saw is the car's driver, not its owner,' she says carefully, knowing that Gelen and every other correspondent of Tella's are going to be retailing this over the entire Authority building in the next few hours.

Tella's gray eyes glitter. 'I'm impressed.'

'It's work,' Aiah says. 'It's a consulting job I've taken to make ends meet.'

'Oh.'

'And I haven't asked the Authority's permission, so I'd appreciate discretion.'

'Ah.'

'And he's married. Well, good as.'

Tella digests this for a moment. 'What does Gil say about it?' she asks finally.

'I haven't spoken to him since I started.'

'Ah.'

'But,' stubbornly, and feeling heat creep up her neck, 'I don't see why he'd care.'

'But this man's rich, that you're working for?' Tella leans across the table.

'I believe he is.' Amusement twitches the corners of Aiah's mouth. 'Though he seems to enjoy complaining about money.'

'Some rich people are like that,' Tella says.

Aiah looks at her. 'How many rich people do you know?'

'*Really* rich? Well . . .'

'He's rich enough so that he doesn't have to count his clinks. But he does, because being rich is still a game with rules, and not being taken advantage of is one of them. I think.' She knits her brows. '*I think* that's how it works.'

'And what does he want you to do for all these clinks he's paying you?'

Aiah laughs. 'God knows. Nothing he couldn't do himself, if he wanted to.'

'And is he happy with his wife, or whatever she is?'

'Personal assistant.'

Tella laughs. 'Personal assistant!' She shakes her head. 'How are they getting along?'

'I believe they are not in agreement.'

'Girl!' Tella claps her hands. 'Wake up! You can have him!'

Aiah laughs, shakes her head, dismissively slides the pads of her fingers across the surface of her scarred metal desk. 'I don't think so.'

'Well – what if you can? What are you going to do about it?'

Take all the money I can, she thinks. *He's my* passu, *damn it*.

By far the safest course.

'Either it will occur to him or it won't,' Aiah says. 'I *think* what happened is that it occurred to him and he decided not.'

Tella looks a little disdainful. 'Takes the pressure off *you*, then. But I still think you should *try* something.'

'Sorry to disappoint you.'

'You'll tell me if anything happens, won't you?'

Tick tick tick . . .

Aiah looks at Tella out of the corner of her eye, and as the seconds click by it occurs to her, a Barkazil notion, that there is more than one kind of *passu*.

'Of course,' she says. 'I'll tell you everything.'

*   *   *

Aiah says goodbye to Martinus, steps out of the Elton, and heads toward the Loeno lobby. Plasm seems to buoy her every step. Her senses dance to the scent of the fresh north-easterly wind that has blown away the previous day's clouds, the aftertaste of wine on her tongue, the astringent scent of the potted chrysanthemums that line the path to the door.

She's just finished a lesson with Constantine. They had concentrated on telepresence technique, invoking and using the sensorium, the battery of sensory perceptions carried from place to place by the anima, the telepresent plasm-body that can be made to fly from place to place, independent of matter. Aiah concluded the lesson with her senses refreshed, hyper-sensitive; the usual wine, fruit and cheese that waited for her in the car seems ecstatic in its power to delight her palate.

Here on the cusp between service and sleep shift, when few people are awake, Aiah meets no one on her route to the elevator. When she reaches the apartment she can hear, through the door, a voice, and she recognizes Gil's tones grating from the speaker of her message system.

As soon as the bolt slams back Aiah pushes the door open and dashes for the communications array, hand out-stretched to snatch up the headset.

'Da? Hello?' Clapping one earpiece to her ear.

'Aiah?'

'I just stepped through the door. I'm glad I caught you.'

Aiah settles the headset in place, then maneuvers back-wards to the limits of the cord, catches the door with her heel, swings it shut.

'Where have you been?' Gil asks. 'I've been calling every second shift for days. I was starting to get worried.'

'Let me stop and catch my breath,' Aiah says. 'I was so afraid you'd hang up.'

'I was beginning to think I should call your sister or something and find out if you were all right.'

'Nothing's wrong. I've been working – I've taken on a consulting job to help pay our debts.'

'Consulting? Who for?'

'I'll tell you when I see you. It's too long a story to waste telephone charges on.'

And besides, she hasn't worked out what to tell him. It might be dangerous even to breathe Constantine's name over the telephone.

'Well, you won't have to keep the job for long,' Gil says. 'The company's finally reimbursed some of my expenses – a lot of the entertainment, and the bed money thing. Hillel went to headquarters in Jaspeer and took care of it personally.'

'That's good.'

'So I'll be sending you a cashgram for eight hundred tomorrow.'

'Thank you,' she says. 'That will be useful.'

There is a little hesitation on Gil's end of the line. Aiah knows that pause, knows the little creases between Gil's brows that deepen when he pauses to think.

'You don't sound precisely overjoyed,' he says.

Two weeks ago, Aiah thinks, she'd have fallen on her knees and thanked the immortals for that money. But now it's redundant, and she can't tell her lover why.

She's made Gil her *passu*, she realizes. And she doesn't want to, but she can't help it, because the truth is too complex, too dangerous.

He can't ever know, she thinks. Because if he ever finds out, he'll never look at her the same way again, he'll never cease wondering if some other scheme has come between them, or endangered them somehow . . .

'I'm just tired,' she says. And even *that* is a lie, with the plasm having scrubbed her weariness away.

'After the cashgram, there'll be money for a trip home,' Gil says. 'I don't know precisely when I'll be able to get away, but it will be sometime in the next few weeks. And then we'll be able to sit down and work out our finances together.'

'Good,' Aiah says. 'But I think the eight hundred should settle everything before you get here.'

She kicks off her shoes and sits down on the carpet and looks up at Gil's picture and wordlessly apologizes for all this, for the deception she's put between them, the situations he'll never understand, the cascade of lies she may never be able to end.

'I love you,' Gil says. 'You don't know how much I've missed you. But I'll do my best to make it up to you once I get home.'

'I love you, too,' Aiah says, and wonders if even this is true any more.

Perhaps, she thinks, she has made a *passu* of herself.

'The money,' Aiah says. 'Just to remind you, I haven't seen it.'

Constantine looks ahead, through smoked glass, as the Elton moves slowly past the Terminal trackline station. He and Aiah sit next to each other on the plush rear seat while the life of the narrow streets presses in around them.

'I was wondering when you'd ask,' he says.

'I thought I'd give you a week.'

'Arrangements have been made with a bank in Gunalaht. I'll give you the codes tomorrow. You can withdraw money by wire, but to avoid the scrutiny of tax officials it might be best to visit the place yourself, by the Inter Metropolitan pneuma, and withdraw in person. Also, you'll need to visit them at least once so they have a record of your chop.'

Gunalaht is a small metropolis known for its banks and casinos. The banks obey strict privacy laws and therefore hold the deposits of half the gangsters and chonah riggers in Jaspeer. The casinos exist to move the money from the gangsters' accounts to those of the government. The metropolis is about half a day away by pneuma, or a day and a half by airship, just long enough to make the journey an inconvenience.

'I may have to take a day or two off,' Aiah says. Her eyes move apprehensively along the busy streets, looking for a familiar form – the skinny man, any of her other attackers. *Forget the man*, Constantine had said. *The problem is over*. But now she can't seem to forget him at all.

'A day off?' Constantine says. 'I wish you'd take a week. What is it you do in that job of yours?'

'At my level,' Aiah says, 'I mostly wait for the people above me to die or retire. They could automate my job completely, but that would mean Authority personnel budgets would decline, and—'

'Ah, yes.' Constantine is bitterly amused. 'The way of officialdom. What is the distinguishing feature of the budget of Jaspeer? Over ninety percent devoted to maintaining *that which is*. Keeping transport moving, maintaining buildings and roadways, paying pensions, keeping people like you stuck at your desks doing unproductive jobs while you wait for your seniors to die off so that you can advance to perform *their* unproductive jobs. And does it change when the electorate vote in a new government? Of course not. Because the people on top really don't hold the power. Everything's really run by a triumvirate of interest groups.' He holds his right hand up, stabs three fingers up toward the car's roof, ticks the fingers off one by one with his left thumb. 'The bureaucracy, the unions, and the Operation. They've divided the budget between them. The first two get everything that's on the books, and the Operation gets the rest. And of these, only the last is efficient, because in the Operation there are penalties for incompetence.'

Aiah looks at Constantine's cynical smile. 'You sound almost as if you admire the Operation,' she says, and remembers the words, *The problem is over*. Something a street captain might well say.

He shakes his head. 'No. The captains of the Operation are vicious animals, with no more concept of the world or their place in it than Sorya's Prowler. And I should know – my family, you remember, *were* the Operation, or anyway what the Operation can become when it runs an entire metropolis. They had the kind of power that the street captains in Jaspeer can only dream about. *Here*, in Jaspeer, the Operation are animals – predators, but smallish ones. Rats, perhaps. They fight over scraps, over territory, over prestige, or at any rate what seems like prestige to a rat. But in Cheloki they weren't rats any longer, they were higher animals, like Sorya's cat, or perhaps more to the point like a pack of dogs, who through numbers and ruthlessness and brute intelligence could bring down game stronger and greater than they.' He smiles, a cold reminiscent glow in his eyes. 'They dined very well, my family, very high off the food chain. They loved power for its own sake, and permitted no threat to that power to exist.' He shrugs, looks offhand at Aiah.

'A person's intent matters,' he says. 'It must. I desire power for myself, yes, I will admit it. But further I will say that I want nothing for myself that I do not desire for humanity at large, and that I desire power only for its ends, not for the thing in itself. The rest of power's trappings are wearisome: the fawning, the flattery, the raking in of tribute and booty . . . it was a mark of my family's merit that such pathetic, unreal aspects of power were all they cared about, while the reality of it, the ability to fundamentally alter the world and all nature, mattered to them not at all.'

He smiles in memory, and the smile is cold. 'They tried to outdo one another in palace-building – horrible places, tasteless and pretentious and shallow, and we may thank Tangid that most of these structures were destroyed in the war – and, with their minds on such earthly glory, it is preposterous what my family overlooked. They had access to all the plasm in their domain, which they used to pursue or crush their enemies, or spy on each other, or create elaborate public spectacles, or engage in the most astoundingly petty intrigues. Plasm is the most perfect transformational agent of the universe, the thing that can *alter matter, alter the fundamental nature of all reality*, and they used it with no more consciousness of its significance than if they had been children. They'd been around the stuff all their lives, and even you, daughter –' his hand finds Aiah's on the plush seat and covers it, 'even you, barely a novice in geomancy, have a better idea of what to do with plasm than they.' He looks at her intently, and Aiah can feel a flush creep up her neck. 'You used it to fly, to liberate yourself from matter. Whereas base matter –' he smiles wolfishly, 'the baser the better, was all my family could find to interest them in the geomantic arts.'

The Elton turns, and the old brick factory's door automatically rolls open to welcome it. Constantine lifts his hand from Aiah's, opens his door, and steps out of the car before it has quite rolled to a stop. The sound of hammering rings off the factory's hard interior surfaces. Aiah looks for a moment at her hand, still warm from his touch, and then leaves the car herself.

The amount of progress in three days is astonishing. The factory floor is covered with plasm accumulators, a few of them unpacked to show their new, gleaming brass and smooth black ceramic, but most of them – those nearest the doors, and the sight of any curious onlooker – still in their packing crates, as if they were being warehoused. Above them a scaffolding has been completed, and contacts are being lowered into place. An even larger scaffolding, a bronze collection web, is being erected around it in order to diffuse any attack. Guards prowl the perimeter, their professional scowls in place.

'I'm amazed by the *scale* of it,' Aiah says. 'Aren't you worried about being detected?'

'The warehouse is being rented by a corporation based in Taìphon,' Constantine says, 'and the accumulators belong to another group out of Gunalaht. The ownership is so complex that no one will ever trace either to me.' His rumbling laugh echoes in the huge space. 'Besides, Miss Aiah,' he says, 'have you ever, in your personal experience, known of a crime that was actually solved by the authorities acting on their own?'

Aiah's laugh answers Constantine's. Her old neighborhood provides the answer every day of the week.

'Of course not,' she says. 'People get caught because they're ratted out.' Her cousin Landro, the plasm diver, had been turned in to the Authority creepers by a friend who'd run short of money in mid-week and couldn't wait till payday to buy a ten-pack of beer. The only people the police caught on their own were the unlucky and stupid, those who committed crimes in plain sight and waited around to be arrested, or those whose behavior afterwards brought suspicion on them.

Like brilliant rain, sparks fall from a torch on the overhead scaffold to the concrete floor. Constantine moves toward the stair leading to the basement, and Aiah follows. 'Every person involved in this endeavor,' Constantine says, 'has much more to gain from our adventure than they ever would from cooperating with the authorities. All my people –' he nods at the dozen or so visible, 'are tried, tested, and loyal. They have served the New City for years, in every manner of peril. The weak links are two: our neighbors here, who at present however have no reason to suspect us, and—' He stops and turns at the top of the stair. His eyes turn to Aiah. 'And you, my daughter.'

A chill drifts down Aiah's spine. 'I have no reason to betray you,' she says.

A cold little curl of amusement touches Constantine's lips. He speaks softly, barely audible over a barrage of furious pneumatic hammering that suddenly rackets up from the basement. 'No,' he says, 'you have no reason to betray me, at least not once you get your money. But – who can tell? – you might be an irrational person. You might inform simply because you are under a neurotic compulsion.'

Alarm chills Aiah's nerves, but she manages to give Constantine a cold Barkazil glare. 'So might any of your people, Metropolitan,' she says.

The hammering sound from the basement dies away, and Constantine's deep laugh booms out in the sudden silence. 'So they might, daughter! But I know them, and you I do not know.'

Aiah's hands make fists at her sides. She wasn't prepared to be made this man's *passu*.

'I don't like this game, Metropolitan.'

He lifts an eyebrow. 'What game is that?'

'I raised a genuine issue of security, and instead you imply that I'm the one not to be trusted.'

'Ah. Forget it then.' He waves a hand dismissively, then turns to descend the stair.

'You said the authorities are keeping track of you.'

He turns back to her. 'No doubt some of the personnel at Mage Towers, or perhaps my neighbors, have been asked to make reports. Probably my fiscal transactions have been scrutinized, at least to some extent. No doubt my plasm use has been monitored. But . . .' he holds up a hand, 'nothing overt. No one has followed me around, no one has been to my apartment to ask questions. Because there is nothing to make them suspicious.'

'People at work have noticed me being picked up by your car.'

Constantine smiles. 'And what conclusions have they drawn from this?'

'That I have a lover.'

He shrugs. 'Let 'em believe it, then. Deny it if you like, but make your denials unconvincing.'

He turns to head down the stair. Aiah, having no choice, follows. Frustration gnaws at her nerves with little rodent teeth.

The basement opens out before her. All the clutter has been miraculously removed, and the room is filled with the smell of fresh concrete dust. Amid a circle of debris and frowning men in hardhats sits a pneumatic drill, a squat man-high egg-shaped machine with four feet braced wide on the floor, and another four long jointed metal legs bolted to the ceiling or pillars.

One man comes forward to report to Constantine. Concrete dust coats his beard-stubble and the bandanna he's wrapped around his neck, and there are two pale sweat-shiny patches around his eyes where he's worn protective goggles.

'We got through the floor all right,' he says, 'and the layer of stonework under that, but now we've hit a layer of concrete reinforced with some kind of alloy rebar, and it's stopped us. We've been trying to drill it for hours.'

'What can you do?' Constantine asks.

The man shrugs. 'Blast, maybe. Get a bigger drill. Hell, I'm not an engineer – the man who rented us this stuff said it'd work, that's all I know.'

'Geomaturgy,' Aiah says.

The man looks at her. 'Well,' he says. 'Of course.'

Constantine looks over his massive shoulder, gives Aiah a frown. 'Fine,' he says, 'you're right – magic is easier. Tell Martinus to get someone to drive you to the Towers. You know where the t-grips are.'

She looks up at Constantine in confusion. 'Are you coming, too?'

'I have work here.' And then, at her silence, Constantine only deepens his frown. 'It's time you managed without me. You'll do perfectly well.'

The concrete dust on Aiah's tongue begins to taste like

fear. 'As you wish, Metropolitan,' she says, and turns to leave.

There is a part of her that wants Constantine to call her back. But he doesn't, and that's that.

The face of the flaming woman burns in her mind, mouth open in a silent scream.

Aiah sits on the couch opposite the arboretum. Prowler, the big cat, stares at her from the other side of the glass wall, a constant unwinking green-eyed gaze of steady interest. Colorful birds flitter in the trees. The solid copper transference grip, as yet unconnected to any power well, sits heavy in her hand.

She takes the little charm from around her neck, holds it in the palm of her right hand and hefts the t-grip in her left.

A wheel of fire, a touch of the burning woman, seems to revolve in her heart. She looks at the Trigram and tries to clear her mind of everything but the task ahead.

Somehow it's very difficult to banish from her awareness the touch of sweaty moisture that beads at the hollow of her throat.

In the last week Aiah has flown. She's taken plasm into her body, projected it from her fingertips, molded it, made it dance in midair. All with perfect confidence. But always Aiah knew the presence of Constantine's hand on her wrist, and her confidence was buoyed by the fact that he was guiding her, that if anything went wrong he could throw the switch and she would return to the safety of the leather couch.

Things are a little different now, with the weight of the t-grip in her hand.

Prowler gazes at her with steady green eyes. Aiah takes a deep breath, looks at the Trigram, and drops the t-grip into its waiting socket.

Raw power blows the breath from her lungs. Aiah's

nerves wake to snarling readiness. Heart crashing, she tries to master the sensation, to direct her senses outward, into her environment. Awareness expands like a ripple in a still pond. The universe pours itself into her like a fall of liquid metal – the carbon-steel skeleton of Mage Towers seems to support her limbs; the transmission horns crown her head with polished bronze radiance; her eyes gaze out from a thousand ports of glass; and the people living inside seem like little atomies that flow through her veins.

Prowler, startled by whatever it is he sees, leaps from his place and flees deeper into the foliage.

Aiah concentrates, narrows her focus to the room. Everything here, the desk, the chairs, the video monitors, all seem unchanged, but somehow ominous, charged with hidden power. Aiah takes a moment to firm her anima and the sensorium by which she will apprehend reality outside herself – she numbers her senses one by one, and makes certain each delivers appropriate sensation – and then her anima floats upwards, towards the transmission horns, and out into space.

She could meticulously follow the road grid to Terminal, but there's an easier way: she knows that Terminal is near Grand City, and Grand City's white granite pinnacles, designed as if to create a shining antithesis to Mage Towers' black fangs, are visible on the horizon. She streaks to them, orients herself along District Boulevard, follows the four-level highway along the outskirts of Rocketman, then turns into the brownstone canyons of Terminal. Still, in the end, she has to descend to ground level to look at street signs before she can find the old factory.

When she ghosts into the factory, Constantine is talking on the telephone and seems unaware of her presence. It's lucky the bronze collection web hasn't been fully assembled, otherwise Aiah's journey would end here, anima diffused into Constantine's plasm defenses – but she threads between the uprights easily enough, moves down the stair, and enters the basement.

The taste of concrete dust floods her senses, and she wonders if the dust still floats through the air here, or whether she has somehow created the sensation for herself because she expected it. The pneumatic drill has been moved back; perhaps they were afraid she'd damage it. Workmen stand near the stair, unaware of her presence, and share food and coffee. Clearly there's been no more activity since she left.

She circles the pit, sees the rubble piled up, fragments of concrete and brick. Below is the scarred surface, glints of bright webbed metal amid pitted concrete. She wonders if this is some kind of centuries-old military relic, a bunker protected from geomaturgic attacks by an intrinsic collection web. If so, her anima will be dissolved once she touches it – harmless to her real body, other than through disorientation to her senses.

So far as she knows there's no way to find out except by trying. She visualizes herself a pair of arms, invisible bone and muscle animated by plasm, and reaches down into the hole, touches elements of the metal web.

Nothing. At least the structure isn't hostile to her.

Aiah doesn't know the type of hard alloy used here, and doesn't know enough chemical geomaturgy to find out, but she reasons that at the very least she can melt the stuff, so she calls for an increase in plasm flow along her sourceline from Mage Towers, and directs the power as heat energy along the arms of her anima.

For the longest time nothing happens. But the metal finally blackens, then begins to burn with a dull red heat, and then at last glows white. Little bits of flame lick up. Drops of liquefied alloy spill from the exposed rebar. Aiah pulls the liquefied metal upwards with a tug of her mind, pulls it out of the concrete, and sees it settle like bright quicksilver in low places in the fractured concrete. She wants to get rid of it altogether, so she lofts it up, a reverse waterfall of bright liquid metal, out the lip of the pit and along the floor of the room. There it can cool and harden for all she cares.

She visualizes herself more arms, each one touching a piece of exposed rebar, and then calls for more power. The concrete cracks with sharp popping sounds as the metal within expands. She extracts more and more of the alloy, then reaches downward with her arms, into the concrete itself, and gathers more metal into her incorporeal fingers. Her awareness reaches out into the structure and she can see the whole alloy web, feel the weight of the concrete, sense, below this layer, the huge beams that support its weight.

Aiah digs into the structure like a burrowing animal, ripping up concrete with her claws, throwing it back into the room behind her while she fountains molten alloy upward. Her awareness effortlessly encompasses the workers who have seen, or probably heard, the activity and are watching with interest while keeping a wary distance. Aiah punches through the concrete layer into the soft layer below, then one of her plasm-fingers touches a support beam.

Aiah feels herself light up like a neon display. The liquefied metal shoots white-hot through her veins. The support beam is a part of what they're looking for, the glory hole, and the huge sleepy well of power leaps instantly to life, the power awesome and inexorable, like a reservoir of energy suddenly burst into flood.

Aiah laughs, and it seems as if all Jaspeer trembles to the sound. Aiah draws her fingers upward, drawing the power up after her, concrete shattering at the force of her power, whirling out of the pit, the remaining rebar twisting at her force, snapping like licorice.

The pit is clear, and the workers can set up their tap now. Her anima hovers over the hole, in a billowing cloud of concrete dust, and she feels herself inflate with power, become a giant with a heart of blazing fire. It occurs to her that she ought to tell the workers that the beam below is part of the plasm well, and that they shouldn't touch it, but she knows they can't see her anima, and she doesn't know how to communicate to them.

She creates a wind to blow the dust away, and tries to fashion a body for herself out of her thoughts; imagine it, the lines of it, the skin and sinew and structure, a heart that pumps glowing plasm through its veins. Aiah wills the plasm-skin to fluoresce, become visible to the workers. She sees them react, throwing up hands to shield their eyes from the light – she can see her red-gold radiance reflecting from the pillars, glowing in the clouds of dust that she's pushed out to the limits of the room. She tries to give herself a mouth, a tongue, a breath, a voice that she can speak with.

'The iron beam at the bottom of the pit is live,' she says. 'You must insulate yourself from it. Nod if you understand me.'

Some of the stunned figures clap hands over their ears, but they all nod. Aiah laughs at her triumph, at the energy that floods her, leaps at the very touch of her will. More hands clap over ears.

Her task is done, but Aiah finds herself reluctant to leave. The energy that floods her mind is exhilarating, a liberation greater than anything she's known. Nothing seems beyond her capabilities. She considers going for a stroll in her current anima – flying into the sky, righting a few conspicuous wrongs, inscribing a poem across the sky, something dazzling.

But no. The workers need to get into the pit, and it would be dangerous to have a live sourceline, charged with plasm, running out of the pit to Aiah's anima. Aiah decides to compel her second sourceline to shrivel, to close off the tap of power, but a few reluctant seconds pass before she can will it to happen.

The radiance reflecting off the brick pillars fades to a dull orange. Even though her original sourceline to Mage Towers is still alive, Aiah feels diminished. To avoid disorientation she prepares herself mentally to return to Mage Towers, then slowly turns the other tap, the Mage Towers sourceline, and allows her anima to shrivel, her plasmsenses, so brilliant and alive, to fade away, to be replaced by the diminished reality and shrunken perceptions of a young woman sitting in someone else's apartment many radii away.

13

Work has ended for the day. Aside from a pair of guards, Aiah is alone with Sorya in the big building. Their heels clack loudly in the narrow spaces between the looming accumulators.

'A flaming woman,' Sorya says. Her long forest-green dress swirls about her ankles; ruby earrings and necklace glow in the shadows with a smoky light.

'You astounded our crew,' she says. 'I must say, Miss Aiah, that you have a greater dramatic sense than I'd given you credit for.'

Surprise tingles ominously along Aiah's nerves as she walks with Sorya along the factory floor.

'A burning woman?' Aiah says. 'Is that what I looked like?'

Amusement glitters in Sorya's green eyes. 'Didn't you know?'

'I wanted my anima to fluoresce. I didn't know what I really looked like.'

Sorya gives a tigerish grin. 'You nearly scorched the eyebrows off a couple of them.'

'Ah.' Aiah is absorbed by thoughts of the burning woman. *Is this how it starts?* she wonders. If she hadn't turned the tap when she did, perhaps she would have become a flaming giant stalking the streets of Jaspeer.

Sorya pauses, lips tilted in a smile. 'Not that the crew

would look away,' she adds, 'since you forgot to give your anima any hint of clothing.'

'Ah.' Aiah glances down at her gangly body and is embarrassed to consider its defects magnified by plasm, skinny legs and pointed elbows and every rib visible – more humiliating, really, than the mere fact of nudity. Now, she thinks enviously, if she'd really wanted to give the workmen an eyeful, she should have thought to clothe her anima in Sorya's body, with its abundant curve of hip and breast, narrow waist and legs of whipcord muscle.

Sorya reaches out, touches the black ceramic surface of an accumulator. It's so polished that Aiah can see the blue eddies of the other woman's reflection in its surface. 'At least we're tapping the stuff now,' Sorya says. 'No more monsters, no more strange effects to call attention to what we possess. Since we won't be needing it, we'll want you to lead a work party down into the pneuma station to seal off that old toilet.'

Entombing the plasm diver's mummy, Aiah thinks. If only remembrance was buried as easily, memories of the empty eye-sockets, the mouth with its silent scream . . .

'Get Authority jumpsuits and hardhats for your party,' Aiah says, 'and let me know when you want it done.'

Sorya's fingers leave smudge marks on the immaculate black ceramic as her hand drifts away. She glances up at the bronze collection web that protects the plasm batteries. As if in response to her glance, one of the factory's pigeons flaps upward from its new resting place.

Sorya's glance narrows. 'Will the cage work?' she says.

Aiah is amused. Sorya is used to the elaborate collection webs built into the architecture of structures like Mage Towers and the Plasm Authority Building; this improvised apparatus looks suspicious to her.

'If the web's extended into the basement,' Aiah says, 'and also covers the tap, yes. But it's hard to make specific judgments without knowing what the web is intended to protect the accumulators *from*.'

Sorya gives Aiah a sidelong look out of her eyes, then looks up to the web again.

'We'll need some way to project our power more efficiently,' she says. 'Transmission horns or something like them, but they'll have to be hidden. We can have a fixed horn pointed straight at Mage Towers to give us power there, but there will need to be other horns with multi-directional capability.'

Aiah gives this some thought. 'Billboards,' she says. 'Put billboards on top of the factory. The scaffolding can disguise your apparatus, ne?'

Sorya looks at her in surprise. 'Very good,' she said.

Aiah grins. '*Warriors of Thunderworld*,' she says. 'With Khorë and Semlin. They used that trick in a chromoplay.'

Sorya laughs. 'Obviously I'm not sufficiently in tune with popular culture.' She walks toward the little office, bright silk skirt outlining her legs at each stride. Aiah follows.

'What's it in aid of?' she asks.

'Say again?'

Aiah waves an arm. 'All this. What's it for? What's the web supposed to be protecting you from? Why is everything being done in such a rush?'

Sorya looks over her shoulder, frowns a bit. She opens the door to the office, steps inside, closes the door after Aiah. The office is a mess, metal furniture stacked in a corner, the floor used as a storage area for a propane torch, bits of bronze rod, cushioned boxes of control equipment that haven't been installed yet. Aiah looks for a place to sit and fails to find one.

Sorya leans her back against the door, folds her arms, looks at Aiah.

'What is plasm but power?' she says. 'And what are plasm and power but reflections of the human will? It's will that controls plasm, and power, and – ultimately – people.'

'What about access?' Aiah asks. 'If you don't have access to plasm, what good is will?'

'The will finds its own access,' Sorya says. 'It did for you, did it not?'

Surprise touches Aiah's nerves. 'I suppose it did,' she says slowly.

'Constantine told you once,' Sorya says, 'that he and I were *not little people*. It is not our wealth that makes us giants in this world, but the force of our wills. And the strong will, ultimately, makes its own rules.' Her green eyes glitter as they gaze at Aiah, and Aiah seems to sense the formidable power of Sorya's will, a constant pressure like that of wind funneling between two buildings. Aiah feels almost as if she needs to lean into it to keep from toppling backwards.

'You and I,' Sorya says, 'are breaking a hundred laws simply by standing here. But laws mean nothing in this place, because laws are made by *little people* – which I, at least, am not – and the laws are made to guard the small against the powerful. Futile, firstly because the truly powerful find their own opportunities; and secondly, because when the small suppress the great, they suppress as well the greatness of their own commonwealth.'

Sorya smiles, sharp teeth gleaming white in the small room. 'Given this, given that the strong find their own place, and do so as inevitably as the water that seeks its own level, then what we intend here becomes clear enough. Specific details are inconsequential, but . . .' Sorya takes a breath. 'We seek to enlarge our scope. Our power. To project our will into the world. And this, inevitably, will bring us into conflict with others that possess the power we intend to make our own. And so, in this conflict of will, we must guard ourselves against those who may seek to attack us.'

Some kind of war, Aiah thinks, *and Sorya's no administrative assistant, she's a general.*

But war on who? An individual? The Operation? Or a whole Metropolis?

Her mind chills at the thought that Constantine had, in one sense or another, warred on all three at one time or another.

'You're guarding against a plasm attack, obviously,' Aiah says, 'or you wouldn't need a collection web.'

Sorya nods.

'If,' Aiah reasons carefully, 'you were preparing to defend against, say, the police or military of Jaspeer, they would have to assault this place very carefully so as not to cause casualties among the population here. There must be ten thousand people living within a radius of this building.'

'Yes.' Sorya's glittering eyes watch her with interest.

'But if, say, your . . . opponents . . . have no reason to care about casualties in the neighborhood, they could do great damage to you and your apparatus as things stand now.'

'Ah.' Sorya's terse monosyllable gives her no clue as to whether Aiah's speculations are the least bit relevant. Aiah bites back on her growing frustration and continues.

'They can't hurt your equipment through the collection web,' Aiah says. 'But they can damage its environment.' She glances through the office windows at the tented ceiling, the high arched windows. 'Hit those windows hard enough and the glass flies in like a thousand knives. Knock the roof hard enough and it falls down on the collection web. It might break the web, and even if it doesn't your personnel are going to take a bad hit.'

Sorya gives a thin, knowing smile, the briefest nod. '*Warriors of Thunderworld*?' she says.

'Common sense,' Aiah retorts. 'A lot of the casualties of the Bursary Street flamer came from flying glass.'

'Indeed,' Sorya says, 'your reasoning is impeccable. Given, of course, your premises.'

And if this place starts getting sandbagged, Aiah thinks, with shields put up over the delicate equipment and work spaces, then I'll know a thing or two.

'Of course,' Sorya says, 'Constantine and many of his people are trained warriors, who would already have considered these matters. Should,' she adds, again with that thin, ambiguous smile, 'they be relevant to our goals.'

'Are *you* a warrior, Madam Sorya?' Aiah asks.

'My battles,' she says briefly, 'have been on a less grand scale.' She turns, opens the office door, then looks at Aiah over her shoulder. 'But on the whole,' she adds, 'mine have been more successful than his. Perhaps I am less distracted by unrealities.'

Aiah follows Sorya onto the factory floor. From above comes the flap of pigeon wings.

'You may as well tell me, you know,' Aiah says. 'I may be able to help you.'

'It's not my decision,' Sorya says. She tosses her streaky hair and offers her trilling laugh. 'Besides,' she says, 'it's amusing watching you try to guess.'

'Thank you,' Aiah says flatly.

Sorya, she thinks, seeks power, and enjoys such power as she has, even if some of it is petty.

But the power of knowledge is a temporary thing, Aiah suspects. She has her own little data points, and sooner or later they'll point to something.

Fire tests precious metal, and grief tests men.
— a thought-message from His Perfection,
the Prophet of Ajas

District Hospital Twelve is of gray stone, centuries old, with sagging floors, windows fixed in their frames by a hundred layers of paint, cobwebs in the high-cornered ceilings, cracked plaster, peeling paint. The building is covered with ornamental stonework, leaf-traceries and statues of the Messengers of Vida flying on membranous wings to the aid of the sick. As a child Aiah had always been afraid of the stern-faced statues with their bat wings, rain-pitted hair, blank eyes and gaping, wordless mouths. Inside, the smell of disinfectant cannot entirely conceal the sad scent of age and despair: too much sickness, too much pain, over too many years.

Aiah catches a heel on a broken tile, stumbles, recovers. She makes a turn into a room, and here is her family standing round one of the room's four occupied beds, and a situation she needs to deal with.

'Hi there.' From the bed her cousin Esmon waves listlessly, hand bulky with wrapped finger splints. His face is badly cut, his eyes masked by swollen tissue.

Aiah remembers the rain of boots and fists in the trackline station, the blast of plasm fire that brought an end to the beating. Esmon hadn't any plasm batteries to protect him. It looks as if his attackers went at him very thoroughly.

Aiah approaches Esmon and bends over to carefully kiss each cheek. She looks to clasp a hand, but one is splinted, and the other, and with it the entire forearm, is strapped into some kind of tape-swathed box. She runs her hand over the top of his head, and her nerves flare as she sees him wince. Even there, he's sensitive.

She remembers Esmon at the Senko's Day celebration, proud in his green-and-gold sequinned coat, his plans to join the Griffins for next year's parade . . .

Aiah looks up at the rest, sees her mother, her grandmother Galaiah, Esmon's witch-lover Khorsa. 'He was attacked?' Aiah says. 'What happened exactly?'

A call from Esmon's brother Spano had come late in her work shift, and she'd taken the rest of the shift off and rushed to the hospital, but the summons had been short on details.

'Don't want to go into it again,' Esmon says in a thick voice.

'Gangsters,' says Galaiah in a fierce voice. 'Gangsters did this to him.'

Surprise stiffens Aiah's frame. She looks from Esmon to Galaiah and back again. 'You've got mixed up with the Operation? Or who? The Holy League?'

'Longnose gangsters,' Galaiah says.

'Don't know it was them,' Esmon insists.

'Let's talk outside,' Khorsa says. 'I'll tell you the story.'

Doubtfully Aiah lets the witch take her arm and lead her from the room. Another woman follows, a stranger in a red turban. As Aiah passes into the hallway she notices that the door has gone from the hospital room, that the doorframe holds only empty hinges. Who would steal a *door*? she wonders.

'This is my sister Dhival,' Khorsa says, nodding at the other woman.

Dhival, Aiah remembers, is a priestess, whereas Khorsa is a witch. She does not know the practical difference between the two, if any.

Tiny Khorsa looks up at Aiah, bites her lip. 'It all has to do with us,' she says.

Aiah is not surprised. Her contact with mages of the caliber of Constantine and Sorya has made her less impressed with back-alley witches than ever.

'Before anything else,' Aiah says, 'how is Esmon?'

Khorsa nods. 'The two men who attacked him gave him a very thorough working over. He's sedated right now, so he's not in much pain.'

'What are the doctors doing for him?'

'We –' Khorsa corrects herself. 'I – I can afford plasm treatments, so he'll get them starting tomorrow. The only reason they're waiting is they want to make sure he's perfectly stable before they begin.'

There's a bitter taste in Aiah's mouth. She remembers Khorsa at the Senko's Day party, the witch's suspicious reaction to Aiah's question about the Operation . . . anger burns hot in Aiah's heart.

'So how have you two got involved with the Operation?' she asks.

Khorsa's eyes widen. 'We *haven't*,' she says.

'They've got involved with *us*,' Dhival says. Her tone is bitter. 'There's this street captain, Guvag, he's been trying to push his plasm on us, and we won't take it. So he's had some of his thugs attack Esmon.'

Aiah isn't sure she believes this. 'You're not in debt to them? You don't gamble?'

'No,' Khorsa says. 'And Esmon doesn't, either.'

'You've never bought the goods from this man? Or sold them? Or walked the streets for him? Or *anything* that would give him a foot in your door?'

'*No!*' Khorsa insists. 'Absolutely not! That's why we wanted to talk to you – you work for the Plasm Authority. Is there someone you know in the Authority police that we can talk to?'

Aiah thinks for a moment. The Authority creepers, the Investigative Division, are a separate jurisdiction that report only to the Intendant.

'No, I don't know anyone specifically,' she says. 'But I can make some inquiries.'

'If you could?' Khorsa says. 'And soon?'

Aiah reaches for her notebook. 'What's the man's name again? And do you have an address for him or anything that would help me track him?'

'I don't have an address, no. But he hangs at the Shade Club on Elbar Avenue with the others in his company.'

Aiah writes this down. 'I'll see what I can do. But the question is: will you testify?'

Khorsa and Dhival look at each other. Dhival licks her lips. 'People don't testify against the Operation,' she says.

'What if I could get you protection?'

'We'd still lose everything, wouldn't we? You couldn't protect us forever. We couldn't keep the Temple going with the Operation after us. We'd be in hiding for the rest of our lives.'

Aiah looks at the two. She knows what their choice will be: testify and lose everything at once, or submit to the Operation's demands and lose everything slowly, beginning with pride and independence and eventually everything else, the Operation slicing off one bit after another, their money, their possessions, eventually the Wisdom Fortune Temple itself.

'We were hoping,' Khorsa says slowly, 'that we could get Guvag arrested for something else other than threatening *us*. He deals illegal plasm — maybe if we alert the authorities to his activities he can get arrested for selling it to someone *else*.'

Faint hope, Aiah thinks. She puts away her notebook. 'I'll see what I can do,' she says. 'In the meantime, I want to see Esmon get the treatments he needs.'

Khorsa looks up at her, eyes wide. 'Of course.'

'And you might also talk to a lawyer. Find out what your options are.'

The two sisters look at each other again. Lawyers, Aiah knows, are not a part of their world. The impersonal mechanism of the law is not something that would ever enter their life unless they'd either been arrested or maybe evicted. Lawyers are the enemy, as are the police and the judges, and the thought of having one on your side is something that is perfectly alien.

Aiah puts away her notebook. 'I need to make a call,' she says. 'Do you know where I can find a phone?'

Khorsa points down the hall, and Aiah follows the pointing finger.

She has to tell Constantine that he needn't send a car to pick her up for her plasm lesson.

Family emergencies, unfortunately, come first.

**EXPERIMENTAL ROCKET CRASHES IN LIRI-DOMEI
2000 PEOPLE KILLED IN BLAZING ACCIDENT
LEGISLATURE CALLS FOR BANNING ROCKET
EXPERIMENTS**

When Aiah leaves the hospital she returns to her office. There are fewer demands on plasm second shift, and there's only one person in the office, Vikar, the plump Grade Six who's inhabiting Aiah's chair during the service shift this week. She greets him and takes Tella's chair. She jacks in her headset, calls Compilation and Billing, and asks for Guvag's records. When they complain, she tartly reminds them that she's working Emergency Response and she needs the information *now*. Forty minutes later it arrives, tightly rolled plastic flimsies in two message cylinders that thunk out of the message system into her wire tray.

She reads the records and doesn't find much: Guvag doesn't use much plasm, at least not officially. Neither does the Shade Club. There's an address, and a red tab, which isn't actually red, or even a tab, just a printed message that reads 'red tab', an indication that Guvag has been convicted of plasm theft and that his file bears watching.

It's pointless to try getting any records out of the Investigative Division, so the next step is probably to get public records from the *Wire*'s information service. She'd like to use the computer in the office, but it's built to Arvag standards while the *Wire* uses the incompatible Cathobeth compression system, so Aiah will have to walk to the Wire office two streets away. Aiah says goodbye to Vikar, finds the office still open, and rents one of the library consoles. She plugs coins into its slot and calls for a complete public records search on Guvag. An hour and a half later she has everything printed out on slick plastic fax paper, and she stuffs the rolled records, still smelling of the developing fluid, into a bag for reading on the pneuma home.

Guvag was indeed convicted of plasm theft twelve years ago, and did a couple years' stretch in Chonmas. The chromograph taken at his conviction shows a bullnecked, mustached man scowling at the camera; extravagant amounts of lace explode from his collar and chest, and he wears an expensive Stoka watch on one wrist, a trademark of connected Operation types. According to the records he's also been accused of assault numerous times and convicted once, though most of the charges seem to have been dropped — probably, Aiah thinks, because the witnesses changed their minds about testifying.

Not just an Operation thug, she thinks, but a violent one. Khorsa and Esmon have their work cut out for them.

Aiah looks again at the printout. Nothing much to go on, she concludes, but she'll see what she can do.

TRACKLINE SCANDAL DEEPENS
CALLS FOR INTENDANT'S RESIGNATION
DETAILS ON THE *WIRE*!

The Emergency Response team has been demobilized. Oeneme's declared victory on Old Parade, and now Aiah's back in the office full time.

A message tube thunks from the pneumatic message system into Aiah's wire basket. She opens it, scans the note — another dreary reminder about personal use of telephones — and then she wads the plastic flimsy and drops it in the recyling box.

Why do they bother?

No one in the Authority seems to have any real work to do. All they do is pass pointless instructions back and forth.

She's heard from Galaiah about Esmon. He's had plasm

treatments and is much better, cheerful even. She'll call him later and talk to him in person.

One of the personal calls the Authority is so upset about. To hell with them.

Over ninety percent of the budget, she remembers Constantine saying, in maintaining *that which is*. Each executive in her little box, bored out of her skull, waiting for someone above to die or move up so everyone can advance. Like a dance in which every step takes ten years.

She remembers the mosaic in the Rocketman terminal, the bright new whitestone city broadcasting rays of golden glory. The mosaic has become her mind's view of Constantine's New City. A little dirtied and chipped perhaps, but worthy of salvage.

Aiah turns to Tella, who is watching little Jayme scuttle about the floor on his stomach. He isn't crawling properly yet, on hands and knees, he's just at the insect stage.

'They don't know what they want,' Aiah says. 'The decorator says something, and suddenly they're ripping out finished cabinets and rearranging everything. And then *I* have to change all the access ports around.'

'At least you're getting paid for all your work,' Tella consoled. Her eyes brighten. 'How's he getting along with Momo?'

'They're in love again.'

'Bad luck.'

'Won't last, though. I'll give it a week.'

Tella looks at the wall clock. 'Break time. You want to go first?'

Aiah shakes her head. 'Go ahead.'

Tella contacts the tabulator and tells her that she's offline for the next fifteen minutes. Aiah smiles – she's invented a false Constantine, a false Sorya, and all for Tella's benefit. She calls them Bobo and Momo. She's been inventing details of their story relationship and inability to make decisions; she's made them the most absurd couple imaginable, a family out of a chromoplay comedy.

Such a couple wouldn't be up to anything illegal, would they?

Tella picks up Jayme, wipes drool from his chin, carries him away. Aiah programs a broadcast into her computer, then sits for a long moment and listens to the distant clicks of the gears.

'May I come in?'

A man stands at the door dressed in a rumpled gray suit. Blue eyes peer at her from a red, lined face, and a cigaret hangs carelessly from a corner of his mouth. She's seen the man around, and perhaps she should know his name.

'Take a seat,' Aiah says. In order to hear him better she pulls back one earpiece of her headset and places it against her mastoid.

The man enters and reaches for one of a pair of metal chairs standing against the wall. 'Not those,' Aiah says. 'Broken – we reported them months ago, but no help. Use my office-mate's chair, she's on break.'

The man nods and cigaret ash falls onto his chin lace. He moves Tella's chair next to Aiah's desk and sits.

'I don't believe we've met, but Mr Mengene speaks well of you,' the man says. He holds out a hand. 'I'm Rohder.'

Alarm sirens wail along the back-alleys of Aiah's nerves. This is the man who snuffed the Bursary Street flamer, who saw with the enhanced eyes of his anima the flamer's sourceline stretching to Terminal.

He's also the man whose phone she gimmicked, making her initial calls to Constantine appear to come from his desk.

Aiah peels back the lace from her wrist and shakes Rohder's hand. 'Good that you're out of the hospital,' she says, and hopes he can't see the pulse leaping in her throat.

Rohder smiles. 'I got a little jangled,' he says. 'I wasn't

expecting to have to deal with a large-scale emergency at my age.'

'Everything's all right now?' Aiah wonders if her voice is too loud.

'Oh yes. Good as new.'

'14:40 hours,' says the voice on Aiah's headset, 'Horn Four reorientation to degrees 033.3. Ne?'

'Ne,' Aiah says. 'Say again, please?' She looks apologetically at Rohder and returns the speaker to her ear. The accustomed actions of programming her computer, the simple movements of fingers and eyes, help her assemble for herself a precarious state of serenity.

As she sets her dials she remembers that both Sorya and Khorsa, on first meeting, had been able to tell she'd been working with plasm – though at least Sorya had been pumping the well at the time. In the last two weeks Aiah has used a thousand times more plasm than she had when she'd met Sorya. Rohder is senior enough to have access to plasm – probably, at his age, using most of it to extend his life and therefore seniority – and might be able to recognize a fellow user.

And he used to be head of the Research Division, Aiah thinks, before he got his funding pulled. So he's probably very good at what he does.

Lies flicker through her mind as her hand jacks the cable into the transmission scalar. Aiah is a bit surprised at the facility of her invention. Apparently deception improves with practice.

My temple lets me use plasm, she decides. *In the rites.* That's the one she'll use.

'Yes?' she says, pulling back the earpiece once more. 'How can I help you?'

Rohder looks in vain for an ashtray, taps a long gray worm of ash into his palm instead, then wipes the hand on his ash-gray slacks. 'You headed the group that Mr Mengene sent east, toward Grand City.'

Aiah shifts in her chair, tries fiercely to will herself into a state of tranquility. 'That's right,' she says.

'And you found nothing?'

'I thought I'd found something promising. But it turned out there was nothing in it.' And get that door bricked up *now*, she thinks.

Rohder leans toward her, a watery light in his bright blue eyes. Aiah wonders how old he is – he seems surprisingly youthful in spite of the white hair and the network of creases around his eyes, but with regular plasm treatments he could easily be over a hundred.

'And that something was?' he says.

Aiah takes a breath. 'There was an abandoned pneuma station called Terminal. The access was right under a building where someone had been gimmicking the meters, so I thought maybe they'd been tapping off some plasm from an unknown structure. But my team searched the station thoroughly and didn't find anything.' She shrugs. 'We took two days at it. So all it amounts to was that someone was gimmicking the meters to hide some plasm use, and that was that.'

'What made you start in this particular neighborhood?'

Aiah decides not to mention the abandoned plastic plant she'd found on the Rocketman transparency. She still has the original in her possession, and she doubts there's another copy of the four-hundred-year-old cel in existence.

'The pneuma station seemed promising,' she says. 'And we had to start somewhere. It wasn't as if there was more than one team working the whole district.'

A flag snaps over on the scalar with an audible click, and Aiah jumps. A transmission ending.

Rohder nods. 'I understand Oeneme thought that Old Parade was more promising,' he says. He nods again. 'But nothing was found on Old Parade.'

'Nothing *much*,' Aiah corrects. 'A few leaks. But they could have built up to a Grade A leak over time.'

Rohder draws on his cigaret meditatively. The bright line of flame, advancing up the length of the cigaret, touches his lips, but he seems used to it. He draws the wet stub from his mouth, looks at it for an uncertain moment, and then balances it precisely on the edge of Aiah's desk, the burnt end overhanging the floor's plastic sheeting. He breathes out smoke, looks at the cigaret butt, and frowns.

'I *saw* the thing's sourceline heading east,' he says. 'I was a little addled when I got into the hospital, so perhaps I didn't explain myself properly, but I know I wasn't wrong.' He gives a little smile. 'Curious how Oeneme chose to disregard this. Old Parade was just so much more convenient for him – right there in public near the Broadcast Complex, to make it convenient for his press releases, and he didn't have that long commute out to Grand Towers.'

He reaches into a jacket pocket, comes out with a cigaret case, thumbs it open.

'Did it occur to you to wonder *why* the pneuma station was abandoned?' he says.

This is precisely the line of reasoning that led Aiah to the plastics factory. She doesn't at all like Rohder's reasoning.

'No,' Aiah says promptly. Then she shrugs again. 'The overlays are full of old structures.'

Rohder methodically lights his cigaret, lets smoke drift upward. 'That neighborhood was built four hundred years ago,' he says. 'I had some people at Rocketman look it up.'

Aiah tries to smile. 'I wish I'd had the authority to tell Rocketman that. It would have saved me a day.'

'It had to have been built on the site of something that had been there previously, though there's no record of what it was. A water treatment plant, a food factory, something big. And when people no longer had to commute to Terminal to work, they closed the pneuma.'

Aiah attempts a thoughtful look. 'If you can get permission,' she says, 'I could resume my search.' And make sure, she thinks, that nothing gets found. 'I've become familiar with the district,' she adds.

Rohder shakes his head. 'Oeneme was in charge,' he says, 'and he's told everyone the problem's solved.' He sighs. 'I could get the investigation reopened, I suppose, but it would be a struggle, and I have too many enemies in this organization as it is. No,' he looks up at her, 'we'll just have to wait, and alert the creepers that work that district. If anyone's tapping that old structure, someone's bound to turn her in sooner or later.'

Her? Aiah thinks. She smiles and feels insects crawling up and down her spine.

Rohder stands and returns her smile. 'I just wanted to satisfy my curiosity,' he says. 'Mengene said you were bright, and I wanted to see for myself.'

Aiah stands to see him off, crouching a bit at the limit of her headset cord.

'I'm glad you're feeling better,' she says.

He shakes her hand, peering at her with his watery blue eyes, and then ambles away.

Aiah wonders if she dares tell Constantine about this. What would be Constantine's response? *Forget the man . . . the problem is over.*

No, she thinks. She doesn't want anything like that on her conscience.

But get a team down to Terminal Station and wall that support brace up *soon.*

Next day, it's done.

ATTACK OF THE HANGED MAN
ALDEMAR'S SPINE-TINGLING NEW CHROMOPLAY
The First Degree of Terror
PREMIERE THIS WEEK!

The day after walling up the toilet Aiah takes off the second half of her shift and head for Old Shorings. Esmon's out of the hospital and she should pay a visit. To that end she's bought a chocolate cake as a gift. But another gift is the information on Guvag she's collected, and she doesn't want to trouble Esmon's thoughts with it.

She'll give it to Khorsa. It's really Khorsa's problem anyway.

The Wisdom Fortune Temple is on the second floor of a brownstone office building. It smells strongly of herbs grown on rooftops and in closets, then packaged neatly in plastic bags behind a glass countertop. Candles stand on shelves, ready to be anointed with special charmed oils and burned for good luck. Packages of reconstituted soup-mixes are ranked on cheap wire racks – people take them home, brew them up, and have a little feast in order to fix what's wrong with them, or maybe what's wrong with the universe.

Above the counter is a picture of Karlo in an ornamented tin frame, identical to the one Aiah has in her apartment.

Through a beaded curtain is the temple itself. There are benches on the walls for elderly or infirm worshipers, but Aiah knows most of the rituals are done round the circle painted on the cheap tiles in the center of the floor, where the worshipers will don their temple garb, kneel on pillows brought from home, and sway back and forth to the sound of chanting. Inside the circle is painted the Branch of Tangid, with a live plasm circuit at its center. On the walls, icons of Tangid, Karlo, and Dhoran of the Dead alternate with the Mirror Twins and the White Horse and other foci.

God, or the Gods, are too remote from humanity really to be worshiped in any kind of personal way; they're far off somewhere, walled off by the Shield. It's the immortals to whom people pray, and who are invoked in the ceremonies. The immortals were once people themselves, and they understand human desires and frailty. They are presumed capable of interceding on human behalf with the remoter divinities, the Gods or the Ascended Ones.

Aiah remembers it all from her childhood: the herbal scent, the chants and drums and hand-claps, the congregation swaying and crying out and calling on the immortals. She knows how some of the worshipers will go into trance and cry out a message from some immortal or other, or sometimes just go into spasms that, to a jaundiced adult eye, look remarkably sexual. Aiah knows that the congregation consists largely of middle-aged women, their children and, for some reason, homosexual men. And she knows all Khorsa's lines, the rhythmic speech meant to lull people into a mild trance, set them up for the special pleas for special sums for some special task or other, healing or redecorating or maybe even sending someone to the Barkazi Sectors to study at the feet of some illuminated seer.

Khorsa sits behind the counter, ready to dispense soup or blessings or advice. She looks surprised when Aiah enters, and rises to greet her.

'How's Esmon?' Aiah asks.

'Taking it easy in our apartment,' Khorsa says. 'But he's fine. The treatments were very successful.'

'I'm on my way to see him,' Aiah says, 'but I thought I'd drop these off first.' She reaches into her tote bag, pulls out all the information she's gathered on Guvag, then puts the thick roll of fax paper on the countertop.

'This is all I could find out,' she says, 'and it's not going to help. I've talked to some people in the Investigative Division about him, and they know his name and would be happy to put him back in Chonmas, but they can't do anything if there's no formal complaint and no witnesses. They've had a lot of witness problems with this one.'

Khorsa bites her lip. 'Would they provide protection?'

'Probably not – not unless you agreed to turn informer and spy, work with Guvag for a while, and get close enough to him to find out some real criminality. I assumed you wouldn't be willing to do that.'

Khorsa gives a little shake of her head, then sighs. 'Well, then,' she says.

'What are you going to do?'

'I won't work with the man. And I won't close down the Temple. Perhaps if I get the right magic working, someone, if I make an appeal to the congregation . . .' Her voice trails off.

'Well,' Aiah says, 'good luck. I wish I could have been more help.'

Aiah picks up her gift cake and walks down the building's worn steel steps to street level. A weary sense of tragedy fills her; this is going to be worse than what happened to Henley, and the dreary inevitability of it all sends a wave of sadness drifting through her nerves.

She walks to the apartment that Khorsa and Esmon share. It's a nice place, with a proper balcony instead of a scaffold, big enough for a nice pocket garden planted with squash, onions, chilies and herbs. Esmon is there, looking much his old self after expert plasm treatments – there's a little bruising visible on his face, and the bridge of his nose has a new hump on it, but he greets Aiah with a smile and invites her in. He cuts pieces of the chocolate cake for Aiah and himself, and asks if she's heard from Gil. She says she has.

Esmon stretches out on the sofa while Aiah tells him more or less what she told Khorsa. She's halfway through her story when there's a knock on the door, and then her brother Stonn enters along with Esmon's brother Spano. Cold suspicion wriggles its way up Aiah's spine.

'Thanks for doing what you could,' Stonn says. He's a practiced felon, with powerful arms and shoulders and tattoos on his biceps. Mostly he's a thief, but he's strong enough to have occasionally hired out as muscle for some of Old Shorings's Fastani gangsters.

'I didn't think anything would come of it,' Stonn says. 'Don't worry, we'll deal with it anyway.'

'What are you going to do?' Aiah demands. She looks from one to another in alarm.

The men shrug. 'We'll take care of it,' Stonn says.

'Take care of Guvag, you mean.'

'Same thing.'

'Stonn.' Pointing at him. 'You'll lose.'

There's a resentful glimmer in Stonn's eyes. 'Not if we do it right.'

Stonn is hopeless; Aiah should have known that. She turns to her two cousins. 'It's the *Operation*,' she says. 'They're *professionals*. They have people who do nothing but kill people. You two have never been involved with anything like that, you'll get chopped down for nothing.'

Esmon and Spano look at each other uneasily. 'Stonn says we can wait for him outside his club,' Spano says.

'There are longnose Operation types in and out of there all the time. You think they're not going to notice three Barkazils standing in a doorway waiting for them? Including a man they just dropped the shoe on?'

'I can get a gun,' Stonn says.

'You think *they* don't have guns?'

'We don't have to go to the club,' Spano adds. 'We can find out where he lives.'

Aiah's frustration boils over, and she tells them exactly how foolish this all is — and that of course only confirms them in their course.

'What else can we do?' Spano demands. 'They beat up my *brother*, ne?'

'All right,' Aiah says, standing, 'fine. But don't do *anything* till you hear from me. *Nothing*.' She looks at Esmon. 'You promise?'

'What are you going to do?' he asks.

She looks at him, anger curling her lips. 'I'm going to take care of it,' she says.

* * *

The anger lasts halfway to Terminal, and is then replaced by anxiety. What, exactly, is she going to *do*? This isn't the sort of situation in which she can improvise and hope to get away with it. And if the Operation traces her to the factory, then Constantine can kiss his whole plan goodbye.

By the time the New Central Line drops her off at Garakh Station near Terminal, she has a scheme halfway put together. As she walks up the station steps into shieldlight, she brushes her hair forward around her face and puts on a pair of shieldglasses. With luck, the Barkazil businesswoman in the gray suit and lace won't be connected with the Barkazil girl in the yellow jumpsuit who fried the face off a local resident a couple weeks ago.

From a public phone she calls Constantine's accommodation number and leaves a message telling him she won't need a ride from her job. Constantine's workmen, accustomed to her presence, let her into the factory when she knocks on the door, then go on about their business.

Aiah's had her most recent lessons here: the plasm is free, even if the equipment is still primitive. There aren't any proper workstations yet, but improvised stations have been jacked into the tap while the real equipment is being assembled. Aiah swabs dust off one of the cheap plastic-and-metal chairs and seats herself. The console consists of a sawn-off plastic plank with gauges and dials cemented on it with a gummy white adhesive. Aiah pulls her chair to it and picks up the dusty copper t-grip that's been sitting here since her last lesson.

Her mouth is dry. Somewhere in the factory a circular saw whines. Perhaps, she thinks, she ought to tell Constantine, get his help and assistance.

No, she thinks. That's not his job. He's paying her for

her knowledge, not to get him involved in some sordid family matter.

Go, she decides. Do it now, before she comes to her senses.

She takes her Trigram token from around her neck and puts it on the table in front of her, then drops the transference-grip into the waiting slot. There's a mental *snap!* as the roar of power fills her senses, an instantaneous shift in perspective, as if she were half-blind before and has only now learned to see fully, to comprehend the essential structure of reality, the power that lies at the heart of the matter.

A thousand Angels of Power sing in Aiah's mind. She builds an anima and leaps from the building, flies under bright shieldlight to Old Shorings, and from there to the Third Ward, the Jaspeeri neighborhood adjacent.

Guvag, Aiah thinks, spends his time at the Shade Club on Elbar Avenue. And if he's not there, she knows where he lives.

Elbar Avenue is a cheerless, dingy little dog's leg only one block in length, overshadowed by old brownstone buildings swathed in scaffolding and plastic. Aiah doesn't understand how any of these places survived the last earthquake. The Shade Club is a small place, discreet, but underneath the chipped black paint of the club's exterior Aiah can see the bronze sheathing that is supposed to keep it safe from plasm assault. The flyspecked window is checkered by a discreet bronze mesh.

Power howls in her ears, urging her just to smash into the club, clear the place out with one great cleansing jet of flame. But that would be impossible – the bronze sheathing would suck her anima dry. With an effort of will Aiah carefully sinks her sourceline below ground, puts the umbilicus connecting her to the factory where it can't be seen. She doesn't want anyone backtracking her to her point of origin.

Carefully she raises her anima to the window and peers in, adjusts her perceptions to the dim light. And there, sure enough, is Guvag – older and fatter than in his chromographs, but clearly the same man. He sits in his shirtsleeves at a round table in the center of the room, a glass of liquor in front of him. A few of his cronies sit round the table, young men dressed with peacock extravagance or old men with expressionless, masklike faces. None of them seems to be engaged in anything in particular.

All Aiah has to do, she thinks, is wait for Guvag to come out.

Plasm growls impatiently in her ears. She might not have time, Aiah thinks; Constantine or Sorya could arrive at any moment. She expands the perceptions of her anima to include the street. The big Carfacin limousine, parked illegally near the fire hydrant, has to be Guvag's.

Might as well start with that. Aiah moves to the car, carefully sculpts ectomorphic hands, places them beneath the vehicle. Power pulses along her sourceline. The car trembles, rises, balances precariously. Aiah feels invisible back and shoulder muscles flex as she lifts the car to head height. Then, impatient, she wraps the entire car in a ball of power and fires it across the street like a round from a cannon.

The club's window explodes inward as the car's massive, chromed front end drives through it. Tables and chairs spill amid a crash of shattered glass. Aiah flies into the building through the gap in its bronze shield and sees Guvag, surprisingly fast for his bulk, already out of his chair and running.

Aiah reaches out a thought like a slap, and Guvag reels. She seizes his collar in invisible hands, hauls him back to the table.

Let him *see* her, she thinks. And she wills herself a body – not her own, she decides, but something much more impressive, a powerful, giant figure with hands like talons

184

and the face of a raging animal. And aflame, alight with a fire that matches her rage.

Fire's reflection shimmers off the walls of the dingy club as her plasm body takes shape. Guvag, on his knees behind his table, stares at her with an expression of sick terror. His friends and servants have fled. Aiah looks at him with the keen, slitted eyes of a hawk.

'Can you hear me?' she asks.

Speechless, he nods. The tablecloth bursts into sudden flame and Aiah sweeps it away with her free hand.

'You have made a mistake,' Aiah tells him. 'The Wisdom Fortune Temple is under my protection. I want that understood.'

'Yes!' he says. 'I understand!' Her flame is scorching his face.

'You do not know who I am,' Aiah says. 'You will never know who I am. But if you do not keep out of Old Shorings, you will meet me again. Understand!'

'Yes!' he shrieks. 'Yes! I'll leave your people alone!'

Aiah releases him and he drops to the floor like a sack. She can see herself reflected in the bar's mirrors, a hunched predator shape, an angel of fire and destruction. Her feet are melting through the bar's plastic flooring. Guvag's car, halfway through the window, rests on its nose. Aiah laughs, and the echoes of her mirth ring from the walls. She has never felt such glory in her life.

'Goodbye, Guvag,' she says. 'Remember that I can come back at any time.'

She would like to stalk out in triumph, but she doesn't dare touch any of the club's bronze sheathing, so back in the factory she just unclamps her hand from the t-grip, and the distant reality of the shattered Shade Club fades from her perceptions.

'Working already?' Constantine's voice. He stands behind her, having arrived at the factory while she was occupied.

Aiah licks dry lips. 'Yes,' she says. 'I was working on my telepresence techniques.'

A tremor runs through her. She feels diminished, a tiny, insignificant figure compared to the flaming figure of vengeance, the Burning Woman, whose fiery existence she had just inhabited.

'With success?' Constantine inquires.

'I believe so.' Either she has just scared Guvag off, or she's killed her entire family. Her display had been spectacular – if that plasm had been metered, it would probably have cost ten thousand dalders – and she hopes the thought of an enemy who can use plasm that extravagantly will cause Guvag to think twice.

'Shall we do something a little more structured?' Constantine asks. He pulls up another of the cheap chairs, tugs at the knees of his gray slacks, sits.

'All right.'

Docilely, Aiah holds out her wrist, and Constantine takes it.

STOKA SEVENTEEN
The watch worn by those whose word is law

Constantine's guard Khoriak drives Aiah home in a little two-seater Geldan. She has him drop her off at the food market, and from there she makes a call on a public phone to Esmon's apartment.

'I've dealt with Guvag,' she says. 'You shouldn't be bothered from now on.'

There's a moment in which Esmon processes this, and then he says, 'What do you mean? What do you mean you dealt with him?'

'If he bothers you or Khorsa again, let me know. But he shouldn't. You don't have to do anything, understand?'

'Ah . . . I suppose. But—'

'And you've got to keep Stonn from doing anything

stupid. That's a lifelong task, I know, but if he moves on Guvag right now it could wreck everything.'

'I'll . . . talk to him.'

Aiah hangs up, buys some soft drinks for the refrigerator and heads home.

A memory of the Burning Woman flames softly in her mind.

THE BLUE TITAN THREATENS . . .
But the Lynxoid Brothers are Ready!
See the new chromoplay now!

Aiah hears the hiss of air and the little tug on her inner ear that signifies the car braking from its top speed of over 450 radii per hour. The InterMetropolitan pneuma to Gunalaht is a high-speed run, and the train spends more time in stations than it does in motion.

Aiah places a bookmark in her text on plasm theory and waits for the deceleration. Regularly spaced soft glowing green lights, all that is visible through the window, shift from a constant blur to a slower, numerable pace. Then Aiah's stomach leaps into her throat as the train drops out of the system and comes to a hissing halt at the station.

The first thing she sees from the train window is a row of bright advertisements for casinos, all with that burnished golden color suggestive of luxury, each promising more spectacle, more indulgence, more ways to win than the last. She puts her book in her traveling bag — it's heavy with Constantine's coin — shoulders it, and steps off the train.

She'd purchased a ticket for a metropolis a stop past Gunalaht. One of the little security procedures recommended to her by Martinus.

She walks past the casino adverts, locates signs to a local train, and then realizes she needs to convert to the local money in order to pay the fare. She converts her money at one of a half-dozen kiosks that all seem to offer the same rate, then takes the local train to the stop nearest her bank.

If she were a real big spender, she supposes, she could have taken a cab. She really doesn't have the reflexes of a wealthy person yet.

The bank is unlike anything she's encountered, a large quiet room, softly carpeted, with silent people sitting at desks. Fluted white enamel pillars support an elaborate fan-vaulted ceiling. A white-gloved usher in a black velvet coat takes Aiah to the desk of a Mr nar-Ombre. He has a voice so soft that she has to lean closely to hear him.

Formalities are dealt with: she gives the codes Constantine provided her, gives her signature and chop, asks for the balance. Nar-Ombre's computer whirrs for a few seconds and produces a total.

200,141.81. A few days' interest to the good.

'Thank you,' she says, and feigns a few seconds' hesitation. 'Does anyone else have access to the account?' she asks.

The banker consults his records. 'We provided the codes to the gentleman who established the account, a Mr Cangene. We have a signature and chop on record for him.'

Aiah represses a smile. Constantine ought to know better than to try to make her his *passu*.

Not that she wouldn't have done it herself, in his place.

'In that case,' Aiah says, 'I would like to withdraw the money, and open another account in my name alone.'

Mr nar-Ombre's expression implies he hears requests like this every day, and perhaps he does. 'There is a penalty for closing this type of account, I'm afraid,' he says. 'And a fee for opening another.'

'I understand,' Aiah says. She hefts her shoulder bag. 'I'd like to make a deposit as well.'

Mr nar-Ombre's long fingers reach for his computer. 'Very good, miss,' he says.

A few more days' interest will offset the penalties, she concludes.

When she leaves the bank, she asks the usher for his recommendation as to a hotel, and when she goes there, she takes a cab.

Learn to live well, she thinks.

She manages her entire day in Gunalaht without entering a single casino. If she's not going to be Constantine's *passu*, there's not a lot of point to becoming the *passu* of an entire state.

GRADE B PLASM LEAK IN KARAPOOR!
HUNDREDS INJURED!
DETAILS ON THE *WIRE!*

Again, that incredibly fast work: over the weekend Aiah spent in transit to and from Gunalaht, the factory has been readied for use. A row of workstations has been built inside the completed collection web, each with a comfortable padded chair and a pair of oval video monitors, side by side like a pair of eyes, to provide an outside feed. A metal shed roof now covers the whole installation to protect it against any attempts to drop the factory's ceiling, and the high windows have been taped so thoroughly that almost all outside Shieldlight has been cut off.

Aiah's lessons in plasm use will take place here from now on. Unlike the plasm at Constantine's apartment, the goods here are free.

Three men are using the workstations, hands clasped around copper t-grips, eyes closed, concentration etched into their faces. Two are Jaspeeris, surprisingly young and with bad skin, but they're neatly dressed in quiet gray, like the uniforms of an elite school, an effect that only makes them seem younger. One whispers inaudibly to himself as he dips the well, his upper body swaying left and right in response to some secret inner pulse. The third is older and black-skinned and looks Cheloki: he has a hard face, a hawk nose placed like a sword between his eyes, and may well be a veteran of Constantine's wars.

Through the as-yet-untaped windows of the office, Aiah glances out at the truckload of sandbags just arrived in the loading bay, then turns to Constantine and lifts an eyebrow. 'Who are you planning on attacking, exactly?' she says.

He glances up from his desk. 'Sorya said you were curious.'

He doesn't seem upset by the thought, but just to play it safe Aiah says, 'Who wouldn't be?'

A trace of a smile plays about Constantine's lips. 'You don't need to know the answer.'

'It's obvious enough you're planning some kind of war.'

'I'm planning a change,' Constantine says. 'An evolutionary transformation. And it should come cheap at the price.' He stands, flexes burly shoulders. His burning eyes are fixed on the workstations.

'Nothing changes in our world,' he says, 'because the cost of change is so enormous. Not the least is simply the cost of *space*. Consider what's needed simply to build a new building. There *will* be something on the site already, so the old building must be purchased, and all the people living or working there moved. All those displaced people will have to go somewhere else, at enormous cost, and even if the builders manage somehow not to pay the displacement fees, *somebody* will. So every new structure is a drain on the economy before it even starts. Few banks can afford to finance such an effort unless it's guaranteed by the government or the central bank, and that just adds another layer of complexity to the whole problem. Jaspeer can afford a new Mage Towers perhaps every dozen years. Nothing can be transformed in any significant way, because the cost of transformation is just so high. So most people can't put up new buildings, just remodel old ones, but that means accepting the older buildings' design limitations, the way they're tied into the infrastructure.

'And so,' he nods, 'I wish to redesign the world. Rethink it. Transform it.'

'So what are you going to do?' Aiah asks. 'Knock a bunch of it down and start over?'

A laugh gusts out of him. 'I wish I could!' He shakes his head. 'They could have used me when Senko and his crowd were setting things up. Ah well.'

Aiah nods at the three intent men at the workstations. 'What are they up to?'

Amusement lights Constantine's eyes. 'Preparing to knock a few things down.'

'Seriously.'

'They are . . .' he frowns. 'Quarrying. Remember when I told you about combat mages? Their short lifespans in action? Well, that is *one* sort of military mage, those used in battle. The kind who turn,' he looks at Aiah and smiles, 'into giant burning women who hammer the enemy with sheer blasts of power.'

That smile makes Aiah uneasy, and she wonders for an uneasy moment if he could have heard about Guvag. But Constantine, apparently unaware of Aiah's anxiety, continues.

'The other kind of military mage is more subtle,' he says. 'Refrains from attacking, and instead tries to worm his way in. Finds weak points in the enemy's defenses, maps them, tries to work out ways to exploit them without alerting the opposition. They are less warriors than spies, and each is worth a hundred of the other sort. These,' he nods at the three men, 'are among the best.'

'Those two boys . . .'

'Naturals.' A smile lights Constantine's lips. 'Like yourself, Miss Aiah. People who have learned plasm use instinctively rather than through formal applications. Young minds are very suitable for that sort of work, being free of inhibiting structures, of overjudicial interpretation.' He nods again. 'They are very successful, those two.'

'Isn't what they're doing dangerous? If they're detected . . .'

He looks at her appraisingly. 'They understand the risks better than you, I believe.'

Aiah rephrases her objection. 'They're young. They can't possibly know what they're getting into. You're using them.'

Constantine smiles with his strong white teeth. 'Miss Aiah,' he reminds, '*you* are young, and I am using *you*. And – I assure you – *you* do not know what you're getting into, either.' He spreads his hands. 'But you find yourself here, do you not? Your will led you here; and *my* will,' he waves a hand, embracing the factory, the huge accumulators, the web and workstations, 'brought this into being. And will shortly bring into being other things, ideas brought to the world of reality.'

Aiah finds herself unwilling to let Constantine escape into metaphysics, at least not yet. 'I'm older than they are, anyway,' she says. 'They can't possibly—'

Constantine's eyes turn hard. 'Why value the lives of the young more than those of the old?' he asks. 'It is the qualities that come with youth that make them valuable to me, or, at this stage, to anyone. Years from now, they will look back on this episode as their golden time, the time when they discovered, as few young people ever do, who they are, and what they are capable of. And if they do not survive to that time . . .' He steps up to Aiah, puts a heavy hand on her shoulder, looks at her with eyes of stone. 'I learned long ago,' he says, 'that the actions of the powerful have consequences. As a consequence of my actions, *thousands* of boys have died, and girls, and babes, and thousands and thousands of ordinary people who had nothing to do with me. I didn't kill them myself, I didn't wish them dead, and if I could have prevented it I would, but they died none the less. And *these* boys,' nodding to the two mages, 'at least volunteered.'

Aiah had forgotten the cost of the Cheloki wars, the destruction of a metropolis as thorough as the devastation that had been wrought in Barkazi. She licks her lips. 'I wouldn't want that sort of responsibility,' she says.

He leans closer to her, his deep voice almost a whisper but still powered by his ferocious energy, a low rumble that Aiah can feel in her toes. 'Miss Aiah, your sentiment is too late. You've given me power, and are as responsible as anyone for what follows. And,' almost offhand, 'there have already been deaths.'

Aiah stares at him in horror. *Forget the man*, she remembers, *the problem is over*.

'They were bad people, I believe, and dangerous,' Constantine says. 'If that knowledge will help you sleep.'

'I don't think it will,' Aiah says.

He steps back, lets his hand fall from her shoulder, gives her an appraising glance. 'I have had sleepless hours myself,' he says, 'but by and by they passed.' He reaches out, takes her wrist as he has in all their lessons together. 'Shall we have your lesson now?' he asks. 'Or were these last moments lesson enough?'

We seek to enlarge our scope. Our power. Sorya's words.

Power, Aiah thinks. Perhaps she ought to get used to it.

'The lesson, if you please,' she says, and lets him lead her to a console.

GARGELIUS ENCHUK WEARS GULMAN SHOES! *Why Don't You?*

'The School of Radritha defines three sorts of power,' Constantine says. 'Power over the self, power over others, and power over reality. And of these, they conceive the first to be the only worthwhile goal, because they consider the only thing a man can know truly is his own mind, and his knowledge of anything else is but a reflection of his inward sight. Which is why I broke with them finally, because their scope was limited only to self-knowledge and self-mastery, without any conception of what the self-mastery is *for*.

'I will agree that power over the self is primary,' he says, nodding, 'because with self-knowledge and self-mastery, power over others and over reality will naturally follow. The School had power – some of the most powerful minds I've ever met – but it had withdrawn entirely into self-contemplation. And was a little smug about it, truthfully.'

Aiah sips at her wine as the Elton cruises away from the factory. The shift's lesson had flushed her with plasm. Power sings in her blood, a chorus of exhilaration and control. But now she finds the wine a little bitter, and Constantine's discourse on power the last thing she wants to hear.

Already been deaths . . . She hadn't wanted to think about it until Constantine's whisper had forced her to confront the fact. And now she is compelled to wonder whether her efforts to educate herself in the use of plasm are worth the loss of life.

'The School desired to give their initiates freedom,' Constantine continues. 'Freedom from passion, from impulse, from – in essence – the world itself. Imagine the reaction of my family,' he smiles, 'when I told them I wished to study there. The School stood in opposition to everything they held dear, and that, I imagine, is why I wished to go.' He shrugs.

'But detachment from all things?' he says. 'Is that not also a trap? To say that nothing matters, or that nothing *should* matter, except that which occurs in the perfectly passionless mind . . .' He utters a black, sneering laugh. '*This* they call freedom? Skulking in their meditation chambers, hiding from the sight of the world, peering obsessively at the landscape of their own minds, terrified they might be caught in an impulse, an emotion, an urge . . .'

Detachment, Aiah decides, seems like a pretty good idea right now. Let us, she thinks, consider the problem dispassionately. People, I am informed bad people, have died. Although I do not absolutely know that these are the people who attacked me, I nevertheless suspect that they are. In which case I have evidence, written on my bones with the toes of boots, that they were in fact bad people, and therefore deserved punishment.

'Avoidance of passion does not conquer passion,' Constantine continues, 'and the School of Radritha, for all the power of their minds, seemed not to know this. They did not conquer passion, they merely denied it. And that is why they were so afraid of power, because they knew it was dangerous to them . . . power becomes a slave to passion so easily, and to an unacknowledged passion easiest of all.'

And, Aiah thinks, if they are dead, I did not kill them. I didn't ask for it to be done, I didn't *have* it done. And so, perhaps, it has nothing to do with me at all.

Colored light floods the car, and a distant scream: an advert tumbling down the canyon of the street, crying its wares with a siren voice.

'Though it is true that a man who is a servant of his passions is not free,' Constantine says, 'neither is a man in flight from those same passions. And, since the passions are an inevitable consequence of our own humanity, it is impossible to eliminate them so long as we wish to remain human. But Radritha was wrong: it isn't passions that make us weak, but rather uncontrollable passions. Harness the passions and reason together, and the person, the *real* person, becomes free . . . and capable of liberating others, which is the only defensible use of power.'

But, Aiah thinks, if these deaths have nothing to do with me, why don't I simply ask Constantine what happened?

Because, she concludes, I am afraid of the answer.

Constantine's flow of words comes to a halt. He looks at Aiah appraisingly. 'I see my discourse has failed in its intended purpose,' he says. 'You remain buried in your own thoughts.'

'Yes.' She is unable, for some reason, to turn her face to him, to achieve any level of personal contact. She stares instead at the seat opposite her. Tries to achieve detachment.

'Perhaps my discourse on power was too abstract for the purpose,' he says. 'I wanted to point out that my ultimate goals are not abstract, but concrete: the New City, power, and liberty. And not for me alone, but for all. And –' he licks his lips, 'sacrifices occur. In a world as entrenched as ours, thousands of years without substantial change, revolution does not happen easily, or neatly, or without consequence. From a strictly practical view, a little ruthlessness now may save much blood later.'

Constantine pauses, then impatiently dismisses his own argument with a contemptuous wave of his hand. Without warning, moving with absolute suddenness and intensity, he snatches Aiah's wrist, the same grasp used when giving her instruction; but now a different power than plasm flows from him, lights the furious energy in his eyes – *passion*, she realizes, startled, but of a different order from what she's accustomed to. A world-eating passion, fierce and hungry and able, without constraint or compromise. No School of Radritha, she knows, could possibly suppress *this*.

'Listen, Miss Aiah,' he says, and she recognizes the powerful whisper again, the deep voice that resonates in her bones, 'if the New City comes into being, then any sacrifice – *any* – will have been justified. Because I see no hope otherwise, anywhere, in our prison of a world.' The hand clamped on her arm is more powerful than a vise; Aiah knows better than to try to break free. Electricity flares through her nerves, as if in resonance with the fury that seems to blaze in his mind.

'And if the New City fails,' he continues, 'then Sorya's

old disciples of Torgenil are right, and we are Damned, and in Hell. In which case –' And the power leaves him, the fierce eyes grow dim, his big hand now without strength; Aiah retrieves her arm, straightens her sleeve. 'In which case,' he repeats, even the voice now without power, 'then nothing matters, nothing. Death least of all.'

Aiah looks into the shrouded eyes that gaze into the bleakness of a hopeless, caged world, and she suppresses again the overwhelming urge to comfort him. Ridiculous, she thinks, that he would need her comfort.

The car glides silently beneath the plasm-streaked sky. Aiah thinks of power coursing beneath the streets like arterial blood, cities lying on the crust of the earth like granite-shouldered parasites, human lives flaring like matches in the dark canyons – a little heat, a brief light, extinction.

'What can I do to help?' she says. A deep ancestral voice wails in her head, *he's your* passu! She needn't give him comfort, only take his money.

Constantine lifts an eyebrow. 'I don't suppose you can breathe underwater?'

She stares at him. 'Are you joking?'

'Not at all. Do you know the apparatus?'

'I've never used it.'

'Can you take two days off this next week? We can get you instruction in the meantime.'

Aiah opens her mouth, closes it. 'I suppose I could take two vacation days,' she says.

She can't believe she's saying yes to this. Constantine had arranged to retrieve her money any time it suited him, and now she is doing him favors.

It's for the New City, she thinks. It's for the dream. Because even a Barkazil girl from Old Shorings needs something to believe in.

14

For a change Constantine is trying not to look like himself. Traveling on passports from Gunalaht that Constantine had somehow materialized, he and Aiah fly in an aerocar to the Metropolis of Barchab, on the shore of the Sea of Caraqui. Constantine alleges himself to be one Dr Chandros, dressed in a simple gray traveling suit and conservative lace, with his famous braid pinned up and a long reddish wig floating off his shoulders. Aiah is Miss Quelger, his assistant. She can't help but think that Constantine with a red wig is even more conspicuous than Constantine without.

Nobody ever looks at the passports anyway.

The aerocar lands with wailing turbines on the rooftop pad of the ziggurat-shaped Hotel Volcano, and as Aiah, head still swimming from the descent, walks along the roof toward the hotel entrance, she stares in surprise at the blue volcanic peaks that overwhelm the western horizon, their cragged snowy crests unmarked by the gray city that advances like a tide halfway up their steep flanks, then comes to a halt. She's never seen a piece of ground that wasn't built on before, not even at a distance.

'They're active, of course,' Constantine says. 'Forty years ago Chukmarkh, that southern peak, blew and killed fifty thousand people.'

'Is that why they don't build on the tops?' It seems a shame to waste that much potential plasm.

'Too dangerous.'

'I'm surprised people don't move up there anyway.'

People are like a flood, she knows, pouring across every empty, available space unless forcibly walled away.

'I'm sure there are a few,' Constantine says. 'But it requires too much infrastructure to support a population for long at that altitude, in those temperature extremes.'

Elevators and a small army of assistants speed them to their suite, all silver and black and mirrors. Sorya waits in the suite in a bright green dress, a vibrant chromatic contrast to the background. Aiah hadn't expected her here.

Sorya seems all in motion, her bright gauzy scarf and blonde-streaked hair floating, the linked gold foci on her belt chiming lightly as she approaches Constantine, then wraps her arms around his neck and kisses him firmly.

Momo loves Bobo again, Aiah thinks, and feels an unaccustomed surge of annoyance.

'Geymard said yes!' Sorya says. Her grin is triumphant. 'You'll still have to talk to him, though.'

Calculations dance in precise sequence across Constantine's face. '*Very* good. Is he still here?'

'I can arrange a meet any time.'

'And Drumbeth?'

Sorya's brows come together. 'He can come across the border, but it will have to be arranged carefully.'

'I want to do my reconnaissance with Aiah first,' Constantine says. 'Then I'll have something to tell him, one way or another.'

Sorya's eyes shift briefly to Aiah, just long enough to nod a greeting, and then they refocus on Constantine. She takes his hand and draws him away. 'Let me tell you about Geymard,' she says. 'I had to use a certain line with him, and you don't want to shift from it.'

Aiah stands by the door for a moment, uncertain where to put her feet, and then one of Sorya's functionaries leads her to her room. It has a private terrace — the advantage of the hotel's ziggurat design — with fragrant orange trees sitting in tubs and a view of the volcanoes.

She misses the solid, reassuring presence of Martinus. But Martinus is simply too conspicuous, a pointer that leads only to Constantine, and Martinus was left behind in Jaspeer.

Aiah dines alone on her terrace next shift, served elegantly on bone porcelain set on a white-clothed table wheeled in by functionaries. The elegant gold leafwork on the porcelain reflects the colors of overhead plasm displays. *Lords of the New City* is as heavily advertised here, Aiah notes, as in Jaspeer. Constantine and Sorya are eating with Geymard, an erect, crop-haired man who, despite civilian dress, looks as if he just marched out of the Timocracy of Garshab. Aiah picks fretfully at her meal and drinks a half-bottle of wine. Orange-scented wind teases her hair. She leaves the table and leans on the bright aluminum terrace rail and looks at the gleaming peaks of the volcanoes, the rooftops of surrounding buildings. A distant airship gleams silver in shieldlight. One of the nearby roofs has a blue plastic foam running track set on its perimeter, and she watches a man in a blue-and-white jumpsuit dutifully, joylessly, circle the track. He doesn't look at the volcanoes once.

Something crosses the sky above the volcanoes and Aiah's heart leaps as she realizes that it's an avian, a winged humanoid. It soars, a winged black silhouette against the Shield, and then folds its wings and stoops like a falcon, diving to someplace unknown. Aiah watches for a while, but it doesn't return.

Aiah returns to her room, brushes her hand down the blue satin bedspread, looks at herself in the diamond-shaped mirrors planted in the walls. She looks ready for an off-shift out. Pity she doesn't know anyplace to go, and she doesn't even know why she's here. Her room has a connecting door with Constantine's and she can hear voices murmur in the other room. They have a terrace as well, but they're dining in Constantine's room to make it harder on eavesdroppers.

Aiah wonders if she's one of the eavesdroppers in question. Alcohol spins in her head.

She puts her fingers on the handle.

There is a dangerous taste on her tongue. Why not? she decides, and presses the handle down gently. She eases the door open until she can see a sliver of the room's silver-and-black decor. Geymard, Sorya and Constantine are seated at a table less than five paces away. Aiah presses her head to the tiny gap.

'The aerodrome's not important,' Geymard says. Aiah can see the back of his head, one ear, a bit of cheekbone. He has a drawling accent that Aiah can't quite place. 'There won't be any reinforcements landing there – all the important units are near the Metropolitan's palace anyway.'

'The aerodrome is important,' Constantine says calmly, 'because we wish to prevent people *leaving*.' Aiah can see him in profile. His face and body mask Sorya, who is behind him.

'Also,' Constantine adds, 'it is vital to be seen to control forms of transportation.'

'It's a diversion of force better used elsewhere.'

'You don't need that much force to control an aerodrome,' Constantine says. 'Just park some vehicles on the runways. A few snipers in nearby buildings can keep the 'drome's personnel from moving them.'

He leans back and Aiah's heart lurches as he unscreens Sorya, who seems to be staring straight at Aiah. But Sorya's expression is languid, her hands are distractedly caressing her wineglass, and there's no sign she's seen Aiah at all.

Not yet, anyway. Very quietly, very slowly, Aiah closes the door, and steps back.

Nothing happens, of course. As if someone would come crashing in with a pistol.

Aiah kicks off her shoes, polarizes the windows to a

perfect obsidian black reflection, and builds a nest of pillows on the bed. She lies down and presses the remote control panel that gives her video. The oval screen blinks on, a drama about a singer who was trying to fight her way to the top while battling the Operation's attempts to control her career.

Absurd. As if they wouldn't just slice up her face with a razor to make an example of her. Plenty more singers where *she* came from.

Aerodrome. The word forms itself on Aiah's tongue.

Constantine's target would seem to be an entire Metropolis. Why else seize an aerodrome? And not for itself, but to keep people from escaping.

Cheloki again? Could he be trying to seize his old home by force?

But that didn't quite make sense. Cheloki was on the other side of the world: why conspire here? Why give Aiah a day's training in underwater breathing apparatus and take her to another metropolis under a false name?

This, she decides, is going to require some reflection.

Aiah rises from the bed and fetches her glass and the bottle from her table.

Maybe the rest of the wine will help her think.

The video is babbling and Aiah doesn't hear the knock at first. When the knock comes again she sits up too quickly and the wine she's drunk takes a sudden spiral curve along the inside rim of her skull. She runs fingers through her hair, takes a deep breath to clear her head, says, 'Come in.'

It's Constantine, still dressed formally. Perhaps in honor of his guest his jacket is of a military cut, though he carries no rank or insignia. 'I'm sorry to have left you alone for so long,' he says. 'Had I given it any thought, I would have had one of the guards take you to see the sights.' He looks at the empty bottle of wine, the smudged glass, and a glint of amusement shines in his glance. 'Should there be any ill effects, a little plasm on awakening and you'll feel good as new.'

'I wouldn't know.'

Aiah reaches for the video control, slaps it off. 'I didn't realize Sorya would be here,' she says.

'We came by separate paths. Safer that way. And I didn't want you at dinner, because that way Geymard would have been able to identify *you*.'

She blinks at him. 'To whom?'

'It hardly matters to whom, but you would be a black-mail target for the rest of your life.'

Aiah doesn't in any case believe they'd have wanted her listening to their talk of aerodromes and the Metropolitan's palace and other targets, but she's willing to give credit to Constantine for an inventive and reasonably gracious apology. She sits down on the bed, arranges her skirt, looks up.

'Metropolitan,' she says, 'why am I here?'

'I have come on purpose to tell you. May I sit?'

She nods like Meldurnë playing a gracious hostess in a chromoplay. He plucks at the knees of his tight pipestem trousers and sits on the wine-colored satin spread. She can scent his hair oil over the perfume of the lavender water someone's sprinkled on the sheets.

'Tomorrow I'd like you to join me on a trip across the border into Caraqui.'

All she knows about Caraqui is the famous Aerial Palace. 'And we're going to dive there?' she asks.

'I would like to show you some plasm connections that are similar to ones I'll need to . . .' He shrugs coyness away. 'To destroy or disable. Disable, for preference. They're underwater cables, all alike, more or less. In the actual target – not Caraqui, you understand – they lead to a combat platform that we'd like to deprive of sustenance. At the core are bundles of steel cable – 164 of them, to be precise – and these are armored with linked ceramic plates. And then they're wrapped in multiple layers of plastic sheathing, and then protected on the outside with a linked bronze collection web.'

Aiah finds herself laughing. 'And you want me to do *what* with this?'

'Offer any suggestions that occur to you.'

Aiah laughs again, falls back against her nest of pillows. Constantine continues in perfect seriousness.

'The traditional method of dealing with these cables is to pack a garland of plastic explosive around them and set it off, but that may not be possible, and it doesn't always work anyway. And there are over forty of these cables on the actual target, multiple redundancy, and even more conventional plasm conduits above the water on bridges.'

Aiah shakes with laughter. 'Why are we bothering?'

'Because the other option,' Constantine says, 'is a surprise attack against the combat platform with everything we've got. And that would kill hundreds, maybe thousands of people who I would just as soon not send to the Shield.'

Aiah's laughter dies away into a long moment of cold silence. She sits up, shakes her head. Not a laughing matter, she thinks, after all. 'All right, Metropolitan,' she says. 'I'll do what I can.'

'Thank you, Miss Aiah.' Constantine takes her hand, leans over her, kisses her lips. She looks at him, wine burning in her cheeks. He stands.

'I'll see you tomorrow,' he says. 'Breakfast on the terrace?'

'Certainly.'

He glides to the door and presses the handle down. 'Have you ever been on a powerboat?' he asks.

'I've never been on any kind of boat.'

'I think you will enjoy it. Sleep well.'

'Thank you, Metropolitan.'

Constantine closes the door silently behind him.

Through the wall Aiah hears Constantine's deep voice, Sorya's trilling laugh, then silence.

She closes her eyes and thinks of floating out with Constantine on a long, slim powerboat, soaring across an endless quicksilver sea, a fantastic body of open water smooth and reflective as a mirror, heading toward a blue horizon such as does not exist anywhere in the world.

The halogen lights of Constantine's speedboat carve a bright tunnel in the darkness beneath the city of Caraqui. Marine engines echo loud in the hollow concrete cavern. Aiah can taste salt in the wind.

The Metropolis of Caraqui forms a skin across the sea like a giant lily pad spread across a pond. Huge pontoons of concrete, linked by hawsers thicker than tree trunks, are spaced across the open water, with buildings atop them. Bridges carry most transportation and utility connections, and the larger bridges have people living on them, urban accretions so much larger than the bridges themselves that it's sometimes difficult to detect the bridge's original purpose. Public transport travels high above the water, and sometimes far below.

There are wide, aquatic thoroughfares here; most commerce moves by water. But the majority of the watery paths are narrow and dark, crowded and overshadowed by the vast slablike sides of the pontoons, the overhanging buildings constructed above, and the overgrown bridges and causeways. Trash bobs listlessly in the dark water. Clusters of barnacles stretch down from the pontoons' waterline, and rusting iron ladders lead upwards at intervals, presumably for the salvation of anyone unlucky enough to tumble into the unwholesome waters.

Coming across the border from Barchab offers no problem. There are hundreds of these watery thoroughfares, and it's impossible to police them all.

Brightness appears ahead, grows larger. The boat shoots

out onto a wide watery canal, turns left. The bodyguards' boat, disciplined, follows a mere half-second behind. The water is a bright green carpet of algae broken only by floating trash. Scabrous-looking waterfowl paddle in the green water. The boulevards on either side are lined with trees. Tall glass-walled apartment buildings and towered temples gaze down at the verdant water. A wealthy district, clear enough, with only a few people in the streets and no commercial traffic on the water except for a few small barges.

'The Martyrs' Canal,' Constantine says. 'The Avians used to tie Delavites together and throw them in.'

Aiah stands in the boat with her face above the windshield, enjoying the flood of wind on her face. She looks for the famous Aerial Palace but can't find it. She looks to her left and sees Constantine standing next to her, the collar of his blue jacket raised against the wind, his black profile cutting the air, hands on the wheel controlling the boat with a light, effortless touch despite the intensity of his expression, as if he were involved wholly with the boat, the water, the very concept of motion, arrowing from one place to another, every second a journey, a transit, from one state to another. The School of Radritha, she suspects, for all that Constantine seems to scorn it now, has nevertheless left its mark, has enabled Constantine to approach everything he does with that same level of intensity, of involvement.

Or maybe it's just being hooked into plasm long enough. Who knows?

Kherzaki's scowling face leaps into existence in the sky above. Another ad for *Lords of the New City*.

Constantine throttles down, his eyes scanning the faded numbers painted on the vast pontoons, the rust-pitted signs hanging beneath the low bridges. He finds what he's looking for, turns right into a cool narrow cavern, the local equivalent of a dark alley. A flock of swallows explodes from nests constructed amid arching girders and streams toward the light. Constantine doesn't increase speed much; his eyes still scan the walls in the vivid illumination of his halogen lights, looking for landmarks. The Shield is a thin bright strip overhead, like a distant fluorescent tube. Engine noise booms off the concrete walls.

After a few moments Constantine throttles down. There's no light visible overhead: the pontoons above have been completely built over, turned into components of a raft. Constantine turns on underwater spotlights. The boat planes on briefly, slows, drifts toward one of the slablike pontoons. The water below is a milky soup in the halogen light. Constantine springs to the foredeck, reaches for a coil of rope, ties it to a rung of one of the ladders placed at intervals along the pontoon. The bodyguards' boat, still under power, comes up slowly and lashes itself alongside.

'Put the sled in the water,' Constantine tells the guards. He turns to Aiah. 'We may as well get ready.'

The bodyguards manhandle the big underwater sled off the back of their boat and into the water. It lands with a slap, scattering spray. Aiah pulls off her sweater and baggy wool pants.

'We've timed this for slack tide,' Constantine says. 'The tide can cause swells, currents, tidal waves rolling up between the pontoons. Sometimes people surf the waves on boards.'

'I saw that on video once,' Aiah says. On the *Oddities of the World* program she used to enjoy when she was little.

Tides are evidence of a universe outside the Shield – Aiah was taught that in school. Because once the sky was supposed to have been dark, except there was something in it called a Sun, and another thing called the Moon, and they both fluoresced or something to make the sky light up, like plasm adverts broadcasting from outside the atmosphere, and their gravity was responsible for the tides

– so they weren't plasm, anyway, but matter, because plasm didn't have gravity. Aiah had always pictured them as big neon tubes twisted into circles.

And now the Shield stands in the way of anyone seeing them, but the Sun and Moon are presumed still to be out there, causing tides. Because so far as anyone knew, gravity was the only force that could get through the Shield.

Aiah supposed she could believe in the existence of a Sun and Moon that predated the Shield and were still in existence somewhere, but some other traditional details of the Premetropolitan world were harder to credit. It was said, for example, that different parts of the world somehow existed in different times. Aiah couldn't understand that part at all, how you could move into the future or past simply by going from one part of the globe to another. And if you could travel from the present to the past simply by moving, for example, from Jaspeer to Caraqui, then could you alter your present by going back in time somewhere else and changing things? The whole business was, somehow, counterintuitive.

The damp chill makes gooseflesh prickle beneath Aiah's bathing costume. Shivering, she begins to drag on the awkward diving suit. The foam plastic clings to her skin like wet towels, making every move a struggle. Despite the chill air she can feel sweat breaking out on her forehead. By the time she zips the jacket up to her chin, she feels like an object securely swathed for mailing.

'Greetings to the glorious and immortal Metropolitan Constantine.'

Aiah's nape hairs crawl as the eerie disembodied voice rises from behind the boat's counter. The hard first consonant of Constantine's name is pronounced as an inhaled click.

Constantine walks to the stern counter and peers over. His burly upper body is bare, with his diving suit jacket dangling above his waist, but still he carries himself with a strangely formal dignity.

'Felicitations, Prince Aranax,' he says. 'Your illumination expresses a magnificent sense of condescension in deigning to speak to me without an intermediary.'

There is a splash from behind the boat. The voice, Aiah concludes, can't be anything human. 'It is best to undertake certain tasks in person,' the voice says, 'in order that certain matters may be communicated in such a manner as to felicitate perfect understanding. We must speak, thus-and-so, concerning this-and-that, and without misapprehension.'

'Your illumination's wisdom surpasses that of the immortals,' Constantine says gravely. 'Surely your brilliance and enlightenment will not be exceeded in ten thousand decades.'

'My pitiful understanding is but a reflection of the glory and the wisdom of Constantine,' the voice says. 'The radiance of your genius illuminates the world as an incandescent ball irradiates the darkness beneath the water, attracting to its magnificent light such unworthy beings as myself.'

'The courtesy that your illumination displays in affording me such a description is exceeded only by your greatness.' Constantine straightens, looks at Aiah. 'Please allow me to introduce to your illumination my colleague, Miss Aiah, whose consummate knowledge shall guide us to our inevitable success.'

Aiah walks dry-mouthed to the stern of the boat. She feels huge as an airship in her thick porous suit, and as clumsy.

And Constantine of course had not prepared her for this. Another of his little surprises.

The dolphin sits in a pool of halogen light, regarding her with small dark pebble eyes sunk deep beneath a bulging forehead. His skin is a pinkish albino white, with scars and blotches and a few open running sores. He seems to be strongly hunchbacked. The nose has been shifted back to the top of the head. His lower jaw is prognathous, hard and beaklike, fixed in a cold, unkindly grin.

Once, she knows, the dolphins were the enemies of humanity, rulers of the world's seas and the belligerents in a ferocious war for domination of the world. Since their defeat the dolphins have been confined to a diminishing role in the world's affairs, and humanity has encroached on their world without hindrance.

The closest Aiah's ever come to a dolphin is watching the Dolphins march in the Senko's Day parade.

She glances at Constantine for support, then licks her lips. 'I am,' she ventures, 'awed by your presence, your illumination. Forgive my speechlessness at, ah, this encounter with your magnificence.'

The dolphin flutters a hand, long spatulate fingers stirring the water. 'The companions of Constantine are beacons of wisdom in a sea of darkness and ignorance.'

Fortunately Constantine takes over the conversation from this point. The ludicrous flattery seems even more absurd in this space, from two exiles hiding from the light in a watery cellar.

Eventually the conversation floats on puffs of extravagant compliments to its termination, and Prince Aranax kicks his broad feet up high and submerges. Constantine and Aiah resume their preparations for their dive. Aiah puts on her buoyancy harness, which contains both pockets for lead weights and inflatable compartments to adjust her depth. Constantine helps her with the flat air tank curved to fit comfortably on her back. In her foam-plastic swaddling, Aiah can hear her heart pounding, the rasp of her panting breath. Just wrestling with all the unaccustomed gear is exhausting. By the time she pumps up her buoyancy, dons her fins and mask, and rolls off the boat into the water, she's relieved simply to be getting underway.

The water tastes more strongly of salt than she expected – she'd done her two hours' training in a freshwater tank. Her suit lets in an insulating layer of seawater, and it seems oily on her skin. She lets the buoyancy harness support her, tries to calm her heart, her breath. Panic doesn't seem very far away.

Constantine follows her into the water, then swims to the sled and climbs aboard. He moves with the same powerful confidence he displays on land, and Aiah feels a stab of envy at his ability to be at home anywhere. Electric motors whine as he tests each propeller. Cavitation bubbles stream in halogen light. Then Constantine starts dumping ballast, air first hissing, then bubbling, from the valves. The raft settles in the water. Aiah's heart gives a leap as something white flashes beneath her feet. The dolphin.

Constantine looks at her. 'Climb on board,' he says, 'if you're ready.'

Aiah concludes she's as ready as she's ever going to be. She kicks up alongside the sled, then wriggles up next to Constantine on the webbing stretched between the two motors. As long as she's on the sled, she can use the raft's air supply. Compressed air hisses as she tests one of the sled's regulators, then puts it in her mouth. Salt sprays across her palate as she takes her first breath.

'Dump the air from your harness,' Constantine says. 'We'll use the sled to provide buoyancy.'

Aiah nods and reaches with clumsy gloved fingers for the pull-valve that will release air from her harness pockets. Constantine dons his mask and regulator, clears his ears, then begins again to submerge the sled. Escaping air sounds loud in the dark watery hollow.

The dolphin surfaces, breath snorting from his nostrils, and looks at the humans with his little eyes for a brief second before submerging once more.

The bubbling water splashes up past Aiah's face.

Claustrophobia claws at her heart. She pinches her nostrils and tries to clear her ears.

Below the surface, the world is an eerie opalescent green. The barnacle-covered hulls of the pontoons stretch down into utter darkness below. Aranax flies in and out of the light, his pale hunched body soaring in its element. He's got a fin on his back that Aiah hadn't noticed before, and he's wearing a sleek harness, with streamlined pockets that won't ruin his hydrodynamics.

The sled sinks slowly. The nose pitches down and the headlights carve an empty tunnel in the gloom. A greenish radium glow illuminates the control panel. Aiah has nothing to do but watch and clear her ears. Her right ear seems resistant, pain mounting as the sled drops, but Aiah clamps down with her teeth on her mouthpiece and swallows, and there's a strange sound, like air squeaking from a child's balloon, as air is forced to her middle ear.

As Constantine starts the sled's motors there is a teeth-clenching buzz that seems to transmit itself through Aiah by bone conduction. It grows darker as the sled moves out from beneath the area of illumination beneath the speedboats. Aranax flies past, his long, outcurved feet pumping together as they propel his hunched body through the water. Constantine steers after him.

There is a moment of claustrophobia, a pressure in the ears and in the mind, as the sled moves beneath the flat-bottomed bulk of one of Caraqui's huge pontoons. Over the whine of the sled's engines Aiah can hear a constant throb of marine engines. With the pontoon above to reflect the sound, the engines sound as if they're right overhead, a grinding pulsation over which Aiah can detect the whine of intakes, the high-pitched shriek of small boats, random metallic clangs that seem to resonate in the water like the distant bang of a gong. In the light Aiah can see hatches, gratings, vents, intakes, all coated with aquatic life that seems blue or gray until touched by the sled's lights, at which point they blaze with color, reds and yellows and brilliant striking greens.

Minutes pass, and Aiah finds herself relaxing, almost enjoying the strange environment. Pale fish swim in and out of the sled's headlights. Pontoons pass overhead, dark and ponderous. Aranax flies to the surface for air, then races down to resume his lead.

The water brightens ahead, shieldlight coming down from above, and the sled slows. As it passes beneath a final pontoon Constantine lets air hiss into the ballast tanks and the sled begins to drift upward. Aiah looks up, trying to see above the protruding rim of her mask. The water is soupy here, green with an algae that seems to coat Aiah's tongue with a taste of copper.

A structure looms above them, a vast shadow, and then the sled rises beneath it. Air bubbles rise as Constantine adjusts buoyancy. The structure slowly comes into focus, a long round flexible connection, like a plastic water main or a huge bundle of communications cable, all sheathed with webbing that winks bright yellow in the light of the Shield.

Aiah's nerves begin to hum.

Constantine stabilizes the sled beneath the structure, pulls off one of his gloves, and reaches out to touch a copper t-grip built onto the sled's console. There are plasm batteries in the structure of the sled, insulated from the sea. His other hand touches Aiah's wrist at the juncture of glove and insulating jacket. Constantine's thoughts intrude delicately on her own.

– You see my problem.

– Yes.

She considers for a moment.

– I'm leaving the sled. I'll have to get closer.

Aiah shifts to her own regulator, then pulls herself forward off the sled, kicks out, and promptly realizes that she's sinking. She flails for the inlet button while her feet thrash in an effort to keep her level, then lets air into her harness and stabilizes her buoyancy. Aranax watches her with his fixed grin. Aiah kicks out with her fins and examines the connection close up, seeing it wrapped in the honey-colored bronze collection web, made flexible and untarnishable by some hermetic process and probably burnished daily by a group of apprentice mages.

Plasm moves through there, huge amounts, heading to Constantine's 'command platform'. And there are supposed to be so many other connections that it amounts to a perfectly ridiculous amount of redundancy.

Aiah's supposed to figure out how to sabotage all this. Wonderful.

Aiah examines the cable from the sides, then kicks up above it. It doesn't look any different. Aranax darts away, diving beneath the nearest pontoon. She kicks along it for a while, but there's really nothing to see — even aquatic life seems to have been kept off the cable. She returns to the sled. Constantine's hand touches her wrist.

— Take me to look at the connections.

Without comment Constantine starts the motors, turns the sled, and moves back in the direction from which they'd come.

— Where did Aranax go? Aiah asks.

— Probably needed to breathe.

— Why didn't he go straight to the surface, then?

— This is a restricted area. He could be shot.

Aiah's startled laugh bubbles out through her regulator. Constantine is full of surprises today.

A pontoon looms up ahead. The cable is attached to it through a complex support mechanism, heavy stainless metal struts that help to support the cable's weight, but they seem redundant. Aiah doubts that it would really matter much if the struts were damaged. And she can't see where the cable goes after it enters the pontoon. She leaves the sled and circles the cable again, but nothing worthwhile comes to mind.

Aranax shoots up from the darkness and does an effortless somersault over the cable. When he slows to a hover Aiah can see that he's eating a fish, his rows of bright triangular teeth worrying at it. Blood blossoms like a red flower from his beak. The fish stares toward the surface with dead eyes.

Aiah reminds herself that she's an alien here.

She returns to the sled, touches Constantine's wrist.

— I don't know, she admits. You could try blowing the connection, but . . .

— We'll give it some more thought. Do you need to see anything more?

— No.

Then, after a pause, she adds, Sorry.

Constantine gives an exaggerated shrug of his big shoulders.

— It seemed worth a try.

The sled follows Aranax back to the welcome pool of light that surrounds Constantine's boats. A thousand little fish circle like moths in the glow. Constantine adjusts the sled's buoyancy to hover beneath the boats for a five-minute decompression stop — Aiah pictures bubbles of poisonous nitrogen frothing in her blood, being nudged reluctantly toward her lungs by each throb of her heart — and then, the safety stop over, the sled rises to the surface in a long hiss of air and a roil of oily water.

Constantine's guards efficiently pluck Aiah from the water by main strength and strip her of her harness and fins. She pulls off her hood, shakes out her hair, gropes for a towel. Suddenly she's quaking with cold. A hot bath is the most desirable thing in the world.

The guards are already attending to Constantine. Aiah yanks off her suit and draws sweater and baggy pants on over her bathing costume. Constantine and the guards wrestle with the sled, drag it aboard the guards' boat and lash it down. Aranax floats whitely in the glowing water, and then suddenly there are more dolphins here, a dozen or so breaking water at almost the same instant, hovering silently in the water, watching Constantine with their pebble eyes. The bodyguards seem nervous. Aiah shivers and looks down at the expanding puddle of water beneath her feet.

Constantine has a long conversation with Aranax then, but Aiah can't hear it because Constantine uses the plasm batteries on the guards' boat and converses mind-to-mind. *Thus-and-so*, Aiah thinks, *concerning this-and-that, and without misapprehension.*

'Your illumination,' Constantine finally says aloud, 'your wisdom is destined to guide my fumbling and uninformed efforts toward success,' and after another exchange of compliments, the conversation is over. The dolphins kick their feet high and vanish.

'That went well, I think,' Constantine says as he returns to the boat's controls.

'Is Aranax really a prince?' Aiah asks. The title has a quaint, musty ring to it, like something out of mythology, from the time of Karlo or Vida the Compassionate.

Constantine grins at her as he starts the speedboat's engines. 'I've never met a dolphin who wasn't a prince. Or a king, or queen, or pasha. They're generous with titles, dolphins. But Aranax is an influential voice among them, insofar as anyone is. And he's honest, as dolphins go.'

'And what is he getting out of this?'

Aiah knows Constantine's look, the sly, confiding pleasure at the sharing of secrets. 'Would it surprise you to know that dolphins have bank accounts?'

'I suppose not, now that I think about it. How do you know him?'

'Ah.' Constantine's eyes gleam in reflected light. 'I've

been here before. I was studying the dolphins' social organization. What they have is too loose to be called a "government", exactly, not with all royalty and no commoners. I thought it might have something to teach us.'

'And does it?'

'Not unless we all become subaquatic, no. But it's an interesting ideal.'

Constantine jumps forward, unties the boat from its mooring, then returns to the cockpit. He maneuvers his boat clear of the other boat, turns, then pushes the throttles forward and begins the return journey. Aiah settles into the seat beside him, hunches protectively behind the windshield to keep the chill from her bones.

'I'm sorry I can't really help,' she says.

'That's all right. You have a fresh perspective which has been useful elsewhere – it was worthwhile to try it here.' He gives her a smiling look. 'Besides, you needed a vacation.'

This is a vacation? she thinks. Perhaps for Constantine it is. But she says, 'Thank you.'

'All I can think of,' she says, 'is to try for the control stations, or maybe the switches. They've got to use switches when they choose which of the cables their plasm is to move along. The switches are electric, and if you can cut the power . . . well, it'll be inconvenient for them.'

Constantine nods, smiles. The look is the sly one again, as if he were in the secret process of having knowledge confirmed.

'Yes,' he says. 'I'll look into it.'

Hair matted, shivering with cold, Aiah returns with Constantine's party to the Volcano, Constantine donning his red wig for his brief public moment in the elevator. Sorya awaits them in the suite. She is dressed exquisitely in delicate gold jewelry and blazing red silk, and the silk matches the fiery anger that greets Constantine the second he arrives.

'Parq is coming here for dinner?' she demands. 'You arranged this?'

Constantine hands the red wig to one of his entourage. 'Indeed,' he says.

'I told you not to trust him!'

'I don't,' Constantine says calmly. 'I'm using him.'

Sorya's long-nailed hands slice the air like knives. 'He's betrayed every leader, every associate . . .'

Constantine nods to acknowledge the truth of this statement. 'And therefore,' he says, 'is perfectly predictable.'

Sorya rages on. The bodyguards tactfully find other parts of the suite that require defense from intruders. Aiah concludes that she had best leave Bobo and Momo to their own devices, and sidles around the storm center toward her room.

She draws herself a bath and soaks for a long time in the hot water, tries to let the scent and texture of bath oil caress her nerves . . . but it's hopeless with angry voices rattling the door in its frame. Aiah can't make out the actual words, but perhaps it doesn't matter, very possibly they're not intended to mean anything anyway, only convey a message of fury. Aiah remembers times in her girlhood where the day's routine was suddenly interrupted by the screams of angry neighbors, their fury clearly audible through thin public-housing walls – or if not a fight, then the unmistakable sounds of coitus, or sometimes one followed inexplicably by the other. Aiah recalls the sensation of embarrassment, not for herself surely, but for those neighbors, people she saw every day, people she greeted in the hallways, who were so carelessly violating their own intimacy, proclaiming their secrets to the world.

Bobo and Momo. Constantine and Sorya. Aiah realizes that she doesn't really know anything about Sorya, only that she's Carveli and rich. Aiah doesn't know how long Sorya and Constantine have been together, or whether they fight like this all the time, or only when they're planning a war. Aiah gives a little laugh at the thought, and washes her neck.

Doors slam, and then there's silence. Aiah washes her hair, sliding down the long porcelain tub into the hot water, submerging her whole body beneath the surface except for the islets of her kneecaps . . . another memory of childhood, looking up at a cracked bathroom ceiling through a blurry layer of water. Only here the ceiling is tiled, little blue-and-white mosaic chips in a swirling abstract pattern.

The hotel furnishes wonderfully plush terry bathrobes with the name of the hotel beautifully embroidered on the front. Aiah wraps herself in one and spends some careful moments unratting her hair. The rest of the suite seems to have been shocked into silence.

Aiah looks at herself in the mirror and wonders if the new memories are somehow visible in her eyes, if strangers can look at her and sense the difference brought by the taste of the sea on her tongue, the stare of the dolphin with its fixed grin, the brilliant colors of the sea-life in the headlights, Constantine's profile cutting air as he stood behind the boat's controls.

There is a discreet knock on her door. She answers, finds Constantine half-dressed for his appointment, black braided pipestem trousers with loops over the insteps of his silk socks, braces, immaculate snowy shirt with the lace not yet buttoned into place. The abashed smile on his face is denied by the mocking amusement dancing in his eyes.

'I suppose you heard,' he says.

'I did my best not to.'

'Sorya's gone.'

'Will she be back?'

He shrugs. 'That will be up to her, I suppose.' Aiah steps back from the door and lets Constantine drift into the room, silk socks purring against the thick carpet.

'There's no manual for what we're doing,' Constantine

says. 'I may never know whether my dealings with Parq make sense, but I know that without Sorya our cause is diminished.'

She looks at him. 'It's Caraqui, isn't it? You're going to overthrow their government. And you need the dolphins for that.'

The amusement vanishes at once from Constantine's eyes, and suddenly Aiah feels herself the focus of his intensity, the full power that radiates from him, as if a tower beacon has just swept over her, then swept back, fixing her in its burning gaze. And what happens, she wonders, if he decides she's unworthy to possess this knowledge?

Thoughtful, his deep voice rumbles out. 'I suppose it's obvious enough.'

'You wouldn't go to all this bother with the dolphins and the trip underwater if this were just a theoretical exercise,' Aiah says. 'Those cables bring plasm to the Aerial Palace, don't they?'

He nods, that intent gaze still on her. Aiah realizes she's holding her breath. And then Constantine nods, and his look softens.

'Will you help me with these plans of mine?' he says. 'I don't think I could abide it if another so exceptional a woman walked out on me today.'

Aiah's mouth is dry. 'Of course I'll help,' she says.

They stand facing each other for a long moment, Aiah's skin prickling under the terry robe. On the mirrored walls there are diamond-shaped Aiahs, diamond-shaped Constantines. Then Constantine, in one of those swift movements so unlikely in such a large man, steps suddenly forward. Aiah barely has time to raise her arms before he has crossed the distance between them, and she has a brief moment of surprise at his size, the simple cold fact of his physical power, before the power is simply *there*, in her arms, and she has to deal with it. She enfolds him, presses herself to the broad expanse of lace on his chest, drives her lips up into his . . . She doesn't want him to think this is completely *his* idea.

The bedsheets are fine soft percale, lightly scented with lavender. Constantine makes love with the same intensity he displays in everything else. Being the focus of all this fierce concentration makes Aiah self-conscious at first – she doesn't want her skinny body the subject of those powerful, all-encompassing eyes – but finally she realizes that the only way to deal with such intensity is to match it. She opens her eyes, looks at him, wordlessly dares him to please her. He seems perfectly willing to oblige.

He refrains from using his physical strength; he meets her with careful delicacy, as if he's fearful she might shatter. She appreciates the consideration but in the end wants more, wants the power of his body against hers, and so she draws him down to her, to where she can feel his weight on her, where she can inhale his scent, taste it tingling on the back of her tongue . . . she is building a sensorium, she thinks, just as she does with plasm, invoking each sense, every possible square inch of flesh, every single impulse of pleasure.

She licks his skin, wanting the flavor of him, and he tastes as rich as the sea.

'I do not wish Parq to see you,' Constantine says. 'For all the reasons I mentioned yesterday. Geymard would not sell you, though he might let something slip to one who would; but Parq would sell you and me and the whole world if he could.' He gives a little smile.

Constantine stands before one of the diamond-shaped mirrors in Aiah's room, adjusting his jacket, his cuffs. One of his functionaries has just called to say that Parq is in the building. Aiah is sitting up in bed, blanket drawn to her chin against the room's machine-chilled air.

'If he's so treacherous,' Aiah says, 'why are *you* dealing with him?'

'Because he's high priest of the Dalavite sect — that's why he's corrupt, of course, they wouldn't give an honest man that job — and therefore, on that account, he controls the only independent broadcasting facilities in Caraqui.' He adjusts his chin-lace and looks at Aiah over his shoulder. 'The people of Caraqui will require *someone* to tell them they have a new government, will they not?'

He crosses the room to the bed, sits by Aiah's side. He touches Aiah's cheek gently, with the back of his hand, and then arranges one of her ringlets more to his liking. 'Would you like to go out later this shift?' he asks. 'We can slip you out once Parq and I are in conference. I can give you a driver and a checktube.'

Chromoplay fantasy flashes through Aiah's mind: a succession of clubs, stage shows, boutiques, jewelers, a limousine filled with wrapped packages, a compliant driver . . . all that was lacking, she realized, was a pug dog on a diamond-studded leash, and why not add one of those to the picture as well?

And Tella thought she was a kept woman *before*.

Aiah pushes her chin into the blanket and gives a little shake of the head. 'I'd rather wait here for you.'

'This meeting may go on for hours,' Constantine warns. 'And yesterday you spent all second shift confined to this room.'

'I'll wait. There's a nice view from the terrace.'

Constantine leans forward, brushes his lips against hers. 'Beautiful Miss Aiah,' he says, 'I hope I will make your wait worthwhile.'

'The flattery is appreciated,' she says.

'Flattery?' He seems surprised. 'Not at all.'

'I'm skinny. You can count my ribs.'

Constantine makes a dismissive sound. 'You have all the muscle you need where it most matters,' he says, and puts a finger to her forehead. 'And remember this — you are at your most beautiful when you take flight. Please don't forget that.'

Surprised, Aiah finds herself without a reply. She watches Constantine leave for his appointment, then wraps herself in the terry robe again and goes out on the terrace. Looks for the avian again, soaring against the sky, but doesn't find it.

In the next twenty-four hours, Aiah discovers some unanticipated functions of beds. Planning to overthrow governments, for one. There are more details to a coup than she had ever thought possible, and Constantine lists them all, from the best way to approach high-ranking officers to the subversion of communications through false messages.

'Caraqui has had hundreds of years of bad government,' he says, 'from the oligarchs who, after altering themselves to an avian form, built the Aerial Palace, to the Kerehorn family who overthrew them with the help of the Delavites and who have now run the place for three generations. Power is concentrated in so few hands now that, these hands lopped off, the body of the state will fall to the first who claims it.'

'And this claimant is you.'

'No,' Constantine says. 'Would it diminish me in your eyes were I to tell you it is not?'

Constantine lies on his back on Aiah's bed. She is half-sprawled across him, arms folded across his broad chest to provide a cushion for her chin.

Constantine explains, to Aiah's surprise, that he is not the prime mover of the conspiracy. 'It was Colonel Drumbeth who first approached me, through some intermediaries he was inclined to trust, members of his own family. Many people so approach me, with some half-brained scheme for violence or conquest or plunder, and I was inclined to put this one off as I had most of the others, but then *you* arrived, young Miss Aiah with your plasm and your demand for a million dalders.' There is a sly, knowing look in his eyes. 'I was inclined to regard you as an omen – and was right to do so, I believe.' He kisses her, suddenly, on the nose. She smiles.

'Who is Colonel Drumbeth?'

A smile twitches across Constantine's lips. 'An admirer of the New City Movement, or so his emissaries tell me. He wants my assistance to set his metropolis to rights. I look forward to meeting him.'

'You haven't?' Surprised again.

'Too dangerous. He is head of military counterintelligence, and cannot move freely. But –' he holds up a hand, 'if anyone in their army suspects a revolt, to whom will they report? Drumbeth. It is a convenience, to be sure.'

He tucks in his chin to look at her. 'We're waiting for him here. He will come when he can.'

Aiah smiles. Blood rises warm in her flesh. She digs her sharp chin into the broad muscles of Constantine's chest, making him wince. 'And what shall we do in the meantime?'

He reaches down with his big hands, clasps her shoulders, draws her up to press her mouth with his. 'I have some notions,' he says, 'if you do not.'

Drumbeth arrives late and alone. He's a short man, made taller by erect military posture and bushy gray hair. His face is carefully expressionless, his eyes slits. With Constantine's assent, Aiah silently watches through the connecting door as Drumbeth and Constantine drink tea, eat cold chicken and plan their strike.

Through Constantine, Aiah knows the army's junior officers will generally favor a coup, or at least not actively oppose it. They're eager to get rid of their corrupt superiors, and if they can give themselves promotions along the way, so much the better. If the generals can't get anyone to obey their orders, they're out of the picture whichever side they ultimately join. The navy is uncertain, but there's little they can do to oppose a coup anyway, with every waterway dominated by buildings that the army can occupy. The police force is large, but they're scattered across the metropolis and their weaponry is light. The Specials — the political police, feared throughout the metropolis for their all-encompassing powers of arrest, their efficient network of informers and the dire tortures they inflict on their victims — are loyal to the Kerehorns, but their numbers are relatively few and their weaponry is militarily negligible. The Specials will be most dangerous before the coup, in that they might detect its preparations, but once the revolt is under way can safely be ignored.

It's the Metropolitan Guard that will cause the most trouble. An oversized mercenary brigade recruited by the Kerehorns and officered by cadet members of the family, they are loyal to their paymasters and have first call on equipment and supplies. The Metropolitan Guard are a third as large as the army, their barracks are adjacent to military headquarters and within a short distance of the Aerial Palace and the main government buildings, their complement of mages is sizeable, and they and their Kerehorn masters have unlimited access to plasm.

The plotters' voices get loud when discussing the Guard. The mercenaries can't be subverted safely, and they're too centrally located to ignore. Any battles fought in the city are bound to cause heavy casualties. Constantine concludes a battle is inevitable, but Drumbeth keeps expressing the hope it can be avoided.

'If we kill enough Kerehorns,' Constantine says, 'perhaps. But we must keep the Guard confined to their compound whatever happens.'

Drumbeth looks uncertain.

'I tell you,' Constantine says, 'it will save trouble later.'

Drumbeth shakes his head, but says, 'Very well.'

Another disagreement arises over the dolphins. Constantine sees them as another resource, but Drumbeth doesn't want to arm them. Aiah can't make out how that argument is resolved.

'Remember,' Constantine reminds, 'tell your people to build roadblocks everywhere about the government center. The psychological fact of roadblocks is more important than their military value. It is a place where one spirit will confront another. *Our* people will be standing behind barricades. All they have to do is remain there. *Their* people will have to nerve themselves to attack people already in position, of unknown strength, wearing the same uniform as themselves, to overwhelm them, drive forward and displace them . . . with luck, they will lack the necessary will.'

Drumbeth nods. 'I worry,' he says, 'that I don't have your military experience. That none of us does, all coming from a nation that has fought no wars in five hundred years.'

'Our enemies suffer the same handicaps,' Constantine says. 'And we have Geymard and his brigade from the Timocracy.'

An unreadable expression crosses Drumbeth's face. 'Yes,' he says. 'So we do.'

The planning session takes only two hours; plans are that well advanced. Constantine shakes Drumbeth's hand, his huge grip engulfing the small man's frail-seeming fingers, and then the colonel leaves. Constantine breezes into Aiah's room.

'Pack,' he says. 'We should return to Jaspeer.'

The aerocar leaps from the Volcano's pad, vaulting over the countless populations below, the billions that cover the surface of the world. It's early in the third shift, Aiah thinks, and most of them are asleep. Aiah holds Constantine's hand and looks out past the clear plastic canopy, watches the world below, at this altitude all undifferentiated gray-brown concrete and brick and the occasional bright flash of reflective glass. A weather system moves beneath them, a dark line of somber cloud dancing with internal electric light, one flash after another that stretch for hundreds of radii.

Aiah turns to Constantine, sees him watching her, amusement in his eyes. 'Thank you for showing me the world,' she says, and kisses him. As the kiss continues, as she inhales the scent of Constantine, Aiah wonders if this is all mere fantasy, a bubble that will burst as soon as they return to the cold reality of Jaspeer.

The turbine pods rotate, and there is a shift in the sound of the engines, from the steady whine to a more earthy growl. Aiah looks out and sees an expanse of cloud that covers everything below like a pall of black velvet. The huge electric display has been left far behind, but lightning can still be seen below, a trembling neon glow. The aerocar drops through the cloud, its lights carving out a bright tunnel ahead like the lights of Constantine's speedboat in the darkness beneath Caraqui; and then suddenly they are through the cloud and Jaspeer is below them. Beneath the black cloud the stormlights glow, bright radial patterns that make the city look like interlocking spider webs, every jewel of light a brilliant drop of dew.

The landing pad is fresh with the scent of recent rain. Sodium stormlights reflect in pools of standing water. Martinus welcomes them, bulking huge beside the big car. The usual fruit and wine wait inside. Aiah powers the window down so she can scent the air. It's deep in third shift and the streets are almost deserted. Her heart grudges the sight of Loeno Towers rising on the horizon.

'I haven't seen where you live,' Constantine says, as if he's read her thoughts. 'May I come up?'

'Of course.' Here in the car with Martinus and the other bodyguard, Aiah's been trying to behave and hasn't given into the impulse to touch Constantine, or even to rest her head on the big shoulder. Her apartment should be the perfect place to say farewell.

And then Constantine, catching Martinus's look in the mirror, adds, 'We won't be seen at this hour. I won't be gone for long.'

The Elton smoothly glides up to Aiah's tower, and then a guard leaps to open the rear door. Constantine kindly carries her small bag. No one sees Aiah and Constantine on their walk past the potted chrysanthemums, through the locked lobby doors – the doorman is asleep in his office, waiting for the sound of a bell. In the elevator, reflected by the mirrored walls, they are free to embrace in a moment of flight as the mirrored box soars upward in the tall tower.

'I have a gift for you,' Constantine says, presenting a flat box.

It's an ivory necklace, with matching earrings. The fabulously rare substance is smoothed into gracefully rounded knucklebone shapes, with a central pendant carved into the Trigram. Aiah is too awed to do much other than stammer thanks. The doors open, Aiah steps out, and Constantine fastens the priceless ivory around her neck. He kisses her nape and the shiver of pleasure tingles to Aiah's fingertips. He must have had Martinus acquire the necklace, she realizes; he hadn't had time to do it himself.

Aiah detects an air of faint curiosity in Constantine as she walks with him down the corridor. He is traveling in Loeno as a visitor, she realizes. No doubt he's been in places like this before, but always with the assurance that he'll be back in his own world before the end of the next shift. He's never lived in this bourgeois world, let alone in a dubious tenderloin like Old Shorings. He's as alien to this kind of life as she is to a penthouse suite in the Volcano Hotel.

'Try to ignore the pile of laundry on the bed,' she says, laughs, and turns her key.

She steps inside, turns on the lights, and a cold certainty

floods her nerves that she's made a mistake, a catastrophic one, even if she can't, at this appalling moment, understand just how.

Gil blinks at them from the bed, hand raised to shield his eyes from the light. 'Hello?' he says.

Aiah finds herself walking into the room, trying to respond normally. 'I wasn't expecting you back.'

Gil blinks, pushes yellow-blond hair out of his eyes. 'I called and left a message, over a week ago. I said I'd be back for the weekend.'

And it's early Sunday now. Aiah bethinks herself of the grinding play head that she keeps forgetting to lubricate, and which seems on this occasion to have let her down.

'I called the Authority,' Gil says, 'and they said you'd taken some days off. And your sister hadn't heard from you, either.'

Which means, of course, that the whole family knows by now.

'And your brother Stonn wants to talk to you. He didn't say why. I didn't know he was out of jail.'

Gil's eyes, slowly becoming accustomed to the light, turn slowly toward Constantine. He is too fatigued to know quite what to make of the large black man, carrying Aiah's bag, who stands silent in the doorway.

Aiah puts her hand to her throat and encounters the ivory necklace. She remember's Gil's pride at being able to afford the bracelet with the single ivory bangle he'd given her, the bracelet Fredho had stolen.

It occurs to her that she has some explaining to do.

'Gil,' she says, 'this is the Metropolitan Constantine. Constantine, this is Gil.' She takes a breath, gives Constantine an imploring look. 'I believe you've heard me mention him.'

Constantine puts down Aiah's bag inside the door and glides into the room with his usual perfect assurance. 'How do you do, sir,' he rumbles. 'Miss Aiah has spoken well of you.'

Gil is still too groggy to quite know what to make of one of the world's most celebrated and controversial figures appearing in his apartment at this desperate hour.

Aiah figures he'll start asking soon enough, though.

15

Constantine takes his leave. Gil stars at the door. 'Was that really—?' he asks.

'Oh yes.' She looks at the door, wondering what, exactly, has been shut off here. 'I'll explain later,' she says. 'I'm too tired right now,' and turns off the light.

The explanation, she reflects as she takes off her clothes, had better be pretty good.

She kisses Gil and curls into a ball on the bed, her back to him. Calculations flood her mind, all ponderous, unnatural-seeming, implausible, probably destined to fade at the first touch of shieldlight. Her nerves are like an array of tight-strung wires, tautly aware of Gil's every breath, vibrating in sympathy to every sigh, every movement, every casual touch.

Hours later, after the turn of the shift, Aiah falls into a kind of wary sleep, intent and restless, from which Gil's arms, enfolding her from behind, wake her with a start. He gently kisses her nape. Sensation shrieks along her nerves.

'Sorry to wake you,' he says, 'but it's late, and this is our only day together . . . and we've been away from each other for a long, long time.'

Aiah turns slightly toward him and he burrows along her collarbone, his jaw-bristle scratching her clavicle. She brushes hair from her face and, out of force of habit more than anything, absently strokes the back of his neck with her hand. 'You smell good,' he says, but she can't think why this would be the case.

A part of her life is beginning, she thinks. Another part is ending. But which? And with whom?

Gil's hands move intently along Aiah's body. He is making a purposeful effort to arouse, perhaps by way of apology for waking her. Every touch of his stubby fingers sets off a kind of cacophony in her high-strung nerves, neurons firing signals for panic, pleasure and flight all at once. It occurs to her that she would probably enjoy this more if she could manage, somehow, to relax. She closes her eyes, tilts her head back, and lets breath sigh from her lungs.

Who, she wonders, has a claim on her flesh? Her heart? Her allegiance?

Gil kneels between her legs, browses her body with his lips and tongue. Aiah tries to relax but her nerves leap with every touch. When he tongues her sex a bolt of sensation almost doubles her up, far too intense to be pleasurable. She cries out and presses her fists into her eye-sockets. Gil seems to take this reaction as encouragement because he doesn't stop.

Aiah hisses through clenched teeth. 'Take it easy.'

Gil's urgency eases – he's always been a perfectly reasonable lover. His tongue makes delicate little lacy swirls about her clitoris. The load of sensation declines to a manageable level. Aiah feels the cold edge of fear – is Gil searching for Constantine there, for the scent or taste of his rival?

No, she thinks. He's a perfectly practical man. If he wondered, he'd just ask.

And this reminds her why she likes him. The way he looks at things, the way he approaches a problem as something to be solved, to be disassembled like a puzzle, taken apart by his stubby fingers and *understood*. If he doesn't comprehend something, he just *asks*. He's not manipulative or dramatic or driven, he's just himself. An optimist who believes any problem can be conquered if you just approach it with the right frame of mind.

Aiah tries to relax again, closes her eyes, breathes slowly. Pleasure expands like a warm plasm tide. Her hips lift to the delicate touch of Gil's tongue. The pleasure rises, flooding, trembles at the brim of the cup, overflows.

Gil rises to his knees, dabbing delicately at his crooked smile with a corner of the sheet. He enters her and she presses herself to his furry chest. Every movement is familiar, unsurprising, a kind of homecoming. Aiah is pleased to discover that she's not drawing mental comparisons between Gil and Constantine. Anyway she knows that no comparison is possible, not between Gil and a fantasy as unreal as her Metropolitan lover, a figure already fading in contrast to the reality of her home, of domestic realities, of the man who lies, secure and genuine, between her legs . . .

They buy fresh bread and pastry at a local bakery, make coffee, fold down their little table from its place in the wall. Tomatoes and cucumbers are plucked from the plants flourishing in the pocket garden. The course of a luxurious breakfast covers the plastic table surface with coffee circles and crumbs.

Gil sips his coffee. 'I looked into our bank account yesterday,' Gil says. 'And there's over a thousand in there.'

'Eight hundred of that is the money you sent from Gerad,' Aiah says, 'and the rest is what I earned from my consulting job.'

Not to mention the six thousand and change, clanking coins, hidden in a bag of fertilizer under the tomato plants.

Little creases deepen between Gil's brows. 'What is this consulting job exactly?' he asks.

A taut fist clenches between Aiah's shoulderblades. 'It's a lot of little jobs, actually,' she says. 'The Metropolitan Constantine wants me to . . .'

The memory takes Gil by surprise. 'I'd forgotten!' he says. 'He really *was* here this last sleep shift?'

Relief stumbles into Aiah's mind. 'Yes. He and I were—'

'Imagine you working for that old gangster!' Gil says. 'What does the Jurisdiction think about it, ne?'

Aiah shifts uneasily in her seat. 'They don't know, and I didn't ask them,' she says. 'We needed the money too much. So if you could keep this thing quiet . . .'

Gil grins and reaches for a pastry. 'How did you meet him, anyway?'

'Well,' Aiah says, 'I sent him a fan letter.'

He frowns, his pastry half-raised. 'Through the *mail*?' he asks, irrelevantly. Letters cost more than wiregrams.

'Yes,' Aiah said. 'I read on the *Wire* that he'd moved into Mage Towers, and the *Lords of the New City* chromoplay is getting all this attention, and I just thought . . .'

Gil looks at her in surprise. 'You mean to say you actually admire him?'

Heat flushes Aiah's cheeks. 'Yes,' she says.

Gil thoughtfully chews his pastry as he gives this revelation some thought. 'But he destroyed his metropolis, didn't he? Cheloki's a sewer now. And Constantine is living high off his loot.'

Aiah is surprised by the fury that flashes through her. She bites down hard on her anger, tries to speak in normal tones. 'He didn't destroy his nation, he was attacked! That whole coalition of gangsters and crooked politicians and—'

'They would hardly have attacked him if they hadn't felt threatened by him,' Gil says reasonably. 'All his moves to strengthen his plasm reserves and build the army – what was he intending to do if not attack his neighbors?'

Aiah's fingernails dig into her palms. 'He was trying,' she says, 'to *help* people.'

'People like Constantine don't help anyone.'

'He was trying to change things!' Aiah waves an arm. 'Things that need changing!'

'Nothing needs changing that badly.'

For an instant a cold hatred floods Aiah's heart. Gil –

smug, judgmental, sitting at the table licking margarine from his fingers – is suddenly no different from the complacent Jaspeeris who have stood, indifferently, dully convinced of their own intrinsic rightness, as an immovable wall between Aiah and her fortunes.

'You wouldn't know,' Aiah says. 'You're a member of the privileged class here.'

An alert glint in Gil's eyes demonstrates awareness that he may have just walked into danger. 'I haven't been particularly aware of being privileged,' he ventures.

'You are,' Aiah says. 'Believe it. And from my non-privileged perspective, I would say, as far as change is concerned, *Whatever it takes*. Because either you make people free, or you don't; and if you don't, what good are you? And if people aren't free, what good is anything?'

These are Constantine's ideas, but the ferocity is Aiah's alone, born of her experience.

Gil's thoughts tread almost visibly across this dangerous ground. He and Aiah have, perhaps incredibly, never discussed this root matter, the difference in their backgrounds, their caste, their ethnicity. Aiah, at least, had told herself that it didn't matter, and now she finds she was wrong, that suddenly it's the most urgent thing in the world.

Gil opens his mouth, hesitates, speaks carefully. 'Do you feel,' he says, 'that I've maltreated you in any way, that I've held you down, or kept you from – I don't know – being free?'

Aiah's anger dies away, replaced by an upwelling of sorrow. He's taken the subject away from the sphere of abstracts and returned it to the two people sharing breakfast over their folding table. Her fingers seek out Gil's hand. 'No,' she says. 'No. You're the only man I've met who ever thought I was all right.'

Except for Constantine. The treacherous thought will not keep to itself.

Gil is faintly puzzled. 'Is that true?'

Aiah nods. 'If other people were more like you, there wouldn't be a problem. But even you could use a few new perspectives.'

Gil offers a faint smile. 'I'm beginning to see that.'

'You don't know what a long, tiresome struggle it was just to get here. To this little place we share. It's natural for you to find a place like Loeno at this point in your life, but for me it's the result of a battle that's gone on for years. And if I hadn't had to spend so much energy on fighting for everything you take for granted, who knows where I'd be?'

He nods, but Aiah can't tell if he understands. That every step upward is a struggle against great weight, against her own family dragging her back, against those above her whose ponderous weight of privilege holds her down; a hopeless, endless struggle, wearying and so full of frustrations that, finally, she'd done something so dangerous she didn't even dare tell him.

Made him her *passu*, which he did not deserve.

The argument, if that's what it is, fades away through sheer weariness. Aiah is exhausted, and Gil had slept badly on the train from Gerad and is tired from overwork. They spend the day at home, leaving only once for a walk.

Gil doesn't ask about Constantine or her job. Perhaps he's wary of starting another disagreement, but Aiah is beginning to think he's genuinely incurious. Constantine is something so remote from the practical realities of his life that he can't manage to raise any interest.

Nor does he recall noticing the ivory necklace that Aiah has by now carefully hidden, but if he had, he probably would have assumed the fabulously valuable thing was an imitation.

Aiah had thought that her relationship with Constantine was so huge that hiding it would have been like trying to hide Prince Aranax in the bathtub. To her increasing amazement, Gil seems to have noticed nothing at all. She wonders about her life and how it relates to other lives, like a circle intersecting with other circles. The common area shared by Aiah and Gil is only a fraction of their whole existence – perhaps, given all this, a smaller fraction than Aiah had ever realized. And Constantine has been edging his wider circle into her own, almost encompassing it, but has only now begun to encroach on the part of Aiah's life that Gil has inscribed as his own.

But that's not what Constantine has done. Constantine has uncovered a part of Aiah's existence that even Aiah didn't know existed.

You are at your most beautiful when you take flight.

But still it's possible for Aiah to enjoy the part of her life that still overlaps with Gil's. They spend the day together, doing pleasant things, among them the repair of the commo board; they make love again, very pleasantly, and then Aiah puts him on the train back to Gerad, and is pleased to find that he's out of her way.

And then she wonders if, the next time she sees him, it will be through the bars of a jail cell.

'This is Miss Quelger. Please tell Dr Chandros that my guest has left, and I'm available for work if he requires me.'

Aiah waits for a moment, wondering if anyone's going to answer, and then takes her thumb off the transmit button. She leaves the phone booth and glances up at the huge bulk of the Authority building, the huge statues that scowl down from their niches, the twisted forest of antennae crowned against the sky. Plasm messages write themselves across the sky, but none is addressed to her.

The number was one Constantine had made her memorize, to leave messages if it was important. She was always to call from a public phone, and not expect a reply.

There's a wreck in front of the Authority building, two cars and an overturned cattle truck. Terrified miniature beeves, scarcely larger than sheep, run frantically beneath the wheels of oncoming traffic. Bemused Authority cops mill about in hope of being helpful. Aiah finds herself wondering if such a wreck could prove a useful distraction during Constantine's coup, draw security out of their positions to a place where they could be attacked.

This train of thought doesn't seem at all strange to her.

Once Aiah arrives in her office, she finds Tella eager to hear about her weekend with the boss. Aiah has long ago worked out what to tell her.

'Bobo made his move,' Aiah says, sitting down to her desk. Tella's eyes gleam. 'But I said no,' Aiah continues, and Tella's expectations crumble.

'Why?' she demands. 'Everything was so promising!'

Aiah turns on her computer and gives it a few minutes to warm up. 'Would you have said yes?' she inquires.

'We're not talking about me!' Tella says. 'Why did you tell him no?'

Aiah puts her headset on, smiles, and dispenses a bit of her grandmother's wisdom. 'Because if he's serious,' she says, 'one no won't stop him.'

Tella considers this thought and reluctantly concedes its merit. 'Well,' she says, 'you'll have to tell me what happens next.'

'Of course,' Aiah says, and thoroughly enjoys the taste of the lie as it crosses her tongue.

Aiah's heart lifts as she sees the Elton at the end of her shift. Constantine waits inside, sealed from his driver and guard by the raised glass screen. There is a chilled bottle of wine, fruit, flowers in cut-glass vases. Constantine is slouched in the far corner, huddled in his black leather jacket, and only nods as Aiah enters the car. The unreadable look on his face sends little pulses of anxiety through her nerves.

'Did yesterday go well with your friend?' he asks.

'Yes,' she says. 'No problems.'

'That's good. I wouldn't want to come between you,' he says, and then, realizing how commonplace and flat untruthful the words sound, he gives a little smile and says, 'Not without an invitation, anyway.'

She answers the secret glow in his eyes, reaches to the seat between them, puts her hand over his. He sighs, shifts on the seat, and stares restlessly forward. 'Sorya is back,' he says, 'and at Mage Towers.'

The impact of the words actually takes Aiah's breath away. Gradually, with effort, she finds it again.

'Ah.' More commonplaces. 'I see.'

Crumpled in his seat, Constantine looks the picture of misery. 'I can't afford to continue in the Caraqui business without her. She's too valuable. I need . . .' He licks his lips, looks at her. 'Everyone.'

Aiah finds words flying in the roaring tempest of her thoughts. 'And what is it you . . . *need* . . . from me?'

There is a moment of thought before he speaks. 'I don't believe I can ask you for anything more than patience.'

'Well . . .' she begins, uncertain.

'But nevertheless,' amusement kindles in his glance, and his hand encloses hers, 'I have had Khoriak reserve a suite at the Landmark Hotel, if you are inclined, after all this, to spend a little time with me. And if not, I certainly understand.'

For a second Aiah is tempted to laugh out loud. So it is to be *her* decision.

'Ah,' she says finally, 'why not?'

There are some preliminary security maneuvers designed to guarantee Constantine anonymity, but after that things are all right. The walls are white, the carpet thick and soft, and the sheets are blue satin. Refreshment is available in the form of sections of blood-orange, grown in the hotel's rooftop gardens, arranged artfully on a silver tray and drizzled with chocolate.

Aiah licks juice off her fingers. 'Things have improved,' she says, 'since the days of sex in stairwells.'

Constantine appears startled by this idea. 'Why?' he asks.

'There was no privacy in the sorts of places where I grew up,' Aiah says. 'Stairwells were as far away from people as we could get.'

'What about the roof?'

'Filled with fenced-off private gardens – we didn't have a key. The only open place was an altar where a local witch burned candles and sacrificed pigeons. Some of the kids used it, but we didn't want to.'

He looks at her with a frown. 'Was it pleasurable, sex in stairwells?'

Aiah is tempted to laugh – Constantine is naive in some matters. 'Not particularly,' she says. 'You had to do it fast, because people might interrupt, and the rail put a groove in the buttocks. Some of the local good-time girls were called "groovers" on that account.' She smiles at the memory. 'I'd forgotten that.'

'Then why do it at all?'

Aiah laughs, not at the question, but at Constantine's seriousness. 'Because there was a boy I wanted, and it was the only way to get him. And of course there was an itch that needed scratching, even if it wasn't scratched particularly well. But hey – poor people are used to their pleasures being compromised. They take what they can, when it's available. And sex is something you can do whether you've got money or not.'

'What happened to the boy?'

'He found another girl, one with a job, so she could spend her money on him. She let him do it without protection, which he preferred, and of course she got pregnant.

They were married for, oh, six months or so, and after that life went on.'

Constantine strokes her cheek with a hand that smells of sex and oranges. 'I feel sad for that little girl, that Aiah,' he says. 'Was she heartbroken?'

'No. I'd got what I wanted.'

'And what was that?'

'A few life lessons. And status – he was a very popular boy. I was an odd child, I should add, and the other kids didn't know whether to accept me or not. I'd won this scholarship to this fancy private school, which made me suspect, and getting this boy made me one of the regulars.' She smiles. 'But I didn't take him to the Secret Place, so I couldn't have loved him.'

'The Secret Place?' Constantine's wistful smile is a mirror of her own. 'Do we find it through anatomy or geography?'

Aiah laughs and picks up an orange slice. 'Geography,' she says, and licks the chocolate off the top. 'The Secret Place was an old temple in Old Shorings, a smallish place, on a tiny lot, surrounded by huge apartments. It was closed when the neighborhood turned Barkazil. I don't even know which immortal was worshiped there. But the place was amazing – gray stone, carved with trees and leaves, birds, flowers, monsters, angels, the most intricate carvings imaginable – and when it was closed it was shut up behind these intimidating steel doors and shutters. But when I was little I *knew* that there were still things going on in there, and that someone, or something, still lived inside. Ghosts, vampires, the twisted, hanged men . . . I knew someone had to be in there, because local people still left offerings in front of those big steel doors, rice or beans or coins. And they'd write their wishes on slips of paper and slide them under the doors, and whoever lived in there would grant them.'

Aiah looks at Constantine, her mind warming to the memory. 'It was my idea of what magic was, when I was little. And I always thought that when I really loved someone, I'd take him to the temple, and we'd sprinkle some rice and push our wish under the door, and it would be granted.'

'What was your wish?'

'The wish varied, but mostly it was to have the temple to ourselves, for one shift. It was the most extravagant wish I could think of, to have some kind of privacy.' Aiah eats the orange slice, feels the flavor of memory burst on her tongue.

'Did you ever take anyone there?' Constantine asks.

Aiah, mouth filled with pulp, shakes her head.

'Not even your Gil?'

Aiah shakes her head again. Constantine touches her cheek again.

'Then I am still sad for that little girl.'

'Don't be,' Aiah says. 'She's done all right so far.'

He nods, but she can still see the tint of sorrow in his eyes. She nudges his biceps with a knuckle. 'And you?' she asks. 'I take it you've never had sex in a stairwell?'

'No. I thought my education had been fairly comprehensive, but apparently that area was overlooked.' He frowns, dismembers an orange slice. 'My uncle gave me one of his girls, one of the younger ones. There was a whole class of them, and they tended to rotate through the family. A number rotated through my bed on a kind of informal schedule.' He chews a bit of orange thoughtfully. 'There's a practical political aspect to it I only appreciated later: if you've already experienced every conceivable combination by the time you're fifteen, when you finally grow into a position of power it's unlikely anyone will be able to manipulate you through sex.'

'I'll have to remember not to try, then.'

He gives her a sly look and pops another bit of orange into his mouth. 'How unfortunate. It could have been fun.'

She smiles, one hand stroking the blue satin between them. 'What next?' she asks.

'Now? I'll take you home when you're ready. Though I hope it's not yet, because I'm just getting comfortable.'

'And then? What after that? Do we keep meeting in hotels?'

Constantine puts down his remaining bit of orange, towels his fingers dry, sits up straighter in bed. 'What happens next,' he says, 'depends on what it is that Miss Aiah wants.'

Frustration hums in Aiah's nerves. 'Why must I decide everything?' she says.

For a moment Constantine seems ancient, looking at her with the distant, knowing eyes of an old man. 'Because you are the one who is most likely to be hurt,' he says.

Aiah's mouth is dry. 'I'm not very easy to damage,' she says.

'What is it that you desire?' Constantine asks. 'To spend time with me for the present, then to return to your life in your black tower? This I can grant you. Or do you wish to hazard everything and follow me to Caraqui? I can't decide this for you, and the decision must be made in, well, in a matter of days.'

Aiah is surprised. She hasn't realized Constantine's timetable is so advanced. 'Say I come with you to Caraqui,' Aiah says cautiously. 'Would I have a place there?'

'A place in the New City? Of course. A place with me?' He frowns, his fierce gaze focused on the ceiling. 'Too much depends on chance.'

'What sort of chance? Will you need Sorya after the coup?'

'Perhaps.' He slumps into the bed and seems unhappy enough that Aiah wants to reach out to comfort him. 'And in any case I would have little time for her, or for you.' He looks at her, a kind of pain in his eyes. 'I can't promise you anything in Caraqui, other than a job in some

243

government office. I am using you most damnably, and one day you will see that and hate me.'

'I can't see that you're using me any more than I'm using you.'

Constantine's gaze burns into hers. 'You're young,' he says.

Aiah can feel herself flush. *I am not your* passu*!* she thinks violently, and turns away. The orange tastes bitter on her tongue.

'I don't know what I want,' she admits. 'I wanted security – money in the bank, not to have to fight all the time – and I never thought beyond that. But now you've given me security, and so much else that I'm afraid I've turned greedy.'

He leans close to her, kisses her bare shoulder. 'You are welcome to what you can take from me, in such time as we have left,' he says.

She looks at him. 'I just told you I'm greedy,' she reminds.

A smile hints that Constantine is pleased by her response. 'Take what you will,' he says. 'I would not limit myself if I were you.'

There are messages from Stonn on her repaired communications array when she gets home, and a call from him comes again as she's eating her breakfast sweet rolls.

'That was pretty good, what you did,' he says.

Weariness falls on Aiah like rain. 'Yeah? And what did I do, exactly?'

'Took care of Guvag. It was on video and everything. The burns sent him to the hospital. He's not going to be bothering *anyone* for a long time.'

'What makes you think it was me who did that?'

'Come on, Aiah. You said you'd take care of it, and you did.'

'It doesn't have to have been me. He had a lot of enemies.'

Stonn gives a little laugh. 'Whatever you say. The point is, I know a way to make some money.'

'No.' Flatly.

'For anyone with access to that much plasm, I know where we can . . .'

'No. I can't.'

'Just listen—'

'*I can't!*' Coffee spills from Aiah's cup as she slaps the table with her hand.

There is a moment of resentful silence. 'You've got to be dealing the goods,' Stonn says. 'That's the only way it adds up. And now you're not willing to share your chonah with your family?'

'Stonn.' She searches for words. *You're going to put me in prison*, while accurate enough, is probably too confrontational under the circumstances. 'Nothing's free, okay?' she says. 'It's not as if I have any plasm of my own. If I accomplished anything, it's because somebody did me a *favor*. And now I have to do favors back, understand?'

'Do the man a favor then,' Stonn says. 'Introduce him to me. I've got this great opportunity for him.'

'It wouldn't work.'

'Well, who *is* the guy, anyway?'

Aiah rubs the pain between her eyes. 'Stonn,' she says, 'I'm sorry, but nothing is going to happen.'

Stonn's voice is full of resentment. 'All right,' he says, 'cut your family out of everything.'

'*I can't help you!*' Aiah says. '*I would if I could!*'

Stonn hits the disconnect button before Aiah gets all the words out. She slams the headset back onto its hook.

Now she's made *passus* out of her family, lying to them as she's lied to everyone else. She wonders what will happen when all the lies start intersecting, if Gil should talk to someone in the family about Constantine, or if Rohder should hear about Bobo and Momo.

Deal with it when it happens, she thinks dully, it's all she can do.

Tella's baby is screaming so loudly — and without any apparent reason, all the normal ones having been looked into and dismissed — that Aiah doesn't hear the message cylinder drop from the pneumatic tube into her wire basket. Suddenly she looks and it's there, and she wonders for how long. The blue-pencil message is signed 'Rohder'. He wants to see her right away.

A cold breeze wafts across her nape.

Aiah doesn't know if Rohder has the authority to give her orders or not. He isn't her immediate boss, but his rank is so high that he might well have authority over her without her even knowing it. She calls tabulator control and tells him she's been called to a meeting and is logging out early. The baby's shrieks are so loud she can barely make out the controller's responses.

She heads for the building's hydraulic elevators, and their peculiar liquid motion makes her nervous stomach queasy.

Rohder's on the 106th floor, which is under reconstruction; walls are torn down or have craters punched in them, bricks and concrete blocks are stacked in piles, there's plastic draped over everything, and temporary scaffolding shores up the ceiling and walls. Despite the disorder the only sound here is the concrete dust grating beneath Aiah's shoes. She has the feeling no one has actually worked on any of this for some time.

Even if Rohder doesn't seem to have a real job anymore he's still senior enough to rate a corner office. The receptionist's desk and chair are covered with an undisturbed layer of concrete dust, but the door beyond is open. Aiah can smell Rohder's cigarets before she enters.

There are monumental statues, ten stories tall, set on the corners of the building, shining bronze hawk-nosed human figures staring down at the city with slitted eyes. They're supposed to be the Angels of Power or something. The windows in Rohder's office give a glorious view of two corner statues' stern profiles turned out to the city below. Rohder, insignificant by comparison, sits behind an enormous bronze-fronted desk covered with a design of rays, a desk that seems to diminish rather than enhance his majesty. He looks as if he's wearing the same ill-fitting gray suit as when Aiah first met him. A cigaret, naturally, hangs from the corner of his mouth.

He looks up at her with his rheumy blue eyes, and for a moment he seems not to recognize her. Then he nods, stands, and brushes cigaret ash off his chin-lace. 'I see you made it through what used to be my department,' he says.

'You wanted to see me?'

'I wanted to talk to you about Terminal.'

The old lavatory is walled off, Aiah reminds herself. The structure is being tapped now, so even if Rohder finds it, he won't find this huge potential well just sitting there. He won't be able to prove it isn't tapped and metered legitimately.

No need to be afraid, Aiah thinks, but as she steps forward she feels insects crawl along her nerves.

Rohder's carpet is covered with plastic sheeting that crackles under Aiah's heels. There is a huge padded chair in the corner of the room, she sees, with copper t-grips on the wide arms. He can access plasm right from here, from a seat that gazes out from two sides of the building.

And there are maps layered atop Rohder's desk, she sees, each anchored on its corners by a brimming ashtray. She recognizes every map.

'Just how do you get down to that old pneuma station?' Rohder asks.

'It's dangerous down there,' Aiah says. 'I'll guide you if you like.'

'Ah.' Rohder's hands wander in and out of his jacket pockets, fail to find cigarets, discover them instead in a drawer. 'Well, that's kind of you, but I thought I might as well do it from here, just use telepresence.'

Terror creeps slowly up Aiah's spine. 'Ah,' she says.

Rohder lights the new cigaret off the old. His ruddy complexion and baby-blue eyes provide a startling contrast with his wrinkled face, every line of which is mercilessly revealed by the shieldlight flooding through the big windows.

It's all down to how good Rohder actually is, Aiah knows. If he can find the structure of the old plastics plant, he can map it, but only if he's good enough to project an anima through solid matter, an act that requires a series of complex skills in which Aiah has no real experience but which seem intimidating enough in theory: to develop a sensorium that can sense in ways that a human could not, sense difference in mass, in materials, to tell bricks from bedrock from steel, to translate all of this into knowledge, and of course to navigate without losing one's path.

But Rohder is good. Mengene said he was a real wizard. Aiah reaches up into her cuff-lace and clasps her wrist with one hand in order to keep herself from trembling.

'Uhh,' Rohder reminds, 'where exactly do I need to look?'

Aiah leans over the desk and looks over the maps, tries to trace her route. Plants her finger firmly on the map to keep the hand from shaking. 'Here,' she says. 'South side of the street. I don't remember the number of the building.'

Rohder screws up his face. 'But there's public access leading in?'

The law is fairly firm on the subject of sending one's anima into 'private domestic space' – various kinds of complicated official permissions are required – but Rohder's allowed to move through what the law defies as a 'public access', meaning in this case the hallways, stairs and corridors of an apartment building.

'I'm not entirely certain of the technicalities,' Aiah says, 'but I suppose it's public.'

Rohder draws on his cigaret and looks moodily at the map. 'Perhaps it would be easier,' Rohder says, 'if I just quartered the district through the air. Any signs of large plasm use could be traced to their source.'

'Wouldn't it most likely be legitimate?' Aiah says. 'How many thousands of people are using plasm at any given moment?'

'In that district?' Rohder mused. 'Very few would be using the goods in any quantity. It's a working-class neighborhood with very little local industry.'

And very few, Aiah thinks, beaming plasm from transmission horns disguised as billboards. She is aware of sweat gathering at her nape.

'Did you need anything else?' she asks.

'Hm?' He's already lost in thought. 'No,' he says, 'I don't think so. Thank you.'

Aiah leaves, feet crunching on concrete dust. She considers dashing down to the lobby, calling the number Constantine gave her, giving Dr Chandros an emergency message.

And then cold fear runs through her veins like ice as she realizes that would be a bad idea. She might *already* be under investigation. Creepers from the Authority's Investigative Division might be tracking her, either in person or through an anima. This could be a trick by Rohder designed to make her panic and do something foolish.

She returns to her office, sweat cooling on her nape. Somehow she gets through the day.

When she leaves, the hydraulic elevator feels hot and close and seems to take forever to reach the ground floor. And then, having rushed from the building as fast as she's dared, she has to wait a few endless minutes at the curb, because her ride isn't here. When the Elton pulls up, she doesn't wait for Martinus to open her door for her, but dives through the rear door and confronts a startled Constantine. It's safe to talk in here: the car has a bronze collection web that would disperse the anima of anyone trying to get inside.

'The Jurisdiction is going to conduct a search for plasm thieves in the Terminal area,' Aiah says. 'You've got to shut down the factory.'

Constantine's brows knit. 'What sort of search?'

The car's acceleration tugs at Aiah's balance, and she sways and then settles into her seat.

'Anima search,' Aiah says. 'Aerial, to look for large-scale plasm use, and underground, to try to find untapped structures. I just found out.'

'When is this going to happen?'

Aiah hesitates. 'Who knows?' she says. 'Tomorrow, most likely, but it could be underway already — heavy plasm use would stand out more during second shift than during first. And if you're firing it off that rooftop . . .'

'Find a public phone,' Constantine tells Martinus.

He calls the factory and tells the people there to shut down operations and head for Mage Towers for an emergency meeting.

As the car speeds for Mage Towers, Aiah wonders if she should tell Constantine that the investigation, if it's not occupying the attention of every creeper in Jaspeer, is most likely being run by one old man, operating on his own.

But she knows perfectly well what would happen, and so she doesn't say a word.

She follows Constantine into his apartment, his broad back moving in front of her like a leather-clad wall. He moves at full speed, his body set in lines of intense concentration, his long legs reaching for the carpet. Aiah hears

Sorya's words – 'What the hell?' – before Aiah sees the woman herself, standing at the base of the spiral stair, tapping a booted foot and pointing her cigaret at the ceiling like a pistol held at half-cock. Her expression is half anger, half alarm, and she doesn't give Aiah so much as a glance. Geymard the soldier is with her, and a thin bespectacled man Aiah doesn't know.

'The Authority,' Constantine says, and heads up the stairs three at a time. Aiah sticks close to his back and Sorya is third up the stair, followed by Geymard, Martinus and others. Once in the plasm control room, Constantine spins like a dancer, his burning eyes focused on Aiah, and says, 'Explain.'

Aiah gives them as much as she dares. She's never had more attention from an audience, from this half-circle of intent, disciplined faces.

'How long will this go on?' Sorya asks. Aiah's skin tautens in alarm at the look in Sorya's green eyes.

'I don't know,' Aiah says.

Sorya's glance shifts to Constantine. 'Obvertag came over to us at breakfast today, and that gives us the Marine Brigade. But if we delay too long, his fears could get the better of him.'

'We won't shift our time, then,' Constantine says. 'Not yet. Any further plasm work,' he turns to the bespectacled man, 'can be done from here. It will be costly, but . . .' he shrugs, 'unavoidable at this point.'

The man nods smoothly. 'Very well,' he says.

Sorya and Constantine then suggest various schemes for continuing the work from the factory, and Aiah reluctantly shoots each one down.

'A lot of things happen when the Authority's not looking,' Aiah says finally. 'There are a million holes in the net. But once something attracts their attention, they – we – don't stop.' She sighs. 'We're very thorough that way.'

Sorya stabs her cigaret into an ashtray. 'So what can we do? Call the whole thing off?'

'Impossible,' Constantine murmurs.

'Find a plasm thief,' Aiah says. 'A big one, somewhere in that neighborhood. And then we wrap him in a big ribbon and hand him to the Authority with our compliments.'

Aiah is gratified to find that once again she has their full attention.

'Who?' Constantine asks.

'Someone in the Operation,' Aiah says. 'Street captain or higher. Colonel, or a general if we can find him. Or Jaspeeri Nation. Or a high-class witch or maybe a priest with a little business selling the goods on the side. Who knows?' She shrugs. 'There has to be someone.'

There is a short, tense silence in which the others look at each other. Then Constantine booms out a deep laugh. 'Very good!' he says. 'Another challenge!'

Disdain tugs at Sorya's lip. 'So now we must put everything aside and go do the Authority's job for them?'

'Not everything,' Constantine says. 'We must form a task group around Miss Aiah, and the rest of us will proceed normally.'

'I'll try to get the Authority to assign me to the investigation,' Aiah says. 'And then I can steer it the way it needs to go.'

'Once we find out where that is,' Sorya says.

There is a moment of silence. 'How do we find the target?' Geymard says, a proper military question.

'You have to know what to look for,' Aiah says. 'I grew up up in a similar neighborhood, let me think for a moment.'

She consults her memories while the half-circle of intent faces gazes at her. She tries to call to her mind images of Terminal, the throb of music, the scent of food heavy with comino, the businesses crowded under the scaffolding, the little old man who sold her the cheap metal Trigram from off his homemade table. 'What's today?' she asks finally. 'Tuesday? Wednesday is collection day in my old neighborhood, I wonder if that holds true for Terminal.'

'What do you mean, collection day?' It's the man in spectacles who asks the question.

'The day when all the illegal businesses make their pay-offs,' Aiah says. 'Those little businesses under the scaffolding, for example. How many of them do you think have real permits, or pay real taxes? And even if they did, would the police protect them? No – they pay the bagmen, who bring the cash to the street captains, and the street captains take care of the cops and then pass the rest up to the colonels and generals. Follow the money, we find where the power is.'

'How do we know it's even happening on Wednesday?' Sorya demands.

Aiah shrugs. 'If anyone has a better idea . . . ?'

Silence. Sorya reaches into her gold case for another cigaret.

'There are other things to look for,' Aiah says. 'Ordinary office buildings that seem to have too much security – exterior cameras and such. Doormen who look as if they might really be someone's bodyguard. The same with apartment buildings, but with some of the buildings in Terminal, you'd go crazy looking for the right apartment, some of them must have a thousand units. And sometimes the Operation advertises. Look in the directory under "social clubs", and though that's probably not where they keep the plasm, that's where you'll find the people who use it. Can you tell who's been using plasm recently just by looking?'

'Aerial anima search,' Constantine says. 'From here.' He turns to Sorya. 'Call our mages, bring them here.'

'That violates security procedure, Metropolitan,'

Martinus says. 'It may not be wise to connect some of these people with us directly.'

Constantine nods. 'Very well,' he says. 'Rent three plasm-user suites in the Landmark Hotel. Use the BMG credit line. I will be there to tell our people what to look for.'

'I would like to get on the ground in Terminal,' Aiah says. 'Can you get me a car and driver?'

'Yes.' Constantine's intent gaze locks briefly with hers. 'Report to me afterwards at the Landmark.'

'I believe Miss Aiah knows the way,' Sorya says, her voice silky. Fear pours like an icy waterfall down Aiah's spine.

Constantine's face is expressionless. 'Let's get moving,' he says.

'Mr Rohder? This is Aiah.'

She's calling from a crowded restaurant halfway between Mage Towers and Terminal. Clatter and conversation aren't quite sealed off by the torn old padding on the heavy ceramic earphones, and she has to shout into a speaker built into the wall.

'Ah? Yes?'

Aiah feels her heart thrashing against her ribcage. She didn't know whether Rohder would still be in his office at this hour, but then, she'd reasoned, where else did he have to go?

Nowhere, apparently.

'I was thinking about Terminal,' she says.

'Yes. I've been looking there.'

Aiah bites her lip to stop herself from demanding to know if Rohder's discovered anything.

'I think I could help, sir,' she says. 'It occurs to me that I could go through the records, see if there's any suspicious activity on the meters.'

'Ah. Yes?' He ponders this for a long moment. 'That

254

will involve many long hours. How will you know where to look?'

'Meters with recent updates. Businesses that have opened in the last few years but which are selling a lot of plasm to the Authority. And I could go out to Terminal and scout around on the ground, then backtrack through the address in the records.'

'Ah.' Aiah hears Rohder inhaling a cigaret. 'Yes,' he says. 'Well. That is most diligent. But I wonder.' And there is a long pause.

'Yes?' Aiah reminds finally. 'What is it that you wonder?'

'Why are you so interested in this task?'

'Because my regular job is the most boring thing imaginable,' Aiah says. 'And this would be a change.'

Rohder sighs heavily. Aiah pictures the cigaret smoke billowing from his lungs.

'I will see if I can get you a temporary transfer,' Rohder says.

'Thank you.'

Another *passu*, she thinks. She seems to be acquiring quite a string of them.

16

Khoriak takes Aiah around Terminal in his two-seater Geldan. Suddenly ravenous, she's taken the basket of fruit from the Elton limo and sits with it in her lap: juice trickles down her wrist as she peers through smoked windows at people and buildings. But when she reports to Constantine after shift change she has little to tell him; they had followed a few obvious Operation types from one address to another, and otherwise had found a few businesses that, oddly, were protected by well-disguised bronze collection webs, a fact that probably meant nothing at all because it was impossible to determine how old the collection webs were, and whether whatever they were guarding had left the vicinity a hundred years ago.

'We have detected someone sniffing about the neighborhood,' Constantine says. He paces as he speaks, and his boot-heels have already trodden an anxious path in the plush carpet. Behind him mages are locked to their t-grips, eyes closed as they navigate over a geomaturgical landscape; security people stand like potted palms in their corners.

'Whoever he is,' Constantine mutters, 'he's good. Very methodical, seems to miss nothing. We daren't use the factory.'

'Tomorrow,' Aiah says. Weariness seems to fall on her like a mist of rain. 'Collection day. We may find something.'

Constantine stops in the middle of his pacing and gives her another of his intent looks. 'Come,' he says, and takes her arm. 'A dose of the goods will set you up.'

The bedroom is familiar, with its plump pillows and blue satin spread, and proves to have cables and copper t-grips lying ready in desk drawers. Aiah imagines she can detect the faint scent of blood-oranges. She takes the Trigram from around her neck and directs it through her body, burning away fatigue toxins, filling every cell with blazing power. She looks up at Constantine, sees his dark eyes intent on her, absorbing her. She feels a resonance, her power and his, like buildings set a precise half-radius apart, building a greater charge of plasm than either would on its own.

Her tissues are flushed with plasm and arousal. Aiah's lips involuntarily draw back in a fierce grin and she laughs. She puts down the t-grip and launches herself at Constantine, suddenly so full of power that she is possessed by the perfect illusion that she can drag his big body toward the bed and fling him into it. The sex that follows is fierce and fearless and leaves the room strewn with discarded clothing.

'You are learning to enjoy your power: good,' he says. He looks at her with lazy approval, eyes half-slitted like those of a cat.

Aiah is feeling a bit feline herself. She draws her claws lightly through the wiry hair on his chest. 'I don't know if I can give this up,' she says.

Constantine laughs, a low, indolent rumble. 'Well, sister,' he says, 'you could decide not to.'

She considers this. 'What is there in Caraqui for me? Nothing.'

'There may be the New City,' he says seriously. 'And I hope that in your measure of value I, myself, am rated somewhere above this *nothing*.'

'You have made me no promises,' Aiah reminds, 'except that you might replace my dull government job with another dull government job, and that perhaps in the near future I may hate you. And Sorya knows about our meeting here.'

He frowns. 'Don't worry for your safety, if that's what concerns you,' he says. 'If you are harmed through Sorya's actions, she will suffer for it. And she knows that.'

Aiah looks into his gold-flecked brown eyes. 'Have you told her that?'

Constantine gives a minute shake of his head. 'No need – she knows who is under my protection and who is not.'

'She could rat me to the Authority, and no one would know.'

'*I* would know. And Sorya knows I would know.' His lip gives a little curl. 'I know things about her that could send her to the Hell her Torgenil family so fervently believes in. I would use them if she compelled me.'

A chill wafts up Aiah's spine. 'If you know these things about her, isn't she dangerous to *you*?'

Constantine's eyelids half-slit his eyes again, and again Aiah is reminded of a cat, a cat contemplating its prey – cruel and predatory and hard, merciless in its calculation, in its perfect objective need. 'Without me,' he says, 'she would revert to the life in which I found her – and that life, believe me, was Hell, little though she knew it. No – she needs me more than I need her, and understands that perfectly well.'

Again Aiah feels a chill. She reaches for the sheets, crumpled at the foot of the bed, and covers herself. She rests her head on Constantine's shoulder and throws an arm across his barrel chest. The silver tip of his braid is cool against her forehead.

'It seems to me there are very many people who need you,' she says.

'And I'm not fair to any of them.' His hand strokes her hair. He sighs, Aiah's head lifting, then dropping, with the breath. 'Well, in another few days, things will be decided – whether I will continue this pointless, rootless life, pur-veying my fading theories of government and geomancy to an indifferent world, or make use of the gift you, my precious one, have given me. It may be that I will yet make the foundations of heaven tremble, and if so I will have you to thank.' He kisses her forehead gravely.

'Thank you,' she says, and hugs herself to him. 'Though I scarcely think I've given you the means to trouble the foundations of heaven.'

Again comes that lazy, rolling laugh. 'You have given me power, which used with care is a means to more power. And the purpose of power, to my way of thought, is to make us free. And what oppresses us more than . . . ?' His words fade away, but the hand, stroking her hair, pauses before her eyes, index finger pointed to the ceiling, and beyond.

Her eyes follow the pointing finger, her thoughts flying up beyond the ceiling, climbing higher, past the realm of falcons and airships, aeroplanes and rockets, high aloft to the place where the air is so thin it might as well not be there, and then, beyond even that.

'The Shield,' she murmurs, and then jolts upright, staring at him. 'The *Shield*? You want to attack the *Shield*?'

'The purpose of the New City is to bring liberty,' Constantine says. 'And what constrains us more than the Shield?'

'But how can you do it? Nothing can survive the Shield!'

'Matter is annihilated on contact with the Shield, or so we presume from the consequent burst of radiation,' Constantine says. 'And plasm is destroyed as well, or so it appears. Electromagnetic energy is absorbed and probably retransmitted. But gravity gets through, so the Shield is not perfect in its hostility to nature. And where there is an imperfection, a weakness can be found.'

Aiah finds herself uneasy at this discussion – probably half the priests on the planet would find it plain blasphemy – and she finds herself casting restless sidelong glances just in case spirits, gods or disapproving Malakas are hovering about listening.

'I thought everything had been tried,' she says.

'No records survive from Senko's time. We don't even know how long ago that was – thousands of years, anyway. Every so often someone takes a crack at the Shield in a kind of half-hearted, disorganized way, but the last time was eight hundred years ago, and a few years ago I bought the records in a surplus sale in an old warehouse and read them, and they only confirm what everyone already knows.'

'So what can you do?'

'A grand plasm assault, perhaps? Senko tried it, but by the available accounts plasm science was uncertain then, and he didn't have any great amount of the stuff to work with. If we can unify more than one metropolis in this matter, take the plasm from many states and direct it against the Shield, we might be able to somehow overload its mechanisms.'

'Why not utilize all the plasm in the world?' Aiah laughs.

Constantine smiles. 'Well, why not? But of course the New City must first gain control of the world, which perhaps is a greater challenge than dealing with the Shield itself, is it not?'

Aiah is staggered by Constantine's treating her facetious suggestion with any degree of seriousness at all. 'Well,' she says, 'let's hope the Ascended Ones aren't listening.'

'If they are,' smiling, 'I'm sure they're laughing.'

Aiah smiles uneasily and restrains the impulse to glance over her shoulder.

'We might also approach the Shield through gravity,' Constantine continues, 'the nature of which we know little, though we know its effects well enough. Perhaps, through plasm, we might be able to amplify gravity, and direct it outward, use it as a method for exploring the Shield or as a weapon directed against its mechanisms.'

'Can plasm interact with gravity at all?' Aiah asks.

'Thus far,' Constantine concedes, 'no. But who has tried? And besides – who knows what the Malakas were thinking of when they built the Shield? Perhaps it is not intended as an eternal barrier, but as an intelligence test.' He looks at her, his voice rolling on like a deep, inexorable river.

'Why hasn't the Shield been breached? One may as well ask why there is still poverty and hunger, why war is permitted, why there is such gross inequality in wealth and opportunity. It is because we, as a political species, permit all these to occur. Perhaps we permit the Shield as well. If we can put aside our foolishness, our shortsightedness and greed, we may discover the realm of the Ascended is in our grasp, and has been all along.'

Aiah feels her head spin with the wine of Constantine's words. The Shield has been there, immovable, irreconcilable, for thousands of years; it is a *fact*, as assuredly a fact as the bedrock beneath the hotel's foundations. And Constantine would abolish it. Might as well, she thinks mirthfully, abolish hunger and war, abolish the planet itself.

Constantine sits up in bed and leans toward her, his voice confiding. 'I would reckon it a favor if you would not confide to anyone this particular ambition of mine,' he says. 'I would prefer not to be laughed out of all respect, or condemned as a heretic by some fanatic. I'm treated with enough skepticism as it is.'

Aiah puts her arms around his neck and kisses him. 'Who would I tell?'

He shrugs. 'Some inquiring wire reporter, I suppose.'

'Maybe when I'm an old granny,' Aiah says. 'The statute of limitations on plasm theft won't expire till then.'

The room takes a sudden lurch, as if a giant had just kicked the hotel's cornerstone. Something in the bathroom falls off a shelf with a crash. Aiah and Constantine scramble erect as the hotel lurches a second time. Aiah's feet nearly shoot out from under her. And then there are a diminishing series of smaller shocks as the building rocks back and forth on its massive floating foundation, a swaying that continues long after the actual earthquake is over.

Constantine is jumping into his clothes before the last shock fades. Aiah stands silent and still, gulping air in reaction to a sudden wave of inner-ear nausea.

'I must check the factory,' Constantine says. 'Have someone take you home—'

'I have to go to the Authority,' Aiah says. 'I'm Emergency Response, remember?'

He nods. 'Tell Khoriak.' And then is out the door into the busy front room, thrusting one arm through a sleeve of his shirt.

It is a middle-sized quake, and in Jaspeer causes only 16,000 casualties, 1,100 of which are fatal, mostly from scaffolding that peels away from buildings in poor neighborhoods and rains down on the off-shift traffic below. Some bridges and tunnels collapse. A food vat ruptures in the basement of a processing plant and drowns twelve workers in a deluge of krill. A few older buildings fall while a rather larger number go up in flames. Among the fallen buildings is a brand-new and very fashionable apartment that will soon be the subject of an investigation to find out which inspectors were paid off and when.

Aiah is assigned to find and repair breaks in plasm lines and spends most of the next twelve hours underground, walking through darkened utility mains illuminated by the jittering flash of her helmet light, old brick and concrete tunnels that smell of disturbed dust. Vertigo keeps tugging at her inner ear, turning the tunnels into distorted, nightmarish places. She performs her job with her heart in her mouth, terrified that a stray spark might set off an explosion in the fine, suspended dust particles in the tunnels, or that an aftershock might bury her and her team alive or flood the tunnel with water.

At least, she thinks, Rohder's anima won't be wandering around Terminal, he'll be busy elsewhere, locating survivors in the rubble of collapsed buildings.

After twelve hours Aiah is allowed to go home. Aside from a broken mirror in the lobby, Loeno Towers is unharmed. The apartment is as she left it. The repaired commo set has logged a call from Gil inquiring as to her safety, and after an hour of trying – commo lines are jammed – she manages to leave a brief message telling him that she is all right.

The plasm energy she'd fed herself at the hotel is long gone. Aiah showers, collapses into her bed, and is awakened only at 1800 when the doorman calls to tell her that her ride has arrived.

She throws on clothing, washes her face, and combs her tangled hair in the elevator on her way down. On the ground floor she finds Khoriak quietly reading a magazine. He leads her to the Geldan and inserts the little car into the late rush-hour traffic. In the wake of the earthquake the sky blazes with advertisements for insurance companies.

'Part of the collection net came down in the factory,' Khoriak says, 'but that should be repaired within twenty-four hours or so. No one was hurt.'

'Where are you taking me?'

'The factory. Everyone else is there.'

'Was there a lot of damage in Terminal?'

'Not from what I saw.'

And indeed there is very little. Terminal is sufficiently far from the quake's epicenter that it's lost none of its scaffolding, and damage seems to have been confined to broken windows and toppled shelves.

A repair crew is already repairing the bronze collection net. The huge accumulators stand gleaming in their rows, reflecting the sparks that fall from welding torches in multiple golden waterfalls. Constantine and Sorya watch from amid a circle of their followers. As the car pulls in, Constantine crosses the stained concrete floor to open Aiah's door for her. The others trail behind him. Constantine is smiling, and Sorya is hunched in a faded green brass-buttoned military jacket of an old-fashioned design. She wears a peaked cap pulled low over sullen, slitted eyes.

'Our people at the Landmark have found something useful,' Constantine says as Aiah steps from the car. 'When the quake hit, two of the Operation men we were surveying left their clubs and dashed to the same address to see if anything there was damaged. We've poked around a little further, and it's their plasm house.'

'Can you tell how much of the juice they are getting out of it?' Aiah asks.

'It's in an office building backed up against a huge public housing project. I'd say they're tapping into the plasm link there.'

A falling bit of bronze rod, cut loose by one of the torches, clangs loudly on the floor. 'Congratulations, Miss Aiah,' Sorya says. 'Your solution looks to be the right one.' The shadowed expression beneath her cap brim is unreadable.

'What's the next step?' Constantine asks. 'An anonymous phone call to the Authority?'

Aiah mentally pages through the Authority's procedures. 'That will just put it in a long queue,' Aiah says, 'and someone may get around to checking the call in a few months, and it's very likely that the call will be assigned to the man who's being paid off in the first place. If you can get someone to lodge a formal complaint for the reward, the Authority will take it more seriously, but if it's you filing the complaint, Metropolitan, or any of your known entourage, they're likely to want to know *how* you know about all this illegal plasm.'

'I see.'

'Best to give me some time, and I'll work out a way for the Authority to discover the building in its own way.'

'We do not have time to spare,' Sorya says. 'Perhaps there could be an accident in that building, something that might expose the heavy plasm use there.'

A cold warning hand brushes Aiah's neck at Sorya's toneless word, *accident*.

'Give me the address,' Aiah says. 'I'll check to see who's registered at that meter.'

'An accident is quicker,' Sorya says flatly.

'An accident is more dangerous for us,' Constantine says. 'We don't want to have our business discovered as a result of a tangential brush with the Operation. Nor do we want to attract *their* attention, having successfully eluded them thus far.' He looks at Martinus. 'We'll take Miss Aiah there,' he says, and then turns to Aiah again. 'But not just yet. You look tired, and it doesn't do my cause any good to have your mind fuzzy. Refresh yourself at the t-grips, and then we'll leave.'

'Thank you, Metropolitan.'

The plasm charges her body, quickens her mind. She wishes she could dawdle, remain connected to the huge well she had discovered, the awesome reservoir of raw power so fundamentally connected to the life of her world, to both its reality and its unreality. But she reluctantly flicks the switch on the operators' console that disconnects her copper grip from the well, then pushes back her chair.

She realizes that she has been aware of Sorya's scent for some time.

Aiah turns to see Sorya standing behind her, hands stuffed in the pockets of her faded green jacket. Aiah rises to her feet, mind and muscle blazing with plasm-courage, and says, 'Yes?'

Sorya's tone of voice carries no hostility but little warmth, either. 'A word of warning, Miss Aiah.'

'Yes?' Aiah repeats. She almost laughs at the whole notion of warning. At the moment she feels capable of taking on an army.

'Constantine and I have been together a long time,' Sorya says, 'and though he and I are no fit companions for one another now, both being so tied, nerve and heart and bone, to this project of ours, and passionate over our differences, we nevertheless, once this endeavor is concluded, will be together for the future.'

Aiah bites back an impulse to reply, a defiant *Are you sure about that, lady?* or something equally refined, equally a product of the old neighborhood.

Sorya's flat green eyes gaze from under her cap brim. 'I bear you no animosity for your interlude here with Constantine,' she says. 'Insofar as you provide him a little release, a little forgetfulness – well,' she nods, 'that is good. You provide a service, if you will, for which I haven't the time or energy myself. But it *is* an interlude, Miss Aiah, and it would be dangerous for you to think otherwise.'

Aiah clenches her teeth. She can feel her hackles rise, her hands trying to form claws. 'Are you threatening me, Miss Sorya?' she asks.

A touch of contempt enters Sorya's eyes. 'Why should I do that? Do you think you're the only worshiper at this particular shrine? For it's worship he wants, make no mistake, and I know him too well to give him quite the credulity he demands.' She shakes her head. 'No, I merely wish to reiterate that he and I are both of the powers of this world, those blessed with greatness and the will and means to use it, and that this fact alone makes us dangerous to our friends as well as our enemies.'

'*This* power –' Aiah gestures toward the contents of the factory, the huge accumulators and consoles and grids, '– *this* power was my gift.'

Sorya tilts her pointed chin. 'Ah, but you gave it away, didn't you? or rather sold it. If you were one of the great,

266

you would have kept it and made use of it to lay the foundations of your own ascendancy.'

'Perhaps it isn't power that I want.'

'Does that make you great? I don't believe so.' She shakes her head. Behind her, sparks fall gracefully to the factory floor. 'I ask you but to look at Constantine's history. How many from the old days are still around him? Martinus and Geymard alone of those who mattered, and Geymard is here almost against his will and only because I worked on him for days.'

Sorya glances over her shoulder at Constantine, who stands in consultation with Martinus and Geymard. Her voice turns contemplative. 'Constantine has a way of being fatal to his friends. It is, in a peculiar way, a measure of his greatness that he survives what they do not. Consider: all his family are dead, even those who took his side in the war. All his old advisors, his companions, those lovers who remained with him for any space of time . . .' Her eyes return to Aiah. 'All but me. Because I can match him, in terms of will and greatness, in talent and power. Because I am no worshiper of his thought or philosophy or –' her lips twist contemptuously '– or his *goodness*, but of his true greatness, his will and power and his ability to dominate others; and because . . .' She leans closer to Aiah, close enough for Aiah to scent the spice on her breath. Sorya's voice turns confiding. 'Because I tell him the truth,' she says softly. Despite the silky tone her eyes are hard, pitiless. 'He *wants* worship, he wants the uncritical adoration of those such as yourself, but after he has glutted himself on devotion, it's the truth he needs, and it's the truth I give him.'

'And you think you're the only person who tells him the truth.'

'There are truths about Constantine that only I know,' Sorya says. 'I know power and wealth and magic, and it is *their* truth to which the greatness in Constantine speaks.'

She fishes in her pocket for her cigaret case. 'Believe me,' she says, 'I have nothing but the best of wishes for you, and that is why I'm speaking to you now. I wish to protect you from disappointment, from any consequences of broken hopes.' Aiah watches the little bright flame leap up from Sorya's platinum lighter to ignite the cigaret poised between Sorya's fingers.

'With all respect,' Sorya finishes, 'you are well out of your depth. In the league in which Constantine and I play, you're not even rated.'

'Thank you for your advice,' Aiah says, managing to speak the words without the sarcasm she feels in her heart, and then simply walks away, toward Constantine and the big Elton.

With an elegant gesture Constantine opens the door. Aiah settles onto the leather seat and Constantine closes the door behind her with that too-solid thunk, that sound of armor falling into place between her and everything outside.

Constantine is buoyant on the way to the plasm house, joking about the dolphins and their pretentions, about the Operation street captains who are about to have an unpleasant surprise. After a few moments of his insistent good humor, and with plasm vitality filling every cell, Aiah feels the tight-coiled anger slowly relax about her nerves.

The plasm house is kept in a nondescript office building, its red-brick walls gone gray with grime. Behind it squats the dark bulk of the housing project, a garden of fortresslike buildings crowned by pigeon coops and roof gardens. As the car pulls up Aiah peers upward out the window to look at the top of the building and sees a thorny, decorative crown of ornate wrought iron. Possibly there are antennae concealed there, possibly not.

She enters through stained bronze doors. Inside the air smells of fish fried in grease. Booming dance music echoes up a tall atrium surrounded by a ramp that spirals all the way to the top. There are young men loitering against the iron rails in the foyer, hoping to find a friend or a girl willing to pay the cover charge for one of the clubs. They look startled at Aiah's arrival, and she feels a warning cry through her nerves. Insulated by drivers, armor and limousines, she's grown careless about Terminal, about the Jaspeeri Nation stickers in the windows. But other than the usual whistles and pick-up lines they're civil enough, and she steps into the building and gazes upward.

The atrium is surrounded by an ancient webwork of wrought iron, an intricate spiral design that, reflecting the shieldlight brought in by the big skylight above, looks like a silvery spider's web funneling up to the ceiling. An elevator, a wrought-iron cage, pilots people to and from the restaurants. Aiah walks slowly up the spiral ramp, mentally calculating loads, distances, masses of brick and iron. She'll have to pull the plasm records for the whole building.

On the second floor she buys some ice cream from a vendor and continues her walk. The businesses here seem to be pawn shops, loan offices, clubs, music stores and bail bondsmen. Pairs of young lovers, pressed against one another in doorways, pay Aiah no attention as she walks by. The plasm house is in an office on the fifth floor, a gray metal door with flaking white lettering, KREMAG AND ASSOCIATES. She doesn't spare it a second glance, but she suspects she sees video monitors concealed in the wrought-iron leaves sprouting from the false iron pillars on either side of the door.

Aiah walks up another couple floors, then takes the elevator back down.

There is power, she thinks as she interlaces her fingers in the wrought-iron elevator wall, and power. Sorya knows of one kind, and Aiah another. And though Aiah wasn't born to Sorya's kind of power, she is learning it.

Is she afraid of Sorya? she wonders, and realizes that the

answer to her question is No. She wonders why, and suspects this is probably a comment on her sanity.

She leaves the building and dives into the limousine. 'Nothing much to see,' she says, 'I'll have to look through the records.'

Constantine nods. 'I can take you home now,' he says, 'but I have a stop along the way. A meeting.' He lifts his head, and Aiah can see a kind of excitement in him, a fierceness in his look, a readiness coiled in his restless body. He looks at her. 'There is an element of danger. You can stay in the car with Martinus.'

'Martinus isn't going with you? It's his job to protect you.'

'With this – gentleman – I'm best protected from here, from the car.'

Power, Aiah thinks. This could be an interesting lesson. 'Does it matter if he sees me? Is it like the situation with Parq, that he might blackmail me if he knows who I am?'

A private smile touches Constantine's lips. He shakes his head. 'No. Blackmail is not a danger here. My principal worry is that if things go awry, the both of us would be swiftly and certainly killed.'

He looks at her, eyes sparkling. The thought of death seems to amuse him.

'May I come?' Aiah asks.

Constantine laughs. 'You don't know what you're asking.'

He is daring her. Cheerful defiance rises in her mind on a whirlwind of plasm, and she grins back at him. 'Why stop taking chances now?' she says.

Constantine's mirth answers her own, and then a hint of caution crosses his face. 'I don't know if I want you to see me with this person,' he says. 'It may injure your good opinion of me.'

Aiah laughs. Constantine takes her hand, laces his fingers

through hers. 'Very well,' he says. 'But you are asking more of yourself than you know.'

Constantine has a way of being fatal to his friends. Aiah remembers Sorya's words, then defiantly dismisses them.

The car takes the Trans-City east, then leaves the highway and heads north. Tall office buildings gleam, white stone and bright metal and glass, on all sides. Off-shift, there is very little traffic. Martinus drives into a parking garage, winds down a spiral ramp to the bottom. He parks but leaves the engine running. Then he drops a panel on the dashboard, takes out a t-grip, and holds it ready.

Surprise floats through Aiah. 'There are plasm batteries in the car?' she says.

'Of course. For protection.'

It's obvious enough, but somehow the idea never crossed Aiah's mind. She follows Constantine from the car.

'Martinus is a mage?' Aiah asks.

'Martinus is a protection specialist. His abilities to protect me against plasm attack are considerable, and have never failed me.'

Constantine leads her to a steel door inset into the wall, takes the handle, pulls, and the door swings open. A loud buzzing sound rattles out of the darkness beyond. Constantine hesitates.

'I must caution you not to run,' he says. 'It may . . . awaken instincts best left alone.'

Constantine finds a light switch and turns it. The room beyond is full of pumps screened off by mesh cages; apparently the garage is below the water table and needs constant pumping. Aiah follows Constantine past them and to another metal door with a yellow-and-red Authority sticker on it. Aiah pats her pockets for keys, but Constantine opens this door as easily as he had the other, and with a chill Aiah realizes that someone else has preceded them.

Beyond is a utility tunnel, hot and humid, with sweat beading its round concrete walls and a rivulet of water at the bottom. Yellow electric bulbs hang in metal cages every quarter pitch. A bulky shielded cable, held to the wall by huge metal staples, carries a fortune in plasm from one place to another. There is a smell of suspended dust. Earthquake anxieties rise in Aiah's mind and she tamps them firmly down as she follows Constantine.

Aiah loosens her collar in the hot air. 'Who lives down here?' she says. 'Who would want to meet anyone here?'

'He said the fourth light,' Constantine murmurs. Even though he has to crouch his pace is rapid and Aiah strains to keep up. The sound of their bootsteps is loud in the small space.

And suddenly Aiah knows something else is there, sharing the tunnel with them, and despite the heat her blood runs cold. She gives a cry and shrinks away, the curved tunnel firm against her spine. It seems to have come in through the tunnel wall just ahead of them, oozing through it as if the concrete were porous.

'Greetings,' Constantine says, his voice firm, but Aiah can see fists at the ends of his arms, fists clenched so tight the nails gnaw at his palms.

Aiah can't tell what it is he's talking to. For some reason, even though there's no obstruction, it's impossible to get a clear view of it. It seems silver, gleaming under the light, and yet also deep black, black as the deepest abandoned pit, and yet there are hints of other colors, whole spectra running fast through its uncertain outlines, like an interference pattern on the video.

And it's cold. Aiah realizes her teeth are chattering. She wonders why her breath doesn't bloom out in front of her, frozen into mist.

'Metropolitan,' the thing says. 'Why do you seek me again?'

'I wish you to serve me,' Constantine says. 'And in exchange, I will give you what you desire.'

'Four each month,' the thing says. 'And for five years.'

Its voice is resonant, seems to vibrate deep in Aiah's belly.

Constantine lifts his head. 'Two. And for two years.'

Aiah huddles in her jacket, nerves crawling with fear, flesh crawling with cold. It feels as if her bones have turned to ice.

'Two?' the thing says. 'And what is it you wish me to do for this . . . *token*?'

Aiah can hear the steel in Constantine's voice. 'I wish to put the Metropolis of Caraqui in my pocket,' he says.

'You wish me to kill?'

'Certain people. Yes.'

'Bad people?' The question sounds like a taunt. Aiah can sense the creature's mirth.

'I believe so.'

'Three.' There is hunger in the thing's voice.

'Two.' Firmly.

'I could kill you,' the thing offers.

Even Constantine's teeth are chattering now. But he takes a step toward the thing, gestures with one fist.

'That would not get you what you want,' he says.

There is a moment of silence. Silver and black run through the thing's faintly humanoid outline.

'Two,' it concedes. The voice is silky. 'And when does the killing start?'

'In a few days. I will send you a message by our accustomed route.'

Aiah gives a warning cry as the creature flows toward Constantine, spreading wide its arms, or whatever it uses for arms, but it's not an attack, it's a kind of submission, the thing bowing down before Constantine, huddling on the concrete floor.

'I will do as you ask,' it says.

Constantine holds out a hand over the bowed form. 'Do this thing for me,' he says, 'and I will give you release, if you want it.'

'Perhaps,' it says, and then, 'Not yet.'

'As you wish.'

And then it flows away, vanishing through the solid wall of the tunnel, and Aiah cries out in relief.

For a long moment, the only sound in the tunnel is the trickling of water. The cold fades from Aiah's bones, and suddenly she realizes she's wet, both from the sweat that covers her skin and from the fact that she's sitting in the rivulet at the bottom of the tunnel. Her knees had folded and she'd slid down the concrete tunnel wall and she hadn't even noticed.

Constantine gives a relieved sigh, then turns, sees her on the floor, and smiles. 'Gone now,' he says, and offers her a hand.

Aiah isn't certain whether her legs will yet support her, but she takes the hand anyway, allows herself to be set on her feet. She's relieved to find them capable of bearing her weight.

The air in the tunnel is very hot. Sweat pours down her face, but her body still shudders with cold.

'Why am I sweating and shivering at the same time?' she asks.

'It's a cold thing, isn't it?' Constantine's tone is light, but Aiah can tell it's an effort. 'The effect is purely mental, though . . . your body continued to respond to the heat and humidity here, even though your mind was convinced it was cold.'

He takes her arm and begins to guide her to the exit. Their boots splash through water. A wave of adrenaline shivers through her body. She looks up at him, clutches at his arm.

'What *was* it?'

'Its kind have different names. Creature of light. Ice man. Hanged man.' He licks his lips. 'The Damned. That's the nearest description, I think.'

'A h-hanged man?' Astonishment trips up Aiah's tongue. Hanged men are a feature of children's stories and bad fright chromoplays, monsters that leap out of closets and bring down their victims in a spray of blood. 'They're real?'

'Oh yes. But quite rare.'

'Thank Senko.'

They reach the door, and Constantine pulls it open. Aiah staggers out into the cool air of a pump room. She wipes sweat from her face with a handkerchief and straightens her skirt. A clammy spot, where she'd sat in the water, clings to her thighs.

Constantine walks past, opens the door into the garage. Aiah follows him out.

'You knew this one,' she says. 'How?'

'There are people who worship hanged men, or make bargains with them. For a time . . .' He takes a breath, lets it out. 'For a time, I belonged to such a cult. It was a period in which I had lost all faith in humanity, and in which I was seeking . . . extremes. But during that time I gained knowledge of hanged men, and what they are and desire.'

'What is it—' Aiah's mind stumbles on the question, and she has to will it to continue. 'What is it that they want?'

'To be what they once were.' They approach the limousine, and Constantine opens the door for her. She seats herself, and Constantine sits across from her. He opens the bar and pours brandy into a pair of crystal glasses.

'Have a stiff one,' he says, and offers a glass. 'It'll do you good.'

Aiah bolts the brandy and welcomes the fiery reality that burns its way down her throat. Constantine sips at his drink with more delicacy. Martinus starts the car, heads toward the ramp leading to the street.

'He was once a man, that creature,' Constantine says. 'You knows about plasm's mutagenic effects, how it can warp things, can create monsters out of ordinary animals.'

Aiah remembers the thing in the pneuma station, the

ripple of silver belly scales that, in memory, now glow with the peculiar liquid sheen of the patterns that ran through the hanged man, and suddenly the brandy wants to come up. She turns away, shuddering, acid burning her throat. She forces the brandy back down.

Constantine, gazing into his glass, seems not to notice. The car spirals up the long concrete ramp.

'It can happen with people, but more rarely,' he continues. 'Scholars, sometimes, or philosophers, those who live in plasm all the time, who practically bathe in it, and never notice when they slip away from matter and become a prisoner of the plasm itself. A few very powerful people, tyrants or captains of industry, people who can afford all the plasm they can consume, have been brought down that way. Some politicians, leaders, but not as often. The day-to-day realities of politics, of decision-making, provide an anchor on the world's reality.

'And then . . .' Constantine's deep voice turns dreamy. 'And then, when they have become plasm only, their material substance gone or used up, they begin to yearn for what they once were. But they can't manage it – they can't work with matter any more, their very touch is hostile to life. They can kill, easily and without thought, but they can't create, can't touch, and life itself, the life of the warm body, becomes a dream, a yearning, an ever-increasing desire they can't fulfill.'

An icy hand touches the back of Aiah's neck. 'So what is it they want?' she says for the second time. The car arrives at ground level, Shieldlight beckoning just ahead, promising a world of normality, safety, the company of human beings.

Constantine looks at Aiah, his eyes hard. 'It wants life. To be back among living things, to know the touch of the wind, the taste of wine, the joys of the flesh. It can't accomplish this by itself, because it's no longer a thing of matter, and cannot work with matter but to destroy. But with the help of a capable mage — my help in this case — it can take a body, occupy it. Use it for a time.'

The brandy tries to rise past Aiah's throat again, and she fights it back down. 'And what happens to the person occupied by this thing?'

Constantine's voice is toneless. 'The body is used up; the hanged man is fatal to life in the long run. In a matter of days the body becomes a husk. And as for the victim's soul, I suppose it goes wherever it is that souls go.'

Sadness swims through Aiah. She leans back, rests her nape against plush fabric. 'And these victims?' she asks. 'Who will they be?'

Constantine sighs. 'Criminals, I suppose. Perhaps some of Caraqui's utterly deserving political class. It is a sad fact of political life that once you concede the notion that certain people deserve death, it isn't hard to find them.'

'And this cult you belonged to? What did *it* offer this hanged man of yours?'

'My cousin Heromë was the priest. He was also in charge of our political prisons. The hanged man did not lack for souls to eat.'

Aiah shudders. Constantine's toneless, objective voice goes on. 'Years later, at my instigation, the hanged man destroyed Heromë and his whole circle. He did not like them, you see, or the things they required of him . . . he is a distinguished personage, even among his kind. Once he was Taikoen, Taikoen the Great, the man who saved Atavir from the Slaver Mages.'

Aiah glances at Constantine in astonishment. Taikoen is one of the great heroes in all history.

'Cults all over the world worship him.' A cold little smile plays about Constantine's lips. 'Would they still if they knew what he had become? The man I most admired in the last five hundred years, and when I met him he was the all-powerful slave of Heromë, a grubby little prison warden. After Taikoen's retirement he lost himself in plasm and now cannot live without it. You thought he came out of the wall? No, he was within the cable. That is where he lives now – he cannot survive for long outside a plasm well.'

Aiah runs fingers through her hair. Sorrow wells through her body. 'I don't know what to think,' she says.

Constantine leans forward, takes her hand between his own. He looks at her for a long moment, and Aiah sees pain and longing in his eyes. 'It's the worst thing I have ever done,' he says, 'or shall do. And for some reason it comforts me that you know of it.'

There is a long silence. Aiah's hand is warm between his palms. 'I have no right to ask you, I suppose,' he says. 'But will you forgive me?'

Aiah licks her lips, withdraws her hand. 'Will you take me to Old Shorings?' she asks.

Surprise glows in his eyes. 'Right now?'

'Yes.'

He turns to Martinus and gives the order. She holds out her glass. 'More brandy, please,' she says. 'A piece of paper, and a pencil.'

It's a long ride, and neither Constantine nor Aiah finds much to say. When they reach the neighborhood, Aiah guides Martinus until she finds the place she has in mind, the gray stone temple on its tiny lot. Aiah props Constantine's notepad on her knee and writes on the thin leaf of plastic: *Let my friend have Caraqui.*

She tears away the paper, takes the brandy bottle and leaves the car. Street hustlers peer alertly from doorways, but when Martinus gets out of the car to stand guard they swiftly lose interest. Aiah walks across the empty street, walks up the steps of the temple, looks up at the carvings, the plants and serpents and creatures of myth. Aiah kneels on the cold stones, feels grains of rice against her knees.

Little leaves of paper flutter in the cracks of the huge door. Faded flowers and a few small coins lie scattered on the stoop. Aiah unstops the brandy bottle and pours it across the threshold as an offering. Then she leans forward against the huge iron door, feeling rust against her forehead, and folds the paper very small and inserts it in the crack between the two metal doors.

'Whoever is there,' she says, 'please forgive my friend, and give him what he wants.'

She lets more brandy trickle from the bottle and repeats her prayer many times. Her knees grow wet with brandy. When the bottle is empty, she leaves it on the stoop and walks unsteadily back to the car, sits next to Constantine, and lets him take her in his arms.

'I would like to go home now,' she says, and as the big car carries her away to Loeno she falls asleep on his shoulder.

17

The scent of bowel hovers in Aiah's nostrils as Tella changes Jayme's diapers. 'I can't understand why you want to leave,' Tella complains. 'Rohder's a spent force in the Authority. He can't get you anything.'

Aiah wraps the cord around her headset and places it on the hook for Mokel, who has this desk on service shift this week.

'Good for a change,' she says. 'Maybe I'll pick up some pointers.'

'Rohder got his whole department flushed,' Tella says. 'How many pointers can he give?'

'Bye,' Aiah says.

'I'm going to be lonely!' Tella wails, and Aiah heads for the 106th floor.

Her nerves spark fire as the elevator rises. Rohder will be her *passu*, and through him, the Authority. Jaspeer's most powerful force will be doing her bidding.

On arrival she finds Rohder seated in his big padded chair, one hand dropped casually on a copper t-grip, the other holding a cigaret to his lips. When Aiah enters, the cigaret points Shieldward in a gesture that tells her to wait.

Aiah waits for a few moments, then a few moments longer. The imperious Angels of Power gaze at her sidelong from their niches on the corner. She walks to one of the huge windows and looks out at the great city, the steep gray grid topped by water towers, roof gardens, cisterns and animal pens. A silver airship two blocks long drifts along the horizon, its belly bright with advertisements.

Rohder lights a new cigaret, smokes it, lights another.

Aiah wanders away from the window, walks alongside a long shelf built against the back wall. Identical sets of thick volumes are laid along it, books bound in red plastic with gold lettering along the spines. *Proceedings of the Research Division of the Jaspeeri Plasm Authority*, it says. Fourteen volumes. Aiah picks one at random and leafs through it. Complex mathematical formulae swarm before her eyes.

'The Intendant found it overly abstruse, I'm afraid,' Rohder says. He's finished his business and is walking around his huge rayed desk toward her. 'But I felt I had to publish the proofs. If you look in the last volume, you'll see our recommendations.'

Aiah closes the heavy volume and returns it. 'Maybe you should have put the recommendations first,' she says.

Rohder blinks as if this is a startling new idea. 'Perhaps.' He walks up alongside the shelf and runs his hand along the long row of volumes. 'It took my department eight years to produce those books,' he says, 'and I've always had the feeling that no one in the Authority ever read them.'

The law of the chonah is for the *pascol* to agree with the *passu* whenever possible. 'That strikes me as fairly typical of the Authority,' Aiah says. 'Spend years and a lot of money on an elite commission, then flush its recommendations the second they're made.'

Rohder looks bemusedly at the shelf of books. 'Would you like a set? I seem to have a few to spare.'

'I don't think I'd understand them. But I'd like to borrow the last volume, if I may.'

'Of course.' His blue eyes gaze blankly at her for a long moment, and then he seems to remember why she's here. 'Terminal,' he says.

'Yes.'

'You think you can help me?'

'What I need you to do,' she says, 'is call Compilation and Billing and tell them that I need to go through the records for that area for the last five years.' She speaks with care, suspecting that Rohder might not follow through unless she spells it out. 'That means I need access to the belts, and someone to handle the belts for me, and a reader-computer. You need to insist that I be given access immediately, because otherwise they'll just put me off forever.'

Rohder nods at each point, as if ticking them off mentally. 'Very well. I'll call Niden first, then have him call his underlings and give the orders.'

He heads back to his desk. Aiah follows. 'How is your aerial search going?' she says.

'I've found some small-scale use that's probably illegitimate, but nothing big enough to cause the Bursary Street flamer.'

'Let's hope I can find something interesting for you.'

'Mmm.' Rohder's look is already abstracted as he reaches for his headset.

All the data are kept in the nearest Authority station at Rocketman, a familiar trackline journey away. The station manager, at Niden's bidding, gives her an alcove with an old Filbaq computer-reader in a room otherwise filled with people busy entering data. Aiah's chosen assistant, Damusz, doesn't seem happy to have drawn extra duty. Digging the old belt out of storage has striped his chest and thighs with grime. He silently and sullenly takes the belt from its case, loads the etching belt's spool on the reader, then stretches the belt onto the secondary spool and tightens the continuous loop. 'Thank you,' Aiah says, as nicely as she can, and adjusts the play head over the belt.

The Filbaq is an old model and has probably been sitting unused in this alcove for years. It's still functional, fortunately, and ozone scents the air as its whining electric motor soon brings the belt up to speed. Dancing dust falls from the reader's ornamental brass fins. The screen hasn't been cleaned in ages, and Aiah swabs it with her wrist lace to no effect. She turns to ask Damusz to bring her a spray bottle of glass cleaner, but he's already disappeared.

Squinting through the smeared lens, Aiah presses worn steel keys, finds Kremag and Associates in the directory, and calls up the data. Disappointingly, it's all perfectly reasonable: the firm is twelve years old, is alleged to offer 'business consulting', and hasn't used an iota of plasm in all that time. Business consultants wouldn't, would they? They just let it flow through the meters.

She needs to come up with a plausible reason why she hands Kremag to Rohder. None seems to be available from the data.

The most likely tampering would come with the matter of dates and names. She asks the reader to search the entire belt for other businesses at that address, a job that will probably take some time. While the read head whines over the long strands of data, Aiah provides herself with some coffee in a cardboard cup and finds a spray bottle of glass cleaner. She cleans the screen and drinks half the coffee by the time the reader comes up with the information she needs: no less than three other businesses occupied Kremag's offices during the years Kremag has supposedly been there. And their plasm use is identical to Kremag's, down to the last millimehr – it seems that whoever retroactively inserted Kremag and Associates onto this belt simply hijacked the earlier firms' data.

It's all suspicious as hell, but still it won't provide Aiah with a reason why she chose this particular address in the first place. Aiah gnaws a thumbnail and stares at the screen and wonders if Rohder will even ask.

Possibly he won't, but at this point she's not willing to take a chance.

If the data were inserted retroactively onto this belt, she reasons, they might not be inserted sequentially with the rest. The idea excites her. She leans forward as her fingers hammer the clacking metal keys.

Yes! she thinks. Triumph skips along her nerves. When data are entered on a belt in the normal fashion, it's done more or less sequentially, one month's string after the next. But Kremag's data for the first years of its existence were layered in separately and lie on the etching belt years out of sequence. Whoever entered the false information should have overwritten the data from the earlier occupants of the office, but either it hadn't occurred to him or he lacked the necessary programming skill.

Aiah leans back in her chair and smiles, and then it occurs to her that, if this particular programmer used this method more than once, she might well be able to find more examples of his handiwork.

She writes down the Kremag data, then starts slowly scanning the data on the belt, looking for data added out of sequence. There's a fair amount of it, mostly gibberish, fragments of information slotted into empty or erased channels, but some of it is laid in whole, months and years out of sequence. Aiah jots these down as well.

The shift is almost over when she remembers that she forgot to eat lunch.

Aiah calls Rohder and asks him to wait past shift change, as she's found some important information.

'I was going to stay second shift anyway,' he says. Aiah wonders if he ever leaves.

Then she calls Constantine's accommodation number and tells Dr Chandros that she will be late, but will have important information when she arrives.

She gets onto the trackline just in time for shift change. The mass of bodies, swaddled close around her, keeps her from losing her footing on the long, jolting journey back to the Authority.

No one works through second shift but Tabulation, Transmission, and the odd emergency crew on standby, and the Authority building is almost deserted; whole decades of stories are vacant. She can't remember the last time she was alone in the building's elevators, let alone for a journey of over a hundred stories.

When Aiah enters Rohder's office she finds him standing in front of his desk, a slight frown on his face as if he can't quite remember how he came to be there. 'Sir,' she says. 'I have a list of possibilities and this one,' she points to Kremag, 'this one is the most promising.'

She explains that she acquired the knowledge by searching for data strings laid out of sequence on the continuous belts. Rohder absorbs the information without comment, his pale blue eyes gazing at her unwinkingly. Finally he nods, his knob-wristed hand rising to stroke his chin.

'Do you think you could find others in this fashion?'

'Certainly. If whoever created the fake accounts made the same mistake.'

He nods and mutters something to himself, then says, 'Perhaps I will be able to give you further employment. Your supervisor doesn't mind?'

'I'm sure Mr Mengene would be happy to assign me here. My job is pointless anyway – I'm just holding down a place in the promotion queue until a real job comes along.'

Rohder considers this. 'I've observed,' he says, 'that here at the Authority the jobs never seem to get *that* real.'

When she leaves, a few minutes later, she carries Volume Fourteen of the *Proceedings* with her.

There's no car waiting for her at the corner, but it doesn't dampen her glow of accomplishment. She happily takes a cab to Terminal and reads Rohder's book along the way.

We therefore recommend the complete reformation of human infrastructure along the following lines . . .

Aiah's eyebrows lift. You had to give Rohder credit for ambition.

Complete reformation of human infrastructure . . .

No wonder no one took him seriously. It cost a fortune just to lay a new sewer pipe, never mind anything more ambitious than that.

She pays her driver, knocks at the factory door, is recognized and allowed to enter. The factory looks like a military installation now, the windows painted black and covered with tape from the inside, an iron-braced corrugated roof over the accumulators and contacts, the control switches and consoles for plasm sandbagged, a half-dozen guards pacing up and down. Even though, given the threat from Rohder, no one uses plasm outside the factory or in Caraqui, there are still a pair of mages at the consoles, warding the factory itself against intrusion.

Aiah hears raised voices, Constantine's voice booming over all. He's in the factory office, raging up and down, arms slashing the air. Sorya, Martinus and Geymard are with him, and two others that make Aiah's skin crawl.

They are twisted: one is small, hairless, with a moist and glabrous skin and huge black eyes each the size of a fist – all pupil, no whites. The other is short, stocky and powerful, with arms like iron conduits that hang to his knees. It looks as if all of Martinus's mass is jammed into a body two heads shorter.

Allies, Aiah thinks, but cannot repress a shudder. She slips into the office and stands in the back, as far from the twisted as she can get – fortunately they seem to have no foul odor – and then she waits to see what the upset is about.

The factory office has been made into a kind of headquarters for the coup: there are maps of Caraqui with pins stuck in them, photographs and room plans of target buildings, tables of organizaton for military units and their commanders, long lists of officers with checkmarks and handwritten notes next to each, detailing whether he was approached, who approached him, his response, and the judgment of the recruiting officer concerning his degree of loyalty to the cause. But something has happened to upset all this careful organization. Constantine argues for launching the attack now, within the next twenty-four hours; but Sorya and Geymard speak against it.

Constantine's booming voice rattles the office windows. 'We daren't give the Specials time to pick our conspiracy apart!'

'Wait,' Geymard says, and frowns at the map.

'Two arrests only,' Sorya says, 'and little folk at that, junior officers who know nothing of the larger picture.'

'And their recruiters are safe, we've got 'em out, and they're sheltering with our friends,' Geymard adds, nodding toward the twisted. 'So the Specials cannot follow the chain upward to people more central to our plans.'

Aiah's breath grows short at the thought of sheltering with the twisted, even if they're friendly, living in their dark warrens, eating their food, surrounded by their odor.

'Someone must have betrayed them,' Constantine insists. 'Someone in our organization.'

'Their own tongues betrayed them, most like,' Geymard says. 'Drunk and boasting of the end of the Keremaths within hearing of some informer.'

'Strike now!' Constantine shouts, and throws up his hands. 'Why not? Everything's in place, awaiting only the word . . .'

Geymard gives a little shake of the head. 'There are *hundreds* in this conspiracy by now,' he says; 'it will take longer than that to alert them all.'

'I cannot guarantee that it will be possible to alert all our people in the given time,' says the smaller of the twisted. His voice is high, gentle, with oddly formal cadences.

'And we can't be assured of the reliability of our plasm supply,' Sorya says, and her green eyes flicker to Aiah, zeroing in like gunsights. 'If you had let me arrange an accident as I wished, perhaps the Authority would no longer be a danger to us.'

Aiah watches the eyes of the conspirators turn to her. She can see an impatient muscle twitch along Constantine's big jaw. Aiah straightens her spine and brings a smile to her lips.

'I've fed Kremag and Associates to the Authority,' she says. 'They'll move soon, I think. And once they're done with Kremag, they'll start looking into a half-dozen other addresses I've given them. Whatever they'll be doing in the next week, they won't be looking for us.'

'When will the Authority move against Kremag?' Constantine demands.

'I've given them enough evidence to move immediately,' Aiah says. 'But they might wish to double-check. Perhaps they won't be able to locate a prosecuting judge willing to sign the warrants on the off-shift, and perhaps the creepers from the Investigative Division can't organize a raid on such short notice. So I wouldn't expect anything till tomorrow.'

Constantine looks at her coldly, then spins on his heel and marches toward the map. Aiah's heart gives a little cry at the sign of his displeasure. Constantine puts his big hand over the center of Caraqui, covering the Aerial Palace and the state buildings with his palm. He leans into the map, putting weight onto it as if he can somehow bring his impatient power to bear against his targets. 'I can feel it slipping away,' he says. 'We had momentum on our side till now. Now we're at a standstill, waiting on events. Any little accident can bring an end to our schemes.'

'That was true all along,' Geymard says levelly. 'And *we're* safe enough, whatever happens. It's Drumbeth who's taking all the chances, not us.'

'The Specials could be arresting our people now.'

'And what could we do to prevent it?' Sorya says. 'Besides, if they do, what will they find? Contradiction, rumor, speculation. Most of the recruits were told what they wanted to hear, which was not necessarily the truth. Their role in the scheme is small, and they know nothing else but their own part. There are very few people who know the full scope of the coup, and they are here in this room.' She looks up at Constantine. 'There are some things even Drumbeth does not know, and the coup is his conception. The fact that you armed the dolphins, for example.'

Constantine doesn't reply, turns to Geymard. 'I want to see your people,' he says. 'I want to know they're ready to move the instant we give the word.'

A hint of exasperation twitches at the corners of Geymard's slitted eyes. 'Very well,' he says. 'Shall we take my aerocar?'

'Yes. At once, if you please . . .'

Constantine launches himself from the office like a hound off the leash, Geymard and Martinus following at a more dignified pace. Aiah's heart sinks – she's abandoned here, with Sorya and the twisted. Sorya watches Constantine go, one brow arched.

'Despite being an initiate of the School of Radritha,' she says, 'Constantine has never quite mastered the value of simply waiting on events.' She turns to her two allies. 'My apologies for his rudeness. He is not himself now, but come the event itself, he will do well indeed. Surpass himself, I suspect.'

'We understand,' says the larger of the twisted, and surprise wells in Aiah at the realization that this massive figure is female.

'We comprehend this is a critical time for all of us,' the other adds in his dancing high-pitched voice.

'I don't believe you have all been introduced,' Sorya continues. 'Miss Aiah, these are our allies Adaveth –' the small, half-amphibian one '– and Myhorn.' The larger. Sorya looks at them and adds, 'Miss Aiah is one of our most valued agents here in Jaspeer.'

Is that what I am? Aiah wonders, and nods at the pair. 'Pleased to meet you,' she says, and tries not to flinch as Adaveth's huge black liquid eyes turn to gaze at her.

'Honored,' Adaveth says simply, and then turns back to Sorya. 'Am I to understand the conference is over? Shall we return to Caraqui?'

Sorya considers this. 'You are welcome to remain, if you desire,' she says, 'but it does not seem possible to make any decisions at this point. We will contact you within three shifts in any case.'

'Then we will return to our homes,' Adaveth says. 'There are always preparations to make.' They shake hands with Sorya, and then with Aiah. Aiah summons her courage, reaches out, and touches Adaveth's moist flesh.

The two twisted take their leave, and Aiah feels herself breathe easier. Sorya escorts them to the door of the office, then closes the door and looks after them through its glass pane.

'They are the Keremaths' great mistake,' she says, 'and our opportunity.' A smile touches her lips. 'The old Avian rulers of Caraqui, twisted themselves, created other twisted to serve them, all adapted for specific tasks. The Avians stratified their society, themselves on the top, their menial creations on the very bottom. And when the Avians were overthrown, the twisted remained on the bottom – but yet they are expected to perform important tasks, among them the maintenance of utility and plasm lines on those foolish great barges the Caraquis live in.' She looks at Aiah. 'Who knows what they will do in exchange for a little dignity, a little honor? Astonishing how the Kerehorns seem not to understand this. I would make of those workers an elite, with pride and esprit, as befits their responsibility.'

'I see,' Aiah says. She wonders why Sorya is being so cordial, perhaps it is merely today's fancy to be pleasant, she thinks, and then remembers, *The law of the* chonah *is to make friends with the* passu, and she feels her mental guard rise into place.

'The consoles are all free,' Sorya says. 'Make use of the plasm as you like – but don't use any outside this building, or in a way that can be detected from outside. After that I will arrange a ride home for you, if you wish.'

'Thank you,' Aiah says.

Her console is a little sandbagged womb, with only herself and the monitors and the t-grip. She uses the plasm to burn away fatigue, then practices some of the exercises Constantine has taught her, visualizations, anima, sensory array. She floats her anima into the basement and strides about in the darkness, past the big iron braces that support the weight of the huge accumulators, the cables and stanchions that feed them power. Conduits for power and reality, and soon for revolution.

And none of it, Aiah thinks, without her.

There have already been deaths. And plots, and arrests, and movements of troops. Alliances made, murders plotted, lies crafted, deceptions practiced, and at least one bargain made, with a creature of purest evil, for the consumption of souls.

None of it without Aiah.

She had been horrified, once, by the thought of deaths laid to her account. But the horror has faded now, replaced only by a fading melancholy at the necessity of it all. What were those unfortunate lives against Caraqui, the New City, the scale of Constantine's ambition?

Aiah smoothly absorbs more power from the t-grips, expands her anima, turning herself into a giant crouching under the brick arches of the basement room. Her sensorium grows, filling the huge empty space until it seems as if she feels the pressure of every mote of dust, hears the dry throb of every insect heart. Aiah calls light into being, illuminating the huge dark cavern with a blazing pulse of power, the flickering orange fire contrasting with the deep black shadows cast by the arches . . .

Aiah floats through the room like a beacon and realizes, with a cold and knowing joy, that she has become a burning woman indeed.

18

Beneath skies filled with adverts for *Lords of the New City*, Aiah luxuriates in the back of the car with her accustomed basket of fruit and wine. She reads Rohder's *Proceedings* in the car on her way home and is progressively intrigued. Rohder claims to have detected something he calls 'fractionate intervals' at which plasm creation can be increased. Similar principles have been known since legendary times, based on the radius, the distance at which plasm effects begin to multiply. Major structures are built at precise distances from one another in order to increase the generation of plasm through 'resonance' – the Great Squares and the Grand Squares, and the Squares of Squares being popular – and the more enlightened and well-ordered metropolises, by statute, have their streets placed a certain distance apart in order to guarantee enhancement.

But the effects diminish at either end of the spectrum: at the large end, the curvature of the planet prevents buildings from being placed in ideal relationships; and at the smaller end, the effects simply fade away into undetectability at distances shorter than about a quarter-radius.

Rohder claims to have detected a smaller unit, equivalent to the radius, that also produces resonance on a much smaller scale, an effect that had previously gone unnoticed simply because earlier equipment was unable to separate the resulting smallish increases from background clutter. He refers to this, in typically uninspiring language, as the 'affective unit', or AU. Fairly large structures have to be placed in precise relationships in order to obtain any effect at all, and the result is a small increase, on the order of twenty percent under ideal conditions.

And therefore, Aiah reads, Rohder blithely recommends a completely rebuilt infrastructure in order to take advantage of the effect. There are a host of recommendations for accomplishing this, mostly impractical. The only realistic suggestion is for new building codes that oblige contractors to put building frames at affective distances from one another.

Still, she thinks, a twenty percent increase in plasm creation is not to be sneezed at.

According to Constantine's system of thought, it is a twenty percent increase in the entire wealth of the world.

She finds herself wanting to see the actual research. She wonders if it was ever published anywhere but in the *Proceedings*.

A message from Rohder waits for her on her return to her apartment. He had investigated Kremag and Associates and found clear evidence of illegal plasm use, and seen plasm in the act of being broadcast from horns concealed beneath the roof.

So much, Aiah thinks, for her theory of the wrought-iron ornaments being used as broadcast horns.

Rohder goes on to say that he's been arranging for a Tactical Team to go into the building. In the meantime, Rohder hopes Aiah would be willing to start a review of the etching belts in the Intendency District, on the sixtieth floor in the main Authority building. The big buildings, public and private, in the Intendency were built much more scientifically than those around Rocketman, and if any plasm is being stolen, it would be in much larger amounts.

Aiah calls Rohder's office. His voice, when he answers, sounds distracted.

'I'd like to thank you for offering to continue my assignment,' she says.

'You're welcome.' Long pause. 'I'd like to thank *you*,' he adds, as if in afterthought.

'I was wondering about what was going to happen with Kremag and Associates, and when.'

'Ah.' Another long pause. The answer, when it comes, is long and drawn out, with pauses for Rohder to breathe cigaret smoke or sometimes just to think. 'Well,' he sighs, 'I've been in touch with the prosecuting judge who usually works with us, and he's granting warrants. Once that's done, we'll send in a Tactical Team, but it helps our case if there's illegal plasm activity going on when we actually storm in, and that means assembling enough mages to guarantee the Team's safety while they're breaking in and making the arrests.'

'How long will that all take?'

'What time is it now?'

'23:00. It'll be Friday in an hour or so.'

'Probably in twenty-four hours or so, then. Late second shift Friday, or early third shift Saturday.'

'That's fast, then. Good.' Aiah is already wondering whether or not to call Dr Chandros on this one.

'I'm doing surveillance right now,' Rohder says. 'I should probably end this conversation.'

His spectral anima was floating somewhere in the vicinity of Kremag and Associates. No wonder he seemed preoccupied.

'I'll see you tomorrow, then,' Aiah says. 'Goodbye, and thanks again.'

She presses the disconnect button and hangs up her headset. An image of Rohder floats through her mind: sitting in his smoky office, the Angels of Power gazing down at him with polished bronze eyes while his mind travels through the city on a stream of plasm.

Aiah looks at the copy of the *Proceedings* that lies on her unmade bed and wonders about Rohder. She knows nothing about him, nothing but what is implied by that red-bound book, the last of fourteen volumes all unread by the audience for whom it was intended, and which nevertheless claims a revolutionary interpretation of the fundamental solvent of matter and mind.

She looks at the end of the book and discovers that all the contributors had appended their vitae. She looks at Rohder's, reads the first few lines, and feels cool surprise run up her spine.

He's over three hundred years old. After some mental math Aiah comes up with the exact figure: 317.

Rohder has been working for the Authority since receiving his doctorate at the age of twenty-five, although he seems to have taken a fair number of sabbaticals in order to teach. No wonder, Aiah thinks, he has too much seniority to be got rid of. No wonder he has such high access to plasm. In a system that runs entirely on seniority, he must be nearly invincible.

Her gaze drifts back to the communications array and wonders again if she should call the number given her by Constantine. If he knew the Tactical Team was going in within twenty-four hours or so, then he could get on with his plans.

And, Aiah thinks, he'd have something else to do besides be irritable.

She sighs, leaves the apartment, and heads for the elevator. There are some pay phones down in the ground-floor recreation area, between the swimming pool and the ball courts. It will be safe enough to make the call from there.

The next morning Aiah finds Khoriak waiting outside Loeno Towers. 'Hello?' she says. 'Is something up?'

Khoriak brushes his blond bangs from his forehead. Behind him, a coffee advertisement unfolds in midair. 'I have a message from the boss,' he says, and hands her an envelope.

'Thank you,' surprised.

'Would you like me to take you to work?'

'Oh.' She looks at the traffic, barely moving, and makes a calculation. 'I don't think you could get me there in time. I'll take the pneuma.'

On her walk to the pneuma the face of the actor Kherzaki seems everywhere, scowling down from his New City in the sky. Aiah considers going to the chromoplay after work and wonders if it's still possible to get a ticket. The hype is so huge on this one that every theater in Jaspeer may well be sold out.

And then, as she opens Constantine's envelope, a pair of tickets drops into her hand. *I would invite you to the official premiere*, in Constantine's hand, *but I fear it would be less than discrete for us to be together in such public circumstances. Take these with my compliments, and use them or give them away, as you please. If you are not too weary, or weary of me, I will be at the Landmark from 0200 on, procedures as before.*

Signed, *Your expectant friend.*

The tickets are for a theater two blocks from the Loeno. Who does he expect me to go *with*? Aiah wonders, looking at the extra ticket, and then thinks, with a smile, that perhaps she'll invite Rohder.

At work she stops by her office to pick up her messages, and finds a pneumatic note from Mengene in her wire basket. *Whatever you're doing for Rohder*, it reads, *keep it up. He was raving about your performance a moment ago.*

Pleasure rises warm in Aiah at the message, though it takes a certain amount of mental effort to imagine Rohder raving – not unless it were a result of nicotine withdrawal, anyway.

She takes the hydraulic elevator to Rohder's office, the elevator doors cutting off the full cry of Tella's baby which had just been unleashed by the opening of a neighboring elevator. It's an event that can only expand Aiah's gratification.

'I took a peek at a couple of the other addresses you gave me,' Rohder tells her, 'and at least one of them looks like a real plasm den. After we finish with this first raid, I'll be looking for another warrant.'

'I hope I'll find you some more today,' Aiah says.

On the sixtieth floor Aiah is treated like the Intendant's personal representative – she's given a clean private office, with a window that gazes straight across the Avenue of the Exchange into another window in the Bursary. The office is equipped with the latest-model Evo-Matic belt reader, and she's given an assistant, a nervous junior department manager in black velvet and lace. Word has pretty clearly got out that she's got some powerful people behind whatever it is that she's doing.

She scrolls through the belts carefully, but the Intendency District is well policed and affluent and is composed largely of government offices anyway. All day she finds only two suspect addresses, both inserted, she suspects, either by the same programmer who had left his handiwork all over Rocketman, or by another programmer using the same methods.

One of the addresses is on Old Parade and probably concerns some fiddle having to do with the new construction. And the second address, she notes, is in the Investigative Division itself, the Authority's own police.

Who watches the watchmen? she wonders.

Herself, apparently. A thought which increases in its amusement value the more she thinks about it.

At the end of her day she reports her findings to Rohder.

'Thank you,' he says. He huddles in his big chair, one foot drawn up beside him, and stares with peculiar intensity at the clutter on his desk while fiddling with his cigaret lighter.

'What about the raid?' Aiah asks. 'Is it tonight?'

'Hm?' Rohder blinks, then gazes up at her with his watery blue eyes. 'Oh yes, probably. The Tac Team will be moving into place at 20:00. After that, it depends on what our criminals are doing.'

'Good luck, then.' Aiah turns to leave, then hesitates, turns. Rohder's staring at his desk again.

'Mr Rohder?' she asks.

'Yes?' He doesn't look up.

'I skimmed through the last volume of your *Proceedings* last night, and I was very interested to read about your affective units. Could I borrow the volumes that deal with them?'

'Seven through twelve,' Rohder says briefly.

Aiah looks at the long row of red-bound volumes. 'Perhaps,' she says, 'I'll start with seven.'

In the end Aiah gives her spare ticket to her work-shift doorman, who goes off duty just as she arrives home. The theater is enormous, holding at least a couple thousand people, with a vast domed ceiling that features a fresco of the Inspirators giving divine guidance to writers, actors, directors and cameramen. The long white expanse of the oval screen seems half a block long. Every seat is full, and each audience member dresses formally for the occasion, even though the official premiere is being held elsewhere.

The chromoplay comes over the wire, premiering simultaneously in theaters throughout the world precisely at 20:00 hours — everywhere it's not banned as subversive, anyway, and sometimes even there, smuggled in on wires strung across borders. There's an hour of programming before the play even starts, live interviews with the cast and with the director Sandvak, with celebrities, with a token historian who, professionally enough, manages to summarize the Cheloki Wars in the thirty or so seconds granted him. And then of course there is Constantine. His modest white lace and black velvet vest contrasts with the extravagance of an ankle-length snakeskin coat. Sorya stands with him, another contrast in silken reds and yellows, the belt of gold linked foci low around her hips, its falling tail curving suggestively over a smooth, carefully posed thigh revealed by the slit skirt.

A reporter is unfortunate enough to ask Constantine what he thinks of a chromoplay based on his life.

'This chromo is one of the signs, I think, that the New City is undergoing a rebirth,' Constantine says. His smile is genial, but there's a yellowish intensity in his eyes, the smallest touch of something feral. 'Perhaps we are at a distance now where we can judge ideas for themselves, and not for the sad and bloody circumstance of their birth.'

The reporter seems not to know what entirely to make of this – he wanted a little bonbon of a quote, something enthusiastic and tasty and instantly forgettable, and not this banquet of prose.

'Do you think the chromo will help people understand your ideas, then?' he interrupts. Constantine looks into the camera and bares his teeth in a carnivore smile, his face looming above tens of thousands of people in theaters worldwide. A cold glow lights his eyes, and Aiah feels a shudder of recognition run up her spine, a recognition of the intensity and passion that, for this instant, Constantine has permitted his audience to see. This was clearly the opportunity he was waiting for.

'The world,' he says, 'has not lost its capacity to astonish. And neither has the New City,' he leans toward the camera, his voice an abrupt, startling theatrical growl, 'and neither have *I*.'

There is a moment of absolute silence in the theater, and Aiah wants to applaud Constantine's pure astonishing craft – and after a second she does so. Others in the theater take her cue and begin to echo her applause, but the reporter, himself slow to recover from the intensity of Constantine's unexpected performance, rises gamely with another question.

'Is this an announcement, Metropolitan?'

Constantine's smile might as well have been borrowed from the cat that stole the cream. 'When I perform a thing,' he says, 'I perform it – others may do the announcing then, if they like.'

The reporter clearly finds all this too alarming, and turns to Sorya for relief. 'And you, Madame Sorya,' he says, 'are you looking forward to the premiere?'

'I expect great things,' Sorya says. 'Both in the theater – and outside it.'

There follows the reportorial equivalent of fleeing in abject rout – the poor man turns to the camera and cuts thankfully to an interview with one of the minor players, who will presumably provide all the bonbons necessary.

The chromo is fabulous, the actor says. Kherzaki is fabulous, and so is Sandvak. The whole experience of working with them was, in a word, fabulous. While bonbons fall thick and fast, Aiah goes to the theater bar and has a glass of wine. She's accustomed to Constantine's vintages and has forgotten how dreadful the ordinary stuff is, and she leaves the glass half-finished on the bar and returns to sit next to her doorman.

The chromoplay, when it finally begins, makes Aiah forget the bad taste in her mouth. The opening scene, a frenzied devotional dance performed in a monastery, is purely riveting – whirling bodies, flaming robes, popping eyes, clashing cymbals – and is followed by a long, smooth, silent pan, through the legs of the dancers as they file out, along the length of a monumentally long room, to the actor Kherzaki seated in a posture of meditation, a tasseled prayer stick in each hand. Red and yellow ritual marks are painted on his forehead and cheeks. There is even more silence – a long, long silence – before the actor rises, still without speaking, and walks away. The only sound is the whispering silk of his robes.

Aiah marvels at a director who knows how to use silence and stillness. She can't remember when she's last seen a chromoplay that wasn't all fast cuts and constant movement.

'My father is dead, reverence.' The first words spoken by Kherzaki. The voice isn't Constantine's, but that of a near cousin: Kherzaki's opera training gives him a resonance and authority similar to Constantine's even though the timbre is different, smoothly flowing liquid rather than tempered steel.

'Everything returns to the Shield in the end.' It's the abbot speaking, a wizened man with a birdlike tilt to his head, a twittering voice, a holy symbol tattooed on his forehead and eerie blue blobs of mascara on his eyes.

'I request leave to attend his funeral.'

'You may have it, child of matter,' says the abbot.

Kherzaki gratefully inclines his head. 'I ask first for a gift of your wisdom.'

'The gift is not mine,' the abbot demurs, 'but that of the Great Path of Superior Perfection.'

'I wish to inquire about evil.'

'Evil is a transient phenomenon that cannot sustain itself. Purify your mind and heart of desire, and evil can gain no lodgment therein.'

The student is persistent. 'And what of exterior evil? Can it be overcome through action?'

'All evil is transient. By its nature it cannot sustain itself. No action is necessary, nor required.'

Kherzaki's deep eyes glitter. 'If evil is transient, then the transience is because evil destroys itself, and that destruction is inevitable. Cannot people of virtue aid evil in its self-destruction, so as to prevent its innocent victims from suffering?'

The abbot frowns. 'All weapons turn against their

owners, child of matter. All desire corrupts. All action is futile. If you wish to aid those who suffer, then teach them to live without desire.'

'Without desire for food for their children? Without desire for hope? Without desire for liberty or justice?'

'Just so.'

There is a long pause, and then Kherzaki turns and leaves. The abbot gives a bemused smile and sips gratefully at his tea.

And Kherzaki, in his room, breaks his prayer sticks over his knee, leaves his robes in the closet, washes the ritual daubings from his face, and goes forth to make revolution.

It's not precisely history – Aiah knows that Constantine left the School of Radritha some years before he made his bid for Cheloki, and that Constantine's father survived, under house arrest, into the civil war that followed. The chromoplay names no real names: Kherzaki's character is called Clothius, the monastery is a fictional one, though characteristic of its type, and the metropolis over which Kherzaki strives is called Lokhamar. The fictionalizations are transparent but somehow aid the chromo's purpose; the characters aren't so much anonyms as literary constructs, a thing in keeping with the entire chromoplay, which is highly stylized, as if inspired by Kherzaki's world of the opera. The actions are grander than in reality, the colors brighter, the gestures more sweeping, the silences more profound. The heightened style transforms a kind of historical outline into a mighty tragedy, a form far more powerful than the merely true.

Kherzaki is never less than magnificent. He attempts no imitation of Constantine, but there are occasional intriguing echoes: an impatient gesture or pantherish glance, or phrases that Aiah remembers falling from Constantine's lips. The actor is particularly effective at the end, after all hope is gone, striving to maintain his brittle dignity while trying to negotiate his own exile and the surrender of his metropolis to the corrupt forces that have brought about the destruction of all his schemes.

Aiah is thrilled to the marrow, and she's not alone, because at the end the audience burst into applause right along with her. She's never seen a biography of such scope, nor a worthier testimony to someone's life and thought.

There's a brief intermission, after which there will be a live report from the huge premiere party. After the five-course dinner that was the chromoplay, Aiah isn't particularly interested in more bonbons from celebrities, so she rises and adjusts her jacket. Her doorman rises to give her room to pass.

'Good chromo,' he says.

'I think Constantine should be pleased.'

'Constantine?' His brow furrows. 'Was he in the cast? I don't remember seeing him.'

Aiah looks at the man. 'It was *about* Constantine, about his life. Clothius *was* Constantine.'

The doorman blinks. 'Oh. Is that why he's famous, then? I never knew.' And then, at Aiah's startled look, he adds, 'I don't much keep up with the news.'

Aiah makes an effort to master her surprise. 'Well, I'm glad you liked it, anyway.' She shuffles past him on her way to the aisle.

'When is that gentleman of yours coming back?' the doorman asks.

Aiah shrugs and calls an answer over her shoulder.

'Who knows?'

Aiah takes a cab to Terminal. At the start of the weekend the streets are fairly full, with long lines outside the fashionable clubs and Shieldlight glittering bright on beads and jewelry. In the poorer areas like Terminal, whole blocks are barricaded off for street dances, with local bands playing atop flatbed trucks and vendors selling food, intoxicants and aphrodisiacs from shops set up in the outdoor scaffolding.

Aiah tells the driver to take her past the building that holds Kremag and Associates, but the street is blocked off – not with a block party, she sees, but by police. Flashing lights throb against the walls of the buildings, and there's a touch of pepper gas in the air that makes Aiah's eyes smart. A line of complaining people, bystanders apparently, lie on the sidewalk with wet towels over their eyes, supervised by indifferent ambulance personnel.

The police would never have used gas so freely in a rich neighborhood.

Still, Aiah is pleased to be able to give Constantine good news. She tells the cab to head for the Landmark, and as it turns away from the barriers, and rolls past the huge bulk of the housing project, Aiah sees Khoriak's blond head gleaming from a shop doorway.

Her news won't be news after all, Aiah thinks.

Security is already in place at the Landmark, along with a meal of cold noodles, pâté, fruit and a fine amber wine. She eats, bathes, banishes weariness with a dose of plasm, and finds a gift from Constantine on the bed: a negligee of golden silk, a matching robe, bottles of Cedralla perfume and body oil. Aiah adds the ivory necklace that Constantine gave her, the carved white Trigram hanging low between her breasts. For a luxurious moment, as Aiah anoints herself, the fantasy of the kept woman floats through her mind again, the limousine, the shopping binges, the pug dog . . .

Pretty silly, she considers. She can't see Constantine long keeping company with a woman so utterly *useless*.

Constantine arrives, face and form concealed in a hooded sweatshirt that makes him look like a retired prize-fighter. 'I believe I've decoyed the reporters,' he says cheerfully. 'A last-minute switch of aerocars, and Martinus dressed in my hat and coat with a little plasm-glamor on his face. He should have led them all back to Mage Towers.'

Aiah congratulates him. He pulls the sweatshirt off over his head and tosses it on a chair. 'Did you like the chromo-play?' he asks.

'It was magnificent.'

Constantine seems pleased with himself. 'They will wonder, won't they, if the chromo was made to promote the coup, or the other way around.'

'So which was it?'

He shrugs. 'It was intended, quite frankly, as a showcase for my ideas. The Caraqui adventure came along quite by accident, and so did you, and these and the chromo jig-sawed together quite nicely.' His rumbling laugh rings out. 'Millions more people will have seen the chromo than will ever have *heard* of the Cheloki wars. For a generation at least, historians will have to spend thousands of hours pointing out just where the chromo was different from history – and no one will really care. That magnificent creation of Sandvak and Kherzaki will be the *me* that people remember.' A mischievous smile crosses his face. 'I'll have to remember to live up to it, if I can.'

Aiah considers this while Constantine pours himself a glass of wine. 'You ... *arranged* this chromo some-how? My impression from all I've heard was that it was all Sandvak's idea.'

'I'm sure that's what Sandvak believes. Sandvak believes intently and passionately and sincerely about *any* idea that takes his fancy, at least till another idea seizes possession of him. He was perfect for the project: he possesses great talent, but has no real convictions save those he borrows, momentarily, for the purposes of his art. I chose him, though he doesn't know it – I even partly financed the chromoplay – and it looks as if I'll make my investment back a hundredfold.'

Aiah is a bit dizzied by all this. Constantine laughs, and with one of his sudden movements sweeps Aiah up – the breath goes out of her in a surprised, delighted whoop. He carries her to the bed cradled against his broad chest. 'So much for passive entertainments,' he says. 'On to better things.'

Aiah has observed that, the more effective the lingerie, the less likely it is to remain on the body. This occasion is no exception.

Constantine is buoyant and playful, for once without the overpowering intensity he's displayed in the past. He seems utterly without care, more inclined to make jokes than sage comments on the world and its workings. It's as if a weight has been lifted from his heart.

'Are you so delighted with the chromo?' Aiah asks. 'Or did something else happen to make you so carefree?'

A warm laugh rumbles deep in his chest. They lie next to each other in bed, propped up on elbows.

'I am lighthearted in part,' he says, 'because the chromo-play was a masterpiece. But also because the business of Caraqui is now in train, and there is nothing I can do to alter it at this stage. The orders have been given, and it's all in the hands of the gods. I may have a few hours of peace and pleasure before my part begins.'

A trickle of alarm shivers up Aiah's spine. She straightens, looks at Constantine in concern. 'When?' she asks.

'The soldiers will roll out of the barracks early Sunday, and should be in place by 05:00. That part is tricky – they all have to start at different times, so as to take their stations at the same moment. The actual attack will commence right at 05:00 whether everyone's in place or not.' An expression of concern crosses his face as he looks at Aiah. 'By this time tomorrow I will be in Barchab making final arrangements. Whatever the success of the strike, I daren't return ever to Jaspeer – not once our secret of Terminal is connected with events in Caraqui.'

A hopeless protest dies on Aiah's lips. Constantine looks

at her soberly, a touch of sadness in his voice. 'This is our last time together, Miss Aiah. I hope you will leave this place with no regrets.'

A knife of pure sadness slices into Aiah's throat, stilling her voice. Unexpected tears sting her eyes. 'I had hoped,' she manages finally, 'to have more time.'

'If the strike works out well,' he says, 'and you come to Caraqui, then we may have time to spare.'

Aiah throws herself back on the blue satin sheets. 'But very possibly no time at all. You make no promises.'

'I can't. My promises are to – well, if it is not too immodest to say so, to the world.' He tilts his head and looks at her, and places one big hand gently over hers. 'You have a full life. You have your young man – who seems a decent sort – and financial security, and a special assignment for the Authority –' there is an amused glint in his eye '– rooting out wicked folk like myself.

'More importantly,' he adds, 'you know how to fly.' He kisses her cheek.

Aiah wants only to cry. She throws both arms around his neck, buries her face in the juncture of throat and jaw.

She hadn't, she thinks with fierce astonishment, known she cared *this much*.

Gently he strokes her back. If he is surprised by the tempest, it doesn't show in his voice. 'I'm sorry for this suddenness,' he says, 'but you knew, at best, we had only days in any case.'

'Of course I knew,' she says, voice muffled by his clavicle while she inwardly curses her foolishness. This is not a time to go to pieces. Not when a perfect chonah has come to its conclusion, the cash dropped safely and untraceably in a foreign bank, and all is well. Any other Barkazil would be dancing with joy.

Aiah leans back, dabs at her eyes with the back of her wrist. 'I'm being stupid,' she says. 'As you say, it's nothing I didn't know.'

'I'm sorry for the upset.'

'It's passed. I – it was the surprise, I think.'

He tilts his head again, considering her from a new perspective. 'You have a grand future, you know. You have intelligence, and a great natural talent, and a fine ingenuity. You have the funds now to get a formal degree, if that's what you want, or to set up a business of your own.'

'And how do I explain where the cash comes from?'

Constantine shrugs. 'A trust set up by a rich grandfather. A scholarship fund in Barkazi. It's unlikely that anyone will even ask – and if you think someone might, you can always apply to a university in another metropolis.'

That would mean leaving Gil behind, she thinks.

But then, perhaps she already has.

'It takes a while to get used to this kind of life,' she says. 'Having so many things to hide.'

Constantine smiles. 'Shall I tell you the secret, then? Of how to survive when you have so much to hide?'

'If you will.'

He leans close, whispers in her ear. '*Tell no one.*' He leans back and smiles. 'It's very simple.'

'Yes.'

'Crimes are solved when people inform. You've said that yourself.'

Aiah smiles, nods. Constantine appears to think she's not taking him seriously, and continues, a little intense.

'You tell your lover or your best friend. And then you have a fight, and they inform. Or they tell someone else, and that person has no loyalty to *you*, and is having tax problems or some other difficulty, and thinks cooperation may help, and so informs. The worst thing is to trust anyone in the criminal classes, as they inform as a matter of course. And therefore the secret, in brief . . .' He leans close to her ear again, warm breath touching her flesh. '*Tell no one.*'

Since he's there, Aiah takes the opportunity to kiss him. 'I haven't,' she says. 'I won't.' And adds, for his benefit, 'I'm a Barkazil, you know.'

'And, when confronted, admit nothing,' Constantine says. 'Make them prove every point. Give them as little as possible, because the longer a story you give them, the more rope they have to trip you up and hang you.'

'I absorbed all this with my mother's milk,' Aiah says. 'But thank you for the advice.'

He gives her a half-amused, narrow-eyed look. 'When it began to look as if it would matter,' he says, 'I inquired into the relationship between Barkazils and Jaspeeris. Jaspeeris, I discovered, are inclined to the belief that Barkazils are a treacherous, conspiratorial, thieving lot.'

'We're only taking what already belongs to us.'

Constantine looks skeptical.

'It's true. My grandma says so.' Aiah offers an assured smile. 'Let me tell you a grandma story. Do you know about Karlo?'

'Karlo's Day is the big Barkazil festival, yes?'

'He's our immortal. We always take Karlo's Day off work, and the longnoses are annoyed. But for the story of Karlo, we have to go all the way back, before the Malakas raised the Shield, and there was a Sun and Moon, to when Senko had invented weapons of iron and steel in the war against the Lord of the Trees.'

'That far back, hey,' Constantine murmurs. His eyes half-close as he prepares to be bored.

'The Barkazils says that it was Karlo who showed Senko the iron deposits, and also that he was Senko's cleverest general, leading the Barkazil people in battle. There are all sorts of stories about him outsmarting the enemy. Now, I've heard Senkoists say that Karlo was an avatar of Senko, but that doesn't make sense, because how can Senko have two avatars at once, even if he *was* an immortal?'

'Good point. Theologically sound.'

'Anyway, after Senko defeated the Trees and commanded them to stay in one place, he began preparing his war against the Malakas. Karlo didn't think a war against the Ascended Ones was a very bright idea, so he approached the Malakas and offered to help them if they would permit the Barkazils to Ascend.'

'Karlo informed on his friend, you mean.'

Aiah slaps him lightly on the biceps. 'Hush! We're getting to the important part. The Malakas offered Karlo the Ascendancy, along with his family, but they refused to allow his people to accompany him, so he declined their offer and gave his armies to Senko instead. But it was too late, and the Ascended Ones destroyed Senko before Karlo could aid him. Still, the Malakas were sufficiently impressed with Karlo's cleverness and his loyalty to the Barkazil people that, when they raised the Shield, they refrained from harming Karlo and gave him regency over the whole world.'

'Metropolitan of the entire planet?' Constantine considers this. 'I've not heard this version before.'

'The other versions are wrong, and my grandma is right,' Aiah says simply. 'According to her, Karlo created an age of greatness. When he became Metropolitan, he discovered how to use plasm, but he kept it a secret he shared only with the Barkazils – we're a special, magical people, as I believe I've told you. Other people were jealous, so they conspired to steal the secret.'

'Most histories name Mala of the Firebird as the person who discovered plasm.'

'She stole it from Karlo. There's a complicated story concerning how there were three attempts in all, but I won't go into it. Anyway, after the secret got out there was a big war, with everybody against the Barkazils, and Karlo was killed and the Barkazils were defeated. Ever since then, the world has been divided up into thousands of independent cities instead of being ruled by the Barkazils as is proper, and anything that Barkazils take by way of compensation is only a way of retrieving our own.'

A laugh begins rumbling deep in Constantine's chest, then bursts from his throat to ring from the ceiling. 'Brilliant!' he cries. 'A license, confirmed in religion, to take whatever you can get your hands on!'

Aiah looks at him. 'I'd look out, if I were you.'

Delight dances in his brown eyes, and he kisses her. 'Dear one, you have already stolen my most perfect admiration.'

Warmth rises in Aiah's cheeks. 'Thank you,' she says.

He kisses her again. The kiss lingers. Aiah's arms coil around him. 'If there is anything you want of me,' he says, 'take it now, while there's time.'

Her flesh prickles at the invitation. She clasps herself to him, feels the imprint of the ivory Trigram pressed between them. One of his large hands encompasses her hip. The kiss ends, and he looks at her smoky-eyed. 'I have a notion,' he says, and leaves her arms briefly. When he returns he carries a t-grip in his hand, a wire trailing from his fist to the desk.

When Constantine touches her again, the touch has the warmth, the warning prickle of plasm. Aiah closes her eyes and lets the plasm flow over her like the wavelets of a warm, shallow sea. Breath eases from her lungs. A thousand plasm tongues lick her nerves and she laughs softly at the sensation.

The nerve-pleasure brightens, grows in urgency. Aiah bites her lip, gasps for breath. When Constantine enters her, she has to open her eyes to make certain this isn't some supplementary tactile illusion sprung to life between her legs. Constantine's face is impassive, a little frown at the corners of his mouth, his mind flown elsewhere, in some concentrated part of him that's reaching out to her with tendrils of plasm. Aiah presses her lips to his chest, tastes him, inhales his scent.

The plasm flows over her – not a gentle warm lake any

312

longer, but an urgent, turbulent swell, harbinger of a storm. Aiah clutches at Constantine's triceps, nails digging in for dear life. She is vaguely aware of her body thrashing like a torn awning in a high wind, but the pleasure transcends any mere fact of the body, transcends everything but the pure fire of the plasm itself, a flaming mass of molten metal that sits on her chest and inexorably burns its relentless way to her heart . . .

When the plasm ebbs she finds herself lying at an angle, her head lying partly off the bed at one of its lower corners. She has no recollection of how she came to be in this attitude. Constantine is propped up on one elbow near her, the t-grip still in one hand. Of his own pleasures, motions and climax she remembers nothing, though she deduces the latter's existence from its sticky residue.

'An interesting way to spend four or five thousand dalders, isn't it?' Constantine observes. 'The lives of the rich are full indeed.'

Aiah reaches for breath and, somewhat to her surprise, finds it. '*What* . . . ?' she demands, and then begins again. 'I have *never* . . .'

'I thought you should experience it once at least,' Constantine says. He leaps off the bed, coiling the wire around his fist as he prowls toward the desk. His movement is economical, balanced, somehow restless, as if the world depended on every step. The relaxed, joyful Constantine she had seen after the premiere has gone; the plasm, perhaps, has focused him, reminded him of the trial to come.

Constantine coils the wire and puts the t-grip in a drawer. He pads back to the bed, sits on the edge of the mattress, and bends to kiss her. 'That was the fifth of the Nine Levels of Harmonious and Refined Balance,' he says. 'I imagine they felt it in the next ward.'

Aiah looks at him in amazement. 'What are the sixth through ninth levels like?' she demands.

'I don't know through personal experience.' He frowns.

'The others seemed rather lonely. The philosophers who developed these techniques hold that only plasm and bodily fluids are divine, and that actual physical contact is inferior to the orgasm of the mind; and their conclusion therefore was that the finest and most refined sexual acts are performed solo. In the sixth and seventh level there's someone else in the room, though one isn't allowed to touch her. In the rest, one is supposed to be alone except, well, with the Godhead or something.'

Aiah rolls onto her belly, draws fingers through her hair. 'They have this sort of thing in – oh – romances and chromos. I never believed it.'

'There are teachers,' Constantine says offhandedly, 'though one should choose them well. There is some small possibility of nerve damage, and therefore a partner with some measure of maturity and training is desirable.'

She looks up at him. 'I could have been injured?'

'Not with me, you couldn't.'

He frowns off into the middle distance, eyes intent, his thoughts clearly elsewhere. He strokes her back and shakes his head.

Aiah looks at him, at the distant calculation in his eyes, and a shiver goes through her as she realizes that, in twenty-four hours or so, he will be at war, a combat in which physical reality, his included, is only an element, and apt, at the intervention of plasm, to be annihilated at any instant.

'Are you already in Caraqui?' she asks. He looks at her and smiles a little.

'I'm sorry.' He rolls his long legs up onto the bed and takes her in his arms. 'We have some time left, you and I, and though problems have arisen, I should keep them off my mind. No amount of thought can anticipate everything, in any case.'

'What problems?' Aiah presses herself to him, kisses his neck.

'Do you recall Parq? That clergyman?'

'Yes. Sorya said he was treacherous.'

'He's utterly faithless. I knew that when I approached him. Well, he's betrayed us, as I thought he would, and so my name is now spoken in the councils of the Keremaths, and I suspect it would be most unwise to be seen in any of my usual haunts for the next day or so.'

Aiah looks at him in cold alarm. 'Why did you trust him at all?'

'I never did.' A smile touches Constantine's lips. 'I lied to him throughout – gave him any number of names, claiming they were part of the conspiracy, and now in good faith he's gone to the Keremaths and handed the names over – or some, anyway, as he's playing a double game. So the Specials are now busy arresting and interrogating people who know nothing, and soon they will conclude that Parq's information is useless, or part of some larger conspiracy of his own. But Parq is maintaining contact with my side as well, and he's got the Keremaths' permission to post his own militia around his transmitters, which of course means that once the action begins, he can jump to whichever side seems to be winning. No,' Constantine shakes his head. 'Parq is not the main problem.'

'What is?'

'There were spreading rumors of the coup – that was inevitable, given the number of people involved, though we took care to spread disinformation whenever possible. The Specials have made inconvenient arrests, and certain preparatory military maneuvers are inevitable and have been seen, and the Keremaths have become alarmed. So they have contacted mercenaries – mages and a brigade of soldiers both – and are moving them into Caraqui. Their deployment won't be at all complete when our strike is launched – it will be inconvenient, I hope, and nothing more – and perhaps Drumbeth is now taking my words concerning the aerodrome to heart.'

'A *brigade*?' Thoroughly anxious, Aiah sits up, coils her legs under her.

Constantine, stretched out beside her, smiles lazily, eyes half-lidded. 'Mondray's Regulars, flying in from the Timocracy just ahead of our own people. Mondray's good, but Geymard's better. And the Regulars don't know the city, and when we strike they won't have deployed their full strength or moved in all their equipment, and they have no real loyalty to the Keremaths anyway. It's Mondray's mages that are my concern. If they're deployed in the Palace or with the Metropolitan Guard, then they'll have no more plasm than the loyalist mages would have already – and we're taking steps to limit that. Possibly they will increase the efficiency of the defense, possibly not. But if the mages are deployed throughout the city, at plasm stations say, or at the offices of the Specials, then they can cause all sorts of mischief, as we won't know where they are or of what damage they're capable until they strike us.'

'What are you going to do about it?' Aiah demands.

'*Do?*' He stretches out along the bed, rolling his shoulders luxuriously against the satin sheet. 'I will do nothing,' he says. 'There's nothing I *can* do. We can only wait on events.'

Aiah gnaws her lip. 'You were less patient last night, when you rushed off with Geymard.'

'The news had just come. I was afraid the whole business would have to be called off. But now that I've looked at the matter I'm confident that we can still pull it off – the odds were nine to one in our favor, but they're still six to four.' He looks at her under his lids, and reaches up to stroke her arm with the back of one large hand. 'Besides, last night I was not in bed with a beautiful woman.'

A tendril of flame licks at Aiah's heart. 'Be careful,' she says.

Constantine reaches up, cups the back of her neck, draws her down to his lips. His kiss feasts delicately on her.

The touch of his breath on her neck makes her shiver. 'There is a thing you can do for me, if you would,' he says.

'Yes?'

'We have mages and soldiers and various kinds of political men,' Constantine says, 'but it disturbs me that we have not enough *engineers*. So much of our plasm will be coming from that factory in Terminal, and there the whole apparatus is cobbled together. I worry that there could be a failure in the equipment, or some unforeseen emergency.'

Aiah looks down into his gold-flecked eyes, and her decision comes at once, an impulse from the heart. 'I'm not an engineer, but I'll do what I can.'

'It will increase your risk,' Constantine says. 'At this moment, mages are going over every inch of that factory, removing all traces of all of us, every fingerprint, every flake of skin, leaving nothing for a plasm hound to trace. They will treat this room likewise after we're gone. There will be another cleansing of the factory at the end of the operation, but very likely we will not be able to make it as thorough.'

'I will do what I can,' Aiah says.

Is *this*, she wonders, what she absorbed with her mother's milk? Returning to the scene after everything's been brought to a conclusion, after payment has been made and safely disposed of?

This is not a *crime*, she thinks. This is politics . . . belief, ideals, necessity . . . different rules apply.

'If you think I will be of use,' Aiah says, 'then of course I will help.'

Admiration glows warmly in Constantine's eyes. 'I salute you, brave lady,' he says, and draws her down again for a kiss. His arms go about her. Apprehension and passion war in Aiah's nerves, and then she kisses him fiercely, determined to possess him entirely, his brilliance and humor

317

and the touch of his body against hers, for as long as the moment lasts.

An hour or so later, bathed and dressed, fatigue toxins burned by plasm, Aiah leaves the bedroom at Constantine's side. The ivory necklace is worn over her evening dress, and the silk nightgown is packed in her overnight bag. He is dressed for casual travel: gray cord pants, boots, his soft black leather jacket. There is a group waiting, a half-dozen of Constantine's associates, and Sorya sitting in a plush chair wearing her military greatcoat and cap, her booted legs stretched out in front of her.

All waiting, Aiah thinks coldly, with the Fifth Level of Harmonious Balance going on just the other side of one thin hotel door.

Sorya stretches and gives a lazy yawn. 'Recreation time over,' she says, and stands, the greatcoat hanging like a cloak off her shoulders. She walks up to Constantine, stands on tiptoe, kisses his cheek.

'The aerocar is ready to take us to Barchab. Geymard is waiting for us there.'

'Then we should go,' Constantine says.

'No luggage to pack? Very well.'

Sorya turns toward the door, pauses, looks at Aiah. A cold, clear warning sounds in Aiah's mind. Sorya approaches, puts her arms delicately around Aiah, and kisses each cheek. 'Thank you for everything,' she says. She reaches into a pocket of her coat, pulls out a jingling velvet bag and drops it into Aiah's palm.

'Here's for all your services,' she says with a smile, and turns away.

In the sudden, shocked silence Aiah stares at the weighty bag. Blood rises in her cheeks and murder wails in her heart. Her fingers close around the money, and she puts daggers in her voice.

'Let me know if you ever need my help again,' she says

quietly, and sees Sorya's spine stiffen as she walks out the door.

The others make haste to follow. Constantine looms over Aiah briefly, his hand squeezing her arm. 'Sorya is what she is,' he says. 'But I thank the gods you are who you are.'

Quickly Aiah traces the Sign of Karlo over his forehead. 'Go,' she says, and kisses him.

Lingering by the door, Aiah watches his big form recede down the corridor, his people marching around him as if already formed in ranks for battle.

19

It's too dangerous to have all this cash around. She takes Sorya's money, and the five thousand she'd stored in the fertilizer bag in her grow-room, and takes it to a money exchange. Except for a few hundred, she cashes every clink in for a checktube, and then hides the tube itself in one of Loeno Towers' utility mains, one she can enter with her Authority passkey.

No more limousine rides; only an arrival time and a password to get her through the doors. Red Line to New Central Line, through Mudki Station, to Garakh Station near Terminal. Aiah knows she'll feel exposed walking along the Shieldlit streets to the factory, but she doesn't dare use a cab for fear some driver might remember her.

She climbs the stair out of the New Central Line Station and then shock rolls through her as she finds herself looking straight up at Constantine's face.

Who is Constantine's mystery lover? The smoky glowing letters must be half a radius high. *Details on the* Wire.

Aiah's foot reaches for a step that isn't there and she almost falls. 'Careful!' A helpful citizen grabs her arm. 'They need to replace this old concrete.' Overhead, Constantine's image fades, replaced by a screaming headline about the lottery scandal and a picture of a politician hiding his face.

Adrenaline pounds at her heart with rubber mallets. Aiah peers into windows as she walks and finds the black-and-red *Wire* sticker in the flyspecked window of a corner diner. She walks into the diner, plugs coins into the machine, punches buttons for the headline she wants, and then waits two minutes, palms sweating, for the *Wire*'s central computer to scroll the story onto the screen.

Constantine, she reads, the controversial former Metropolitan of Cheloki and subject of renewed interest as the fictionalized hero of the chromoplay *Lords of the New City*, is said to have left his long-time companion, the socialite Sorya, at the chromo's premiere in order to spend the next several hours in the Landmark Hotel in the company of an unknown woman. He is said to have spent several off-shifts in the Landmark recently, presumably with the same lady, whose identity has piqued the curiosity of millions. Sorya's reaction to the revelations has not been revealed, and both she and Constantine are incommunicado.

Does she want a printed copy of the story? Aiah savagely jabs the *No* button. Reporters, she thinks, use plasm hounds if the story is big enough, but on the other hand Constantine said he'd have a mage sweep the hotel room clean of all traces.

Well, she thinks, there'll be a better story about Constantine by tomorrow. Maybe everyone will forget about this one.

And then she thinks, *socialite*. And smiles, imagining Sorya's reaction.

Aiah leaves the diner and makes her way through the Saturday dinnertime crowds. By coincidence the route takes her past the building that held Kremag and Associates. The faintest taste of pepper gas touches her nostrils and she glances up at the building's ornamental wrought-iron crown. Pedestrians walk past without giving the building a glance. The arrests are yesterday's news.

Aiah heads on to the factory. She's got more news to make.

The factory is quiet and dark and filled with the tension of waiting. Aiah has been here five hours and feels perfectly useless. Probably she should have brought a book or magazine to read. Possibly she shouldn't have come at all. Even the pigeons seem to know it's sleep shift and drowse on the roof beams.

The two young Jaspeeri mages are dipping the plasm well – teenagers, Aiah thinks, mere children – but they're not part of the attack, they're helping to guard the factory. Another mage is due to arrive later to help coordinate the actual assault.

There are a half-dozen security people, but they're second-string – Aiah doesn't know any of them, and they don't move with the same unobtrusive, watchful confidence she's experienced with Constantine's personal guard. A group of communication specialists huddle around their equipment, monitoring radios and ground links. They're dressed in civilian rig, but their posture is military, just like their spit-shined shoes. Aiah is the only woman present.

Aside from the two boys, Aiah hasn't met any of these people before. Everyone's known by code-names, which imparts a silly sense of chromoplay melodrama to the whole proceeding. Aiah is Lady, which is at least logical. The boys are Wizards Two and Three – Wizard Two is the one with thick spectacles, and Wizard One is the mage who is yet to arrive – and the rest, manning the commo board or the radios, all have names like Red or Trucker or Slim.

'Insertion's proceeding,' Red says to no one in particular. He's listening to radio traffic, headphones clamped over his ears. The announcement is perfectly unnecessary, because a jerky video feed from Geymard's helicopter shows the mercenaries flying toward Caraqui from their bases in the Timocracy of Garshab. Shieldlight splashes off rotors as the gray machines arrow through the sky, ordnance patient in streamlined pods. Bulletlike aerocars, packed with munitions, follow at a discreet distance. Geymard is still hundreds of radii away from his destination, and will refuel in midair before the final jump to his targets.

In Caraqui, army units are already on the road. The First Brigade started late, with some officers having to be arrested or won over at the last minute, but the Second and Marine Brigades are on schedule, and the Marines made their move without a single officer over the rank of captain, having slipped out from under all its senior commanders while they were sleeping off a celebration honoring one of their number, a celebration carefully arranged by the coup leaders.

This last is the subject of much mirth when Red reports it. Aiah smiles and pictures herself, Tella, and the other junior executives turning buccaneer and commandeering the Plasm Control Authority while Mengene, Oeneme and the other seniors are off at a party honoring the Intendant.

Adjusting the surgical gloves she's been given to keep her fingerprints to herself, Aiah wanders toward the office. The maps and the lists of names have gone, but in their place are a checklist, a carefully compiled master schedule for the entire operation, complete with handwritten addenda in pencil. All names are in code, including all personnel, units and objectives, so it's pretty opaque even to someone who knows what's going on. Opaque or not, the schedule isn't meant to be left behind, and for that reason it sits in a metal safe on which squats a slab of pure thermite: pull the pin and white-hot metal melts right through the safe and slags everything in it. All paper is to go in the safe on evacuation, along with the surgical gloves and t-grips, and everything will then be cooked to atoms.

Aiah looks at her watch – two minutes after four – then at the list. *04:05: Team Seven-A reaches Point Barometer en route to Point Windvane.*

Team Seven, she knows, is the absconding Marine Brigade. Seven-A must be one of its units.

'Seven-A is at Barometer,' Red reports. Aiah looks at her watch again. Seven-A would seem to be ahead of schedule.

There's a clumping of security men at the big street door, an exchange of passwords, and then the door opens and a red Gharik two-seater enters. The woman inside doffs her shieldglasses and steps outside, and a rush of surprised recognition goes through Aiah.

It's Aldemar, an actress who plays a mage in a lot of second-rate chromos and is alleged to be a mage in reality. Aiah had never really believed it, or for that matter any of the other hype concerning this woman, whose absurd adventure plays were supposed to be inspired by her real life. *Attack of the Hanged Man* is her current release; Aiah's seen the ads for it, and it sounds ghastly. *This is who we've been waiting for?* Aiah wonders.

Constantine, she thinks, has not lost his capacity to surprise.

Aiah waits in the office and is surprised by the other woman when she arrives. Aiah is used to seeing the actress forty feet tall in chromos, and in person she's tiny, over a head shorter than Aiah, with dainty wrists and delicate ankles cased in clinging leather boots. Her dark hair is bobbed, with bangs across the forehead, and her refined features have the enigmatic caste that comes with years of plasm rejuvenation treatments. She seems surprised to find Aiah here.

Aiah holds out a hand. 'Hello. You must be Wizard One.'

Aldemar smiles and takes the hand. 'You are . . . ?'

'Lady.'

'Ah. Fine. Appropriate, I'm sure. And what's happening so far?'

One of the communications techs leaps in to answer. 'First Brigade had some problems sorting things out, but they're on their way.'

'Air refuelling's commenced!' Red calls helpfully from his console – he seems miffed that his headset cord won't stretch all the way to the celebrity.

Aldemar sits on the end of the old metal desk, is presented with the checklist, and goes over it carefully. Aiah watches her: even though she's dressed in old cotton jeans and a worn quilted jacket, with no makeup or jewelry, there's still an aura of glamor here. For years her skin and hair have been beautifully cared for, and she moves with the perfect, unhurried poise of an actress used to presenting all the most flattering angles. She responds to the techs' clumsy attentions with grace and an expression of perfect attention so studied it might as well be real. Her identity as a celebrity is so ingrained by now that even though she's made the attempt to suppress it, she was still recognized by everyone at the factory the second she stepped from her car.

Constantine, Aiah thinks, *uses* his celebrity, it's a weapon, or a tool, he employs to get what he wants, a table at a restaurant or access to the powerful. Aldemar's fame seems much more a part of her, and perhaps it's all there is.

One of the techs scurries to make her a sandwich.

The mage senses Aiah's appraisal, looks up at Aiah from under her bangs. 'Did you need to tell me something?' she asks.

'No. But they didn't offer *me* a sandwich.'

The corner of Aldemar's mouth twitches in amusement. 'Perhaps one of these gentlemen will get you one.'

One of the gentlemen does.

04:12: *Team Eight-C reaches Point Window on its way to Point Pillar.*

Aiah remembers all the stories of the Barkazil War she heard when growing up, all the old soldiers drinking their beer on the sidewalk and reminiscing. She imagines trucks and armored cars in silent, disciplined columns, rumbling engine noise disturbing the sleep of Caraqui's citizens. Marines in their gunboats speeding through the darkness beneath their city's huge concrete pontoons.

Looks up to the video feed to see Shieldlight glinting off rotor blades and the blunt noses of rockets.

Thinks of dolphins darting in the darkness beneath Caraqui's barges, weapons in their sleek hands.

And considers Taikoen, the hanged man, living in the pulse of plasm, ghost-hands reaching out to smother life.

She wonders who will die according to the neat dictates of the checklist and who will not, will die instead in the sudden, flaming knowledge that all schedules have gone awry, all agendas are voided, all programs canceled.

04:40: Factory goes live. All goods moved to Paperhanger.

Aiah knows the hardware as well as anyone, so she throws the switches herself. Copper contact arms descend to the sockets atop the huge accumulators and capacitors. Plasm fills the circuits, leaps in a beam from the transmission horn concealed in the billboard atop the factory.

Paperhanger is a silver airship floating along a precise radio heading that intersects the factory's broadcast beam. A linked bronze mesh, designed to absorb plasm, covers the ship's vulcanized skin. The ship's own horns, synched to spinning gyroscopes, redirect the plasm to where Constantine's mages are ready to use it.

Aldemar lies back in a padded chair, eyes closed, a copper circlet around each wrist – military-type t-grips that can't be dropped by accident. It's her job to ride the plasm beam, make certain that Paperhanger gets every mehr of energy. If Paperhanger gets attacked, she's supposed to help defend it.

'All circuits live!' Trucker reports.

'Mage attack! Mage attack!' Red yells. A wave of adrenaline hits Aiah's body, racing through her veins like fast-moving columns of troops, but there's nothing she can do but feel the pulse pounding in her throat.

There's a tap on Aiah's shoulder. One of the techs, holding in his gloved hand a military helmet of high-impact plastic. 'Better put this on,' he says.

'Accelerating all schedules!' Trucker shouts. 'All units advance to seize objectives *now*!'

On the oval video screen, the image jolts as the cameraman hangs on for dear life, copters put their noses down and peel away from flight lanes toward their objectives. The fantastic towers of the Aerial Palace appear on video through the shimmer of rotor blades.

The mage attack is on the First Brigade. Because the brigade is late, the mages who were supposed to protect it haven't joined it as yet, and the moving columns are helpless beneath waves of fiery plasm.

04:55: trackline cars moving.

It's actually 04:51. The schedule's been advanced, or possibly just dissolved altogether. The 'trackline cars' – in actuality artillery shells the *size* of trackline cars – sit under canvas at railway sidings in neutral territory. Plucked from their cradles by giant plasm hands, they commence their flight to their target, directional fins deploying in midair.

The trackline cars rumble through the air on the way to their targets, a faint line of vapor trailing from each fin. The huge shells are flung from their mages' ectomorphic hands like darts into corkboards, plunging into the huge concrete barges that support the headquarters and barracks of the Metropolitan Guard and the Aerial Palace, which itself is defended by detached Guard companies. Aside from the damage the shells can cause, the shells are supposed to disrupt communications, stun the defenders and punch holes in the bronze collection web that guards the buildings, making it possible for the attackers' plasm to enter. The Guard's buildings are also splashed with incendiaries, in part to mark their location with columns of smoke to aid Geymard's air assault.

A loyalist mage locates another column of the First

Brigade, and the lead armored car erupts in a spectacular display of fuel, ammunition, and plasm fire.

Aiah looks dry-mouthed at her dials and sees them feeding a constant supply of the goods to the airship Paperhanger that hovers gracefully over neutral ground a thousand radii away. A staccato adrenaline pulse beats time in her throat. A drop of sweat courses down her cheek from beneath her helmet.

She's as useless as any bystander, helpless to alter the situation one way or another, but she's *not* a bystander. The whole thing is her *fault* – none of this would be happening if not for her.

She looks up at the video screen and sees smoke columns rising above the Metropolitan Guard complex – huge square-shouldered buildings, all concrete and gunslits, bombproof roofs, transmission horns, radio antennae – and then white trails of rockets reach into the jittering image like smoking fingers . . .

Team Four-A commencing strafing attack.

Explosions wink red against the massive Guard structures.

Aiah can't take her eyes away.

06:05: Judiciary and Popular Assembly occupied. Team Seven reserves deployed as necessary.

Good news, bad news. Visible on a new video feed, rebels of the Marine Brigade stand proudly in front of Government Harbor buildings, having occupied the seat of government without resistance. But it's all symbolic, for the cameras; nothing of importance is going to happen in those buildings in the next few hours. Much of the Marine Brigade pushes forward to aid the Second Brigade in storming the Aerial Palace, where companies of the Metropolitan Guard are putting up a stiff resistance. Live feed shows the battle from a half-dozen angles, the extravagant architecture of the Aerial Palace bright with reflected tracer fire.

The rest of the Metropolitan Guard is still confined to its base, sheltering in the massive concrete buildings. Parts of the buildings are on fire, coils of thick smoke rising from the gunslits, and a fierce battle is being waged, with both gunfire and plasm. Geymard's mercenaries, on the high buildings adjacent, have the Guard surrounded, but can do little but pour more ammunition into the fight without any clear indication that it's doing any good. Their gunships have exhausted their ammunition, but fortunately the big aerocars with munitions and heavy weapons all arrive without interference, crushing neat roof-garden rows as they drop to disgorge cargo.

'All gunships have exhausted their ammunition. Returning to base.'

'Report from Jewel One,' Red says. 'The necklacing was only a partial success. Mages guarding the cables.'

Jewel One was Prince Aranax, the necklacing his attempt to blow the cables carrying plasm to the loyalists. Aiah thinks of dolphins drifting downward into darkness trailing mute streams of blood and bubbles . . . plenty of plasm for the defenders.

'Four-A's being hit again! Foreign troops!'

Clearly the First Brigade has no luck at all. Now Mondray's Regulars, the mercenary troops imported by the Keremaths, are racing to the rescue of their employers. The First Brigade was supposed to seize bridges between the mercenaries and the Aerial Palace, but now they're too late.

Aiah tastes blood in her mouth and realizes that she's been gnawing her cheek.

She looks up in alarm at a throaty cry from one of the plasm consoles: Aldemar sounds as if she's just been punched hard in the solar plexus. Her body thrashes on its padded chair. Her perfect white teeth are clenched, and her eyes are closed in concentration.

Slim's eyes go wide. 'Paperhanger's under attack!' he

shouts. 'Wizard Three, Wizard Two – abandon security duty and defend the ship!'

No crushing plasm assault destroys Paperhanger, but rather a series of raids, the government mages running at the airship for a slashing attack, then fading away to attack from a new direction. Most of the attacks fail, but a few get through. The airship's condition slowly worsens: enough gas cells are punctured so that the ship slowly loses altitude and stability, more and more water ballast must be dumped to keep the vessel on an even keel, and eventually its captain announces that its crew will have to abandon ship. The crew drag their wounded to the emergency aerofoils and the long glide to the surface of the world.

'*Shift the plasm beam to Red Bolt!*' Aldemar's voice, boosted by plasm, rings off the roofbeams of the factory. Pigeons flutter nervously on their perches.

Red Bolt is the backup, a converted cargo plane cruising in neutral airspace. But its facilities are more limited than those of the airship: its slim, aerodynamic profile is less likely to soak up the entire plasm beam, and its broadcast horns are smaller and less accurate. These handicaps can all be overcome with care and attention on the part of the mages attending to the plasm transmission, but the care and attention could be diverted to better things.

Aiah licks her lips, tasting adrenaline in the sweat dotting her upper lip, and reaches for her dials. 'Does Red Bolt know they're getting the goods?' she demands.

'Yes! Panther's told them!'

Panther is Sorya's all-too-apt code-name, as Constantine's is Big Man. Aiah checks the orientation of the reserve horn again – correct for Red Bolt – and readies her hands on the switches.

'Shifting to Red Bolt on my mark!' she says. 'Five! Four! Three! . . .'

On her mark she throws the switch; overhead she can

hear the clatter of rotators as the main feed is shifted to the roof's secondary transmission horn. Her dials show the plasm going out, but it's not clear that Red Bolt is actually receiving the goods until word comes from Trucker at the commo board.

'*You* – Wizard Three –' Aldemar's voice lashes out, stumbling on the code-names. 'Keep the beam on Red Bolt! You – the other one – we've got to ride security. Or . . .' Her eyes, all whites, roll toward Aiah. 'Lady – can you keep the beam on target? That would free one of us.'

Aiah's heart is in her mouth. 'I will try,' she says, and with feigned calm and pounding heart steps toward one of the consoles, connects the circuit that feeds plasm to it, pushes the gloves and closes the copper military t-grips over her wrists.

A demonic roar of plasm fills her senses. It's as if she can sense, on this end of the circuit, the war and death and desperation that resonates through the whole plasm circuit. Perhaps she's receiving scattered sensation from mages in combat.

'*Hurry!*' Aldemar's plasm-enhanced cry seems to imprint its urgent message on the inside of Aiah's skull. Aiah has no time to go through the careful steps of building an anima and sensorium, instead her mind leaps straight into the circuit and out the directional rooftop horn. Her impressions are diffused, uncertain, yet filled with thundering glorious power and occasional intense flashes of brilliant sensation, as if the plasm itself were alive and transmitting its inchoate sensations to her.

Aiah makes an effort to sharpen the scattered sensation and finds her senses coming into focus, the world resolving itself into an image of startling clarity as if through a miracle of optics: Red Bolt itself as seen from the rear, cruising twelve radii above the planet's surface, white vapor trails stretching from each of its four engines.

Aiah restructures her sensorium until she sees the beam

itself, the directed plasma burning bright gold through the sky to surround the plane like a diffused aura, with other, smaller beams firing from the plane's broadcast horns toward the ground. Consciously she tries to manipulate the beam, and finds a wilful resistance that, with a start, she recognizes as another mind. She attempts to communicate with it.

– This is Aiah . . . No! Lady, she tries. I can take the beam from here.

– You sure? The answer is twinned, the mental communication echoed by a vocal one from the sandbagged console to her right.

– Yes. No problem.

The task proves simple. Red Bolt continues to fly imperturbably above the endless gray city mass below. Aiah builds her sensorium until she sees everything in ultra-clear focus: the silver-skinned aircraft with its studded bronze collection web, sharp white clouds far below, the golden lines of plasm firing down on Caraqui, the metropolis so distant that from here Aiah can't even see the shimmer of its sea or the violet outlines of its famous volcanoes.

'Keep alert!' A ringing command from Aldemar. 'If they could find Paperhanger, they can find Red Bolt!'

And if they can find Red Bolt, Aiah thinks, they can find the factory. Her fingers fumble with the strap of her helmet and snug it in place under her chin.

The job of keeping the beam focused is dull enough that she can spare part of her attention for the news coming from the commo board. The unlucky First Brigade has been routed by Mondray's mercenaries. The rebels are trying to make a stand on the far side of the Martyrs' Canal, where Constantine and Aiah had once raced toward their meeting with Prince Aranax.

Elsewhere the news is better. The Aerial Palace has been entered by rebel troops, and they're fighting their way upward. Detachments of rebels have seized plasm stations and begun switching their plasm horns to rebel receivers. The government mages are capable enough, judging by their attacks on Paperhanger, but now they've less raw material to work with. And when Aiah slits open her eyes to catch a glimpse of the video display, she's astonished by the change at the Metropolitan Guard complex – several of the buildings are ablaze, pillars of fire around which whirl the hurricane debris of war. Armored vehicles burn on a bridge ramp, remnants of an attempted breakout.

From the Keremaths themselves nothing is heard. No broadcasts to the population, no appeals to loyal troops, nothing. It's as if no one's in charge at all.

Perhaps no one is. Aiah thinks of the hanged man creeping like a vein of methane ice through the plasm conduits – no bronze collection web can keep him out, because he enters along the plasm circuit itself.

You wish me to kill?

Certain people. Yes.

Bad people?

I believe so.

Aiah wonders if Constantine's cold ally, in exchange for a reward of warm human bodies, disposed of Caraqui's rulers before the fight even began.

The rebels manage to raise some drawbridges on the Martyrs' Canal – it's wide enough to provide a substantial obstacle – and Mondray's troops are halted till they can find an alternate route. Elements of the Marine Brigade are being pulled back from the Aerial Palace and sent to the canal by speeding gunboat. Over the wide stretch of water, mages reach for each other with outstretched fingers of burning plasm. Resistance in the Aerial Palace has almost collapsed.

'*Attack on Red Bolt!*' The high-pitched scream comes from Wizard Two, and snaps Aiah's attention back to the silver areoplane cruising on its Great Circle course high over neutral ground.

Aiah can see it coming – with her senses attuned to plasm, and nothing but many radii of air between her and the attackers, it would be hard not to – and there, below and northward, she sees a blazing gold serpent streaking toward the aircraft, backtracking the plasm beams that Red Bolt's transmission horns are sending to Caraqui.

Aldemar's mental voice, invading Aiah's senses, is surprisingly calm.

– Wizard One, remain in reserve near Red Bolt. Wizard Two, try to cut off its sourceline.

The attacking serpent suddenly rears up like a cobra about to strike.

Bits of Aiah's own plasm beam break off, like military aircraft peeling out of formation, each trailing its golden sourceline behind it. One heads for the intruder – Aldemar, Aiah thinks – another darting low as if to snip the serpent off near its tail. If the attacker's sourceline can be interfered with closer to its point of origin, then the attack itself will evaporate.

The hovering cobra strikes, spitting a hundred flashing plasm missiles at its target, self-contained bolts of fire. Flame streaks the sky. Missiles splash against a shield that Aldemar stretches across the sky at the last instant. And then both the missiles and the cobra are gone, and Red Bolt flies serenely along its course high above the clouds.

Aldemar's grim voice float's into Aiah's consciousness.

– He'll be back. He's just gone to get his friends.

A notion occurs to Aiah.

– Can we put Red Bolt on another course? I can bend the beam to keep it on track, and eventually reorient the transmission horn.

Aldemar's answer is decisive.

– Yes. Let's do it.

In her normal voice she orders the commo techs to relay orders to the pilot, and Red Bolt dips a wing, throttles up, and rolls away from its original path, diving slightly to increase speed.

For the moment the sky is peaceful again. Aiah finds it easy enough to keep the beam on target: she follows Red Bolt's path, the plasm looping behind her in the sky, and then straightens the kinks in the beam when she has the opportunity.

She glances up at the video through slitted eyes. Half the Metropolitan Guard headquarters is a flaming holocaust, but there's still resistance, shellfire crunching against the crumbling concrete walls. Resistance seems to have completely collapsed at the Aerial Palace, and rebel troops are moving up stairwells without opposition.

But the Martyrs' Canal seems to be living up to its name. Mondray's mercenaries managed to find or seize a bridge, and they're pushing as many troops over it as possible. The rebels don't have enough troops to stop them ... calls for reinforcements are continuous ... and the only rebel superiority seems to be in numbers of mages. The mercenaries have very little magical protection.

If you can't send troops, send plasm, Aiah thinks urgently. But she's not in command.

'Red Bolt's under attack!'

Aiah's perceptions snap to the sky. And the war goes on.

07:55.

Red Bolt had managed to move over three hundred radii before the enemy found it again. It's hard to say whether Aiah's maneuver made any difference at all, and Aiah wonders if that is typical of war, if a commander never really knew whether the care she was taking was ever worthwhile. And now battle is joined, the air covered with writhing plasm serpents and arrows of fire. Red Bolt corkscrews through the sky, trying to dodge the swift oncoming attacks. The defenders are agile, but the government mages keep coming, raking in from different directions, and though Red Bolt is a smaller and more maneuverable target than the airship Paperhanger, it's also more fragile, with far less redundancy. And when it dies it dies swiftly, an irruption of fire, wings folding toward its flaming body in one last sad gesture as it streaks like an arrow in a long arc toward the gray metropolis below.

Aiah never even saw what hit it.

They died right in front of me, she thinks, *and it's all my fault.*

'Out of the well!' Aldemar yells.

Aiah pulls her awareness out of the plasm. Her eyes open to scenes of carnage – the Metropolitan Guard complex afire, a jittering camera regarding a distant bridge over a wide stretch of water all orange with burning, doubtless the Martyrs' Canal. Aiah's eyes go wide with awe and terror.

'Lady! On the board!'

Aiah jumps at Aldemar's command, strips the copper bracelets from her wrists and races to the master switches as she wipes tracks of sweat from her face. Plasm is still pouring out of the reserve transmission horn, aimed uselessly at the all-absorbing Shield.

'Shut it off! *Now!* They can track us!'

Aiah throws switches. With a clack, overhead copper contacts retract to the neutral position. Her eyes stay glued to the video, the jittering images of holocaust. The rebels have lost a large percentage of their plasm, and she's expecting horror to erupt on video any second now.

'Who needs the goods?' Aldemar tips her chair back, looks over her shoulder, at the commo crew. 'And how do we get it to them?'

'Ride the beams in ourselves!' Wizard Two is happy to state the obvious. There's a twitchy glow of battle behind his thick spectacles. A crooked grin reveals a gleam of steel braces.

Trucker presses big hands over his earphones. 'Big Man and Panther are demanding all we've got. He wants to finish off the Guard.'

'But look!' Aiah can't stop herself from pointing at the screen. 'The real fight's at the Martyrs' Canal!'

Her words are punctuated by an explosion, a mushroom of flame and smoke rising near the canal.

Red nods. 'They've been calling for more plasm all along.'

Aldemar looks up at the screens, bites her lip. 'Who's the mage in charge of that fight? Where is he?'

'He's an army mage,' Red reports. 'He's at the Qinchath Plasm Station, and I think the only plasm he's got is the stuff generated locally.'

'Big Man wants the goods *now*,' Trucker reminds.

'Qinchath needs plasm,' Aiah says. 'Are the coordinates on the charts? Can we ride a beam there?'

Aldemar flips hopelessly through the paper printout. 'Crap! Is it on the list or not?'

'I can use the video!' Wizard Two bounces up and down on his chair. 'I can just jump there with the goods! If I can find our Qinchath man, I'll hand the stuff to him, and if not, I'll just kick some ass myself.'

Aldemar cocks an eyebrow at him. 'You can do that?'

'I've got the training – yeah! I can do it!'

'Excuse me!' Trucker shouts. 'But Big Man is chewing me a new asshole *right now*! What do I tell him?'

Aldemar turns to Aiah. 'Give Horn One to Wizard Two. Half our product.' She looks resigned. 'I'll get the rest to Big Man myself. Give me Horn Two.' Sweat patters on Aiah's console as she spins knobs, throws switches. Aldemar continues with her orders. 'Wizard Three – run a security watch around the factory. We might have half a battalion of creepers out there for all we know.'

A charming thought.

Copper contacts clack into their cradles. 'Wizard Two!'

Aiah calls. 'Powering Horn One on my mark! Two! One! *Mark!* Alde – *Wizard One* – powering Horn Two on my mark! Two. One. *Mark!*'

Aiah stares at Wizard Two. The purpose of the live video feed is to enable precisely what the boy is attempting: a mental jump from one location to another, dragging the anima's plasm tail along with it. The mage visualizes the place he wants to go, then tries both to leap his transphysical presence to the spot and to carry his plasm supply with him.

Wizard Two stares intently at the video of the Martyrs' Canal. His staring blue eyes are enlarged by his thick spectacles. His body gives a jerk, hands clenching into fists.

And then, above his head, the video image jitters, as if something's just jostled the camera. '*Yes!*' the boy shouts.

Aiah licks sweat from her upper lip, her eyes darting from the boy to the video feeds and back. Other than the brief nudge to the camera, nothing visible occurs for a while. And then the boy's body curves in a perfect arc as water fountains from the river right in the center of the bridge, gushing upward as if from a broken main. The center span rocks, then lifts as if a giant invisible hand were beneath it. The span strains, rocks and finally is flung bodily to one side, girders snapping like twigs. Personnel and armored vehicles spill into the water. The camera jerks again as if in surprise or terror.

Explosions march along the approach span of the bridge, Mondray's vehicles cooking in their own fuel or ammunition. This is followed by a series of flashes in midair – Aiah concludes it's invisible mages battling each other. And then, slowly forming over the bridge approach, is a figure, tenuous at first, then gaining in solidity and size, outlines rippling with fire.

The Flaming Man.

Fear chills Aiah's spine. She stares at the video display, helpless with terror and awe. The flamer, taller than any of the surrounding buildings, stalks into the city. Flashes fill the air near him, but they don't seem to slow him down. Buildings explode into flame at his approach. Prisms of light flash in midair from flying glass. Debris spirals skyward in a whirlwind of rising heat.

My fault, Aiah thinks. The accusation catches in her throat and stops her breath.

Aiah rips her eyes from the video and looks at Wizard Two. He's slumped in his chair, head cocked to one side, one arm dangling almost to the floor. Aiah runs to the chair and her heart leaps into her throat as she stares aghast at the ruined, shriveled face, already an old man's, lolling atop a body shrinking slowly into its clothes. Behind misty lenses the blackened eyes are sizzling in their sockets, evaporating, and from the slack mouth comes another hiss, a wisp of vapor – the tongue and palate are being consumed.

My fault.

Noradrenaline fury seizes Aiah. She snatches the wires connecting the boy's t-grips to the console and yanks, pulling them from their sockets. '*Help!*' she yells. '*Is anyone here a medic?*' And then her knees give way and she sags against a wall of sandbags. Sand drifts gently to the floor at her feet. On the video feed she still sees the Burning Man, holocausts leaping into being at his touch. A cold hand twists Aiah's nerves as she realizes the flamer's self-contained now, and will live as long as there's plasm to feed him. She throws down the wires and runs back to the command console. Her boots skid on concrete as she pulls herself to a stop, and she slaps at the switch cutting off plasm to Horn One.

'*Medic!*' she yells.

The Burning Man's image fades, crumpling into itself the way Wizard Two shrank into his clothes, and relief sings through Aiah's mind, a relief that fades into horror as she realizes that, while the flamer is gone, his funeral pyre is not. A firestorm still rages in Caraqui, flames swirling skyward, and no one is in a position to put it out.

Two of the security men, so maddeningly unhurried that Aiah wants to shriek at them, stride to where Wizard Two lies on his chair, look at him for a moment – one offhandedly checks the pulse of the trailing hand – and then they look at each other and shrug. 'Toasted cheese,' one says.

'I'm getting a message from the Qinchath mage,' Red says. 'He says our side's running like hell, but it doesn't matter, because the enemy's *annihilated*.' He grins up from his console and savors the word. '*Annihilated!*'

'Annihilated, shit!' Aiah cries, gesturing at the flaming chaos onscreen. 'Look at the video!'

My fault.

'Where the hell is my plasm?' Aldemar yells. 'What's going on?'

Aiah looks at her dials and simply stares. The capacitors and accumulators are empty, drained, and so is much of the old factory structure underneath. The buried structure at Terminal will generate more over time, but for the moment even its awesome resources are strained.

Aiah turns dials. 'Wizard One, I'm giving you all there is. We're depleted!'

'Oh, crap.'

'The Aerial Palace is secure,' Trucker reports almost anticlimactically. 'They haven't found anything on the top floors but bodies.'

'Silver is trying to transmit a surrender demand to the Metropolitan Guard.' Another announcement. 'No reply yet.'

Silver is the code name for Colonel Drumbeth, the leader and instigator of the coup. This is the first Aiah's heard of him since the whole action began.

She looks up at the screens again, the buildings burning. *My fault.*

*   *   *

The security men are quietly gathering up papers and equipment for the burn safe. Vehicles are being readied for a fast exit.

Fire fills the video screens. The Metropolitan Guard hasn't replied to any of the repeated surrender demands, leaving the rebels with no option but to continue their attack. Resistance has almost ceased — some scattered gunfire is still directed at attackers — but for the most part the Guard receive their pounding in silence, without reply. All the Guard's plasm connections have been broken. Their mages have ceased action and may well be dead, cooked alive in their bunkers. No one can tell.

The waters of the Martyrs' Canal reflect a wall of flame, a fireball eating its way outward. Panicked residents choke the quays and the bridges, most of which have been broken or blocked in an attempt to keep the mercenaries from crossing. The Qinchath mage, or someone, is lifting the waters of the canal to pour on the burning buildings, but the fires are beyond his control.

'I can see police cars,' Wizard Three reports. Aiah is too mentally exhausted to react to the announcement. 'Cars coming down Eleven-ninety-first Street, but the weekend crowds are slowing them down. I don't detect anyone observing us through plasm.'

'Shut down the transmission horns,' Aldemar says. 'Leave my station live, but everyone else get out.'

Aiah throws the switches for the last time.

'Gloves in the burn safe,' a security man reminds.

Aiah peels off her gloves and throws them into the burn safe, then moves toward the cars. Aldemar stands up at her station and calls out.

'I'm going to cover your withdrawal, and then I've got to give this place a quick-and-dirty cleaning. Get out as quick as you can.'

'This way, miss!' a guard says, opening the sliding rear

door to a small van. His tone shows impatience. Aiah jumps into the back along with Red and Trucker. In the instant before the door slams she glances up at the screens and sees only orange fire.

The van is in motion before the factory door has completely slid open. Aiah balances herself against a violent turn as the van swings into traffic, its horn bleating to clear pedestrians out of the way.

The driver looks at Aiah through mirrored shieldglasses. 'Where do you need to go, miss?' he says. 'We haven't been left instructions.'

'Take me to Rocketman trackline station,' she says.

'I don't know where that is. I need directions.'

Aiah makes her way forward and slides into the passenger seat. In the rearview mirror she can see two other vehicles in convoy behind. Startled pedestrians are jumping out of the way of the vehicles.

'How are you people getting out?' she asks.

'InterMetropolitan Highway,' the driver says. 'We'll be out of Jaspeer in less than ninety minutes, traffic willing.'

Aiah stares at a flash in the rearview mirror, a bloom of orange and black. Her heart gives a cry of anguish.

'The factory!' she says. 'It's on fire!'

The driver gives her another expressionless look. 'When mages clean,' he says, 'they clean.'

09:00.

New Central Line to Mudki Station. Mudki is huge, and Aiah makes a point of wandering through a lot of it, making it difficult for any plasm hound to trace exactly where she intends to go. She buys fresh bread and rolls from a vendor, then takes the Red Line home.

10:44.

Aiah walks through the door of Loeno Towers. She had hoped to enter unseen but the doorman – not the one she'd taken to the chromo — smiles and opens the door for her. She offers him a roll and tells him she'd gone out for breakfast supplies.

In her apartment she depolarizes the windows to full light, makes breakfast and watches the video news. A new military government in Caraqui, she hears, much fighting and loss of life. A burning aeroplane crashed in a crowded residential area of Makdar, creating an explosion and fire that killed over 160 people. A punctured airship had draped itself over several buildings in a district of Liri-Domei, but no one has been injured. An old factory building on fire on 1190th Street, the neighborhood threatened, no deaths reported.

Scarcely tasting it, Aiah eats slice after slice of the bread. She's never been hungrier in her life.

She wonders if Aldemar made it out of the factory. She doesn't see how.

13:02.

The hourly news broadcast shows Caraqui's new government, little Drumbeth in a fresh uniform, Parq in full clerical regalia, red and gold, wearing the Mask of Awe that demonstrates he's acting in his official capacity as head of the Dalavites. Apparently he joined the winning side in time. A third figure in the triumvirate is a spare, disdainful civilian she's never heard of, a journalist described as a 'leading dissident'.

All the cameras are on Constantine, though, looming behind the three in his long snakeskin coat. Sorya stands next to him, a self-satisfied smile on her face.

And standing on the other side of Constantine is Aldemar, her face neatly made up, eyes gazing complacently at the cameras from under her level bangs. Aiah stares and wonders how she escaped from the factory that she herself had set on fire, let alone got to a Caraqui still in the midst of a revolution.

Teleportation, she thinks. The rarest and most dangerous of mage skills.

Aldemar, it would seem, is a much better mage than even her chromos ever made out.

Almost all the journalists' questions are addressed to Constantine. 'This is not my moment,' he finally says, 'but Caraqui's, a metropolis that has been rescued from generations of government by bandits. Please address your questions to Colonel Drumbeth.'

This, Aiah comforts herself, is her responsibility as well.

15.20.

A feather touch in Aiah's mind, a stimulation of the senses — the scent of soft leather, musk, a deep voice that speaks gently to the inner ear.

— Precious Lady, can you hear me?

Aiah touches her throat and sits down suddenly on her unmade bed.

— Yes. Yes, I can hear.

— I wish to thank you. Aldemar says that you did very well today. You were right to divert plasm to the Martyrs' Canal, I was too close to the fighting to realize that.

There is a lump in Aiah's throat.

— That boy. He died.

— You were not responsible for that. He overestimated his own abilities.

— So many others must have died.

Constantine's tone is matter-of-fact.

— Yes, certainly. But compared to what happened in Cheloki, I think we got off lightly.

Aiah cannot entirely find ease in this thought. Constantine continues.

— You were brave and most resourceful, he sends. I wish to give you a reward if this can be done safely. There will be money in a bank account in Gunalaht, and I will send you the numbers and a chop when it's safe.

– Those people who lost their homes, Aiah sighs. Take care of them first.

– Yes. Yes. I am, finally, in a position to do that.

A phantom hand seems to stroke Aiah's hair. Constantine's scent rises in her nostrils.

– Farewell, brave Lady, he sends. I will not forget your brightness.

Constantine fades from Aiah's mind as tears spill across her cheeks.

Some dreams have come true today, she knows, but not her own.

18:22.

The police are at Aiah's door.

20

Police have a knock louder than anyone else in the world, and there's no mistaking it. Aiah stares at the door while fear grips her throat. Then she walks to the door and tries to calm herself.

There are at least three different kinds of police outside: the two in suits and subdued lace are plainclothes Authority creepers, big men who threaten to fill the doorway. Behind them are a pair of district police in their brown uniforms, and a blue-uniformed Loeno security woman who seems bewildered by the whole thing.

Aiah suspects there may also be a mage floating invisibly overhead on a plasm sourceline, there to guard the cops in case Aiah dares to smite them with magework.

'May we come in?' the first creeper says, brandishing his ID. He has fatty eyelids that fall over pebble eyes like curtains.

'No,' Aiah says.

Something else she learned at her granny's knee. Once you let the cops in, you can't get rid of them.

'We can go to a pross judge and get a warrant,' the creeper offers.

Aiah shrugs. 'I'm sure I can't stop you.' There's a tremor behind her left knee that threatens to capsize her at any moment. More for support than anything else, Aiah leans a shoulder against the door jamb, though she tries to turn the movement into a confident gesture.

She looks up into the creeper's eyes.

'What's this about, exactly?'

The man looks at his partner, and it's the partner who speaks, a man in a worn green suit. 'Your name is Aiah, right?'

'Yes.'

'Where is your place of employment?'

Aiah smiles. 'I work at the Plasm Control Authority headquarters on the Avenue of the Exchange.'

The cops look at each other again. Apparently they hadn't known this.

'What do you do there?' says Green Suit.

Aiah's smiled broadens. Somewhere in the back of her brain is a nasty little imp who's enjoying this more than she should.

'I'm a Grade Six. Right at the moment I'm assigned to Mr Rohder, the head of the Research Division, engaged in a special project solving major plasm thefts.'

The creepers seem to sag, the big shoulders crumpling inside the worn suits, and Aiah knows she's won, at least for the present. She knows just what's going through their minds: some hopeless bungle, one division of the Authority chasing another, lots of reports to file and probably someone's ass on the hot seat.

Aiah's imp tells her to follow up while she still has the advantage.

'Does this have to do with the arrests at Kremag and Associates?' she asks.

Her interrogators give her blank looks. 'Where?'

'An Operation plasm house down on 1193rd Street, near Garakh Station. The Authority took it down late Friday. I provided the information that secured the warrants.'

'1193rd?' Fat Lids makes an effort to retrieve the situation. 'How about 1190th? Were you at the factory that exploded first shift today?'

Aiah narrows her eyes and opens her arms, inviting them to feast their eyes. 'Do I *look* like I've been through an explosion?'

'Were you there,' patiently, '*before* the explosion?'

'Possibly. Late Friday. I went down to look at the Kremag raid, but there was a lot of pepper gas and not much to look at, so I wandered around the neigborhood for awhile and then came home.'

Aiah considers herself lucky that the creepers are Jaspeeris who probably wouldn't consider how implausible it is that any Barkazil would wander around Terminal by herself at an odd hour of the sleep shift.

The creeper starts again. 'This factory—'

'I don't really remember a *factory*,' Aiah says. 'Although it's possible that your factory might be one of the plasm houses I reported to Mr Rohder. I don't remember all the addresses, and I never actually saw any of them – except for Kremag, I mean.'

'Our plasm hound,' the creeper says, 'led us from the factory straight to your door.'

Aiah shrugs. 'Well,' she says, 'I *was* in the neighborhood.'

'And you had nothing to do with the plasm station in the factory on 1190th that was used to assist in the overthrow of a foreign government?'

Aiah tries to look impressed. 'I don't *think* so,' she says. 'Not unless it was on the list I gave to Mr Rohder.'

The creeper circles back to the beginning.

'And you won't let us in?'

'No.'

'Why not?'

Aiah folds her arms. 'Because there's obviously been a fuckup at the Authority,' she says, 'and whichever of our superiors is responsible will be looking to foist the blame on someone else. Why should I cooperate in cutting my own throat?'

The creeper gives up. 'We may have more questions later.'

'I'll be at work tomorrow. You can talk to me then.'

The creeper nods.

'Till next time,' he says.

GRADE B EARTHQUAKE IN QELHORN MOUNTAIN DISTRICT
100,000 FEARED DEAD
DETAILS ON THE *WIRE*!

Just act normally.

It isn't hard. Nothing in Aiah's life is abnormal any more.

While brewing coffee early Monday she listens to the early newscasts. The casualties in the Caraqui coup are in the 50,000 range, divided about fifty-fifty between the firestorm victims on the Martyrs' Canal and the Metropolitan Guard, who died almost to the last man. By now the authorities have connected the crashed plane in Makdar and the deflated airship in Liri-Domei with the coup, and some of the airship's crew are being held pending charges.

There's plenty on the news about the factory – neighboring buildings went up in smoke, and hundreds are homeless – but the reporters, as opposed to the police, haven't as yet connected the building with Constantine or his coup.

At least there's no mention of Constantine's mystery lover. It seems clear to the reporters that, whoever he was meeting with in the Landmark, it was to plan his attack.

On the pneuma, she reads Rohder's *Proceedings*. At the kiosk on the Avenue of the Exchange, Aiah buys a lottery ticket, then heads for work. She stops by her office to pick up messages, and finds the office empty: no Tella, no Jayme. The message tube in her wire tray, from Mengene, informs her of an emergency meeting at 09:00.

She takes the elevator to Rohder's office on the 106th floor. Rohder's sitting at his desk, his pink face in his hands. It's the first time Aiah's ever seen him without a lit cigaret. When Aiah walks in, he straightens and looks at her with his head cocked to one side.

'The Investigative Division's been onto me about you.'

'Yes. The creepers showed up at my apartment yesterday.' She walks up to his desk. 'What's it about? They asked a lot of questions but they didn't tell me much.'

'That plasm well in Terminal we were looking for, the one that probably caused the Bursary Street flamer ...' His pale blue eyes gaze up at her expressionlessly from behind his thick spectacles. 'Well,' he continues, 'someone used it to kill fifty thousand people yesterday.'

The shock that clamps a cold hand on Aiah's throat isn't feigned. She hadn't considered the facts in quite this brutal light before.

She clears her throat. 'Was it one of the addresses I gave you?'

'No.'

'Well – at least we were looking for it. If those others had backed us, maybe we'd have found it before this, ah, disaster happened.'

Rohder nods slowly, his eyes fixed on her. 'Since I last saw you I've procured two more warrants, by the way. There was another big arrest late yesterday.'

'Well,' Aiah restrains an impulse to wave her arms. 'What more do they *want* from us? We were *looking* – and that's more than the creepers ever did!'

'Ah. Yes.' Rohder frowns and looks at his hands. 'As it happens I had a call from the Intendant earlier today. He congratulated me on the way I – *we* – had managed to discover so many plasm houses in such a short time. But he pointed out – nicely, I thought – that it wasn't really my *job* to find criminals, and that we should really share our methods with the Investigative Division, who could then finish the work for us.'

Anger buzzes through Aiah's brain. It's all going to *waste*, she thinks.

'Did you point out that one of the plasm cheats we found was *in* the Investigative Division?' she asks.

'Well. No. Not as yet.'

'If we give the creepers our method – *my* method – any investigation in the district plasm stations will likely be carried out by the same corrupt officials who were paid off in the first place. And if word of the method gets out, the crooks will know that all they have to do is program a little more efficiently, and then we won't catch them.'

Rohder frowns, then reaches for a pack on the table and thoughtfully draws out a cigaret. 'I know,' he says. 'And I'm sure the lesson's been learned before, over the decades. Someone like you comes along, the thieves get cautious for a while, and then they get careless again and a few get caught and the rest learn again to be more cautious.' He sighs, looks at the cigaret for a moment, then puts it in his mouth and lights it.

His eyes shift restlessly; he won't look at her. The cigaret bobs up and down in his mouth as he speaks. 'What I'm saying is, well, fine, we caught a few. And the creepers will catch a few more with the information we gave them. But as far as developing any more leads goes, well, the Intendant doesn't want it.'

'We make the Investigative Division look bad.'

'That's a part of it, yes.'

Anger and frustration crackle through Aiah's nerves. She doesn't have to act this part, she knows, all her anger is perfectly genuine. The truth is bitter on her tongue as she lashes out.

'Doesn't it strike you as odd that I find a plasm thief in the Investigative Division, and within two days the creepers are trying to pin some kind of major crime on me?'

'I didn't tell anyone of your discovery. I was going to

approach the Intendant properly when the moment suited. Did you tell anyone?'

'No.'

'Your office mate? Anyone?'

'No one at all.'

Rohder stares uneasily out the window. 'Do you think someone crept in and read the notes on my desk? Most odd, if true – no one's expressed an interest in my work in years.'

'How many years has it been since you uncovered a major crime being committed in our own headquarters building?'

'Oh, thirty years or thereabouts,' he waves a hand airily while Aiah stares at him in surprise. 'I had forgotten, till this business reminded me.' Rohder draws in smoke, his watery eyes fixed on the distant horizon.

His glance lifts and, finally, he looks at her. 'I have exerted myself on your behalf already,' he says. 'I spoke rather forcefully to the creepers, and I will also speak to Mengene and the Intendant.'

Aiah tries to conceal her glee. Like every other division of government, the police are stacked heavy with layers of officialdom anxious to protect their jobs and their privileges. If Aiah can win the bureaucratic war on the top floors of the Authority building, she can stifle the investigation below before it properly starts. Unless they get more physical evidence, Aiah thinks, the creepers are out of luck.

'Thank you, Mr Rohder,' she says.

He cocks his head again, blue eyes blinking, and Aiah feels as if she's being regarded by some strange, hunched waterfowl. 'I am sorry to have to return you to your job. It doesn't seem to be a particularly rewarding one. I looked at your record – you've never had any education in live plasm use?'

'No. I couldn't afford it.'

'Your advancement here would go faster with a degree in plasm engineering.'

'Perhaps you know a millionaire I could marry.'

'Ah.' Cigaret ash falls on Rohder's lace. He brushes at it absently. 'I have occasionally taken leaves of absence from the Authority to teach,' he says, 'and some of my students have kept in touch. One is now chancellor of Margai University, and there are scholarships that are within his prerogative. If I were to recommend you, you would almost certainly be accepted, and the Authority would be more than pleased to grant you a leave of absence. When you returned with the degree, your career prospects would be enhanced.'

The offer takes Aiah's breath away. She stares at Rohder for a long moment and makes an effort to compose herself before answering. 'Ah,' she says. 'Yes. Yes, I'd be grateful for the recommendation.'

'Well then.' Rohder swabs at his lace again as he stands, and then he offers his hand. 'It was a pleasure working with you. If you have any more of these little projects in mind, do call me.'

Aiah takes his hand. 'Thank you again. I learned a great deal.'

Rohder looks puzzled. 'I can't see how, Miss Aiah. Good day.'

> *Obedience is the Greatest Gift*
> — a thought-message from His Perfection,
> the Prophet of Ajas

'Creepers!' Tella reports. She's nursing Jayme, and for once the office is quiet. 'I just spent half an hour with them! What the hell is this about?'

'What did you tell them?'

'Nothing!' Tella's eyes are guileless. 'I don't tell people things, you know that.' She leans closer and lowers her voice, and Aiah hopes there isn't some mage hovering in the room, overhearing every word. 'I didn't mention your little after-hours thing,' Tella whispers. Or course she'd told maybe a hundred other people in the building, but maybe the creepers wouldn't know to ask any of them.

Aiah wonders how many people had seen her driving off in Constantine's limousine.

'The folks upstairs are covering their asses,' Aiah says. 'They're trying to lay blame on me because they wrote off the Bursary Street flamer without a proper investigation.' She drops into her gray metal chair and it sags about twenty degrees to the right. Anger flares in Aiah's heart. She swivels the chair left and right, but the list remains.

'*Shit!*' she shouts, stands and kicks the chair across the room, where it crashes into the other two disabled chairs. All three chairs tumble onto the cracked tile floor. Fury flares in her veins. 'I don't know how many reports we've filed with Maintenance in the last year!'

Urgency enters Tella's voice again. 'But the *investigation* . . . what are you going to *do*?'

Aiah restrains herself from giving the chair another kick. 'Tell me,' she demands, 'if I should be afraid of an organization that can't even fix a chair.'

TRACKLINE INTENDANT RESIGNS!
MAINTAINS INNOCENCE
SCANDAL CLAIMS ITS GREATEST VICTIM

Aiah walks into the 09:00 emergency meeting pushing her broken chair in front of her. While the others watch, she places the chair against the wall and then sits in one of the comfortably padded chairs at the long boardroom table. The others observe but do not comment.

Oeneme is present in person, testifying to the seriousness of the meeting. 'I'm not interested in facts,' he says. 'I'm interested in *impressions*.'

354

Oeneme's subordinates duly supply him with their impressions, relieved of the duty of mentioning the fact that it was Oeneme himself who ignored Rohder's report that the flamer's sourceline was eastward and instead ordered Emergency Response to Old Parade.

The meeting drags on for three hours and, as no one is willing to say anything pertinent, accomplishes nothing.

In the New City, Aiah thinks darkly, all these people would be thrown out onto the street to beg for their bread.

When Aiah leaves the meeting, she drags her plush chair behind her and takes it to her office. Everyone sees, but no one says a word.

Her office smells of urine and baby stool. Two creepers wait for her there, small, polite men in neat suits, a different style from the street bruisers she met yesterday. 'We'd like you to come with us,' one says, speaking over the wails of the baby.

'Are you going to buy me lunch?' Aiah asks.

They look at each other. 'No.'

'Then you can wait till after midbreak.'

She plants the stolen chair in front of her desk and leaves. Outside, she buys a bowl of savory broth with rice noodles from a vendor and eats it while sitting on a bench on the Avenue of the Exchange. She reads *Proceedings*, making notes, for the rest of the lunch hour, then collects the deposit on her soup bowl and heads back to her office.

A curious sensation of invincibility trickles like wine through her veins.

The creepers are waiting when she returns. Tella leaves for her own lunch, taking the baby with her. For the next hour Aiah answers the creepers' patient questions. When they start to ask the same questions all over again, hoping to catch her in some contradiction, she calls an end to it.

'Unless you have anything new to ask, I have a job to do.'

Somewhat to her surprise, the creepers put away their notes, thank her pleasantly, and leave.

'15.31 hours, Horn Six reorientation to degrees 114. Ne?'

'Da. 15:31 hours, Horn Six reorientation to degrees 114. 9:34, confirmed.'

'15:31, Horn Six transmit at 800 mm. 30 minutes. Ne?'

'Da. 15:31, Horn Six transmit at 800 mm. 30 minutes. Confirmed.'

IS ALDEMAR CONSTANTINE'S NEW LOVER?
SPECULATION SWEEPS MEDIA!

Her yellow message light blinks furiously in her apartment. All the messages are from relatives approached by the creepers: they all want to know what they should say, if anything, and simultaneously demand to know what she's really up to.

No messages from her mother; maybe the creepers haven't located her as yet.

Aiah goes out to buy supplies for supper, and while at the grocer's uses a pay phone to call her grandmother.

'What's happening?' Galaiah demands. 'Did you do something stupid? Did that *passu* of yours get you in trouble?'

'I haven't done anything stupid. I haven't done anything at all. It's some people above me who are trying to cover up their idiocy – too complicated to explain, really.'

'You're a Barkazil. They'll sell you out without even thinking about it.'

'I know.' Aiah looks at the grocery customers standing in lines with their sacks of food and wonders if she's being followed. There are some Jaspeeri men loitering by the exit, but then on the other hand there are always people loitering there, and they don't have to be creepers.

And of course if some mage is following her on an invisible plasm tether, she'd never know.

'Nana,' she says, 'I'd appreciate it if you could just ask everyone in the family to tell the police they don't know anything, and they think I'm an honest person. I don't know if it would help, but at least it wouldn't put anybody in jeopardy.'

'Your mother,' Galaiah says darkly.

'Yes,' Aiah says, heart sinking. Gurrah would tell the creepers anything that came into her head and worry about incriminating her daughter later.

'I'll tell her to throw them out and say nothing,' Galaiah says. 'That way she can play a scene.'

Aiah is relieved. 'Do that, please. If I suggest that, she'll just do the opposite.'

'True.'

'And tell people that I . . . well, someone may be listening on my phone, so they should be careful about the messages they leave me.'

'Yes. I'll tell them.'

'Thank you, Nana.'

'You be careful. You can't trust longnoses.'

'I know.'

'Don't you talk to them, either.'

'I don't have anything to tell them, anyway.'

On the way home Aiah buys a few pieces of fruit from a street vendor – a battered orange and a pair of plums. At home she washes the plums carefully with water and chlorine bleach – that's what you do with street fruit – and eats one. The pulp is strangely tasteless, full of juice but without savor.

Constantine's arboretum, she thinks, has spoiled her for the ordinary stuff.

Aiah makes a sauce for vat curd out of freeze-dried vegetables and some spring onions from her pocket garden, then watches the video news. Disaster teams from other areas are pouring into Caraqui. Drumbeth, spokesman for the new triumvirate, speaks about the need for aid and compassion, his voice firm, his tone a bit fierce. A member of the Keremath family, who as ambassador to another metropolis escaped the coup, denounces the new government as murderers and proclaims a government in exile. The few surviving Mondray's Regulars, having surrendered, are being air-shuttled back to the Timocracy.

Considerable air time is devoted to speculation about Constantine, even though he hasn't appeared in public since yesterday. There's much more interest in Constantine than in Drumbeth or any other member of the actual government.

Aiah swallows a mouthful of pasta and curd. In Caraqui, she thinks, things are *happening*.

GARGELIUS ENCHUK ON TOUR
TICKETS AVAILABLE ON THE *WIRE*!

'09:00 hours, Horn Two reorientation to degrees 040. Ne?'

'Da. 09:00 hours, Horn Two reorientation to degrees 040. 9:34, confirmed.'

'09:00, Horn Two transmit at 1400 mm. 10 minutes. Ne?'

'Da. 09:00, Horn Two transmit at 1400 mm. 10 minutes. Confirmed.'

COUP SURVIVOR DENOUNCES CONSTANTINE
CALLS FOR WORLD COUNCIL INTERVENTION

By midbreak the *Wire* has found out about the burned

factory's connection to the coup in Caraqui and a pack of reporters sits in the Authority lobby demanding information. Another emergency meeting is called.

'Simple,' Mengene says. 'We blame everything on Constantine. The factory fire, the Bursary Street flamer, everything.'

'There's no evidence connecting him to either,' Oeneme points out.

'Who else could it be? And even if it wasn't, who cares? We're not judges, we don't *need* evidence just to smear him in the media. It gets us completely off the hook.'

Oeneme smiles. 'All I have to say is that our investigation is aimed at making a connection between Constantine and the factory.'

'Exactly. Let the reporters do our work for us.'

Aiah glances up from the spilled-coffee circles she's drawing on the glass tabletop, looks at the broken office chair leaning against the wall's gold-plated chrysanthemum pattern, and smiles.

If the official blame is laid on Constantine, she thinks, that means they can't lay it on *her*.

DOLPHIN APPOINTED TO MINISTRY
PAYOFF FOR SUPPORT IN COUP

No one has explained this line of reasoning to the creepers, however, who show up after Aiah's lunch break for another round of questions. They've got ahold of her finances and have discovered that a few weeks ago she paid off debts totalling over six hundred dalders.

'I paid them,' Aiah says, 'because my lover phoned to tell me that he was sending a cashgram for eight hundred. And if you've got my bank accounts, you'll see that he did just that.'

'Where did you get the six hundred? Your bank balance had only forty-some dalders in it.'

'From the emergency fund under my mattress,' Aiah says. She leans back onto the plush cushions of her stolen chair and forges ahead with the story she's readied ahead of time.

'I play the lottery. Every so often I win – not much, never more than twenty – and I put the winnings away.' She reaches into her pocketbook and picks up the ticket she'd bought before work.

'Why don't you put the money in a bank?'

'Twenty isn't worth a trip to the bank.' She shrugs. 'Besides, it's a Barkazil thing. We don't trust banks much. My family lost everything when the banks failed in the Barkazi war.'

The creepers gaze down at her with perfect skepticism. 'But when the eight hundred came,' one says, 'you left it in the bank. You didn't put it under your mattress.'

Aiah shrugs. 'It wasn't *my* money. It was Gil's. I still have a hundred-and-some stashed in a bag under the mattress, though.'

Which is perfectly true. If they've got a mage with a warrant, he'll find it there.

They try to shake this story for some time, but Aiah digs in her heels and insists on the truth of her story. They can't *prove* she never had cash stashed in her apartment.

After the questions circle back to this point for a third time, she tells them she needs to get to work.

Again, they leave when she tells them to. Perhaps, she thinks, she's getting the upper hand.

LOTTERY SCANDAL WIDENS
INTENDANT PROMISES FULL INVESTIGATION

'14:20 hours, Horn One reorientation to degrees 357. Ne?'

'Da. 14:20 hours, Horn One reorientation to degrees 357, confirmed.'

'14:20, Horn One transmit at 1850 mm. 20 minutes. Ne?'

'Da. 14:20, Horn One transmit at 1850 mm. 20 minutes. Confirmed.'

The office rings with Jayme's screams and smells of dirty diapers and warm milk. There's a numbing series of calls for plasm. Her ears and skull ache with the weight of the heavy headset.

In Caraqui, she thinks, things are *happening*.

CONSTANTINE LINKED TO FACTORY DISASTER IN JASPEER
DETAILS ON THE *WIRE*!

As she leaves the Authority building, Aiah looks up to see the gold letters unfolding across the sky, and her heart gives a leap.

Try and blame it on me *now*, she thinks.

CONSTANTINE IN HIDING
NO WORD FROM COUP MASTERMIND

The news is all about Constantine, even though no one's seen him since Sunday. He's been appointed Minister of Resources in the new government, a job that will put him in charge of plasm. Weekend business for *Lords of the New City* makes it the largest-opening chromoplay of all time, despite the fact that twenty percent of the planet's population weren't allowed to see it by their governments.

And authorities in Jaspeer have now officially linked him with the factory disaster. Much air time is absorbed by the government's indignation.

Aiah's communication rig chimes as she's halfway through her leftover vat curd. She turns down the audio, leaving on video the image of Constantine overlaid with a red banner screaming *Under Investigation*, and then she picks up the headset.

'Yes?'

'Hi. This is Gil. Good news.'

'I—'

'I'm coming back. In ten days or so. We're wrapping everything up in Gerad. And I'm getting a promotion to assistant vice-president, which will bring us another five thousand a year.'

'I—' The message sinks in, and Aiah finds her heart hammering, her eyes darting wildly from one corner of the apartment to the next, as if an iron cage had just dropped over her. She swallows hard.

'At last,' she says.

'Don't jump up and down with joy or anything.'

'Oh.' She swallows again. 'I'm sorry. But there's a problem here. I'm under investigation because some people think I helped Constantine launch this coup against the government of Caraqui.'

'Malakas! Did they find out about—'

Aiah shouts over Gil's inconvenient question. *I didn't do it! I didn't do anything!*

'Well.' Taken aback. 'Of course you didn't.'

'I've told them I don't know Constantine, I've never met him, I've never helped him.'

'Ah.' Aiah can almost hear the wheels click over in his mind. 'Okay.'

'It'll turn out all right,' she reassures. 'Their investigation doesn't make any sense and they'll have to drop it. The only problem is,' she tries to soften her voice, 'I can't tell you over the phone how much I want you, and what I'd do to you if you were here, because somebody might be listening.'

There's a moment's pause. Then, 'Really? They're on your phone? It's that serious?'

'It's not serious because nothing will come of it. But the Investigative Division can be very thorough when they want to be, and Constantine made us all look pretty foolish, so they may feel they've got to try to pin it on me if they can.'

There was a long, thoughtful pause. 'I'm going to try to come home sooner. They don't need me for the wrapup as badly as they think.'

'You won't be able to help.'

Gil's voice is firm. 'I can be with you. That's what matters. Let me talk to Havell.'

Aiah knows she should receive comfort at this, but all she can feel is a bleak hollow where the comfort should be. 'I've got other news – good news,' she says. 'I've been doing some work for a man named Rohder – kind of a detective job, locating plasm thieves – and it's gone well, and Rohder thinks he can see a way to my getting a degree.'

'You already have a degree.'

'But this will be a degree in plasm engineering. I'll be qualified for much better jobs once I get back to the Authority.'

Let any eavesdroppers know of her long-range plans, she thinks. Let them know she plans to be with the Authority for a long time.

Let them know her life is just fine.

TWISTED DEMAND CIVIL RIGHTS IN THEOCRACY
OF CHANDRAB
300 KILLED BY ZEALOUS POLICE

'12:31 hours, Horn Six reorientation to degrees 114. Ne?'

'Da. 12:31 hours, Horn Six reorientation to degrees 114. 9:34, confirmed.'

'12:34, Horn Six transmit at 1200 mm. 30 minutes. Ne?'

'Da. 12:31, Horn Six transmit at 200 mm. 30 minutes. Confirmed.'

'Incorrect. Incorrect. 1200 mm. Not 200.'

'1200 mm. Confirmed.'

The news is filled with images from Caraqui. The thousands of dead are being loaded onto barges and will then be towed to a deep part of the Sea of Caraqui and sunk.

Aiah makes herself watch the video, watch the rescue crews in their gauze masks, the stretchers with the blackened bodies curled in the prayer position, wailing relatives hoping for a miracle, icons of Dhoran of the Dead raised high, clergymen in their robes and masks muttering blessings and splashing each body with holy aloe. So many clergymen they could form an assembly line.

That plasm well, Rohder had said. *Someone used it to kill fifty thousand people.*

Rohder, Aiah's friend and benefactor.

A tug tows the first barge down the wide Martyrs' Canal, past a vista of hollow building shells and survivors sobbing their last farewells.

My fault, she thinks.

And then Constantine appears and Aiah's heart leaps. He's prowling along the waterfront, dressed somberly in black velvet and dark mourning lace, face etched in a scowl. The reporters surge toward their target, scattering mourners. Constantine looks at the cameras, and Aiah recognizes at once the brooding intelligence in his eyes.

When his mind is working, she thinks, you can *see* it.

There is a chime from Aiah's communications array. Clenching her teeth, she ignores it and fixes her attention on the video.

'No one intended this tragedy,' Constantine says. 'Neither our forces nor those of the previous government. It is the task of the new government to make certain that all these lives . . .' Constantine's eyes lift slightly and scan towards the canal, towards the barges piled with their dead. Good dramatics, Aiah thinks. In her apartment, the chime continues.

Constantine's gaze returns to his audience. 'That all these lives,' he continues, 'will not be written off as an unfortunate accident. These, no less than those who died to capture the Aerial Palace, are the honored dead of the revolution. Their survivors deserve no less than the soldiers who died in the fight against the Keremaths – they deserve a better Caraqui, prosperous, free and just. They deserve the New City. And I am here to pledge on behalf of the government that they will get it.'

Nicely done, Aiah thinks. If Constantine had simply made a speech in the normal way, it would have been ignored or cut into snippets by news editors. But by hiding out for a couple days, then showing up on the quay and pretending his appearance was spontaneous, he got his message across to the world without it being filtered.

There is an art to this, she thinks. Because he enhances his words with art doesn't mean they aren't sincere, it just gives them more force.

Fifty thousand dead, Aiah thinks, and Aiah is at least partly responsible, and Constantine has promised to do what he can to give meaning to all that, and meanwhile Aiah is in Jaspeer preparing for her college career.

The commo rig stops chiming and begins to speak in Gurrah's voice. 'The police were here,' she says to the recorder, 'asking about you.'

Aiah drags her eyes from the oval eye of the video and jumps to grab the headset and punch the answer button.

'Mama?' she says. 'I just came in the door. What happened?'

'The police were here. They asked me about you, but I just told 'em to clear off.'

'Good for you!' Aiah encourages. With Gurrah, it's usually a good idea to reinforce good behavior as often as possible.

Aiah steps back from the commo rig so that she can see the video screen. Constantine's appearance is over, and the program has cut to newly appointed members of the new Caraqui government arriving at the Aerial Palace for a meeting. Aiah recognizes Adaveth, the twisted man, his huge liquid eyes gazing at the reporters while he marches past battle-damaged doors carrying his briefcase.

'There were two cops,' Gurrah says. 'One of them had a white leather jacket, like he got it from some streetwalker. What kind of cops wear white leather jackets?'

'The kind you shouldn't talk to,' Aiah says.

Gurrah's voice rises in pitch, a tone Aiah knows all too well, and Aiah's heart sinks. 'I *knew* you were going to get in trouble,' Gurrah says. 'I knew ever since Senko's Day.'

'Ma—' Aiah warns.

'After you made that scene and called me all kinds of names—'

'*I didn't call you names!*' The words burst out before Aiah can stop them.

'In front of your grandmother and everything,' Gurrah says. 'Why are my children so disrespectful?'

Gurrah's tones are sulky, but Aiah thinks she recognizes a tone of triumph. Her mother, Aiah thinks, knows her too well, knows exactly how to get the reaction she wants.

'Ma,' Aiah says, 'we probably shouldn't talk about family matters over the phone. The creepers might be listening.'

'You *are* in trouble if they're tapping your phone!' Gurrah says. 'I knew it!'

On the video, members of the Keremath administration are being hustled off to jail by Geymard's mercenaries. Police officials, members of the Specials, high-ranking military men, being shoved into their own dungeons.

'I'm not in trouble, not really, because I haven't done anything,' Aiah says. 'The administration is trying to cover up its own idiocy.'

'They always blame the Barkazil,' Gurrah says. 'You know that.'

'It makes it convenient for them,' Aiah says, 'but it won't work.'

'You should talk to your mother more. I can help you.'

Aiah makes an effort to change the topic. 'Hey,' she says brightly, 'I have some news! I may be going back to college for a degree!'

'More longnose education,' Gurrah says darkly. 'What good is it?'

'Education is education,' Aiah says. 'What university in Barkazi is going to give me a full scholarship?'

Aiah tries to disguise her satisfaction at the argument being channeled into such familiar paths. She lets Gurrah score a few points, then says she has to get supper ready and brings the conversation to an end.

Aiah shifts to another station. More images from Caraqui, more Special Police being dragged off to the subaquatic basements of their own prisons.

And more dead, presumably.

Later that shift, while buying bread at the local bakery, she sees a man in a white leather jacket hanging in the doorway drinking a soda. Later she sees the same man, without the trademark jacket, following her home.

Interesting, she thinks.

CORRUPTION ALLEGED IN POLICE
'MILLIONAIRE COMMISSIONER' DENIES KNOWING OWN WORTH

'15:31, Horn Six transmit at 430 mm. 6 minutes. Ne?'

'Da. 15:31, Horn Six transmit at 430 mm. 6 minutes. Confirmed.'

Aiah thinks of fifty thousand dead, the barges nosing out to deep water with the cargo of ash. *Their survivors*, she remembers, *deserve no less*.

She thinks of Constantine, his big hands stroking her skin.

She looks at the picture of Gil in its wetsilver frame, and sees the face of a stranger.

STRIFE ALLEGED IN OPERATION
TWO STREET COLONELS ASSASSINATED

Another creeper turns up in her office and asks her a lot of familiar questions. Aiah answers patiently, her answers consistent with everything she's said before, and she looks up into the scowling face of her interrogator and thinks: *You may have a new boss soon, courtesy of me.*

She settles into her stolen chair. 'I thought the government was officially blaming Constantine for this one,' she says. 'Why are you bothering to question me at all?'

'Constantine may have had accomplices.'

'Constantine's accomplices aren't lousy Grade Sixes in Jaspeer,' Aiah says. 'Constantine's accomplices are being appointed to run whole departments in Caraqui. Do you really think if I knew Constantine, I'd be stupid enough to stay here when I could be in Caraqui living like a queen?'

Asking the question leaves a bitter taste in Aiah's mouth. Sometimes, she thinks, a question implies its own answer, its own perfect truth.

'Maybe you don't want to leave Jaspeer,' the creeper says. 'You were born here and have lived here all your life, and you have a lover here. Jaspeer is your metropolis.'

'*My* metropolis,' Aiah says, suddenly in passionate love with the truth, 'was destroyed before I was born.'

After the creeper leaves, Aiah puts on her headset, logs in, and, between calls on her computer, begins to plan her escape.

If the ID is really going to follow her everywhere, she thinks, that's going to complicate everything.

Aiah gives it three more days. The creepers are still following her at least part of the time; sometimes they're easy to spot, particularly after she starts recognizing faces, but sometimes she just can't be sure. Any plan she develops has to deal with the possibility that she might be tailed without knowing it.

Aiah calls the Wisdom Fortune Temple and finds out the times of their services.

The easiest way to follow her, she knows, is through telepresence. From the back of one kitchen cabinet she takes one of the plasm batteries that, all those weeks ago, she carried in her tote bag to and from Terminal. She takes it to her plasm meter and fixes the battery's alligator clip to the live well wire.

Dials click over as the battery fills. It's the first time Aiah has ever used the plasm connection in her building.

She puts a finger on the contact and feels her nerves cry at the touch of plasm. The sensation takes her breath away.

She had tried very hard to forget what this was like.

Aiah recalls how plasm turned gold in the sky when she was feeding it to Red Bolt. She takes a breath and expands her sensorium, tries to attune it to the presence of plasm. Carefully she scours her apartment.

Nothing other than the glow she's generating herself.

But any hypothetical mage following her might have guessed what she was attempting and flown his anima somewhere else. So she pops her own anima out into the hallway outside – nothing there – and then looks in the apartment across the hall, above, below and to either side.

Still nothing, saving the knowledge that the lady next door is cutting her toenails.

Aiah takes the finger off the contact, makes certain the

battery is full, and detaches the alligator clip. She looks at the meter and realizes she now owes six hundred dalders to the Authority.

She puts the battery in her tote along with a dark blue jacket, her ivory necklace, Volume Fourteen of *Proceedings*, a floppy hat and her passport. She takes the money from under her mattress, hesitates for a moment, then adds the portrait of Karlo. Then she dons a light beige jacket, picks up a pillow and leaves the apartment.

In one of Loeno's basements she uses her Authority passkey to open a metal door leading into the utility tunnel. Once inside she puts her finger on the battery contact again, checks for watchers, then takes her checktube from its hiding place behind the plasm main, wipes off the gritty dust and stows it in her tote.

She leaves Loeno Towers by her usual door and almost at once sees the creepers' car drifting down the street after her. When she drops into the New Central Line Station, the two creepers have to exit in a hurry and follow her.

New Central Line to Red Line to Circle Line. The last car jolts so badly it nearly puts her back out of joint. She leaves the trackline at Old Shorings and almost dances to the surface.

Childhood memories rise along with the scent of food and the sound of music rolling out of open windows. The buildings lean on their scaffolds like old friends bending over her to wish her well. Chardug the Hermit greets her cheerfully from his pillar, and she drops a little change in his basket.

The last time, she thinks, she'll see any of this.

For good luck she buys a bowl of hot noodles flavored with onions and chilies, her favorite. Above her head, plasm Lynxoid Brothers battle the Blue Titan in an advertisement for the new chromoplay. Glancing down the street she can see the unhappy pale faces of the Jaspeeri cops standing out like neon displays amid the brown Barkazil population, and Aiah has to turn away to hide her smile.

Aiah climbs the worn metal stair to the Wisdom Fortune Temple, passing two elderly women in white-and-blue temple garb who have stopped on the landing to catch their breath. The steel door is open and Aiah enters, breathing in the scent of the packaged herbs behind the store counter. Behind the counter is Dhival, Khorsa's sister, dressed in red-and-gold velvet robes, her face dramatic with heavy cosmetics.

Dhival looks surprised, but comes out from behind the counter to give Aiah an embrace and a kiss on each cheek. 'Have you come for services?'

'Is Khorsa here?'

'In her office. I'll get her.'

'I need to speak to her privately, if I might.'

Dhival looks surprised. 'Fine. Just go back, then.'

Aiah finds the office and knocks on the open door, and Khorsa looks up from a thick ledger. Splendid in her scarlet temple robes, she rises to give Aiah a hug. At the touch of Khorsa's cool cheek on her own, Aiah feels a degree of tension ebbing from her.

Khorsa looks at the pillow Aiah carries and says, 'Can I loan you a robe?'

'The pillow's camouflage. Actually I was hoping for some help.'

Khorsa draws back, looks at Aiah, and shows no surprise at all. 'Of course, after everything we owe you. What do you need?'

'There are two Jaspeeri men following me. I want to evade them for a few hours.'

Khorsa tilts her head and considers the problem. 'Evade how? I can send a message to the Vampire clubhouse and have those two sent to a hospital, if that's what you want.'

'No. That would only get people in trouble. All I'd like is to get out the back way, if there is one, and for you to make certain I'm not being followed till I get to the pneuma station.' Aiah reaches into her tote, pulls out the full plasm battery. 'Can you or Dhival use telepresence technique?'

'I'm better at it than she is,' Khorsa said. 'But you don't have to give me plasm. I can dip my own well.'

Finger-cymbals begin chiming from the temple. Aiah holds the battery out. 'Take it. It's too heavy to carry with me.'

Khorsa looks at the battery, reluctance on her face, then takes it in her many-ringed hands. She looks back at Aiah. 'Dare I ask what this is about?'

'It's very complicated,' Aiah says, hoping she won't have to make a *passu* out of Khorsa, but the tiny woman keeps looking at her, and finally Aiah gives in.

'Those two are police,' Aiah says. 'I found out some things about their department – it involves corruption – and now I want to get away from them for a while.'

Khorsa absorbs this and shifts at once to practical matters. 'Do you need shelter?'

'Oh no. Thank you. If I can get a few hours away from them, things will settle themselves. I just need to know that no one is following me – neither those two, nor a mage.'

Khorsa nods. 'I'd best go into the temple and let them know that someone else will have to beat the drum during the service. Wait here. I'll be back.'

Khorsa puts the plasm battery on her desk and bustles out. Aiah takes off her beige jacket and puts it into her tote, then takes out the blue jacket and puts it on. She pins up her long hair, then pulls the floppy hat out of her tote and puts it on.

A drum beats tentatively in the temple and Khorsa returns. She looks at Aiah, reaches up to tug the hat brim more firmly into place, and then nods. 'If I see anyone following,' she says, 'I'll give a signal. A red glow right in front of your face. I'll try to make certain you're not blinded, but I want you to see it.'

Aiah nods.

'If they follow you, what will you do then? Will you need protection?'

'I'll come back and attend the service. Then I'll go home, and I'll know that they're better than I had reason to suspect.'

Khorsa purses her lips and looks thoughtful. 'I wish I could give you more help.' The drum beats steadily now and Aiah can hear Dhival calling for everyone to enter the temple. The worshipers begin clapping and chiming finger cymbals as they file in.

'Might as well get started,' Khorsa says. She reaches behind the desk, opens a small door, reveals a plasm connection and contacts. Khorsa produces a t-grip from her robe pocket, jacks it into the connection, and then settles herself into her chair.

The battery remains on her desk. Perhaps she means to return it to Aiah later, or maybe she just wants the city's well because it gives her more flexibility.

'I'll scout the outside of the building first,' she says. 'If someone's watching the back alley we may have to rethink everything.'

Khorsa closes her eyes in concentration, and Aiah uneasily shifts her tote from one shoulder to the other. She can feel perspiration gathering under her hat brim.

Music rises and falls, an invocation of Dhoran of the Dead. Aiah pictures it spilling out into the street through the open windows, the Jaspeeri cops looking up and wondering.

A laugh bubbles up from Khorsa's lips. 'They're both out front,' she says. 'They are looking *very* uncomfortable. What kind of cops are these? You'd think they'd be more at home on the street.'

'Authority cops.'

'Oh.' Dismissively. 'No wonder.' There is another moment of silence. 'No one in the alley,' she says. 'No one watching that I can see.'

Jump to it, girl, Aiah thinks. But her feet don't move, she stands in place and looks at Khorsa and suddenly wants never to leave, to shelter here forever amid the sweet smell of herbs, the music and chanting . . .

It is Dhoran of the Dead they are invoking, she remembers, and thinks of the barges trailing little wisps of ash as they move down the Martyrs' Canal.

Her legs jerk as if hit by an electric shock, and take her out of the room faster than the speed of thought.

Down the stair, out the back hall. The tote bangs against her hip. She hits the back door, pushes it open against resistance. Something clatters as the door opens, and she steps out into an alley that smells of urine and rotting food.

The alley is filled with broken glass, old furniture and piles of human feces. Whoever lives here doesn't seem to be around at the moment, and Aiah darts around the worst of the mess. The sound of chanting follows her like a friendly memory. Once out of the alley she heads east in order to put several streets between her and the Authority cops, and then turns north to the pneuma station. The pneuma isn't really in this neighborhood, being almost a radius away, but with brisk walking she thinks she can probably make it in ten or twelve minutes.

She crosses a street and marches halfway down the block before she recognizes the big building coming up on her left, the old temple covered with stone carvings, the vines and monsters that loom at her out of her childhood. The porch before the steel doors is dusted with rice and other offerings.

Aiah slows as she passes, then dips a hand into her pocket, pulls out some coins, and flings them at the steel door. They splash like the silver drops of a fountain as they strike, a series of clean ringing sounds; and Aiah turns her back on the place, laughs and runs onward.

She hopes Khorsa is amused.

No red lights appear in front of her face.

There is a long, anxious wait on a cold, empty pneuma station. A stray sad thought of Gil sticks like a lump in her throat: he will return home to an empty apartment, to bills his salary won't cover. She will have to send him money from her bank account, twenty or thirty thousand, something that will pay for half the apartment.

She climbs aboard the pneuma once it arrives, and it takes her straight to Gold Town InterMet, where she buys a ticket for Karapoor. Anxiety tingles through her thoughts as she has to show her passport to the sleepy-eyed ticket clerk to prove she can get into Karapoor – there might be a watch out on her. But the clerk doesn't even glance at the picture, punches the button on her console, and Aiah's token spins down a gray metal slide into her hand.

From Karapoor she can get on a high-speed pneuma that will take her halfway to Caraqui by noon tomorrow.

She steps into the InterMetropolitan and looks at her fellow travellers, mostly glassy-eyed commuters heading for home, and finds a seat by herself. The doors close. The wind whistles across the smooth surface of the car as the system inhales, and then there's a kick to her spine as compressed air spits her out into the world.

Constantine has a way of being fatal to his friends. Sorya's words flash through Aiah's mind.

Well, she'll just have to take her chances.

She takes out the fourteenth volume of *Proceedings* and opens it. Rohder's research will be her gift to Constantine when she arrives.

There's no sign at the border to let her know she's left Jaspeer, that she's made her escape – there's only the hiss of pneumatics as the car slows, as it drops out of the system and glides to a halt at the Karapoor InterMet station.

And then, as the weary passengers gather their belongings, the car is filled with sudden light, little glowing flecks of plasm fire that drop from the ceiling, that fall like particolored snow on the wondering, uplifted faces of the passengers. A gift from Khorsa, who has followed Aiah all this way.

The magical snowfall, Aiah notes, is every color in the world but red.

The Collected Stories of Robert Silverberg
Volume 3

Beyond the Safe Zone

'A master of his craft and imagination'   *Los Angeles Times*

'When one contemplates Robert Silverberg it can only be with awe. In terms of excellence he has few peers, if any. *Beyond the Safe Zone* is not just a desirable thing, it is a necessary addition to the archives'   *Locus*

Volume 3 of the Collected Stories of Robert Silverberg, one of the eminences of science fiction, gathers together work from a vital and fertile period, the 1970s. Herein: the Nebula Award-winning story 'Good News from the Vatican', in which the first robot pope is elected; the Jupiter Award-winning novella 'The Feast of St Dionysus', about a burned-out astronaut finding ecstasy in an ancient cult; more secrets are revealed in 'Capricorn Games', the sign of the goat and of Christ; in 'Many Mansions' an exquisite time-travel paradox is made up of many murders. A total of 26 dazzling stories from the master of the craft take us on a voyage to a wealth of different cultures and futures from which no one will return quite the same.

'Where Silverberg goes today, the rest of science fiction will follow tomorrow'   Isaac Asimov

ISBN 0 586 21371 6

The World Jones Made
Philip K. Dick

'Dick was perhaps the first real genius to have worked in the science-fictional mode since the days of Stapeldon'

Brian Aldiss

After the war, amid the radiation and rubble, a world government is established based on Relativism. People can do whatever they like – take heroin, fornicate in the street – and believe whatever they like, so long as they don't tell anyone else what to do or what to believe in.

Underground police enforce the new Law. Dedicated people such as Cussick. Cussick hopes that God is a thing of the past, along with war – at last. What he doesn't expect is the rise of the devil.

Philip K. Dick remained a cult figure until Hollywood translated two of his stories into movies, *Blade Runner* and *Total Recall*, which defined for a generation a terrifying, and totally plausible, future. *The World Jones Made* is a hauntingly sinister place.

ISBN 0 586 21844 0

SCIENCE FICTION IS *NOT* DEAD!

Life's too short for the mindless spectacle of most modern visual SF. The chances are you got interested in science fiction because you like the mind-stretch you get from new ideas – and you only find that in the written word.

LONG LIVE SF!

Science Fiction is alive and kicking in the UK. Every month half a dozen challenging new science fiction and fantasy tales appear in Britain's best SF magazine –

INTERZONE